Brenna

A Christian Novel

When my father and my mother forsake me,
then the LORD will take me up.
Psalm 27:10

Paula Rae Wallace

Order this book online at www.trafford.com
or email orders@trafford.com

Most Trafford titles are also available at major online book retailers.

Scripture quotations marked KJV are from the Holy Bible, King James
Version (Authorized Version). First published in 1611.

The events and characters of this novel are fictitious!

Printed in the United States of America.

ISBN: 978-1-4907-4881-8 (sc)
ISBN: 978-1-4907-4872-6 (hc)
ISBN: 978-1-4907-4873-3 (e)

Library of Congress Control Number: 2014918314

Trafford rev. 10/21/2014

 www.trafford.com

North America & international
toll-free: 1 888 232 4444 (USA & Canada)
fax: 812 355 4082

Additional Titles by Paula Rae Wallace

DWELLING BY THE WELL A daily devotional

DAZZLING Volume 1
TREASURES Volume 2
WEALTH Volume 3
MAGNIFICENCE Volume 4
RADIANCE Volume 5

THE ANDERSONS Volume 1 of THE ANDERSON Trilogy
FAMILY FORGED Volume 2 of THE ANDERSON Trilogy
GAINING GROUND Volume 3 of THE ANDERSON Trilogy

THE PRAYER AND PRAISE JOURNAL

TABLE OF CONTENTS

Chapter 1: APPLICATION

'Hamilton, Brenna Renée'! Brenna surveyed the employment ap. critically! It only asked for middle initial, but she liked her middle name! She sighed. Neither did she want to look like she couldn't follow simple instructions for completing the form~she scrambled around in a derelict-looking, crochet tote for white-out, eradicating all but the initial.

Copying from a scrap, she filled out the address part! She fought tears as miserable events of the past twenty-four hours crowded into the elegant office space now surrounding her! So, she could still be living out of her car, but without a physical address, how could she expect a prestigious firm like *GeoHy* to hire her? So, consequently she spent money she couldn't afford, to rent an extended stay 'suite' for a week! A nasty place; terrifying actually! She fought tears and nausea! So the manager had taken her money, failing to mention that the available unit's plumbing didn't work! Her bitter and probably loud complaints fell on a deaf ear! The place didn't refund rent; the plumbing was, 'being worked on'! Leaving her with a toilet which had been used without flushing, and water now cut off! So after a few hours wasted trying to sleep on a thin and lumpy mattress, she had dressed and taken a city bus into the Tulsa city center, finding a fast food restaurant where she washed up the best she could. Then she wandered aimlessly, even after locating The Sullivan Building, where her dream job stretched upward beyond her reach.

Returning her attention to the application, she filled in slots that asked for her educational background: Somerville High School in Somerville, Massachusetts! Where, in spite of turbulence and turmoil, she actually managed to do well enough to be pinned for National Honor Society! No

1

place on the ap. for that accomplishment, although the grades helped her acquire some scholarship money! The next line: four year undergraduate course in Geology from Boston University! No hours toward a Master's degree! Not a stellar GPA! Just, she made it! She worked hard, and she made it; avoiding the pitfalls of both partying and student loans!

The door opened and a beautiful young woman breezed in, wafting perfume and an aura of confidence.

"Did you get some coffee?" Her voice was pleasant enough as she filled a mug for herself and someone else. She was gone without waiting for an answer.

'Alexandra'! Brenna knew who she was. She knew everything there was to glean about Daniel Faulkner; his company, *GeoHy*; and his family! Almost weird to the point of stalking! She was just fascinated with them! They seemed to epitomize what she wanted; what she had never had! Her troubled gaze fell on a crystal clock atop polished mahogany mantel. The rest of the ap asked about professional organizations she belonged to. None! And then the typical three references. When she finished, it looked anemic! Her reason for not mailing a resumé across country, rather than making the grueling road trip to appear in person! For all her hard work and striving, her life on paper wasn't impressive!

She caught sight of her reflection: a thick main of honey colored hair, the color repeated in sparkling eyes and groomed brows! From a world where everyone taunted, 'Brenna; you ugly!' she got plenty of attention that attested to the opposite! Not that it mattered, either way! If she did have good looks, she hoped she had more going for her than that!

And Alexandra's lingering fragrance-Brenna felt like the stench from her few hours in the-whatever it was-clung about her-And Alexandra was dressed up to the hilt! Doubtless, an ensemble from the hands of her mother, Diana, and *DiaMal, Corporation*! Brenna's thinking had been that if she dressed in jeans, plaid shirt, pony-tail, and no make-up, she would come across as a no-nonsense Geologist, her gender not an issue in a male-dominated field!

"Finished?" Alexandra Faulkner's voice, with a clipped edge, accompanied her appearance.

Brenna sighed. "Yeah, I guess."

Alexandra sank into a chair across the table, turning the paper toward her, while making a point of checking her wrist watch. "Okay, you didn't complete the 'Next of kin'. Do you not have any family?"

"I do; I-"

"Well, finish filling it-"

"Okay, I can give my step-dad's last-known address! He bounces from place to place since my mother died! He may be in prison! I have siblings; they bounce around in foster care!"

Alexandra pulled a Mont Blanc from the inner breast pocket of her suit and wrote a notation, making the interviewee feel smaller than ever! Her phone buzzed, and grabbing it, she jumped up! "Sit tight! I'll be right back!"

⚑ ⚐

Brenna studied her surroundings in awed curiosity! No shortage of Lladro figurines! And original oil paintings graced the walls! She wouldn't know Lladro, except for the past year's roommate who was blown away with anything expensive and prestigious! The conference room exuded class, but she couldn't help comparing it to the other Geological firm she had considered applying to: *DiaMo, Incorporated*. Mallory Anderson, the CEO of that company, themed her office décor to Geological samples! Her conference table was glass topped, supported on beautiful pieces of crystalline Rhodochrosite in matrix!

Her gaze rested on her application, left in Alexandra Faulkner's hasty exit! Suddenly the folly of showing up here swept over her! Her beater of a car, stripped during the night, of her one decent tire and all four hubcaps! A complaint about that to a different property manager who informed her they took no responsibility for personal property-

She needed to forget this futile process and get back before someone helped themselves to the belongings inside the car! Not much, but all she had, including nearly eighty dollars in cash! She could live in her car, nail down a job waiting tables-Grasping the application, she bolted!

⚑ ⚐

"I'm sorry Daddy, but I don't need her!" Alexandra's eyes stung with tears under her father's reprimand! "Why don't you hire her?"

The good-looking Daniel Faulkner studied his daughter carefully before responding slowly, "Okaaayyy Alexandra, we've tried to teach you that there's never a call for being rude and high-handed with people! And

3

with all due respect to your new-found independence, I'm not sure you know what you need!"

"Okay, well, she reeks, and her GPA isn't that impressive! And she left half of the ap blank!"

Daniel frowned. "Like I said, go make a humble apology for your discourtesy to her, and make sure she's on your payroll before noon! Don't forget whose name's on the line underwriting your mining venture! Geologists don't have to smell good!"

"Well, you'd think that to interview for a job~"

"Was I unclear?"

⚜ ⚜

Diana Faulkner spun in surprise as a sobbing young woman dashed past her in the *the Sullivan Building* lobby!

"Are you okay?" Her compassion and nursing instincts fired up as she studied the beautiful girl who had nearly sent her sprawling!

"Yes Ma'am! I'm fine! I'm sorry for nearly knocking you over~um~sorry~"

Brenna made the freedom of the nearly-empty city street and flattened herself against the granite façade of the ground floor, sobbing! She needed to get her bearings and locate the right bus line back to her hotel! The Tulsa Public Transit System didn't make as much sense to her as Boston's! Suddenly, Tulsa, the city long dreamed of, seemed loathsome! Homesickness flooded over her! 'No way back! No way back! No way back!' The finality of her actions rocked her as her dream shattered around her feet!

Brushing tears on her sweater sleeve, she drew in rasping breaths!

"You're sure you're okay?" Mrs. Diana Faulkner's voice at her elbow made her jump! "Have you eaten anything today, or in the past several days? Fluid intake~ There's a good Bistro around the corner; will you let me~"

Brenna summoned all her courage! "I told you I'm okay, and I apologized for nearly running~over~Thanks anyway!"

She jumped onto a coach as it braked at the curb, sinking into the first seat with a sigh of relief! Except that the fare was two dollars, and she was heading the wrong direction!

⚜ ⚜

Puzzled, Diana reached into the garbage container for a balled-up sheet of paper! An application to *GeoHy*? Reentering the office building she ascended to the *GeoHy* suite!

"What's going on?" One who preferred order to chaos and turmoil, a chagrined Diana took in the scene in Daniel's private office!

"Come in, Honey, and close the door. What's that?"

"It's an application~"

White-lipped, he reached for it! "Where did you get it?"

Diana's big blue eyes searched the expressions of husband and daughter. "Well, this little gal~she was running~she looked like she was on her last legs~what~"

"Well, I didn't want to hire her," Alexandra's defensive stance.

"Oh, I see!"

"I was interviewing her, and Daddy called me in here! When I went back out, she was gone!"

"What did you expect?" Daniel's frustration erupted!

"I expected her to finish the interview! I told her to sit tight!"

"Well, did you offer her anything to eat or drink?" The memory of the girl's haggard appearance worried Diana's nursing persona!

"Look; I just didn't like her! I can't afford anyone else on my payroll right now~but, she ran, and Daddy told me I have to go find her and apologize!"

A sudden perception, and he questioned Alexandra sagely, "Is this connected in any way to Tommy Haynes?"

"No! It's just~" she crumbled into Diana's arms. "I'm sorry, Mom! You have taught me better manners!"

"Okay, Alexandra, stand up, and dry your eyes!" Daniel felt no sympathy. "This is about Haynes!"

"Well, no Sir; not really! I mean, I keep hoping that one of these days~"

"One of these days; what? Write him a letter! I want to see it before you send it, though!"

His daughter came alive with a screech, "Really? I can send him an email?"

"I said a letter!"

"Yes, Sir, that's what emails are; except they're faster and you save postage!"

He laughed and color flowed back into his face! "Okay, an email then! I'm not sure he's worth postage!"

Ire flashed in Alexandra's gray eyes! "You're more snobbish about him than I was to that applicant!"

"Alexandra~" Diana's mild rebuke. "Your father and I have invested ourselves and all that we have into you and your brothers and sisters! We're particular about who waltzes into your life expecting to sweep you off of your feet~"

"Yes, Ma'am; I'm sorry!" She turned her attention to her father. "Can I send the email before I go look for her?"

He studied the wrinkled page before him, dismayed by the address. "On second thought, I think I better go with you! This is~uh~a scary area of town!"

"I'm coming with you," Diana's determined tone!

"No, you're not! I probably shouldn't take Al, except~"

Diana could only guess at the turbulence behind handsome features! "You know, she~uh~what's her name~" she lifted the ap to read the name. "Brenna, oh, that's cute~uh~she wasn't going this direction-I tried to slow her down to get her something to eat! She hopped the first bus that stopped, to escape from me-headed toward TU!"

"Let's go, Al! Honey, go home! We'll keep you in the loop!"

"Well, get some nutrition into her-and be careful!"

Grim-faced, he nodded. "Yeah, the last thing I want to do is shoot someone else! I will, though, if it comes down to it!"

⚑ ⚐

Brenna rode, studying the city pensively, fighting panic.

"End of the line, Miss!" The driver's voice roused her, and she scrambled to her feet.

"Which line takes me to~" she gave the shabby address, and he squinted at her strangely.

"That's way out the other end of town! You'll have to take this line back to city center, then it's a bit of a walk south to catch three-o-six."

She nodded numbly. Friendlier and more helpful than Boston drivers! She had heard that, about the people, 'Out west'.

"Thank you, Sir. Have a nice day." She hopped down and he fell in beside her as she loped back the way they had come.

"Ma'am, ya have ta cross the street up with the light and wait on the other side, over there where that stop is!"

"Right!" she forced a laugh. "I guess I'll get a bite to eat before I head back!"

"Well, suit yourself, but there's no restaurants or nothin' for miles up this way! Gettin' the bus back uptown gives you your best options for fast food."

⚐ ⚑

Daniel and Alexandra followed the transit route to Tulsa University, and then backtracked.

"How long are we going to keep at this? I mean, how much do we owe her, when she's the one who jumped and ran?" Alexandra made a good point, but her attitude still miffed him.

"Oh, that's right! You're extra-eager to get back so you can compose your email! Just go ahead and do it on your phone."

She stared at him dumbly, "Really?"

"Yeah, Al, because I want to keep looking"! He glanced as her fingers flew on her keys.

"I guess you know his email address then," he challenged.

"Yes, I do! He's in my contact list! But I don't contact him." She met his gaze with a return scowl. "Okay, how's this?"

Hey, Tommy
What's up? I'm doing great! My dad said I can drop you a line!

"Yeah, that's great! Send it, and then help me, will you?"

Alexandra pushed send, and returned her attention out the window. "I have been helping you."

"I know. But try putting yourself into her shoes. Where would you go?"

Alexandra considered. "Well, I didn't see that she had any electronics with her. Maybe she went on campus to use the library-"

"Good thinking! I mean, she can't get on TU's campus without a student ID! She could get a visitor's pass, but that wouldn't allow her that kind of access. Maybe she found a public library! She seems desperate for a job, and I don't think she wants anything more to do with us."

Alexandra nodded. "Okay, I'm accessing all of the public library branches." She studied the schematic. "Okay, uh, there's one, like-" she pointed, and he frowned.

"No, it's getting colder, and there's no bus line up that direction!"

Tears sparkled on Alexandra's eye lashes. "She didn't have a coat with her, did she? Because it was fairly warm earlier-"

He agreed, "Something deceptive for someone from Boston. Maybe she thought our weather's always balmy. Or maybe she heard the forecast, but her coat looked too ragged for a job interview."

"She doesn't have any money, does she?" Al's worry-filled voice, "and not even a credit card- I guess I-uh-really take a lot for-granted-" She patted delicately at tears with manicured fingertips.

Daniel sighed. "I guess that makes two of us!"

Her phone buzzed and she met his gaze, blushing.

He frowned. "Haynes?"

"Yes, his name's 'Tommy'!"

"Well, answer your call, but keep it to five minutes. We have a job to do."

⌣ ⌣

Brenna shivered, stretching her sweater sleeves over her hands and clamping them with her fingers. Friendly! Over-friendly, making her homesick for the indifferent rudeness of Boston Transit! She struggled against a stiff breeze. She knew he had meant well, but good grief! She didn't have any money to cross the street and catch the return bus! Meaning she was walking back uptown and her excuse about getting something to eat had been a lie.

"Lord, I'm sorry! They just slip out! I know that's no excuse-just please forgive me-again-for another one!"

Seeing a stately-looking church complex, she headed toward it. Maybe the sanctuary was open; she could pray and warm up a little bit! Maybe there would be someone to recommend a shelter. That idea made her cry! Finally having earned her coveted and elusive degree, she had to search for a homeless shelter now?

"Lord, You know all about it," she whispered. "I can find a warm place to sleep, and tomorrow I can get my car and get a waitress job while I wait for a career choice to open up. It won't be that much longer; will it? Help me to trust You and keep being patient." Finding the complex locked tight with no one in sight, she settled into a sheltered spot between what looked like the auditorium and the Sunday School Annex. *Honey Grove Baptist*!

She recognized the name from her fascination with the Faulkner family! This was where they served the Lord together! Where they served with their musical talents! Tears flowed and memories of her mother overwhelmed her~

⚔ ⚔

"Well, yeah, sure, go ahead." Alexandra sounded puzzled as Tommy, 'wanted to get something off his mind'.

Daniel kept both eyes out for the run-away Geologist, and one ear tuned to the phone conversation.

Alexandra's indignant response! "Well, what's your problem with my having the silver mine?"

She listened to 'what his problem with it was', before responding.

"Well, I didn't have a chance to run it by you first! What did you think I was majoring in Geology to do? Why do you have a problem with it?"

She listened some more.

"Well, what if I don't want to be like your mom? What if I want to be like my dad?"

Another response from the Haynes kid that Daniel couldn't understand!

"Oh, Tommy Haynes! That is so not true! I am still feminine!"

Color stained her cheeks and stormy gray eyes rolled in exasperation. "I go by, 'Al' because it's my name! I like it! My daddy has called me that since day one!" She paused, listening. "Okay, I'll reevaluate if you will! Ciao!"

She disconnected and whirled toward her dad, "I saw her! I thought I did! Go back around!"

He eased over in increasing traffic, but it took a couple of blocks before he could ease into the right lane to turn.

"She was at the church!"

Handsome features questioned. "Why~"

"Uh~I guess I~still wasn't focused~when you asked me before~where~"

Emotions welling up, he nodded agreement! "Well, her locating a computer to do a job search; that was good thinking! But, you're right, you would find a church~"

⚔ ⚔

"Oh God! I'm sorry! I'm so~so sorry! It's all my fault; and~hard as I try~I can't fix it! Oh God, oh~Dear God, please forgive me and~help me! I do love you, and-it's my fault! I was trying to-do- the right thing! Why do things- always- backfire for me?" Words streamed forth amidst hiccuping sobs! "Oh, God, I'm sorry for abandoning the kids! I thought-I thought that Mama's finding You as her Savior would help her! I didn't know-I didn't know-we'd all be left without her! I should have seen it-but-uh-I didn't! Why-did-I come here? Oh, I couldn't wait to get here-unhhh-and now I hate it-so bad! I-I guess-I got way out ahead of You-doing what-I-"

"Brenna?"

Brenna thought she heard her name, but no-no one in Tulsa knew her! She glanced up, and to her dismay, the elegant Alexandra Faulkner stood looking at her.

⚞ ⚟

"Come in; welcome to our home." Diana stood back to let husband, daughter, and newcomer enter the kitchen.

Brenna tried not to notice the scale of the kitchen; the rich gleaming polish of the rooms beyond. "Thank you, Mrs. Faulkner," she gritted. "But the last thing I want to do is impose on anybody. I just need to get home to my apartment! I have laundry to do and calls to make." (More lies, but what could they expect? All she wanted now was to be free of them! To gather some shambles of her dignity)!

"Okay, well that's not going to happen tonight!" Diana's nursing professionalism took over. "As a health-care professional, I'm obligated to step in when I see a medical crisis. Your options are staying here and starting immediate intake, or going straight to an ER!"

Raging honey-brown eyes traveled from face to face of the threesome blocking her flight. She trembled, clenching and unclenching her fists! And every other muscle in her overtaxed body!

Diana's voice quieted to soothing mode. "Okay, Hon, actually, we're not such bad ogres-as ogres go!" She laughed softly. "Okay, relax for me, because you're not going to flee, nor fight! Please sit down." She pulled out a kitchen stool and gave a gentle nudge, before opening the biggest refrigerator on the market, brimming with groceries beyond imagining!

Diana surveyed the inventory, "Okay; wish I had a sports drink! Uh-cranberry juice, or Sprite"?

From cranberry country, Brenna weakly requested the juice. "Thank you, but then I really do-"

"Need to go," Diana finished for her. "Yes, we heard you. Sip slowly; if you get started vomiting, you're on the way to~"

"Look, I don't have any health insurance~"

Alexandra perched next to her on an adjoining stool. "See, another reason for you to accept my job offer! I provide a great benefit package!"

⊨ ⊨

"Hi, Shay! To what do I owe this rare pleasure?"

A rueful laugh from Shay O'Shaughnessy to his cousin, Mallory Anderson! "Hey, sorry I don't stay in touch better! And I can't say I'm calling now without an ulterior motive."

"Everything's okay with Grandmother?" Mallory's worry-tinged voice at her cousin's unexpected call!

A rolling laugh, "Feistier than ever! And Emma and the baby are doing great! We're about to emerge from our trauma; sorry to be so out of the loop~"

Mallory nearly went limp with relief! Shay and his wife had endured a traumatic experience during a business trip to South America! On making it home safely, their response seemed to be withdrawing into a shell. "Okay, all great news! Now for your 'ulterior motive'! What's going on?"

"Well, we have this friend; well, more of an acquaintance, actually! We met her at church. To Grandmother's horror, she decided to drive straight from here to Tulsa, hoping to be hired at *GeoHy*. She's~uh~pretty broke, we think, but fiercely independent~"

"So, you haven't heard if she made it okay?"

"We haven't! She had this convoluted plan set up with Emma, that if Faulkner hired her–well, he'd contact the phone number, Emma's phone! Brenna doesn't have even her own cell phone~"

Mallory pictured her cousin and his cute wife, "And this girl; what's her name, is driving cross country, alone?"

"Well, trusting the Lord! Her name's Brenna!"

"Okay, I'll look into it and get back with you! Thanks for your call. Love you! Give Grandmother my love!"

Chapter 2: *REWARDED*

Brenna stirred a cold bowl of oatmeal, listlessly. "Look, Alexandra, you're wasting your time. And your money! I told you I'm not hungry! You could have given me a ride to my apartment easier than coming back down here! I keep telling you, I've changed my mind about pursuing employment here! If your mother would have turned me loose last night-"

"You might be dead somewhere! My mother is very good at what she does, and she doesn't play that, 'medical professional', card without good reason."

The new geologist sighed, "I'm sure, but, you could have advanced me a couple of bucks for bus fare, rather than paying ten dollars for oatmeal and toast I told you I don't want!"

"I get that! You sound like your needle got stuck in a groove! But, my dad told me to hire you; so could you at least listen to the employment package I've worked out?" Alexandra's eyes widened as a newcomer approached! Brenna turned in response! And froze! This could not be happening!

⊰ ⊱

"Weston, special invitation to visit the warden"!

Warren Weston's eyes narrowed suspiciously, and he grinned sardonically around the table at other hard-timers. "Yeah, heard he's having a tea party, and that I've made his social register! I hoped I'd get an engraved-"

"Can the chatter, and move it! I ain't got all day!" The guard advanced threateningly and the felon shrugged casually! Yanking these guys' chains was one form of entertainment he enjoyed, knowing just how far to push.

"You sure I shouldn't stop by my cell and change into my tux?" he grinned wickedly. "You did pick it up from the tailor, didn't you, Maximilian?"

Scoffs from the others indicated a mild approval of the comedy act.

"You're a million laughs, Weston! Git it goin'"!

⚞ ⚟

"What are you doing here?" Alexandra's question came out, more bluntly than intended.

Brenna just stared in horror, trapped!

"Well, invite me to join you, and I'll explain! You two look jolly!" The stunning newcomer scooted Alexandra over so she could join them in the booth! "Hi, I'm Mallory Anderson!" She extended her hand across the table in characteristic friendliness.

Brenna sat staring, trying not to let her jaw drop, and not to cry!

"You must be Brenna? You know my Grandmother and cousin? Shay called me last night to find out if you made the trip okay! I have a guy working on getting your car! That sleazy place had it towed; their words were that with it sitting on the property stripped, it was running off business! Otherwise, as we know, the place is a tourist magnet!"

Mallory turned her coffee mug up, indicating 'yes' to coffee before continuing! "Hi, Al; great to see you too! How's Silverton?" She hugged Alexandra warmly.

"Buried in snow"!

"Yeah, that's what I thought! So, why does your dad want you to hire another Geologist right now?"

"I guess, so we can be ready to go when the snow melts~if it ever does~"

Mallory's gorgeous features contorted into a droll expression. "So, you'll be throwing money down the drain while snow melts in Colorado? May I remind you that this is only January?"

Brenna lowered her eyes demurely, trying to mask a gamut of emotions! Mallory Anderson was actually **the** Geologist she admired! Even more so than Daniel Faulkner! And she was gorgeous! And everything about her screamed money and success! And, although Brenna had convinced herself she would refuse Alexandra's job offer, she resented Mallory Anderson's suggestion; that hiring her would be money wasted.

Alexandra's frustration boiled over. "Well, don't tell me! Tell my dad!"

Mallory chuckled! "Well, I would! Except he scares me!" Her words meaning that her former legal guardian held her respect! "I mean, if he said to hire her, you better do it!" She paused to survey the menu, opting for a Denver omelet.

"Beautiful pin," Al complimented reluctantly.

"Thanks! Actually, my idea! Last fall, there were three trees near our church that looked just like this! All lined up! Gorgeous! One so deep crimson it looked purple in places; one oranges and golds; and then one, still pretty much, this golden green! So, I took a picture and sent it to Herb! Voila! Executed in garnets and rubies, and sapphires, and peridots~I'm not sure what all else! Then, he was so proud of it, he displayed it on his web site and Face Book fan page! It got him a thousand 'likes' in one day, but now I'm a target! Any of Herb's designs bring a hefty price!"

Alexandra laughed for the first time, "Well, then don't sit with us!"

Mallory ignored her. "And then your mom came through with the outfit! As she always does"!

Brenna was forced to admit to herself that she had never seen anyone so elegantly turned out as the Dallas-based executive! Of course not, with her poverty background! But even faculty members at Boston U~ Brenna was aware of Diana Faulkner's clothing design and manufacturing business in addition to her skills as a nurse! The outfit inspired by the jewelry was chic beyond imagining!

⊰ ⊱

"Mr. Anderson, with all due respect are you sure you know what you're doing?"

David Anderson, Mallory's husband of four years, maintained a serious countenance. "I think I do, Your Honor! Miss Hamilton has worked extremely hard to complete her degree so she could apply for custody of her siblings. You probably don't remember~"

"You are wrong, Mr. Anderson!" The Middlesex County family court judge contradicted, "I do remember my cases! They are heart-breaking, usually with few good options! Or outcomes! I recall Miss Hamilton's pleas in my courtroom immediately following her mother's demise! I've kept an eye on her progress~and would be inclined to grant~"

"Except that Miss Hamilton moved out of state!"

"I'm capable of completing my own sentences; thank you, Mr. Anderson!" The judge's eyes snapped warningly; her tone crisp!

David covered a grin behind his hand and a pretend cough. "My apologies! My wife and I always finish each other's-well, I digress!"

"Yes, you do!" The Honorable Marilee Wilkerson studied the documents before her. "You and your wife live all over the place! What agency would guarantee the children's welfare? And, I'm afraid you haven't met the children; they are not without behavioral problems!"

"Well, here's the deal. I have three kids of my own! And one on the way! I'm not seeking a position as a foster parent!"

With one long, final look at the paperwork, she met his earnest gaze with a sigh! "When she gets settled in one place with steady employment, I'll strongly consider her request! Then there will be innumerable details to arrange. It will be costly, requiring a family attorney. And Mr. Weston will undoubtedly fight her tooth and nail!"

⚔ ⚔

"Let me see the ap!" Mallory doctored her coffee and sipped cautiously.

"I'm not sure why you need it." Alexandra produced it from her attaché, and Brenna cringed as Mallory reached for it.

"Oooh"! Mallory laughed. "Stingy little pig, aren't we? You can't afford her and don't want her, but you don't want anyone else-"

"What? You're hiring?" Alexandra scowled.

"No! You know I hardly hire!" Mallory smiled at the server, and bowed her head for a prayer before taking a bite; then ran her gaze and a manicured finger down the application before meeting Brenna's gaze. "So, what happened to your mother?"

The other young woman seemed stunned by the directness of the question. "Uh-she passed away-a-little more than two years ago!" Her face twisted. "It was-uh-my fault! I didn't-I thought-"

Mallory nodded, waiting troubled, for Brenna to continue.

At last, Mallory broke the silence. "I still feel responsible for my Dad's death! It's been nearly ten years ago, now; and people tell me my guilt's irrational! But I miss him, and I still feel-" She blotted her eyes gently with her napkin.

"My mom was a drug user-but don't judge-" Sobs racked her, but the Bistro was empty; between breakfast and lunch crowds.

"She was the sweetest, and people took advantage of her~and she~reality was too painful for her~she lived in~a dream world~her own private~dream world! Sometimes she needed drugs~to take her there~when imagination alone~She had her demons~but I loved her~ I needed her! We~all did~"

Mallory's expression grew troubled. Poverty, Mallory could relate to; although it was something beyond comprehension for the privileged Alexandra! But the world of drug-abuse-something-that, as a Christian, Mallory insulated herself from! Therefore, the request, not to judge~ "Go on." She prodded softly.

"She used, she OD'd; she used, she OD'd, she used, she OD'd! But they could always~and then~just once~and there was~nothing they could~do! Can you believe that?"

Mallory nodded, although it was inconceivable to her how anyone could ignore such dire warnings! She sighed softly. Things were so black and white to her, and this~

"Okay, uh~so how do you make that your fault?" Alexandra's typical brashness!

Mallory shot her a startled look, but Brenna laughed through her tears at the snobbish directness.

"I'll excuse that, and chalk it up to your bad mood about your boyfriend!" She turned her gaze to Mallory.

"I've waited tables since way before it was legal for me to! And one night, this guy stiffed me in my tip!" She snorted derisively. "Nothing new with that! He left me this religious gobbledygook instead!"

Mallory cringed, remembering the pleadings of two different pastors, for church members not to do that! Her father-in-law, John Anderson, had stood up in the pulpit one day, explaining that one of Calvary Baptist's members had done it, leaving a tract imprinted with the church and his information! Sort, of, 'If you're too cheap to tip, get fast food, and don't leave my name and phone number for someone to take their ire out on'.

"I'm sorry to hear that," she murmured.

"Whatever! Well, it made me mad, so I balled it up and pitched it in the garbage! Never thought anything more about it; but then, this miserable hag, Doris, who did the accounting was suddenly all smiles! I mean, she was so cheap she went through the garbage to make sure we didn't throw away any tickets~and found~ *Are You Sure if You Died Today, You'd Go to Heaven?* We never liked her, so it took a while! But then, I decided, there must really be something to it. While I was trying to decide where to search, some church people-came to our door-and asked if-the kids could ride-a church bus." She grinned suddenly, although tears flowed freely! "The little kids laughed them out of the apartment-but-I followed them down a couple of building units! Because I always worked a double shift on Sundays if I could, I couldn't figure out how I could work on Sundays, and still find God, and what Doris had found."

"Wow, that's an amazing story-" Mallory's spirit rose.

"Yes, I received Jesus within a few days of that, and I started trying to make it to at least parts of the services. Candy Milton, the pastor's wife gave me a Bible! It's uh-in my car! The truths I was learning! Well, Candy told me that God could take the desert of my life and make it a watered garden! I knew that my mother-that this was-what she was-seeking, although-she didn't realize it! The church had this amazing program, too-with a genuine track record-for helping the-addicted-" She paused to blow her nose and sop copious tears. "I just knew-Jesus was the answer-for my whole-family! Well, Mom and the kids and me! I would have been scared to-So Candy came over, and she explained to my mother-but she was strung out-I was-ashamed! People-don't understand."

"So your mother overdosed before she understood-" Alexandra's tears flowed freely as she tried to guess the outcome.

Brenna's voice changed to a weaker, more childlike tone. "No, she accepted Christ, I think! I hope so! But Candy and I did such an amazing job picturing Jesus and His love, and heaven-"

"Ah," Mallory's soft sigh as she grasped Brenna's torment. "So, of course, it never occurred to you that it might seem like a beautiful, ultimate escape to your mother's painful existence! That she might commit suicide"?

Sobs tore loose. "I didn't know! I didn't know! Instead of being the answer for us! It tore us all apart! I was wrong! Everything I do-is wrong-How can-every step-I take, be-the wrong step?"

੨੮ ੮੨

"There; I hope she likes it." Diana stepped back, paint roller in hand, to survey her handiwork, her comment addressed to Cassandra, her fourteen-year-old violin virtuoso daughter, and now partner in stealth interior decorating.

"It looks great! I never knew Wal-Mart had cute stuff."

Diana sighed. "Yes, well, I still stick with what my grandmother always told me, 'That you get what you pay for'. But it does look cute for the moment! I doubt it will launder well."

Cassandra suppressed a smirk at her mother's words. It wasn't like she ever stuck with bedspreads and drapes long enough to require laundering; or dry cleaning!

"You ladies ready for me in here?" The deep voice of Shank, the custom drapery guy Diana favored.

"We are. We'll move out of the way and let you work! Then we'll come back in~"

"I'll hang the pictures and mirrors if you'd like! Just show me what goes where."

"Wow! Thanks! We can be on our way then! Add the miscellaneous~"

I got the proper tools; won't take me thirty extra minutes. You've been an immense help to my business with your recommending me! How's that ornery brother of yours? I hear nothing but good things~" Shank referenced one of Diana's younger brothers who was a missionary in Nigeria.

Diana laughed. "Then you hear more than I do! Thanks again for finishing up." She paused in the doorway to take in the lovely space, finished in monochromatic purple to lavender color scheme, offset by white trim.

Daniel met them in the front yard. "I was just coming to check on your progress! I can't believe the change in this place."

Diana frowned. "Were you ever in here?"

He blushed guiltily, "A few times! I helped Hig move in, and then we met here for a few poker games. Most of the time, we hung out at my parents', or~"

Diana raised both hands defensively. "Sorry I asked."

He sighed heavily, "Yeah, me, too!"

He hated reminders of past failures!

⊱ ⊰

Mallory accessed her phone for a couple of emails. One was Brenna's university transcript; the other, a police report. Brenna's grades were overall, mediocre to poor. And the police report was troubling, primarily because Brenna had answered 'No' on the application about ever being in trouble with the law! The lie was more troubling to Mallory than the actual incident! Although the incident looked bad!

"You don't have to stay." She addressed her comment to Alexandra. "I have a few more things to delve into."

Brenna's brows drew together as she wondered why she stayed. Mallory's earlier statement was pretty clear! She hardly ever hired anyone!

"Yeah, I have some calls to make."

Mallory searched Al's features closely as she squeezed out of the booth, worried about Brenna's comment about a boyfriend. That must mean something was up with Tommy Haynes. "Okay, talk to you later?"

"Yeah, y'all take it easy."

Brenna was shocked at her relief of being alone with her idol! Mallory was amazingly personable, just calm and compassionate.

Mallory checked her watch and proceeded, remembering Diana's warning that the girl was near a, 'psychotic break,' and to tread cautiously. She wasn't sure what that meant, but it sounded bad. With a frown and a sigh, she continued.

"So, this is slightly unusual! Majoring in Geology with a minor in elementary ed.?"

Brenna nodded. "So I've been told! Repeatedly! My faculty advisor pitched a fit to me about it! Like they know you and care anything about what you want to do! Until you cross their opinions"!

Mallory studied her phone information, wondering why anyone would doggedly oppose sage advice. "So, you must like working with little kids?" she ventured.

"I don't want to teach high school! I actually want to be a field Geologist!"

Mallory frowned, "Then why take ed. classes at all?"

"It's hard to explain."

"Okay, one more thing, and then this inquisition will be over." Her bubble of laughter was met by a hard stare.

"What about this case of aggravated assault?"

"You have the police report? That's what happened. What more is there for me to say?"

Mallory bit on her lip and her deep green eyes probed her devotee. "But on the ap~"

"Yeah, I said, 'No'. I hoped no one would check!"

Mallory laughed suddenly. "Yeah, I get that! But in this day and time~"

"Yeah, it was stupid!" The admission came as the exhausted girl began to tremble visibly. "I can't figure out why you're putting us both through this! If I can just get back~"

"Well," Mallory touched the hand resting on the table. "Please, I want you to know that we're your friends. Uh~I have some good news~uh~and some bad news!"

Brenna sat, bracing herself without answering.

"Okay! First the good news! We hired a private investigator to check into the place you rented the room from, and to locate your car and belongings! The good news is, that he found quite a bit of your stuff chucked into a dumpster a few blocks away! The bad news is that he can't locate your car beyond its having been towed. He assumes it was chopped! I guess they use the frames for dune buggies, or something?"

Brenna clamped her teeth together, trying to control their chattering as the shakes overtook her.

⛩ ⛩

William Beckwith scowled as he stashed his high dollar camera and prepared to ease into traffic a few car lengths behind his quarry. 'Very odd'! He needed to return and chat up Brenna's former roommate. For now, he considered it the best strategy to stick with his guy! His phone rang, and he scowled as he accepted the call.

"Hey!"

"Beckwith, what are you up to now?" followed by an angry tirade which included a good deal of profanity!

With a careless laugh, the private investigator responded, using unsavory words in turn. "Hey, this case is considered closed, Detective. Except now this girl, you say is the perpetrator, whom her friends see as victim, well~she and her friends want it expunged."

"She's lucky to have gotten probation! Maybe she should be grateful and not stir the pot! She attacked Steve Elwood like some crazy wildcat!"

"Right! I get that! After she spent an evening serving him the finest booze money can buy! She wasn't impressed because he didn't seem to be that much of a high roller! More of a wannabe! So, she was keeping an eye on him to skip and stick her with his tab!"

"Yeah, and that goes with the territory! They know that!"

"So, you're saying that this guy guzzling up five hundred bucks and skipping without paying, is fine, because the waitresses know if that happens, it's up to them to make it good? This gal's boss didn't even back her! He testified that she had a few screws missing!"

"Yeah, well bad stuff happens!"

"Well, it's baffling to me why the city's finest are okay with that!" Beckwith sighed. "Sorry! You're right; she should have stopped shy of laying her hands on him! But she chased him for a block and then he laughed at her!"

"Yeah, and then his story was that he was so drunk he forgot about paying, and he laughed at her because he thinks everything's funny when he's soused!"

"Why that would wash in America's courts of law~He even tried to get Hamilton into trouble for continuing to serve him! But that bar's manager gives strict orders not to pull the plug on anyone who's still paying! A violation of the law, but hard to prove! Why does the department have an issue with me checking this guy out?"

"Because her piddling little case is done; she keeps her probation terms without any further assaults on people, maybe she can still gather her little chicks from foster care! To my thinking, she should cut her losses and start clean. Since you want to know, Elwood has upped his ante from walking on bar tabs, to major fraud."

"Well, surprise, surprise! And if she doesn't consider abandoning her younger siblings as cutting her losses, she seems pretty charactered! At least loving"!

"Well, I don't know what money hired you, but I'm sure they failed to tell you the truth about getting the case expunged! The companies she's interviewing with give their people guns and train them to use them! Imagine that crazy woman~"

"Gotta go, Webb! I won't be in the way of the Boston PD!" He hung up as the detective growled that he better not be!

⊰ ⊱

David Anderson supervised a work crew from a masculine office in a high end RV. Delivery trucks arrived with hastily purchased furniture! Although crews had completed renovations on an older house acquired from Professor David Higgins several weeks earlier, it had stood empty.

Now, with Mallory's sudden idea of moving Brenna Hamilton into it, crews were doing double-time to get it revamped and furnished! One of his crew members, familiar with assembly of loft beds, was putting three of them together.

"Make sure you don't cut corners," David warned. "We don't want them collapsing with anyone!" Still, to be on the safe side, he checked the joints, knowing employees often don't do what you expect, but what you inspect! He nodded to Shank who completed the draperies, and then sighed in relief when his brother and valuable assistant, Jeff, arrived on scene! At Jeff's direction, workers carried new linens and groceries in. Jeff's girlfriend, Juliet Prescott, stepped in, "I'll oversee the kitchen and grocery stocking! But I need a helper!" She addressed David. "Where's Alexis?"

He laughed, pleased for her interest in his girls "Glad you asked; she's stirring around now, from her nap."

"Okay, I'll change her; Amelia and Avery can help me, too." She pulled the cuddly toddler into her arms and snuggled her before digging in to help!

⚑ ⚐

"Where are we going?" Brenna realized she was out of options, but fretful at not being in control.

"Some place safe and warm and comfortable," was all Mallory would say. She really liked what she saw in the newcomer, in spite of a couple of warning flags. But, before she committed to the plan formulating in her mind, a few details needed clarification! "You can calm down! If none of us can actually hire you, we'll give you a chance to regroup and make a plan when you aren't in panic mode. I guess 'trust' comes hard for you?"

Brenna laughed nervously. "Yeah, I guess! I mean, I try to trust the Lord, but-um-Hey, I'm sorry I made your grandmother worry. She's a sweet lady! I'm not used to people caring about what happens to me!"

"Yes, Grandmother's the best," Mallory agreed warmly.

The SUV pulled in at a discount store and Mallory pulled a hundred dollar bill from her wallet. "Why don't you go in and shop for something else to wear? I'm not sure exactly how much of your clothing they actually salvaged."

Brenna's brown eyes were a study in fear and anger.

"Please, you can pay me back, once you get on your feet!" She watched the girl limp into the store, figuring she had blisters from her uptown walk the previous day. She pressed a button on her phone. "Have you gotten anything new?"

"Yes, as a matter of fact!" William Beckwith responded. "Two crucial items of interest! Elwood, the so-called assault victim, is up to his eyeballs in serious financial and credit card fraud! Evidently, realizing the hammer is about to fall, he has fled!"

"Where to? Does that make his case federal?"

"Sadly, not yet! Only Massachusetts! And it takes yet more serious offenses to get the feds to take notice! This is a heads up! This guy is headed your way! One way ticket to Tulsa from Boston Logan! Brenna Hamilton's ex-roommate, Jill, told him where she is!"

彑 彐

Brenna pushed her cart slowly. Seeing children and aisles of toys dragged at her, pulling more tears from the depths of her heart! Wishing she could use the money to send little gifts to her brothers and sisters, she shook herself! Not an option at the moment! But, maybe-Mallory Anderson seemed to think she had some potential! If neither Mallory nor the Faulkners hired her, they had a network of people-maybe coming here wasn't such a mistake!

A pair of purple jeans caught her eye! Her favorite color! In her size and on clearance! Into the basket they clunked! Then, a pair of faded denim, an ivory, zip hoodie with purple writing and emblem, a lavender crew neck sweater! In the limited accessories department, she found a purple and lavender scarf in a *Fair Isle* look! Not like anything Alexandra or Mallory wore, but these were cute and new! It came to eighty-five dollars, and she was horrified! Mallory didn't tell her to get two outfits! And a scarf!

"Hi! Any problems"? Mallory's greeting as Brenna slid into the back seat with her package.

"No, did I take too long?"

"Not at all! Show me what you found!" Mallory grabbed mischievously at the bag! "Oh wow! You done good! Cute! Oh, I love the purple!"

"Me, too; it's my favorite!"

Brenna surveyed the neighborhood curiously as the vehicle turned down an older, narrow, tree-lined street! It didn't appear that they were en route to the Faulkner's! A truly gorgeous and cavernous home! Where she had never in her life felt so out of place, nor like she was being held prisoner!

Mallory wasn't sure what to make of the chaotic scene! David's, "Just about finished", meant that furniture trucks still blocked the driveway and Suzanne Bransom's flats of pansies made the sidewalk impassable!

"Hey, Mom"! Mallory hopped out to hug her mother! "Thanks for coming to the rescue! Your flowers are always such a nice finishing touch!" She refrained from asking her if she had seen the kids yet, figuring she hadn't! Which, always hurt her feelings! Still, Brenna's heart-breaking story about losing her mother, made Mallory grateful to still have hers, whatever her foibles might be! "Mom, this is Brenna! Brenna, my mother, Suzanne Bransom"!

Brenna hopped from the SUV, extending her hand shyly. "Pleased to meet you, Mrs. Bransom! I love pansies! Is it not too early to~"

Suzanne laughed. "Well, in Boston, it would be! They should do okay! You probably know they tolerate cold much better than they do heat!"

Brenna shrugged. "I didn't know that! I generally prefer rocks to flora and fauna!"

Suzanne omitted a mock sigh! "Yeah, another one! I despair!"

Mallory laughed. "Better watch out, Mom! We got ya outnumbered here!"

"Yea! Mommy's back! Mommy's back! Mommy where have you been? You been gone all day and now it's almost night time!"

Mallory swept her first-born up into her arms and planted a kiss on pouty pink lips! "I know! I'm sorry! Mommy missed you, too! Have you been a good girl for Daddy? Say hello to Miss Hamilton!"

Mallory released Amelia to greet her other girls, Avery and Alexis.

Amelia obediently and grudgingly greeted the newcomer.

᎐ ᎏ

Brenna crowded shyly behind Mallory as she led the way past workers scurrying with last minute jobs. Enviously, she wondered who the home owner was, who had such a gorgeous home; plus all of the new furniture and gadgets; even a robotic vacuum cleaner scooting around the gleaming wooden floors! A new office, with state of the art everything! A washer and dryer coming in through the garage on dollies! Obediently, she preceded Mallory through a doorway!

"Believe it or not, everyone's nearly finished up. I guess these are your things they found in the dumpster." Mallory surveyed the derelict little pile dismally. "If you'd like, you can get a chance to clean up and try on your new stuff! By then, all the crews should be cleared out! There's plenty of stuff here to snack on, and we're going out for steaks later!"

Brenna studied the master suite reflectively! Wow! Walk in closet! With no clothing in it! Everything done in lavish purples! Her favorite! They were so lucky! She caught her breath sharply at the lavishness of the bathroom! Thick purple towels that yearned to be touched, yet she dare not muss anything up! Picking through her few personal possessions, she grasped her Bible. Sure enough, tucked beneath the securing flap of the worn cover, was her small stash of cash! Reluctantly, she realized that she owed it to Mallory for the recent shopping. She would return the stuff and get her money back, and be gone, as far as the modest amount would take her! And she could fall back on her waitressing skills! Glumly, she picked up a DVD, turning it over slowly! It looked okay; hopefully it still worked. She needed to find a library and access a computer, to be certain! After all, a lot of her work and hope were invested in it! She should have made a backup!

No way was she running water in spotless sink, or using such luxurious towels. Hating to even risk rumpling the satiny purple bedspread, she slid onto the floor and opened her Bible!

⚔ ⚔

Brenna fought panic as she joined the elegant group filing behind a hostess to a private seating area in a dark, richly-paneled restaurant! The prices made her heart lurch, but she did at least have the cash with her! Not that she wanted to spend it all on one piece of meat! And she felt foolish, that Mallory had been forced to wake her when it was time to leave! A puzzled Mallory, Brenna knew, at why she had neither cleaned up, nor fallen asleep on any of the inviting furnishings!

"Relax," Daniel whispered. "Don't forget you're among friends!" Then, he was gone, taking over the boisterous group, directing seating, laughing and at ease!

She was shocked at the place he directed her to! Right between Diana and an attorney, Clint Hammond! As awkward as she felt, she was still glad she hadn't changed into the new things. She needed the money back!

David and Mallory settled in on the other side of the attorney, and she watched as the wait staff approached and the meal progressed. Reminding herself of Mr. Faulkner's words, she relaxed, although she tried to opt for the less expensive chicken entrée!

David leaned around Clint Hammond! "Get a steak," he insisted.

Diana frowned. Her main hope was that the exhausted and mal-nourished girl would eat whatever she ordered. "You should try the bread! We particularly like it here."

Smiling wanly, Brenna dabbed thick butter, then paused to see if anyone would give thanks.

"We usually attack the bread and then pray once the orders are turned in." Diana took a nibble to back up her words, and Brenna followed suit!

A people-watcher, she forgot her own self-consciousness to watch how the wait staff operated, and also how these amazingly successful people handled themselves! No orders for wine or beer, let alone hard stuff! She was impressed, enjoying the gentle din of the camaraderie! Still, she was shocked when David whispered to the Captain to put all the orders on one tab and give it to him! Well, that simplified everyone's asking for separate checks! Still, she didn't want to assume anything!

True to Diana's words, as beverages arrived and the wait staff retired, Daniel asked for everyone's attention. He was so commanding in his presence that he didn't have to ask twice!

"Okay, as all of you know, except for Brenna Hamilton, she's the reason we're all here for this business meeting!"

She blinked in amazement!

Daniel continued, "She made a rather bold move from her roots in Boston, to show up and apply to *GeoHy* a couple of days ago! Well, I wanted her, but I thought Al needed her more! And then, Mallory got wind of it-as she usually does-" He paused with a laugh. "Well, as Mallory pointed out, the snow at Al's mine in Colorado is still deep, and getting deeper as we speak!" Another chuckle!

Brenna listened breathlessly as he continued, "So, with David and Mallory's problems with Del Waverly's drinking, they need a good Geologist weeks ago!"

Brenna cringed! She was a green Geologist, not necessarily a good one! Her expertise very much remained to be seen. And the last thing she wanted was to challenge a drunk, experienced, male Geologist for his job!

So, of course the wisest way to proceed, for the benefit of all of us, is~if you know Mallory at all~you can guess!"

The buzz grew; it seemed everyone in the room knew Mallory enough to guess~

"That's right! To incorporate Brenna into her own entity, and contract with her!" He leaned past Diana to make eye contact with the stunned young woman! "Let's hear it for the CEO of a brand new company!"

When the excitement abated slightly, Daniel thanked the Lord for great friends and a marvelous meal together!

Chapter 3: ENTHRALLED

Alexander Grayson Prescott scrutinized the worried countenance staring back at him in the gleaming mirror! Dropping in at a haircut joint was taking longer than planned. The stylist whose turn it was, yacked endlessly! And it wasn't like she could talk and cut at the same time! So he stared at the reflection; seriously thinning hair and mild gray-blue eyes behind wire-framed glasses.

"Is that enough off?" She snapped chewing gum as she waited for his response.

With a wince, he nodded. 'Too much, actually'! "Yeah, yeah, it's fine!" He hated it, but it wasn't totally her fault.

He paid and tipped before pulling on a woolen/cashmere blend top coat! Something he had paid way too much for! His sister, Diana Faulkner, with contacts in the fabric/fashion world, doubtlessly could have provided him with better fit and quality at a better price! It was just that ordinarily, he didn't care! And now, time was of the essence.

⚜ ⚜

Brenna hopped from the city bus at the Sullivan Building, a stop she was becoming accustomed to! Another summons brought her down here, and nerves brought waves of nausea, reminding her that she should have eaten at least a piece of toast! *Prescott, International.* She spotted the listing on the mezzanine directory! These people were somehow related to Diana Faulkner, and they specialized in helping international workers and travelers! She was here for the primary purpose of obtaining an expedited passport and visa for Chile! But the receptionist had also said something about this company doing much of the bookkeeping and payroll services for the related corporations! Not a CPA, but a company that took these responsibilities to free the executives for focusing on their key missions! She sighed; she wasn't great at keeping records, but she had always done what she had to, where the IRS was concerned. She figured she could hang onto receipts! She didn't need any unnecessary expenses in her start-up! Still, she felt like she was facing a pressure pitch. Since her first contract was with *DiaMo*, she had considered running this summons past Mallory!

⚔ ⚔

"I hate the way the picture turned out!"

"Have a seat, please," Preston Banks Prescott's voice and personality filled the sizeable space that was his office. "Passport pictures are always horrible! Like driver's license pictures and other ID's you're stuck with for ten years!"

Brenna obeyed reluctantly! Evidently, there were no retakes! And now with the visa application completed, she assumed the pitch was on for the financial services. To her amazement, he handed her a packet with instructions to look over the services they offered, to keep in mind as her responsibilities grew! That made sense!

⚔ ⚔

Gray moaned! Typical of the way his morning was going! Leaving from the haircut, and his car wouldn't start! He had waited for the dealership to come for it and provide a loaner, which was in need of being thoroughly cleaned; and now one elevator on the front side of the Sullivan Building was being worked on, creating a backlog for the other!

"Lord," he whispered, "why is all this happening today? I can't figure out if You are against my plan, or if the devil's messing with me!" He sighed! Probably neither! Just one of those days! "Lord, I guess I forget to praise you when my days go smoother than oil."

He hit the door into the stairwell and loped up two stories. The top coat was definitely warm! Two more flights and he exited to frown into a large decorative mirror, at a strange sprig of hair! Oh well! Gathering his wits, he stormed into the *Prescott, International* office suite, past a startled Denise sitting at reception, and into his father's private office!

29

A beautiful woman standing there preparing to leave, stared at him in bewilderment! Practically knocked off her feet by the force of his entrance!

He stood staring stupidly while angels played harps, and a choir erupted into the *Hallelujah Chorus* in his brain! Brenna Hamilton was beautiful beyond description! And he had nearly smashed her with the heavy wood door! His father stared at him strangely.

"Is everything okay, Son? Miss Hamilton, I'd like you to meet my eldest son, Gray! Gray, Brenna Hamilton!" Even as Preston retained the presence of mind to make the introduction, worry hit him about his son's odd entrance! Gray was the unflappable one!

After long moments of electrified silence, Gray extended his hand. "Actually, I'm Alexander! My parents sometimes call me, 'Gray'. My first-born niece, Alexandra, is actually named in my honor!"

Even as he spoke, he remembered that Alexandra hadn't exactly hit things off royally with the newcomer! And he was still holding her slender hand in both of his. Reluctantly, he turned loose and managed a shy smile. "But you can call me Gray, or Grayson; that's my middle name!"

Brenna recovered herself, backing away slightly. "Very pleased to make your acquaintance, Mr. Prescott! Have a nice day!"

He blocked her exit! "Sorry to burst in like this! I wasn't aware my father was in an appointment! My car wouldn't start earlier, and I was going to talk to him~"

Brenna frowned! "Oh, that's the worst. What do you think's the problem?"

He responded with what the service manager had suggested it might be.

Her countenance lit into a smile! "Hey, I know how to wire around that! Just a re-circuit~"

He laughed, "Well, if it weren't under warranty, I'd be tempted to take you up on your offer!"

The smile faded and she paled! How foolish! Of course! Everyone around here had brand spanking new, shiny, glitzy cars! All under warranty! What a different world she was from! With her beater and retreads! And even that seemed to have disappeared!

Not one normally to be at a total loss, Preston's hearty voice boomed too loudly! "Nothing like a young lady that knows how to be resourceful! And you've helped me with another problem by your analogy! I've run up against a wall; maybe I need to back off and figure a way to 'recircuit'! Listen, we're burning your valuable time! Denise will give you a call the second the passport and visa are available! Have you checked on inoculations?" He studied her. "None are required, but I suggest Malaria for anyone traveling to South America! Just a precaution! Better to be safe-you probably haven't located a GP yet, since you've barely been here a week!" He buzzed Denise to locate and provide information for the Prescott family doctor!

With a troubled thanks, Brenna managed to exit.

"Gray, what's up?" Preston tried to close his office door. "Did you get in a wreck? Maybe you should go to the hospital and get checked out! You-uh-don't seem yourself!"

"I'm fine, Sir!" Gray spun on a well-heeled loafer and sprinted after the Geologist!

⚔ ⚔

Warren Weston surveyed his handiwork with mock satisfaction! Although his hands trembled, he took a sculpting tool and poked a couple more indentions into a clay mug! Craft time! Making clay stuff! Still, gazing around the wintry grays and browns of the working ranch, he was once more glad for this reprieve!

Jeff Anderson walked between the two long tables, examining the pieces carefully. "Okay, time to wash up for chow! Just leave your projects to dry a bit! Then, you can glaze them later before they're fired."

He paused behind Weston! David had held some reservations about bringing him here; afraid he might be trouble! To this point, he was the most pliable and helpful of any of the camp men in a long time! Jeff stopped to study the mug. It was unbelievably cute, featuring an angelic little face! One of the guy's little girls, evidently! As the men filed out, he snapped a photo to forward to David!

⚔ ⚔

Brenna tried to remain patient as she waited for the elevator! There were probably security cameras in the hallway, and she didn't want her picture taken revealing her total annoyance, but in a building this nice, the elevators should work better! And she needed to catch her bus so she wouldn't be stranded down here for an additional half hour! She was getting hungry, and the building's Bistro appealed. But she couldn't start blowing money like that! Well, she didn't have any to blow! She jammed the button a couple more times, "Come on; come on!"

"Ah, I've managed to catch you! Because, they're working on the elevator"! Alexander Prescott's voice startled her.

"You have a great talent for making me jump, I guess! Why did you need to catch me?"

The doors slid open and he followed her onto the crowded car.

"Well, I've gotten dreadfully hungry, and I hate to eat alone in the restaurant here. I can go over the contents of the packet with you."

Brenna felt herself flushing. She hated to say she had to catch the bus. "I thought your father told me it's pretty self-explanatory! I apologize for the dumb thing I said about your car-"

The doors slid open into the lobby, and she allowed herself to surge forward with the crowd.

"Brenna, wait! Please!"

⚔ ⚔

"He-he just ran off, then? And he didn't give you any updates on Parker and-" Diana could usually keep calm, but the panic in her father's voice was disturbing. "Maybe he was that upset about his car! He-he wasn't hemorrhaging?"

"Well, no; nothing like that! Or I would have taken him to hospital!"

"Is there a chance he's in a financial bind?"

"Who? Gray?"

"Yes Sir! That's who I thought we were discussing!"

"Nah, he still has the first nickel he ever made! And all the other ones since! And he's earned lots of nickels! He tore in here with what hair he has, standing on end; his face red as a beet; and panting like-and I was in a meeting with that new girl! He nearly knocked her flat with the door, bursting in without so much as a tap-I'm thinking he got exposed to something in Nigeria, or on the return flight! And we still don't know how his visit went with Parker and Callie!"

"So, where is he now? In his office"?

"No, Sis! He took off again! He's-just-not-himself!"

⚔ ⚔

"Why order an egg white omelet? Diana isn't here."

32

Daniel laughed at his dad's sneaky observation. "She doesn't have to be! She has her ways of finding stuff out! And I'm getting used to them! As long as they're drowned in salsa! Which, I know, has too much salt in it! You should try one, Dad! We need to keep you around as long as we can!"

"Well, thanks, Son, that's good to know! But why live long if you have to live on sawdust?"

"Good point! So, an exciting year; huh"? Daniel's eyes glowed with wonder at the oil flowing from a freshly discovered field. "And you counseled us to run from Patrick O'Shaughnessy!"

"Yeah, in fairness to me, he seemed a little off his rocker! And you and Diana were having kids so fast, your mother and I didn't think you needed to agree to take in an extra!" Daniel Jeremiah, Sr.'s stern countenance gave way to a grin! "But you prayed and did what you thought the Lord wanted! And Mallory has proven to be a treasure in a multiplicity of ways!"

They paused to bless their food, and Daniel continued. "Yeah, and to our immense relief, even David seems to be turning out okay! And Diana and I weren't having kids fast, Dad! We kept losing them!"

The senior Geologist nodded. "Yeah, well your mom and I questioned the wisdom of bringing you into the world at such a seemingly turbulent time! And you and Diana, and the Christianity thing, and reproducing like rabbits, as society ratcheted up its craziness, seemed cultish to us!"

Daniel shook his head in amazement. "Thanks a lot, Dad! How did we get here from discussing the oil production?" An odd expression flitted across his handsome features, causing the senior man to look over his shoulder.

"Ah," he turned back to face his son, "your hermit of a brother-in-law! Never seen him frequent this place before! With the new Geologist"?

"Yeah, Dad, how weird is that?"

⚎ ⚎

"Morning, Diana!" Mallory's tone bright as she recognized the number. "Do you have word about Parker and—"

"None; that's what I'm calling about! Gray made it back on schedule this morning, but he's-well-he has my Dad-worried-and Daddy isn't-a worrier!"

Mallory listened to the story as Diana comprehended it to be.

"That doesn't make sense! If the car's a lemon, he's traded with that dealership for five or six years. They'll accommodate a trade-maybe it is something about Parker and Callie, and it has him too distressed—"

"No, whatever it is, it's totally made him forget his mission visiting them! I mean, Gray is just so steady and unflappable! We're thinking he's ill! Just, I need to call Daniel, but will you guys pray?"

≒ ≓

Brenna managed to eat most of her half sandwich; and the cup of soup was delicious! Mr. Prescott, for claiming to be so hungry; had yet to take the first bite of lunch.

He paused in his gossipy family chatter, blushing apologetically. "I'm not sure why I'm telling you all this."

Brenna wasn't sure why he was, either! But it was interesting! Maybe too much information, but enlightening! And he was back and forth with laughing at funny incidents from his past, to weeping at some of the trauma!

"So, you've still resented Daniel Faulkner? All this time"?

He shrugged, trying to shrug off his own guilt for not 'getting over' some things, and his continuing bitterness at his brother-in-law!

"You would have had to experience how perfect our world was!"

Having never experienced a 'perfect world', or even a perfect day, Brenna frowned. 'Yeah, hard to fathom, all right!'

And yet he had already painted for her the magic of the idyllic world of his childhood.

"I always assumed MK's had it tough and hated their lives!"

His laughter rolled, a pleasing sound, "Only occasionally, when we were forced to visit some of our supporting churches! Then we felt like bugs under a magnifying glass! But the time actually on the field in Africa! We liked many of the African kids we ministered to, and we would play with them at church functions, VBS, camps. But mostly it was us brothers and sisters! We had chores and stuff we helped out with, but we helped each other with those, and they became like part of the never-ending game to us!"

Brenna sighed. "So, your father's actually the one who insisted on sending you off to England to study! Why do you blame Mr. Faulkner?"

"It's complicated. I guess he's all right now, finally! But things were never the same for us kids when Diana left! I went for a semester, and came back to a different world! She was the spark of the family! She left a gaping hole! And the fact that we wanted her, and he was treating her~Anyway, the Lord smacked him in the head a couple of times, and it got his attention~the fever~"

He broke off suddenly. "Tell me about you!"

"Just a little girl from Massachusetts! I claim to be a Bostonian, but~I have this problem sometimes~with~" She blushed.

"Embellishing the truth?" He finished. "Well, calling yourself a Bostonian isn't that much of a stretch! And you got your degree from there!"

Brenna was keenly aware when Daniel Faulkner and his father departed. She was sure he hadn't overheard the conversation, but wondered if it made his ears burn.

"I'm not sure how you have that information! So," she smiled mischievously, "we've determined that I'm a Bostonian with a Bachelor of Science in the field of General Geology! I've never been out of the state of Massachusetts until I drove here! And I'm thrilled to no end to be getting a passport and visa! And, I guess I'm headed to Chile?"

She sparkled at the prospect of the adventure.

⇇ ⇉

"Hey, what's up?" Daniel's voice, anxious, as he responded to a dozen missed calls from Diana! "I was down eating lunch with my dad and didn't realize I'd left my cell phone lying on my desk! I'm sorry, Honey," he continued, to bridge the silence! "Are you~is everyone~okay?"

"No!" the panic in her voice caused his heart to dive into his Italian leather loafers. Before he could ask, she continued tearfully.

"Something's the matter with Gray! Father said he arrived this morning, and he was all askew! And then he bolted away! And~no one~"

"Okay, Di, Honey! Take a breath! He's fine! Dad and I just came up from the Bistro. He was down there having lunch!"

"Who was?"

"Grayson! Your brother! The one you're worried about! He seemed fine! Well, except that he was with a girl!"

"Grayson was? Well, I guess it's about time~" she paused in absolute confusion. "Did it seem like a business appointment? What did she look like? You're sure it was Gray?"

Daniel laughed. "Actually, he was talking to Brenna Hamilton! Maybe it was business! Your dad was taking care of the passport and visa; who knows?"

❧ ❦

David laughed at Mallory's intensity! "What now? With the receipts? We haven't yet completed the mission set forth by your last discovery!"

She smiled. "True, but it's been a profitable venture so far! Now, if we can get Brenna on board, to finish things up~thank you for all of your heroics~it's coming together, I think! I hope! Maybe we should pray about it again!"

David nodded, reaching for her hand. Not a bad idea; some of the loose ends defied being tied up! "Yeah, getting her siblings transferred to Tulsa~it'll take a miracle~actually, they're halves and steps!"

Mallory nodded. "She's an amazing person, I think! To care and to fight so hard for them! And about my daddy's old receipts! I had a hard time sleeping last night."

"Yeah, I thought so. You were moaning and getting restless, and I thought the nightmare was coming."

Amused and startled deep hazel eyes met his intense dark brown ones! "Come to think of it, that hasn't happened in a while! For me, or Amelia! That's an answer to prayer!"

"So, you couldn't sleep because of the mountain of receipts? And now you're going through them again?"

"Well, I was dreaming I was in a car! Just not in the trunk this time! I don't remember seeing my dad in the dream, but~do you remember my telling you about the day when he and I were supposedly on our way to the mall in Little Rock to shop?"

"I remember. It was his object lesson warning you to steer clear of me! Glad it didn't work!"

"It worked, David. He opened my eyes! After I got over being so mad at him! He drove me all over the country-side! Now, today, I can hardly catch my breath! I'm so excited! My dream was about our final turn around that afternoon, before he was suddenly able to drive right straight back to the house! That spot wasn't random! Nothing he did was ever random!"

"We've tried to retrace that route, before, though!"

She shrugged slightly! "Yes and no! By my foggy memory"!

Doubt showed on every feature. "But the dream cleared it all up?"

"No! The dream was of the place we turned around! It didn't speak to me that day, but now~I know with certainty~it was a Lamporolite dike!"

"We couldn't find it, though!"

She laughed brightly! "Because we didn't follow the map"!

⚔ ⚔

Brenna tried to sneak a peek at her watch. She didn't want to appear rude, and it was cheap compared to Mr. Prescott's expensive chronometer.

"Look, Brenna," Gray taking a desperate tone. "I don't want to put any pressure on you, but-uh-what do you think?"

"What about"? She lifted the packet neither had mentioned. "I thought I'd wait until my company grows more complex-and then-I don't know! I'm confused to suddenly be a CEO! A CEO of nothing, mind you-but-" she laughed self-consciously.

He squinted at her, nice straight-forward eyes behind his glasses. "No, you and your company will make it! You're CEO of a viable entity! I don't doubt that! What you've done-that's been the hard part! The waiting tables, and making your way through to earn your degree. And I wasn't talking about the accounting we do-"

She met his gaze, clueless.

"Look, I know I'm older than you are, by a good bit-" He wasn't the Prescott blessed with the gift of gab, and reining in emotions he barely grasped himself didn't add to his eloquence! "This may seem kind of sudden, but would you do me the-honor-"

She couldn't stop a giggle from springing forth! "Sudden! That's an understatement! Whoa! Whoa! Are you-a-serious-?"

Tears sprang up in her eyes at his consternation. "Look-umm-this has been a-an-amazing afternoon! Marriage; it's been the last-I-I have plans-"

He nodded. "I know! I want to be part of them-with your siblings-I want to help you take care of them-"

She scoffed. "Uh-I'm pretty sure you don't know-"

He sat there, regarding her in his solid way. "Maybe I know more than you give me credit for! I've been single this long-because I've never before met-anyone who made me-want to not-be single-"

She stared, trying to grasp the magnitude of the situation. Of his admission! He knew more than she gave him credit for? "Okay, what, exactly, do you know?"

Grave eyes met her faltering gaze and held her steadily. "I know you have a degree from Boston University with a minor in Elementary Ed. No one can figure what your thinking was behind that–I assumed it meant you like little kids–in addition to your family members! I know that customer stuck you with his bill, and you ended up with an arrest and assault charge! That's utterly mad!"

She stared, enchanted with the slightly British-gentlemanly accent and demeanor!

"So, you want to take on a project?"

"If you're a 'project', then yes, the answer is emphatically a 'Yes'! Although I just see an enchantingly lovely woman! And I shared all of the foibles of our rather large Prescott family to pave the way toward making you understand–"

She nodded slowly and patted gently at tears. "Understand you know what you're bargaining for with kids under foot–"

"Kind of! I know it isn't the same thing! But the things you're worried about, their behavior; might require a firmer hand than you have to give!"

She smiled. "So, having lots of brothers and sisters makes you the one to know how to discipline a houseful of toddlers to teens?"

He laughed, and his features lit up! "No, that I learned from my father! Just say, 'No', to everything they ask!"

Her laughter bubbled and then she grew serious, regarding him in wonder! "I-I should pray about it!"

He slid his hand onto hers and warmth coursed through her! "I already have!"

Chapter 4:   CRAZINESS

"Now what"? Mallory knew what Diana's words were; she just didn't like the implications!

"They're getting married! And fast!" Diana's usual aplomb forsaken, she practically wailed into the phone. "It's just so unlike Gray! Usually, he's so methodical and deliberate!"

Mallory figured Diana's brother was old and wise enough to order his own life; her concern was for the Geologist the Chilean government required for her exploration project! Brenna had seemed like the answer! She hated to address her spin on it when Diana was in such turmoil! "Okay, well, could you please slow down, and give me more of their plans that you're aware of?"

"Okay, Gray's pastor has agreed to a vow exchange in his office, on Friday! The legal waiting period! We can hope he comes to his senses~"

"Yeah, in case he doesn't; what then?" Mallory figured it was a done deal! And Gray and Brenna didn't seem like a bad match! Except to his overly-protective, big sister!

"Well, then, assuming her passport arrives, they're going to Niagara Falls for a honeymoon for a couple of days; then to Boston to deal with her criminal~" Diana broke down, unable to finish!

"Criminal charges that should have been brought against the drunk thief! Instead of Brenna! That would have made me mad, too! As a matter of fact, it makes me feel like finding the guy and punching him one, myself! A private investigator told us he followed her to Tulsa! How weird is that?"

"That's what I'm saying! Gray doesn't need to get mixed up with a girl like Brenna!"

Mallory laughed, although she realized her friend's distress was real! "That makes me glad David and I are from a town that's too small to have a right and wrong side of the tracks!"

Diana emitted an annoyed, something between a sigh and a, hmmmpf! "Don't get me wrong! I'm not a snob!"

"I know you're not! It's just, that he's your brother! No one could be good enough for him in your eyes. Just like no one can be good enough for your kids~ Uh, that reminds me; did something happen to Al and Tommy?"

"Her name's Alexandra! And Daniel told her she could correspond with him by letter. Thomas phoned her and reamed her out for her mine!"

"He did? What was his problem with it?"

"I don't know! They were too young, anyway! And Gray's plans are to deal with the charges against Brenna and then make it happen for her to bring the other kids back with them! Then, they'll have a week or so to establish a routine before Brenna flies out for your exploration! Gray plans to play father while she's gone!"

Mallory cringed, relieved that her plans seemed to be on go, but also questioning the staid bachelor's foray into parenting! "Okay, that's interesting!"

⊰ ⊱

Brenna paced; the hour was late, but she was too keyed up to consider going to bed! Well, hours of sitting and consuming coffee while they talked! She stared at the sparkling diamond in her new engagement ring! How could Gray not have noticed how ugly and unkempt her hands were as he slid it onto her finger? How could he help noticing she wasn't in his class, at all? She loved him! What was not to love about him? Steady and solid, but then dissolving into laughter at a story they shared. He made her feel special, something new! And satisfied, like she was home! She couldn't say he was her ideal, her dream man! She had never dreamed about men, assuming they were all sorry, and that she didn't need the grief they brought! That there could be a good man, or that she would have anything to offer in the event of that rarity, had never occurred to her! She had simply tried to finish her degree and trust the Lord, with the hopes of re-gathering her pitiful, torn-apart family!

Her happiness brought memories of her mother flooding in! She was grateful for Gray's desire for a vow exchange in the pastor's office! That way there wouldn't be the sad comparison between the bride and groom's 'sides' in the church sanctuary, where he had tons of loving family members and well-heeled friends! And she didn't have friend or relative one! The reason why she had left the space on the *GeoHy* employment ap, blank, that asked about next-of-kin.

From the Bistro, they had taken a taxi to a prestigious jewelry store! Hence the beautiful rings! And a watch with a price in a stratosphere she didn't know existed! A watch telling her it was past one a.m., and she couldn't afford to grow lazy and off-schedule! Could anyone be so perfect? From the jewelry store, they had strolled a couple of blocks to a hole-in-the-wall that served amazing Italian, quiet, with a leisurely pace! Then, as though he couldn't bear parting either, they went to a little bakery for coffee and dessert! Then, like a true gentleman, he escorted her home in a cab before being taken back to his loaner car downtown!

During the course of the day, she had divulged the story of her mother's taking her own life, as a result of Brenna's description of her Savior and the beautiful mansions He was preparing in heaven. Gray was the first person to give words that really brought her comfort! That if it was suicide, there was no note, and over-dosing wasn't anything new! And, that suicide wasn't an unpardonable sin! And that the likelihood of its being intentional wasn't quantifiable!

"Hey, she's saved! She's in heaven now! Think where she would be had you not brought her to the knowledge of Christ when you did! It's a trick of the deceiver to load you up with guilt about so much that's not your fault! And that makes you feel like you don't do anything right, when you're doing so much good!" She had even shared with him her anguish at serving liquor, telling him how earnestly she had prayed for a better job!

"Do you think I should have quit, by faith? I just couldn't see a way~"

"Well, all that's in the past now! You got your degree, and you beat all of them! God gave you the victory! But you haven't stopped long enough to savor it!"

She sank into the midst of the lush purple that was the queen sized bed, grasping her little Bible and studying her reflection in a heart shaped mirror attached to a dresser that matched the bed frame! When had she ever been surrounded by new stuff that matched?

"Lord, Gray is right! I've been going at it so hard and fast for so long-it is hard to realize I've made it! Well, You did it for me! And Gray said my new company is real, and that I've got what it takes-! As a matter of fact, I don't think I've had as many nice things said to me in my whole life, as he said to me, today! They kind of flew right over the top-I need to remember them all and write them down!"

On her knees, she prayed, "Dear God, I don't know how to be a wife, let alone a good wife-especially-he's just so high-calibred-and I'm pretty sure his family won't accept me-I don't measure up-"

She opened to a passage in II Corinthians that she liked when she felt too many rungs down her imaginary ladder! About people that compared themselves among themselves and by each other, being unwise in so doing! And another passage came to her about how, 'fearing men and their opinions', brought a snare!

"And, Lord, if I please You and Gray, the rest isn't that important! Thank You for loving me and lifting me up! Help me not to fight what You are doing, because I'm like the little pilgrim, *Much-afraid*. If You have brought me to these positions, as being Gray's wife and president of a company, I guess You can give me the capabilities I'll need!"

⇜ ⇝

It was late, but sleep evaded David! It probably didn't matter, in the long run, in God's scheme of things; but he had really put himself into the remodel of their *DaMal, Inc.,* property, acquired from Professor David Higgins! Even before the extra work and expense of furnishing and preparing it for Brenna Hamilton! And her siblings, in the event that the judge should okay their relocation! And he was okay with six months rent-free, while she got on her feet! Of course, he hoped Mallory would compensate the losses on his side of the balance sheet-He sighed! But now, Gray Prescott, the personification of *Scrooge*, in David's estimation-was sweeping Brenna off her feet! David was suspect of the man's motives! That his actions were spurred by his being a taker, so he could live rent-free! On David's dime! That was bad enough, without the huge mutt, Chauncey, the Great Dane! Of course, Mallory was relieved that the couple's plans were for Brenna to sign her contract with *DiaMo* to join the exploration off the Chilean coast! Probably Prescott had plans for Brenna's company and income! Diana thought Brenna was the gold-digger, but David liked Brenna more than he did Diana's brother!

He moved quietly through the north Dallas mansion, checking on his sleeping kids! Tucking covers tenderly and kissing precious little faces, he crept down to the sports bar and brewed a decaf mocha. Then sitting in the charming space with the extravagance of the frothy drink, he chuckled softly! "Lord, forgive me! Help me to mind my own business! I have plenty of my own! And not be so caught up with what others are doing, and judging motives I really have no clue about-You are the righteous Judge-it's just-that horse of a dog!"

He laughed inwardly. "I had to get the last word in, didn't I, Lord? Even with You! Guess I'm the one Amelia gets that from!"

⊰ ⊱

The Honorable Marilee Wilkerson paced in her chamber. When did a block-buster attorney like Lawrence Freeman ever appear in her courtroom? She studied the adoption petition. Alexander Grayson and Brenna Renee Prescott, appearing to adopt all seven of the children and relocate them to Tulsa, Oklahoma! Wow! High-powered! She wasn't sure what to make of it! Evidently Brenna had managed to land some guy with money! But convincing him to adopt the menagerie she called brothers and sisters, sight unseen? Maybe stranger things had happened, just never in her court room! She scanned down the document at the background checks! Brenna's legal trouble wasn't there! And the man seemed squeaky-clean!

She pressed an intercom button. "Have the children all arrived?"

The judge and attorney were both shocked at the children's appearances! Their foster families were supposed to want to see the children be adopted! The children were dirty, all wearing ragged and out-grown clothing. Judge Wilkerson considered banning the foster families from the system. Sadly, they did as good a job as most! Brenna seemed shaken at their appearance, but the husband simply smiled good-naturedly, answering her few questions more than satisfactorily! With a few warnings about the gravity of the adoption process, the papers were signed. He drew a checkbook from his breast pocket and wrote a check to the clerk for the court costs!

Those costs, with what he must have paid to the attorney, were quite substantial! Maybe there could be a good outcome! Not that money was a guarantee!

☲ ☵

Mallory studied a travel blog! It featured new pictures of Professor David Higgins and his wife, Nanci, aboard a Danube river cruise! The couple were newlyweds and new Christians; consequently, Mallory wanted to give them space to grow in grace and make adjustments to their new life! To her chagrin, the Professor was on her payroll! Nanci was still doing her job for Deborah Rodriguez, while the Professor followed her! Brenna's timely appearance, taking up the slack for Higgins, and his over-imbibing buddy, Waverly, was a huge blessing! And Brenna was a contract, rather than a hire! The ideal situation!

She answered her intercom. "Hi, Marge, is Brenna here? Send her on in."

She smiled as Brenna entered, followed by Marge with a tray of coffee and pastries.

"Welcome back, and congratulations! On all fronts"! Mallory's voice infused with sincere warmth!

Brenna laughed. "Thank you! It's good to be back, but now I'm raring to go!" Her eyes were alight with anticipation.

Mallory knew the feeling, almost wishing she were going, herself! She quickly went down through her bulleted checklist, before finishing, "Look, if anyone tries to give you any trouble at all-"

"Yes, Ma'am, that's what Gray told me, too!"

Mallory laughed. "I'm sure he did! But tell me first, so I can have a chance to fix things! I don't want him pulling you off the job! I have a lot of confidence in you, though-" she paused. "I know things have been tough for you-"

Brenna regarded her steadily. "Yes, Ma'am, they have been. But it's made me tough and pretty much taught me to handle myself." She turned to the large monitor. "What is that picture?"

Mallory sighed. "That's my chief Geologist and his wife-"

In a bound, Brenna was at the device, studying it, fascinated.

Mallory fought annoyance. She had nearly spilled her frustration with Higgins to the newcomer! Something she made a habit of never doing! And Brenna was changing the subject from the important briefing!

"Where is this taken?"

"I think somewhere in Germany! Nanci models Deborah Rodriguez' fashion line among cruise clientele, and also has started a successful travel blog! Her blog advertises Diana and my fashions, as well as Herb Carlton and Davis Hall and their jewelry lines!" As she spoke, the facts dawned on her, that in spite of *DiaMo's* losing out while Higgins loafed, Nanci's ads were bringing in orders for clothing and jewelry! Maybe a trade-off! Like if she tried to be nice to people and help them out, the Lord always took care of her!

Brenna seemed not to have heard her answer, but stood transfixed before the screen!

Mallory sipped coffee and bit into a Danish, then leapt from her chair with a yelp!

⇥ ⇤

David pulled in front of the rent house. To Mallory's relief, Brenna was en route to Santiago! Assuming no one would be at home, David had come by for an inspection of his property. But there were lights on! Maybe another time~From his drive-by, it was evident that Suzanne's flower beds were meeting a cruel fate~No telling what transpired inside! He was curious how the old bachelor was making it with his instant fatherhood, but decided it would be best to find out via the old grapevine! He drove slowly to the corner to make a U-turn, and was chagrinned to be caught on his spy mission!

He lowered his window as Gray appeared from a neighboring house with an elderly woman in tow! Maybe the guy was kidnapping himself a nanny!

"David! Meet my neighbor, Anna Kinsey! She's joining me for a spot of tea! Join us?"

'A spot of tea!' Really? Why couldn't the guy drink coffee like a normal person? Still, curious about the state of the new family, and his property, he agreed.

To his shock, all of the children were assembled in the family room around a large screen, watching Tommy Haynes teach a math course! It was pretty elementary, but they were intent, not even getting out of line while Gray was at the neighbor's!

"Children"! At Gray's quiet voice, heads turned his direction.

"Yes Sir?" A chorus in unison.

"Turn that off for a few moments. I want you to meet these people, and then it's tea time! Say 'Pleased to meet you,' to Mrs. Kinsey and Mr. Anderson! And say their names! Look them in the eye and smile as you offer your right hand~"

He paused as he took note of a grimy, outstretched hand. "Hold it! Go wash up before tea! Don't forget to use soap and leave the towels straight!"

David tried not to be impressed! After all, Brenna hadn't yet been gone four hours!

☙ ❧

Brenna's terror gave way to pure exhilaration as the jet gained altitude and banked in departure from DFW! New to flight, she still felt apprehension at take offs and landings! When a bong announced they were at altitude for electronics, she eased the business class seat to a comfortable position and opened her new laptop! Excited about a fresh quest, she still gave herself over to a tide of emotions! A verse from The Psalms flooded her mind: And she softly quoted it to herself:

> *Psalm 68:13 Though ye have lien among the pots, yet shall be as the wings of a dove covered with silver, and her feathers with yellow gold*

She studied her screen saver: a new photo celebrating the birth of the Alexander Grayson Prescott family! The kids hastily made presentable following an emergency trip to Wal-Mart for clothing that fit better and was clean. She ran the tip of her index finger lovingly across Gray's attractive features, then tracing down: Jacob, Summer, Luke, Lindsay, Terry, Emily, and Misty!

Glancing up at the attendant, she welcomed a cup of coffee! She savored the strong brew, slightly less than hot, but she could enjoy it at room temperature! She allowed herself time to reflect on the quick-fire series of events since earning her diploma! A cross-country drive in a beater car, fighting wintry conditions! No cell phone, little money in case of break-down (a strong possibility), or other emergencies! To arrive in Tulsa and rent a deficient 'suite'! And then to run in panic from the *GeoHy* offices~right into a startled Diana Faulkner! And then~Grayson! Her attention refocused on the screen before traveling to her sparkling rings on manicured hand! A smile tugged at the corners of her mouth! And the criminal charges against her–with her boss, Murphy, being arrested on an outstanding hit and run case, before he could appear to testify–And then Gray's hiring Lawrence Freeman, for both the assault charge and the adoption–a lot of money!

And then a snug, but cozy fit, into the house! Having the kids tested academically, to learn that they were all alarmingly behind! And Grays' stolid determination to oversee a home schooling course to bring them up to speed.

"They all have extremely bright minds," he assured her, within their hearing. "They'll catch up in no time at all, and join their classmates!" Then with that, he devised a <u>schedule</u>, as he pronounced it with his English accent, and a few family ground rules! He was right about starting out with firm control, something she knew she could never have established without him!

The kids were overwhelmed at being wanted and loved, and being back together– Once they were asleep the previous evening, she and Gray had enjoyed a long talk about dreams and goals! He changed his accounts quickly to everything's being joint; his understanding of business and estate planning being beyond her! Now she carried some cash and credit cards, as well as sharing a checkbook!

He had confessed to additional ambivalent feelings about his brother-in-law, admitting his envy that his own paper assets grew slowly, and then took hits at the whimsy of 'the markets', while Diana and Daniel added a third story to their already ostentatious home! Then were given a luxury cabin on the Andersons' ranch/camp property in Arkansas! And then, hit an oil gusher–and Alexandra owned a rich Colorado Silver mine that looked favorable for production of other noble metals, also! Later in the year, Brenna's new corporation would contract with the mine in an attempt to locate the source of the alluvial Platinum nuggets!

He had gazed around the purples of the modest bedroom. "Sometimes, I've felt the Lord nudging me to be bolder and have more faith in Him, to branch out into Real Estate! I've been wondering if David and Mallory would consider selling us this house! The one across the street is also for sale, as well as a few others I've noticed in the neighborhood! I'm not a fixer-upper, but I could hire David's crews to update the places to earn rental income. Real Estate provides tax advantages, and I'm not sure why I've hesitated! While you're in Chile, I'll acquire some properties! We need a bigger place; this barely accommodates our children, and then-are you sure you don't mind Chauncey?"

She smiled, thinking about the moose of a dog! She loved him, and so did the kids! But, a bigger house? How could things get better?

⊰ ⊱

Jacob and Summer brewed and poured the tea, a new skill, and their nervousness showed. Lindsay used tongs to place scones on small china plates. Over all, the scene was charming!

"Thank you, Children! Jacob, please refill for our guests, and then return to your studies!"

David and Anna exchanged awed glances.

"David, your driving past couldn't have been timelier! Brenna and I talked late into the night last night, about expanding our investments into real estate! I was just gone over to ask Anna about her 'For Sale' sign-uh-her husband has been-gone-for seven years,-and so-um-naturally-"

David's friendly gaze met the shy neighbor woman's, "She has trouble keeping it maintained, and ready to show at a moment's notice," he finished.

She nodded tiredly. "There's no way I can do all that real estate man told me I'd have to-"

David nodded understanding! An aging neighborhood! Hard to tell if investments into the properties would reclaim the block or go down the drain. He wasn't sure what to say to Gray, either! Over all, investing in real estate was wise; but there could be real clinkers!

"Well, I realize there are always some risks!" Like David read his mind! "This is what Brenna and I discussed! Offering you fair market value on this house, including your recent upgrades and furnishings! And purchasing Anna's home, if I can hire your company as remodeling contractor! Then, we have found a larger, but older home not far from my parent's house! We would continue to live here while you modernize and make improvements on it! Then, we will live there until we can build! And we would like you to design our dream home and draw our blueprints!"

David's resentments toward the man were crumbling! Unless, he expected the labor he described at some super beneath market rate! He hesitated to speak!

"I know someone else could do it cheap! I admire the quality of your work! Give me your estimates, and I won't even take further bids! And name your price for this home!"

David considered. "Okay; give me a chance to run it all past Mallory, and I'll get back with you by tomorrow morning." He turned his attention to Anna! "What are your plans?"

Gray's laughter rolled. "You leave Anna to me, Anderson! I'm thinking to lease her this house, for lower rent than her mortgage payment has been! The rental income will help toward our payments! This way, she can still be around the same friends and neighbors who all look after one another!" He laughed again! "And I'll have a nice quiet tenant who doesn't have seven children and a Great Dane!"

David laughed, draining the tea cup! "Guess ya got me!"

Anna rose, too, and they moved toward the front door!

"Children, our guests are leaving!"

The lesson muted and seven voices chimed, "Good bye, Mrs. Kinsey and Mr. Anderson! Thank you for coming!"

⚔ ⚔

Brenna worked avidly at a fresh project she had assured Mallory she could figure out! Her fingers moved nimbly; then she referred to the map in the flight magazine, then back to her Google map! She sought for a news article about a recent forest fire in Germany! Amazing how scarce world news was; mostly local stuff! School boards and county commissioners and their little soap operas! Still, some coordinates came together! Annoyed, she became aware that the attendants were more willing to offer Champagne to the business class travelers than the repeated cups of coffee she requested! Evidently, they just wanted everyone to nod off! Head aching from resisting sleep, she finally dozed.

⚔ ⚔

With a quick check of Brenna's research, Mallory was inclined to agree with her about the coordinates of the Higgins' photo! She accessed the travel blog, to note that the picture, the most recent posting, was still up! Sad, that Professor Higgins, being right on the spot, failed to notice what Brenna picked up on in the background of the picture! Mallory was forced to admit that her frustration with Higgins caused her not to see anything else, either! She already liked Brenna! A lot! Passionate about Geology, and from a Creationist world-view! A switch Brenna had made half-way through her studies, when she received the Lord! Higgins, as a brand new convert, still sought to make the rocks support a false premise; while Mallory, and now Brenna, just tuned in to what they actually said!

She turned to greet David as he appeared in her office doorway! "Tammi's coming to have lunch with Kerry in the café! We're invited!"

Mallory grinned. Tammi, David's younger sister, was married to their corporate attorney.

"Which means we're buying, but she is really good help wrangling the kids! I think it's a majorly great trade-off!"

He nodded, "And as always you look so sensational! A shame to hide you away in your office"!

"Thanks! I already feel as big as a house! And, I have plenty to do! Not to change the subject, but did you go do your drive-by?"

"I did~and got caught in the act!"

"Who by? Brenna's well into her flight! I'll be glad when she navigates entry and reaches the ship!"

"Well, Gray caught me, and trust me, he went over and over every scenario in the book with her, about passport control, her visa, and clearing customs! All my worry about our rent house was for naught! I'll tell you all about it later: for now, I'm going to go gather up the girls!"

Mallory frowned as he departed, wondering why he had been worried! And what had happened~to ease his mind!

⚐ ⚐

Brenna studied other travelers as she waited in the Santiago, Chile, airport, for her flight backtracking up to Iquique where she would join the *DiaMo* exploration ship, *The Rock Scientist*, studying the Peru-Chile, or Atacoma, Trench! Stilled buoyed from a Skype session with Gray and the kids, she purchased a Coke and munched from her stash of American snacks! Just a few days previously, she had been awed to live in the cute house as a single, rent-free tenant! Now, owning it with her new husband seemed likely! And yet, as well off as Gray was, he encouraged her to form the company and pursue her professional dreams! She sighed! Surrendering herself to the Lord was certainly not a mistake! She remembered some of the girls

50

from her Somerville church grumbling about the pastor's words to let the Lord lead them to the spouse of His choice! What rebels they were! But was her attitude as rebellious, in affirming she wasn't ever going to marry at all? That men were self-seeking problems! She would be contented to do whatever she could to help her brothers and sisters; that would be enough! And her plan was a good one! It's just that God's was better! Like the verse about His thoughts being as high above our thoughts as the heavens are above the earth! Literally measured in light years!

She kept her Bible out as she boarded the local carrier, but she was asleep before takeoff!

⊣ ⊢

Mallory called her grandmother with the update about Brenna's safe arrival in Santiago! Delia was extra-concerned for Brenna's safety following the previous year's scare with Shay and Emma in Bolivia! Colored by that incident, Delia seemed to consider the entire South American Continent suspect!

Mallory understood her mindset! Globalism presented risks! Not every country was like the US, although, the US seemed to be sliding away from the values that had always set her above the rest of the world!

David buzzed her, "Okay, Waverly made it to the Ranch! It's not necessarily a rehab facility~"

"No, but it's turned lots of lives around in amazing ways," Mallory responded. "Since he left, the crew can't do any exploration until Brenna gets onsite! Let's pray for Del, that~he understands the gospel~but even as I say that, I have an ulterior motive~"

David sighed! Well, in a way! If he gets restored to profitability and productivity, and stays with us, he'll be an asset~to us! But, it will do more for him than for us! It's just something that would be good all the way around! Don't feel bad about your desire to see him squared away! Why is it, the worst criminals don't feel guilt for their acts, and guilt racks us day and night, when we're trying to please the Lord? It's because the devil is 'the accuser of the brethren', (saved people). He accuses us to God in our shortcomings, and makes us loathe ourselves when we shouldn't! Do I sound like my dad?"

She laughed. "Not yet, but you're getting there! And I got you started!"

"Yeah, I eventually tried not to get my dad started! It helped reduce his daily number of sermons, exponentially! Can't believe I just delivered that little lecture to you"!

⇥ ⇤

Brenna retrieved a flashlight from her cabin and returned to a project in the cargo hold! Her understanding was her predecessor, Waverly, was to have offloaded the core samples at Iquique and shipped them to the various analysis labs *DiaMo* contracted with! And then load up with empty cases for the samples now being drilled! With Waverly's being gone, she wasn't sure who to check with! She hated to email Mallory first thing, with a problem! She straightened, massaging the small of her back! A shadow with an accompanying rustle made her freeze with terror!

"Who's down here?" She shone her light toward the sound, but the weak beam didn't pierce far into the gloom. "Hello?"

Alarmed, she was positive she wasn't alone! When no one answered, and she sensed no further movement, she eased backwards toward the companionway, and to the deck above! Eerie! Whoever was down there should have come forward and identified himself!

Chapter 5: PANIC

Mallory's concern deepened to dread as she watched the information coming live on the drilling logs! Nothing! Nothing! Nothing! And then, still more nothing! She should know when to say, 'Uncle', admit defeat, and pull the plug! How much more money should she sink, in the face of the facts? Day after day, and miles apart, the samples showed more of the same in monotonous fashion! She turned her gaze to a map of the South American Continent! Most of the Andes' watershed coursed eastward, across the vast expanse of the continent! And drained into the Atlantic! Being on the Pacific side, off the Chilean coast, barely made sense now! Something about the sameness of the data snatched at her consciousness! Maybe more than the same? Identical? What were the odds of that's happening? She inhaled sharply, then noticed the time stamp on the data feed! It wasn't coming live, as it should be! The same core sample data reran–but someone had grown careless about updating the time!

She sat, trying to comprehend how that could be! And who could be behind it. She was pretty certain that neither the ship's crew, nor the drillers on board, possessed the capability for such a sophisticated deception!

Two realizations struck her simultaneously! That her drilling was on target, with valuable discoveries coming in! And, that, that fact might have Brenna in peril!

Rather than buzzing for David, she sprang toward her office door in search of him. Before she could touch the knob, he stormed in! "Have you eaten anything since day before yesterday?"

She turned guiltily toward an untouched donut on her desk! "I can't remember! You need to see what I just figured out! Brenna might be–"

"Okay, don't change the subject, because I thought we had an agreement about your eating!" He moved purposefully past her, to place a container of soup on her desk, easing the lid off carefully!

She couldn't stand having David mad at her, and she really was doing a lot better! She obediently sipped a spoonful of the broth; then opened a cracker packet, shoving a saltine into her mouth!

"Okay, take it easy! Don't bring anything back up!"

Tears filled her eyes as she nodded, trying to swallow the big bite, and gagging instead! It seemed like long moments before her will power won out and the food decided to go the right way.

"Okay, I'm sorry! But, keep eating! What were you on your way to tell me?"

"This data feed is fake! Meaning we have no idea what's really beneath the sea floor; and that I've possibly sent Brenna into a huge corporate conspiracy!"

His handsome features grew troubled. "So, we keep hoping Halsey and Pritchard will change; and they do! They keep getting worse!"

She rose to indicate the monitor with the wrong time still showing on the feed. "I keep wanting them to realize it's the Lord that blesses us, and leads to these amazing-"

He shrugged. "Yeah, and whether or not you convince them the Lord has anything to do with it, they do realize you're their ticket to wealth! Let you walk with the Lord and figure things out, and they'll be ready to steal what you find! Keep eating!"

⊰ ⊱

Brenna's attempt to return to her cabin for her possessions was blocked by a tight knot of men in the narrow passageway! They were looking for her! Her heart thudded in her ears, and she shrank back! Her sat phone vibrated, and she figured it was Gray! No time to talk now, or make any sound! Maybe he would understand that she was in peril! She paused. Maybe she wasn't! Maybe she was easily spooked and paranoid! The snafu with the samples' not being off-loaded was probably due to her predecessor's drinking problem! Unable to take care of business properly! The reason for his being pulled off the job and her being sent in! Whatever was going on, she needed to appear at the noon meal-notice if anyone acted strange- Sadly, she already knew the answer! She was the sole female onboard! The rest, about thirty men, evenly divided between the ship's crew and the drilling crew! If they were up to anything, it stood to reason that they were working in collusion with one another! And they didn't need her here at all, down going through things, with direct comms to the *DiaMo* offices!

"Lord," her prayer in total silence. "If I'm being a silly scaredy-cat, help me to trust You and snap out of this! If my danger's as real as it seems, I'm seriously outnumbered~ Lord, please protect me! I have to get back to Gray~and he's legally bound himself to all the kids! I have to be in it with him~

A voice carried to her, above the hum of the engines and the clanking of the drill rig, "She'll show up for mess!"

"Yeah, but she can call out for help!" came a voice of caution!

"Okay, well the laptop's here! We'll take that! She probably doesn't have a clue about anything; hasn't made any outbound calls! She's pretty green! We can just keep an eye on her~"

"Hmmm! Ain't that sweet? I say, we don't take any chances!"

∺ ∺

"You need to call Sam Whitmore, and explain everything you can to him!" David's logic kicking into high gear!

Their genius IT contact could get them some intel about who had hacked their system to override the drilling logs!

"I'll call Cade and see if any of the samples have been analyzed, showing different results from this data feed!"

Mallory agreed glumly. "Yeah, see if Jeff can get Waverly brought in here! I'll call Erik, too! I know the FBI doesn't reach a hundred miles off the Chilean coast, into the Pacific~"

David met her anguished eyes. She relied more and more on her mother's husband, FBI Agent, Erik Bransom! "Great idea," he approved! "Maybe he should be your first call! If he sends agents to confront Gabe and Nate, maybe they'll~uh~ fold the operation up before anything~uh~ happens! And you're right about seeing if Waverly realized anything was amiss! Maybe he played a worse sot than he is, so they'd decide he's harmless~and let him come home!"

"I hate this so bad, but Gray needs to know!" Her normally lilting voice filled with deep dread!

Before David could offer to make the tough phone call, the intercom buzzed, "Mallory, Grayson Prescott is on line one!"

❧ ☙

Brenna felt totally exposed with her every movement aboard the ship! State of the art security that should give her comfort, presented a huge threat! Skirting the cameras she was aware of, she slipped back down the companionway into the welcoming darkness! Pausing, she replayed the ship safety video through her nearly photographic memory! Her best bet was escaping the ship in one of the large evacuation rafts! A scary thought, since she would be like a duck in a shooting gallery from the ship's decks; even if they didn't utilize the chopper!

Oh well, she didn't have much choice! Shaking the negativity, she scrambled in the dusky space until she located a pair of oily coveralls and a huge wrench! Peeking into the engine room, she listened to the rhythm of the twin diesel engines! The space was empty of personnel, evidently at mess! She wished she was in readiness for her evacuation. A fire down here would keep everyone busy while she made her getaway! Not that the ship surveillance crew ever left their posts! Even as the gloomy fact presented itself, she wondered how she could take down the system! And if she managed to do serious damage in crippling the craft and escaping safely to be rescued at sea-would the Anderson's believe her ludicrous story? Could they sue her for her actions? Would Gray be by her side, no matter what? She sighed. She thought he would be! "But, Lord, if not-You are on my side! And I don't have anything worth suing over!"

❧ ☙

Sam listened seriously before attacking the problem with all of his skill and considerable equipment! Not even any jokes! And to Erik's amazement, Dawson, his superior, backed him in an operation to send agents into the Dallas offices of *Pritchard and Halsey*! The surprise visit yielded some evidence, although both of the corporate officers denied knowledge of any wrongdoing, before hiding behind powerful corporate attorneys!

❧ ☙

"Hello, David!" Cade Holman's answer to the *DiaMo Corporation* executive's call. "Why are you asking me if we've analyzed any of your samples? We haven't received any! I've watched for them to begin arriving, wondering if the delay is due to its being South America!"

"Nada? Zip?" Although, David half-way expected such news, he was still surprised. "Samples should have started arriving three weeks ago! Jeff's on the way here with the former expedition Geologist! Maybe he has some tracking information on where the boxes got routed."

⚑ ⚐

Using the flimsy disguise of coveralls and stocking cap favored by the crew, Brenna returned to the upper decks, counting on most everyone's being in the mess area! The captain always wore his sidearm, but she scooped up a handful of .22 shells from her foray into his cabin, before grabbing three bottles of his highest proof hooch! In the lounge area, she found a couple of partially used books of matches! Lowering her loot into a garbage can, she pushed it along on her supply gathering mission! Sad, that alcohol seemed more readily available than fresh water, and if she were to survive aboard the raft for several days~ She forced fear aside!

⚑ ⚐

Gray rose courteously as his parents approached the table where the children were settling in. He hugged his mother as he strove to get his group under enough control to make a good first impression!

"Hi, Honey!" Rainne Prescott clasped her eldest son in a prolonged embrace! "How beautiful your family is~" she released him with a delighted ripple of laughter! "Wow! When you finally make your move~"

He agreed softly, "Yeah, things move fast! Tell me about it!" He turned his attention to the disorderly culprits vying for position in a new environment! "Children~"

"I want to sit by Summer!" Lindsay's gritty warning to Emily.

"Children, I'm speaking to you; I would like to introduce you to my mother and father. Remember how we respond to~"

"Wow! You have a mother and father?" Jacob's amazement that Gray could have surviving parents didn't seem humorous at the moment! And,

57

of course, Gray was the only one aware of the danger Brenna was facing alone, thousands of miles away!

"Hello, Children," Rainne's musical, humor-infused voice brought a small measure of response! My name is Rainne Prescott, and I'm your new grandmother! My other grandchildren call me Mimi! Let me see," Her eyes sparkled as she placed her finger on her chin contemplatively! "Uh-Jacob," she guessed.

With a delighted blush, Jacob nodded shyly! "Yes, Ma'am! I'm very pleased to meet you!" Recovering slightly and struggling with the new manners, his voice was hesitant! "Rainne-er-Mimi, may I present Summer, Luke, Lindsay, Terry, Emily, and Misty?"

Each child raised a reticent hand as their 'brother' announced their names!

'Mimi' clapped her hands joyously, making gold charms on her bracelet jingle! "I am charmed to no end to make all of your acquaintances!" She nodded toward Preston, who was assisting café staff in delivering trays of food to the table! "And I would like for you children to meet my husband, Preston! You may call him, Pop!"

Gray winced. Since his admiration for his father was unbounded, he as the older single uncle, always cringed when Diana's kids used the affectionate grandpa endearment! He was relieved to see the food appearing! Grilled cheese sandwiches and tomato soup all around reduced confusion by miles! His parents brought years of wisdom to the table, literally!

Mimi frowned as Pop answered his phone! He could at least say the blessing; instead, he stepped out of earshot!

Gray's serious eyes followed him before he returned his attention to the crowded table! "Mother, Misty says grace nicely!"

"That's lovely, Sweetheart!"

Misty repeated her two line prayer and Gray beamed proudly!

⚜ ⚜

From viewing the ship's safety and evacuation DVD, Brenna knew that using the better choice of escape, the motor launch, was out of the question! In the video, it took two men to operate the winch system to lower it! And then, who knew how much fuel it had, or if there was an ignition key she would need! That left four sturdy inflatable rafts! The plan for an emergency was, to send the chopper with two men from the drilling company, to alert rescue personnel! That, following the initial mayday call from the ship! Then, more people by rank from the drilling company would evacuate in the motor launch! The rafts were for the ship's crew to use, in the event they couldn't keep the ship afloat! Gathering MRE's and a life jacket, she pushed her garbage can toward the position where the rafts were stored! From the janitor's closet, she grabbed a stack of rags and found two aerosol cans of stuff for removing tar and gunk! Perfect!

Securing a life jacket in place, she tugged at the heavy bulk that was the raft! The weight was a shock! Aware that once she opened the bay to release the raft, the security system would sound an alarm, she hesitated! Timing was everything! "Help me, Lord, please!" With a mighty jerk, the raft budged; not too far from the bay~Using a hatchet from the fire-fighting area, she chopped at the rubber of the other three rafts~probably silly because the chopper and launch would present more of a threat to her~

At a dead run, and with no attempts to avoid the security cameras, she approached a smoker the cook used for smoking fish and meats! Barely pausing, she placed one of the aerosol cans at the end farthest from the heat source. Dumping three of the .22 shells into the cooking glove, she placed it where the heat was more intense!

To her amazed delight, the bay opened as smoothly as the video had promised! Alarms clanged! Now or never!

⛻ ⛻

Preston Prescott greeted each of the new family members jovially, assuring them how welcomed they were~and longed for! Then, "I'm afraid something has come up that needs my attention! I must go make some calls! I'm guessing that these boys will be able to make short work of my lunch! I'll catch a bite later!"

Gray watched his father stride purposefully away! If anyone knew the international scene, it was his father! He knew people in the *State Department*, personally! He probably had connections in Chile, although he would do nothing to put missionaries at risk to assist a corporate entity! And, better than those advantages, he was a seasoned prayer warrior! Masking a heavy heart, Gray took pride in his new-found family and his mother's loving acceptance of his little brood!

And, as a practical parent, she distracted him slightly, with her list of things for him to take care of in Brenna's absence! The kids needed their inoculation records, they needed medical and dental check-ups, they needed to sign up for sports, and start music lessons!

He laughed. "I do have another job, if you remember!"

"I remember! Now maybe you'll finally learn to delegate!"

He frowned! Rainne was a delegator from way back! Like, having put Diana in perpetual charge of all of them! "What exactly are you getting at?"

A ripple of laughter, "Well, it's healthy for the children to have responsibilities, and they're capable of taking responsibility! However, I was thinking about that Joe Hamilton-"

"The insurance guy that drives David and Mallory nuts?"

"Well, yeah-he's a bean counter, and you're not!"

He regarded her steadily as the kids grew restless. He considered himself an accountant, or 'bean counter'! He liked what he did at the family company! "So how do you see Hamilton fitting?"

"Well, Joe is great at the policy comparisons, analyzing and researching! He isn't self-motivated or a salesman, which limits his ability to support his family with insurance sales alone! If he keeps his license up, he would be even handier to our company! He keeps begging the Andersons for a job because he knows he needs a nine to five, with oversight to keep him at it! David and Mallory don't want anyone they have to stand over, cracking the proverbial whip! He's not a threat to your position, for goodness' sake, Son! But he could handle a lot of-"

He turned a stern eye toward kids growing rowdier, and they settled down. "Maybe I'll give him a call!"

⚔ ⚔

"What?" A shocked question followed by sailor-caliber profanity! Drilling foreman, Vance Johnson, leapt to his feet as the ship's Klaxon blared an alarming jangle! Spewing profanity, he turned angry eyes at the tables circled by men finishing mess!

"The bay's been breached! Seriously, none of you could find one woman with few options for hiding places?" Still muttering savage curses, he kicked his chair to reinforce his anger! "Get below, find her, and take care of it!"

⚔ ⚔

Suddenly calm, Brenna watched the craft inflate on the pitching waves! Although tethered, it resisted her attempts at controlling it long enough to load her meager supplies and get onboard! And then, she was free, well sort of, with the tether chopped and the waves increasing the distance between her and the *Rock Scientist*!

⚔ ⚓

First Mate, Ed Devine was the first one down the companionway in an attempt to stop the Geologist from whatever crazy stunt she was trying to pull! Females! The sound of shots halted him, and he dove for cover! Crazy woman must still be on board, taking pot shots! Three! That meant her clip wasn't empty, wherever she was holed up! A small explosion made the craft shudder, and the Klaxon wailed again! Just as Devine relaxed with a mocking jibe about the 'mini-bomb', a secondary explosion rocked the ship violently, and heavy black smoke burst from the engine room!

Brenna stared up into the sites of a rifle! Nowhere to run or hide! If they missed her, the bullet would rip through her rubber craft, sending her helplessly into the cold ocean! Amazingly, one of the other guys clasped the shooter's arm, indicating for him to abandon the idea of shooting at her! She trembled with relief when both faces disappeared from the deck beyond her! Gratified, she watched as black smoke rose, and she heard frantic voices from the crew as they fought the fire!

⚔ ⚓

Preston Prescott's number came up on Mallory's caller ID and she grasped her phone quickly, "Hello, Mr. Prescott, I guess you're aware of the situation~"

"Yes, Mallory, and Gray's holding up for the sake of the children. I must admit to you that I'm worried! If Brenna manages to be rescued~it's such a male-dominated culture down there! I've been talking to a guy who speaks fair English, but he'll, doubtless, believe the male crew members' slant on what's happening! Especially if the guys point out Brenna's legal situation in Boston! If she gets arrested in Iquique, she may wish she were back on a raft floating endlessly on the rolling tide!"

"Okay~well, do I need to contact a Chilean attorney?" Mallory was unsure how to cope with this fresh worry! But Mr. Prescott's evaluation was spot-on! Chilean law enforcement or military would take the word of twenty or thirty men, over the voice of one woman!

"Well, they don't exactly have a legal system like ours! This may be delicate to broach with you, since the Geological exploration side of your companies, is directly your responsibility! But due to this gender bias, if David could talk to the authorities down there, instead of you-I know it probably sounds crazy~"

"Oh, that's good thinking! I mean, it shouldn't matter who tells the truth~me, or David! But I certainly don't want to jeopardize Brenna in a greater way! Yeah, David can handle all the calls! Do you have his cell number to give them?"

⇄ ⇄

Sam paused in his hacking and clacking to phone Agent Erik Bransom! Satisfied with his progress, he wasn't giving up! Just making a report!

"Hey, Sam; come up with anything?" Erik's tense voice!

"But of course!"

Erik chortled! "Okay, no offense intended. What~"

"Inter-office memos and emails! Pritchard signed his John Hancock to a direct order to keep the samples on-board and falsify the feed! Two days later~"

Erik listened to the report. Interesting as the information was, it wasn't obtained according to the letter of the law! As a matter of fact, he wished Sam hadn't divulged as much to him as he had!

"I didn't hack their system illegally, Agent! Not that I wouldn't have! In the scope of their corporate espionage on *DiaMo, Halsey & Pritchard's* tech guy broke through Mallory's fire wall! Everything I picked up that incriminates them, I got from their illegal hack on her! Their cleverness boomeranged back on them! Should I wire you a copy or do you prefer hard copies?"

A broad grin split Bransom's face! "How about both? Great work, Whitmore!"

⇄ ⇄

Michael Cowan and former US Army Lieutenant, Ward Atchison met at a café in the Tocumen International Airport in Panama City, Panama!

62

"Nice to finally meet you in person," Atchison extended a big strong paw in an awed but friendly gesture!

Cowan's eyes narrowed suspiciously, always amazed at Americans' need to bond! "You have seven men, and I have two, besides myself!" Cowan's confidence in his personnel left no question in Atchison's mind, that he and his American mercenaries were barely more than a contingency plan for the Israeli!

Whatever! The mission was to rescue and return Brenna Prescott to the US! By legal means, if at all, possible! Otherwise, they had a clandestine operation in the works!

"My intel is that the Geologist evacked the ship on a raft-" Atchison sipped coffee as he offered the latest!

Clearly displeased with Atchison's being in an information loop he wasn't in, Cowan frowned! "You sure about that? One girl fresh out of school? Against the odds of two crews of mean and fit men? What even tipped her off that she was in trouble? Anderson didn't have time to get word to her, once she discovered the scheme!"

Atchison met the glowering eyes. "I'm not sure! Do you think it's true what they say? That sometimes females have a sixth sense?"

Cowan snorted. "I don't think females have any sense! First or sixth!" He sighed, smiling for the first time! "And if you tell my wife and mother I said that, I'll deny it, so help me!"

⚔ ⚔

Relieved to see the gap of water widening between the smoldering vessel and her raft, Brenna sensed a terrifying isolation! Nothing but rolling blue in every direction! And once the sun sank beneath the horizon, there would be nothing but blackness! She shivered!

Chapter 6: PACIFIC

Brenna observed warily as the *Rock Scientist*, with the fire extinguished, resumed power! Her relief at their not shooting her ebbed away with the vanishing vessel! Doubtless, they assumed she couldn't survive! The vast billowing carpet stretched beyond her bobbing, state-of-the-art raft, in all directions! Awesome in its infinity! She wasn't sure she had ever felt smaller or more alone! In all of the small and lonely minutes of a life offering little but hope off in the distance! Make good grades! She was smart and attractive! Surely, she could-and now- All of the struggle seemed to have been in vain!

Maybe remorse at their actions and the consequences of abandoning her at sea, would bring them to their senses! Surely, the ship would reappear at any moment, flying a white flag of surrender! She scoffed! If that happened, would she be foolish to trust and re-board? In vain, she tried to conjure Gray's image! Strange, it had sustained her all day! Now, she could hardly remember the chiseled features, the eloquent blue-gray eyes behind wire glasses, the smiling lips closing on hers! It all seemed like a sweet dream lacking fruition! Turning to ferocious nightmare, trying to free screams from a parched throat!

⊰ ⊱

"Linds, focus!" Luke's whisper at Lindsay's elbow brought a stern frown from eighteen year old, Jacob!

"I'm trying to, but I want to talk to Brenna! She said-"

"Sh-hhh, Mr. Gray said she's in a meeting! Pay attention to this review; the test's coming!"

"That was hours ago, and Brenna promised we could call her~"

Jacob paused the curriculum and hit reverse! "She'll call when she can! Let's be able to tell her we finished this session~" He returned his attention to the monitor.

⊣ ⊢

Mallory paced! Yes, it was great news that Nate and Gabe's corporate snooping into *DiaMo's* confidential files had provided enough evidence to arrest them! But, still, there was no word on Brenna! If anything happened to her~she paused, nearly too numb and exhausted to word a cognitive prayer.

And there was no further word from her two mercenaries! They were lying low, on hold~for the moment, until they received definite intel on Brenna's location! So it was wait, wait, wait! Even the law enforcement personnel in Iquique hadn't called for David!

⊣ ⊢

Brenna mumbled, rousing slightly. "Jill, your~" Forcing her eyes open, she took in the bright iridescent green of her ceiling! "The phone~ringing~"

She fished the sat phone from deep coverall pocket! "Hello, Brenna!"

"Hi, Brenna," a little voice sliced across the four thousand, plus, miles~

She sat up straighter, suddenly alert! "Emily, hey Sweetie! Everything going okay?"

"Uhn-hunh, but we miss you~"

"Oh, I miss you, too! How are the other kids?"

"Okay! We're working on our school! We kinda understand it, and we're all helping each other! Well, most of the time!"

"Mmm-hmmm," Brenna's tone grew firm. "Y'all aren't doing a lot of fighting for your father, are you? Remember, I just promised to bring you something back if~"

"Em, stop playing with the phone!" Terry's voice was aggravated. "We missed this part again~" He made a grab for the extension and Emily wrestled free with a screech!

"Children." Gray appeared at the arched entrance to the family room. "Emily, who is on the telephone?"

"It's Brenna! I called her because she said~"

"Brenna? Are you quite certain?" He moved dazedly toward the six year old, but she backed away. "I called her, and I'm not done talking! Hi, Brenna! What are you going to bring me? Did you get it yet? Are you still gonna be gone long?"

Gray sank down dazedly on the end of the sofa, barely discerning the familiar voice on the other end of the line! It seemed an eternity before Emily obediently handed him the phone. "She didn't shop yet! She has to go back into the meeting! She wants to talk to you!"

"Brenna, my Love! How's the meeting going?"

She answered him by giving him the coordinates showing on the emergency beacon equipment!

"So, how's your cabin on the ship? Are you quite comfortable, Love?"

"Spacious! Designed for six! And I have the whole place to myself!" She lowered her voice so the kids couldn't overhear! "Safe for now with food and rations! The raft's a bright lime green! Is anyone looking for me?"

"Be assured of our love, Dearest! Best save your batt'ry! Children, tell Brenna 'Good night'!"

She smiled as the little chorus chimed together, "Good night, Brenna!"

"Night, kids; sweet dreams!"

⊣ ⊢

Mallory relayed Gray's update to Erik Bransom!

"Yeah, I already got the update, and we've been speaking to Pritchard and Halsey in lock up! I guess their defense counsel warned them not to contact the ship to order the Captain to stand down on this! Their attorneys thought it would look like an admission of their complicity! It's against maritime law and all standards of decent behavior, to leave anyone stranded like that on the ocean! Let alone a girl!"

"Okay, but there's a search and rescue under way? The beacon's functioning, and they should be able to fish her out soon; right?" Mallory cared about getting Brenna home safely, far more than about the criminals' actions, or even justice for them! She frowned when she received silence rather than confirmation of her hope!

"Well, we're trying to slough through red tape! If she were off the US Coast-I guess the weather report's that there's a big storm brewing down there-"

"Okay, thanks, Erik!" She blinked back desolate tears! "Lord, You're the Master of the sea! Please don't let a storm come now! That-that-will help the bad guys! Lord, You know Gray and Brenna love You, and they have such great plans! If You separate them this way, now-I can never forgive myself! Lord, I'm sorry! I-I had no idea-that-this-"

David appeared in the high doorway of their master suite, his arms opened invitingly!

She moved toward him resolutely, longing to be comforted, but knowing that nothing short of Brenna's appearance would lift the weight from her heart!

"One of the little girls called her sat phone, and she answered! How crazy is that!"

Mallory nodded. "Yeah, so we know she's alive and bobbing in a raft! Erik said there's a bad weather report, and no one will attempt a rescue mission!"

"Yes, confirmed by Atchison and Cowan who are still in Panama waiting for a go-ahead! It's every bit as bad, or worse-"

"So, they're not doing anything either?" She freed herself angrily from his arms!

"Mallory, they can't! They're willing to take risks, doing what they do-but we don't want to multiply our losses!"

"Well, they're highly trained! This is the kind of thing they do-"

He studied her sympathetically! "True, but they aren't bullet proof! They're just men! Some things are beyond their control! They take risks, but they take measured risks! We'll just keep praying! The raft is state of the art, and stocked with good supplies-"

She whirled on him! "Would you want to be on it alone? With a huge storm brewing? And, I've been praying! So many people are praying that it just seems like-"

"It seems like there shouldn't be a storm! I've been thinking the same thing! You know, sometimes God doesn't keep the storm from coming-He shows Himself strong through the storm-And as much as we dread to think about it, He may not choose to-"

"But, it's my fault!"

"No, it's Pritchard and Halseys' fault, and their team of drillers-"

"And the crew of our ship! It seems like they could be loyal to our interests! Since we're the ones paying their salaries!"

He nodded, "How things should be, and how they actually are~sometimes, are two completely different~uh~"

Her turbulent eyes met his! "Reality check! I~I guess~I've gotten~kinda~spoiled~"

"Maybe we both have! God's so good to us, and He answers so many prayers the way we want, when we want~I mean, we deal with a few hiccups, and think we've had it tough!"

"Yeah, you're right! I should be being grateful to Him instead of angry~All the times He's helped and delivered when we've thought it was impossible! That we were at the end!"

She paused to mention so many close calls they'd experienced, that David laughed! "Those you just mentioned are the kind of miracle we need right now for Brenna! God has certainly delivered in impossible situations before! His hand isn't shortened now!"

Her eyes sparkled as the tears paused abruptly! We should sing like Paul and Silas did in the Philippian jail! She started tentatively, a little Sunday School chorus:

With Christ in my vessel, I can smile at the storm~

He joined in, but they were both keenly aware that they weren't the ones in the little vessel! Brenna was! And it was going to be a rough ride!

Still, when they finished, Mallory spoke softly! "Well, dwelling on past deliverance and miracles helped! Complaining and whining weren't getting me anywhere! As a matter of fact, it made me feel as if praying was a waste of time!"

⚜ ⚜

Captain Winslow McKenzie watched bands of rain on his radar screen! She was coming in fierce and sideways! Everything was battened down, and the massive oil tanker shouldn't have much to fear other than a rough ride! Still, there was always that possibility! He strolled to the galley for a fresh cup of coffee!

"I would have brought it to you, Captain," one of the crew members reminded.

"Yeah, weather makes me pace! Thanks, though!" He frowned at a big plasma screen before heading back to the bridge.

✄ ✄

Brenna moaned weakly as the raft pitched upward before plunging dizzily once more! Never again, would she enjoy amusement park rides! She scoffed! As if the opportunity would ever be presented~She tried to control pessimistic thoughts, trying rather to focus on Emily's little voice, then Gray's, and all of them as they bid her good night! Maybe it would be fun to take them to an amusement park! So much had been denied them; now with some money~ She laughed softly, imagining their joy and excitement! For a moment of calm, she could see their glowing faces and hear their peals of laughter! Then, her cocoon soared heavenward, twisted and smashed down furiously! She dry-heaved~

✄ ✄

One thing about the children, when bed time came, which they were realizing was non-negotiable, they fell asleep instantly! Gray tiptoed through the quiet house, checking locks on doors and windows! In the purply plushness of the bedroom, he pulled his Thompson Chain Reference onto his lap! It fell open where their family picture saved his place! Like the others, he struggled with the untimeliness of the cyclone! He sat, neither reading, nor focusing on the faces of the photo! A sigh escaped, but he fought giving way to hopelessness! His children needed him! If there wasn't good word by morning when they wakened, he must tell them the truth, hoping his deception to this point, wouldn't hurt his rapport with them! Making the right decisions regarding them was less cut and dried than anticipated. Still, he would do the best he could by them! They were God's gift, even if He chose to take Brenna away!

✄ ✄

Heavily armed and cloaked in ponchos against the ravaging storm, members of a Chilean National Police agency, coordinated with members of the Iquique Port Authority, watched *The Rock Scientist* limp into port! Both the ship's crew and the drilling crew were taken into custody, as a Lieutenant of the national agency, leading a crew of techs, boarded to investigate the crime scene!

His instructions to be thorough were hardly necessary! He led some real professionals, on the cutting edge of criminal investigation! Still, with international implications, possibly involving a murder of an American at sea, he didn't want any crucial evidence overlooked or misinterpreted. He frowned as he noticed a slim, new laptop in the drilling foreman's cabin! Pulling on latex gloves, he opened the cover and switched the device on! As he assumed! It matched the photo sent to his agency from the American owners of the exploration ship! A belonging of the missing female Geologist! He pointed it out, and it was duly photographed, bagged and tagged!

⚮ ⚮

Shivering violently, Brenna surveyed the small interior of her prison/refuge! A lot of water coming in! She tried to remember the intro DVD for evacuation and survival! She bailed listlessly! A wind squall hit the raft and spun it viciously as more splats of rain pelted her! She zipped the window opening securely, not certain when it had unzipped! Oh-her original attempts not to vomit into her space~ She stared blankly at the life jacket beside her in the deepening water! Who removed it? With fingers that refused to cooperate with mental commands, she tried to wrestle it back into place and fasten the buckles! Tears mixed with rain drops on her cheeks! She was going to die!

⚮ ⚮

"You staying up all night, Captain?" First mate, Abe Burkhalter's voice filled the bridge as his frame loomed in the hatch!

"That, I haven't decided! I guess I'll let you take the helm for a couple of hours!" He swore in reference to the intensity of the storm! "I'm getting more joe and doing a visual inspection! What was that I saw on the news headline when I got my last refill?"

More profanity interlaced with the answer! "Some woman Geologist went overboard from an exploration vessel! The story said she just graduated from college and she's twenty-three! But she has a whole bunch of kids almost as old as she is!"

Captain McKenzie rubbed a hand over bristling stubble! "Yeah, I couldn't make any sense of it, either! If she went over in this storm~"

"Guess she's in one of the sturdiest rafts afloat~"

McKenzie rolled his eyes sarcastically! "You'd think they could unscramble the facts before they air a story! 'Man overboard', doesn't mean, 'with a raft', to seamen!"

"Yeah, maybe more caffeine'll clear your brain, and you can make sense of it for all of us! Watch yourself, making the inspection! Secure a line!"

Mc Kenzie winked, "Sure thing, Mate! But I issue the orders on this tub!"

ᵴ ᵴ

With judgment totally lapsed in the final stages of hypothermia, Brenna punched frantically on the buttons of the sat phone! Why disconnect from her family, to 'save the 'batt'ry', only to end up with the device water-logged? Through a fog, she couldn't imagine her lapse of not keeping the phone dry, at all costs! At the mercy of the raging Pacific, with deluges coming from every direction, clarity grasped her with icy fingers! This was it! She was going to die!

Chapter 7: SICKBAY

Whiteness everywhere! Blinding, unending whiteness! Long eyelashes fluttered back down, casting shadows on pallid cheeks.

⚶ ⚶

Diana's gaze met Daniel's haggard eyes! "She's stable!" she announced. "Captain McKenzie is coming out of it, too! What an ordeal he went through–"

Daniel nodded, barely able to speak! "Uh–he really put–his own–life on the line–"

"Brenna's core temp is nearly back to normal, and so far, no cardiac symptoms–" relief in both Diana's words and body language! "You know, it's a blessing–well, the whole thing–but Mallory's forethought in insisting on such a state of the art infirmary is making a crucial difference for both Brenna and her rescuer!"

"Yeah, the sick bay on the oil freighter was barely adequate for initial first aid!" Daniel supplied details he was aware of! "The First Mate ordered to put in at Iquique, rather than trying to make their appointed entry to the Canal! Although the *Rock Scientist* was still roped off in the criminal investigation, the Lieutenant granted access to the sick bay!"

⚶ ⚶

After nearly twenty hours of going over the ship stem to stern, investigators removed crime scene tape! Local law enforcement personnel studied the ID's and approved list of those waiting to board! An insurance adjustor, a rep from a marine repair company, family members of the patients, and various members from *DiaMo, Corporation's* management!

To Gray's immense relief, Brenna looked remarkably beautiful~if pale! Seeing him, she burst into tears. His efforts to gather her into his embrace and give comfort met stiff resistance! Baffled, he backed away!

"Shhh~hhh, Love, there there, now; don't fret! You're safe now, from further harm! Shhh, now! The children are here and dying to see you~"

Reaching for a tissue, she nodded. "Um~I ~want~to~"

He frowned. "Are you certain you're up to all of them at once? Because if you're not, they'll make a dreadful row over who comes in first~"

She laughed through tears. "Forgive me for deserting~"

His steady gaze met her wavering one. "Nothing to forgive! I love the children; they are God's gift to me; along with you~We got on famously~but not to say, they won't be at each other's throats about who visits you first"

She nodded, still sobbing and fighting an inexplicable range of emotions! "That's exactly~how~I feel!"

⊰ ⊱

Diana moved silently but authoritatively to the cubicle where medical personnel had withdrawn from Captain McKenzie's bedside! Though in the water a much shorter time than Brenna, he was suffering more acute symptoms from hypothermia! She frowned at the monitor showing he was still in a-fib, despite the efforts of the team!

"Who are you?" The question muttered between clenched teeth!

"Hello, Captain McKenzie! My name's Diana Faulkner! Oh, look, your rhythm just converted!"

"Yeah," he drew a shuddering breath! "Feels better! Guess I just needed to gaze on a pretty woman!"

Diana nodded acknowledgment of the off handed compliment without responding to it. "I wanted to thank you for what you did in saving Brenna!"

His face contorted, "Well, I gave it my best shot, Ma'am~uh! If you're under the impression I succeeded, I guess it's my duty to inform you~"

"What happened?"

Tormented blue eyes beneath shaggy gray brows met hers before dropping guiltily. Large gnarled hands picked nervously at the sheet's hem. "Picked up the raft's beacon on our radar! Couldn't raise any closer vessels to effect a rescue! We'd been seeing the story on the news about-her-some corporate theft and greed she got caught up in the middle of! Shame! So, we changed course! I'll catch the devil over it; it took us into a storm we would have pretty much skirted, if we had steered course for the Canal!"

"Well, you saved a life! You're a hero!"

"Storm's like none I ever been in in all my days! And I've put in quite a few days at sea in my time! My First Mate couldn't get response from the raft, and it looked kinda the worse for wear- but I launched in the inflatable skiff, anyway! Craziest stunt I ever pulled! I didn't expect to live long enough to make it to the raft, but a wave picked me up, and landed me down like a next door neighbor-I attached my skiff by cable and boarded the raft! But the second my weight was out of the skiff, the waves rolled it over and over sideways, broke the cable like a piece of thread! Well, probably some of the hardware failed-Left me stranded on the beat up raft! I'm sorry, Ma'am! The girl was-gone-"

Diana's expressive brows rose. "Gone? As in, deceased?"

"Yes'm! Stone cold and tinged with blue-it was a really sad realization for me-No one notified you?"

"Brenna somehow managed to survive; do you feel well enough to finish the story?"

"I don't remember the rest of it! I mean, I boarded, thought she was dead, but that maybe I should try to warm her up! Ma'am, I swear there was nothing more to it than that! I got a daughter older'n her! I thought I was going to 'Davy Jones's Locker' for sure, so I didn't want any sins like that on me! And, honestly-I-I thought she was dead-"

Diana nodded, still perplexed, "And then, somehow, your crew managed to pull you both aboard?"

The weathered face showed signs of exhaustion. "Yep; guess so!"

⚔ ⚔

Gray led the children from their visit with their sister, to the empty mess hall. "So, there, you see now, nothing to worry about, children! In a few days, she'll be returning with us to Tulsa! Look at the sunshine! It's like the storm never-"

Evidently coming to the same conclusion, the kids were scattering with plenty of noise and confusion! "Hear now! Straighten up before one of you goes overboard!" He sighed as they continued with their rowdiness!

Dread welled in his chest! Brenna's emotional state and resistance to him filled him with nagging worry! Perhaps being free of him for a few days had caused her to decide her hasty marriage was a mistake! He loved her more than ever, if that were possible, following the terrible possibility of losing her!

His fourteen year old niece, Cassandra, came to the rescue with a handful of printer paper and some pens and pencils from the Skipper's office! Challenging each kid to expend some time to make a 'detailed' picture, she offered a dollar prize for the best! When little Emily complained about unfair competition from older siblings, Cassandra simply insisted everyone do their best!

"Gray, are you okay?" Daniel's appearance startled him. "I'm not sure you could look any glummer if you'd lost her."

In his heart, he felt as though he had. "I guess I'm too much of an old bachelor to know what to do when they cry!"

Daniel's hearty laugh filled the space, interrupting the children's studious concentration on their projects. "Welcome to the club!"

⚖ ⚖

Gray looked up as David and Mallory approached on the gangway! "Have you talked to the insurance adjuster yet? Damage looks pretty serious to me!" he assumed the damage Brenna had inflicted on *The Rock Scientist* was one of the things hanging heavy on her.

"Not yet," David responded. "I'm pretty sure our insurance carrier will sue *Pritchard and Halsey's* insurance company to pay for damages. How's Brenna?"

Gray shrugged noncommittally! "I've seen her in better spirits. Mallory, she wants a few words alone with you!"

David thought Mallory blanched visibly at that! He hated what Brenna had been through, but it wasn't Mallory's fault! "I'm coming with you! You're not going to get raked over the coals by yourself!"

Mallory's panicked gaze flitted between the two unyielding men! "Okay, Gray said she wants to talk to me alone! It'll be okay!" She squared her shoulders resolutely, but David knew that emotionally, she was on a roller coaster! He watched her slender form until she disappeared around a corner, hoping she'd walk out if Brenna got too accusative!

⚖ ⚖

Out of sight, Mallory paused to free a tissue! She could hardly blame Brenna for being upset! For now, she was relieved that the other Geologist was still drawing breath to be upset with!

⊣ ⊢

Brenna was stunned at Mallory's sudden appearance in the cubicle! Although, she had told Gray that she needed to talk to Mallory, she felt suddenly speechless, and more bereft than ever! She scooted up, still taking in every inch of the beautiful business executive! The most gorgeous lavender suit, with cute feminine details compliments of Diana! And lavender was her favorite-

"Hi," Mallory's voice would barely come! "Gray said you want to talk to me! Listen, Brenna; I apologize! I had no idea-well, my experiences with both Gabe and Nate, should have-I-guess! But, I didn't knowingly send you into trouble! As soon as it dawned on me-but then, the storm-"

"Yeah, I know! Listen, I'm sorry for the damages-"

"Okay, the damages are on them! They're the ones who decided to break the law! Please don't worry about anything, and just get well!"

"I'm well! I guess I wanted to talk to you about my being under contract- Gray wants me to come home with him to Tulsa!"

"Well, yeah; you had a close call! He thought he was going to lose you after waiting so long to find you-I'd say what's happened to you is enough to nullify your contract! We'll still pay it out, of course!"

Brenna sat up straighter and dabbed at tears! "I want to finish it out! I signed, and, I didn't major in Geology simply because I couldn't think of anything else to study! I want to work as a Geologist! I have to work as a Geologist! I'm not sure how to make Gray understand that! So, I need your words of wisdom!" Her countenance reflected the inner conflict. "Gray wanted to adopt the kids, and I don't want to stick him with them while I see the world! But then again, I do!"

Mallory could barely absorb the significance of the other woman's words, and as the light dawned, she tried to temper soaring hope! "So, you're saying you want to stay and see this project through?"

"I do, but I'm not sure how to talk to Gray about it! Marriage is a new arena for me! Mallory, I love him; don't misunderstand! He's like beyond anything I ever dreamed of-well I never dreamed about a husband! His voice and face sustained me when I felt like giving up! But, there are a couple of other issues~" she broke down in sobs!

⊰ ⊱

David paced! Maybe Brenna wasn't flaying her alive! If she were, Mallory didn't have to stay and take it! As usual when he wasn't sure what else to do, he made his way to the galley to look for edibles!

"Hey, David; I didn't realize that you and Mallory made it in!"

"Yeah, and then the second we boarded, Gray informed us that Brenna wanted a 'word with Mallory, alone'!"

Daniel frowned. "That sounds ominous! Tell me, what do you make of Brenna?"

David laughed. "What I think doesn't matter! Gray's smitten, so you might as well welcome her to the family! Along with her assorted sisters and brothers"!

David fiddled with an oversized coffee maker, managing to start it brewing! He opened a package of cookies and began to munch as he waited for the brew light to go off. "Mallory is like, really blown away by her! Well, Waverly has been such a zero with the ring erased, so Brenna's appearance has been timely! Mallory kind of sees the possibility of a friend and confidante; which she's usually cautious about trying to bond!"

Daniel frowned, wondering why Diana and David's friendships weren't enough!

David grinned! "It's the Geology thing, and kindred minds! She keeps her distance from you because you're married, and so is she! Alexandra~is like a sophomore and acts like she knows all there is to know~Mallory and I are good friends, but rocks don't excite me that much! That's why I'm worried about Brenna telling her off! Most people she can blow off~she didn't know she was sending her into an ambush!"

⊰ ⊱

Mallory retreated from Brenna's cubicle with her emotions whirling! Brenna's story seemed strange and alarming; she texted Diana:

Do you have a few minutes to talk? Can you meet me on the bridge?

"Did she blame you?" Diana's tone, more strident than intended, when she made the rendezvous!

Mallory closed the hatch, grasping both temples and panting for air! "No, Ma'am! She said, that~um~that Captain~"

"What?" Diana's worried voice!

"Well, she can't remember how he got into the raft with her, but he took her clothes~and~uh~he didn't have much on~either~She doesn't know if anything~happened; or what to tell~Gray! Her wedding rings are gone, too~ Strange; hunh?"

Diana stood regarding her steadily! "Maybe so; maybe not so much~"

"How, 'Not so much'?" Mallory's mind seemed made up on the Captain's guilt.

"Okay, well, hear me out! Captain McKenzie nearly died, too! The hypothermia put him into A-fib, a condition he struggles with, anyway! When his heart rhythm converted, the first thing he told me was that, 'nothing happened'!"

"Well, maybe that's a sign of his guilty conscience!"

"Maybe, but he was pretty sure he got to her too late! He said she was cold and blue; he didn't say if he checked her pulse! He said she didn't have anything on!" Diana held up a hand to continue, as Mallory started to object! "Okay, listen to me! A classic symptom of hypothermia is that as the brain starts to swell, it sends wrong messages! People who are freezing to death, suddenly think they're too hot! They remove their clothing in the harshest elements!"

"So, you're saying she took off her own stuff and threw it out of the raft?" Mallory's expression was dubious! "And then Captain McKenzie, he got the same 'wrong brain message', and took his off, too?"

Diana couldn't help a wry laugh! "He was on the raft for less than an hour! Brenna survived on it for six! Mallory, he said that hour was the most terrifying he's ever spent in his life! He said it was like a tilt-a-whirl and roller coaster combined~on steroids! As one who has long since adjusted to life at sea and ordinarily never affected by seasickness, he began vomiting immediately! Let's suppose that Brenna vomited all over herself, early on; maybe she did try to rinse her things out! The raft spun in circles, then pitched upwards and plunged down again, capsizing and then righting itself! The Captain said the raft was empty of all the supplies: water, rations, first aid equipment! Maybe she thought it would stay afloat longer if she threw everything out!"

Mallory sat crying! "I don't think she was lying!"

"No, but she nearly died of hypothermia, so her confusion is a given! She may have been trying to put her rings in a safe place! Captain McKenzie removed his outer garments because they were wet from the moment he launched in the skiff! The raft was battered, and he figured it wouldn't keep them on the surface much longer. He knew he couldn't swim in heavy boots and clothing! From what I can tell, his actions are heroic, and I hate for her to make accusations when she doesn't know anything for sure!"

Mallory nodded, still emotional! "She's heartbroken about losing her outfit! The purple jeans and lavender sweater-"

Diana made a cute face!

"I know." Mallory smiled a slight agreement. "She's hardly had it off since she bought it!" More emotion, making it difficult to finish the story! "She said that's the prettiest outfit she's ever had! And that she never had anything brand new before! She's grieving over-"

Diana's eyes filled with responsive tears.

"You know," Mallory continued, "I promised myself and the Lord, that I would never forget what it was like-to be poor! I mean, I got 'new' things from time to time! And when I did, I wore the daylights out of it! And it was 'new' until I managed to get something else 'new' to replace it! She can't imagine that as much as she loved that outfit, she let something happen to it! I've really gotten spoiled with having something expensive and new every day! I think I take it for granted! Thank you so much for all of the beautiful designs! I didn't want to tell David any of this, but-"

"Well, I think you can tell him what you've told me, but remember to give the Captain the benefit of the doubt! I'll go find Gray and talk to him!"

⊰ ⊱

Brenna and Mallory sat visiting on deck! Straight-backed metal chairs on the work boat had to do! No lounge chairs on this deck! Mallory considered changing that! Surely, when members of the crew completed their shifts, there could be a pleasant environment for relaxation, without jeopardizing productivity! She made a notation on her phone to run the idea past David!

Brenna ruffled through thick, luxurious tresses of honey-gold hair, allowing the sun and gentle ocean breeze to dry it naturally!

Mallory admired it before proceeding with business. She admired Brenna as both colleague and potential friend! "Well, I inquired with the German government and got a hot letter in response!'

Brenna's eyes widened with surprise, "Really?"

"Yes, I guess they tracked the picture to David and Nanci Higgins and checked their German entry visas! Since the Higgins have taken several river cruises, it's raised red flags for members of the German Cabinet for Mining and Industry! They've accused Higgins of 'Industrial Espionage'!"

"So, will he be arrested?" Brenna's expression was a mask.

"Well, let's just say they have him on a watch list to ban his reentry! If it didn't create me such a problem, it would be nearly comical!"

"Well, since he can't go back, maybe I can do it," Brenna suggested eagerly!

Mallory studied the other woman thoughtfully. "Well, the problem is that Nanci's travel blog and the European River cruises together, are getting fashion orders for both *DiaMal* and *Rodriguez*-Higgins has actually brought more to my table as Nanci's travel companion, than he has as a Geologist! If he's spying on Germany as a Geologist, their natural resources are quite safe, I'm afraid! The last thing I need is for him and Nanci to be barred from the cruises! And I can't send you in as a Geologist, as long as they think I'm sending spies in to plunder their resources. I think I need to make a trip to Berlin and try to talk to this gentleman! You still had a good eye-amazing, actually!"

"Could I ask you an unrelated question?" Brenna hated to change the subject as though she hadn't been listening.

"Sure! Depending on what it is, I might answer it." Mallory's standard dodge for avoiding personal questions!

"Well, it may be dumb, but what are, *DiaMo*, *DiaMal*, and *DaMal*?"

"Ah, good question. *DiaMo* is the original corporation founded by my father! Based on Diamonds discovered along the Little Missouri River in Arkansas! *DiaMal* is the design business started by Diana! It was going well, but we incorporated and expanded on it; the name's a combination of her name and mine! Then *DaMal* is David's and my real estate holdings corporation!"

Brenna grinned. "Okay, not as confusing as it sounded! Thanks for clearing it up!"

Mallory smiled past her as Gray approached.

"Hello, ladies, may I join you?"

Mallory hopped up. "Certainly! I'll go hunt up another chair!"

"No, no; please keep your seat!"

Mallory wasn't sure how, but she thought Gray had the most calming effect of anyone she had ever met! She sank back onto the uncomfortable chair.

"Are you two in a corporate planning meeting that I'm interrupting?" He pulled Brenna up, sitting on her chair, and pulling her onto his lap.

"No, far from it," Mallory responded. "Whenever the doctor releases her, she's free to go home!"

He sighed. "Well, we haven't had a chance to discuss it, but I'm pretty sure, if I know Brenna, she'll be eager to be back on project the moment the repairs are made!"

Brenna turned toward him with a joyous screech, and he laughed. "So you can relax; I've been on-line and located the last pair of purple jeans in your size, in the United States! The sweater was easier! They're being shipped to Tulsa overnight, so they'll be waiting when we get home! I do need you to come home while *The Rock Scientist* is under repair! We have more paperwork we both need to sign, for the real estate deals! As for your finishing your contract, I would ask you not to; if I felt the danger was still great!" He grew emotional! "I thought I had lost you!"

Mallory excused herself under the guise of looking for David, giving the newlywed couple an opportunity to talk privately.

He found her! "Are you okay? Did she really light into you?"

Mallory allowed David to pull her into his arms! "Not at all," she answered, her eyes meeting his deep, expressive ones. "She was embarrassed and concerned about her-uh, -rescuer! And she was afraid to talk to Gray-uh-you know-"

David nodded. "Well, Daniel and Diana talked to me about it, and we're all of the consensus that all of Captain McKenzie's actions were honorable! The sea was so tempestuous, he could barely hold onto her to try to warm her up-it was terrifying-"

Mallory interrupted. "That reminds me, I thought those life rafts were top of the line-"

David laughed. "They were almost top of the line! McKenzie was amazed that she kept afloat as long as she did! It's a miracle! The insurance adjustor plans to send a check the second the repair bids are in! You were amazing to change insurance companies when you did!"

"And Brenna wants to finish the job~"Mallory's voice effervesced with joy!

David frowned. "Has she bounced that off Gray? He's so ultra-cautious that I'm surprised he let her sign the contract to begin with!"

Mallory smiled. "Maybe, but he's a lot like you in giving her latitude to be herself! That's one of the many things I really appreciate about you!"

"Well, thanks," he acknowledged the compliment before continuing, "so having a Geologist still on board with the exploration is a good thing~"

Mallory's smile faded and she paled! "So, we'll have a repaired boat and a Geologist-but our ship's crew and drillers are headed to the US under arrest!"

He nodded glumly, "Afraid so! And look at the disaster we got with our carefully vetted crews! No telling what we might get trying to fill the positions cold!"

"Here's something else Brenna shared with me! She was absolutely heartbroken, not just about being pulled aboard the freighter with little on, but that she lost track of her purple jeans outfit!"

"Maybe for the best"! David's sense of fun always bubbled up.

She laughed before growing sober again! "Okay, listen to what I'm trying to say-it was on sale at Wal Mart, and nothing I'd choose-but she didn't have much time or money, and all of the purple colors are her favorites!"

"Doesn't mean they all look good together~" He couldn't resist!

"I thought I grew up poor~"

"You did! We both did!" Spoken matter-of-factly!

"Well, yeah, especially compared with what we have now! Brenna loved those jeans and that sweater so much because they were the first new things, just for her, that she's ever had! I promised the Lord I would never forget where He's brought me from-but her broken heart at her carelessness for losing such a treasure-to her a treasure-Well, I guess I needed the reminder! Speaking of that, maybe we should pray about replacing the crews! I didn't mean to be haughty about Gabe's guys-but I didn't pray! I thought I had everything under control!"

He nodded, then, sighed in mock relief! "So you're admitting this fiasco is your fault? That's a load off my mind because I thought I was to blame!"

Chapter 8: THE RANCH

"Can we stop at a restaurant?" Jacob's cajoling tone!

Brenna turned in her captain's chair. "No, we've barely been on the road for an hour! Make a sandwich or get a glass of milk! Look at the scenery!" She enjoyed the wintry landscape where the winter's kill exposed more rock faces, than when summer's foliage concealed interesting Geological features.

"We like eating at restaurants," Lindsay piped up.

Brenna laughed. "I'm sure you do! Your father spoiled you quickly while I was gone!" She shook her head with wonder! When had this bunch ever had snacks available like the ones they seemed already to disdain?

Gray shrugged good-naturedly at the mild accusation! "I've never had anyone to spoil before! I guess I like taking them places because I'm so proud to finally be a father! I may do what I do, more for what it does for me, than any benefit to them."

Brenna regarded his distinguished profile, amazed that he could find pride in the undisciplined mélange! She kept thinking he'd wake up, come to his senses, and ask himself what in the world he had done!

"Still, children, if you're hungry, it would be better to find something in the Frigidaire for now! You will really like The Ranch, and we'll get there more quickly if we can minimize the stops!" His patient reasoning brought a grudging acquiescence.

"Can we watch a movie?"

Gray shot a questioning glance at Brenna, and she answered. "No, you've seen too many movies! Start the science class and watch it! When we get to The Ranch there's lots of outside stuff to do, and you won't want to work on your schooling."

Despite the grumbling, they were soon engrossed.

"Jacob."

Gray's summons brought the oldest child forward. "Yes Sir? More tea?"

"No, thank you! There is something Brenna and I need to talk with you about before we reach our destination!" He focused on passing a truck before his gaze met Jacob's in the rear view mirror. "You know, that for me to adopt you, your real father signed papers~"

"Yeah! Guess that shows~"

"He didn't want to; just so you know!" Gray's tone and serious blue-gray eyes met the stormy ones once more in the mirror.

"But you paid him off, and then it was easier for him?"

"Okay, Jacob, Gray didn't 'pay him off' so he could adopt! That's illegal! And it wasn't easy for him! He was in torment about both you and Emily!"

"Don't make no diff'rence, I guess! He's in prison anyhow! I guess that should make me glad that my new daddy is scared to do anything illegal! At least maybe he'll stay out of jail!"

"Okay, Jacob, could you just listen?" Brenna tried to control aggravation.

"Well, he's listening, Brenna, Love! I don't mind that he has feelings to express~" He directed his comments from Brenna to Jacob again. "But that's what I want you to know! Your father signed for me to adopt because he thought I could give you a better chance at life! You should believe he genuinely wants what's best for you and Em~"

"He never tried too hard!" An angry sob erupted, and Brenna sighed before coming to Warren's defense:

"He didn't know how! He~didn't have the tools, or the example, or the opportunity! And he's out of jail~"

"That's what we're trying to brace you for, Son!" Gray's voice caressed the word, but the endearing term brought a sarcastic snort.

"David Anderson works with ex-cons," Brenna strove for patience, "with a good success rate! He convinced the judge to allow him to bring Warren to The Ranch!"

Jacob's head jerked up, and his features were a study in confused emotion! "I don't want to see him! I never want to see him again! He just turned me over to a stranger like a~a~"

౽ ౾

"You ask! You're his favorite!"

Cassandra frowned at her big sister's catty hypothesis! "You only say that when you want me to get yelled at, instead of you!"

Jeremiah stretched his long legs and tipped his head back into his interlaced fingers. "Well, he doesn't yell!" He grinned knowingly, "He will, however, have a long list of reasons why not!"

"Yeah," a sighing agreement from Cassandra! She straightened suddenly. "Let's get Zave to do it!"

Daniel Faulkner listened good-naturedly to Xavier's carefully coached sales pitch.

"That's a great idea, Son!" He noticed the three eldest do their classic glance-exchange thing! "See if you can get the others on board with you, and you can show the new cousins the ropes; the tree house, golf carts, chow hall, alpaca, and the stable! Time to get acquainted! Without a lot of snobbery"!

"Well, we figured you would want us to keep our distance until you figure out what they're like! Their language, and everything!" Jeremiah tried to conceal his ire at misjudging his dad.

Diana entered with a sunny laugh. "Parenting isn't that easy, you know! We've home schooled you and made the choices we have~" she fished for the appropriate words.

"Yes, Ma'am," Alexandra agreed, "to shield us from riff-raff and bad friends! What do you think about Uncle Gray's sudden family?"

Diana shrugged, perplexed. "Well, he certainly seems happy! I hope it lasts! For now, we hope we've taught you to be good enough Christians to influence Gray's bunch for the kingdom~"

"And not let them be bad influences on us~" Cassandra chimed!

Daniel nodded. "That's basically what the Christian life is about!"

⊰ ⊱

David looked up in response to the hesitant rap on his open office door.

"You sent for me, Boss?"

"Yeah, come on in, Warren. Help yourself to a cup of coffee and some cookies! Then take a seat!"

The man moved awkwardly and suspiciously! For the first time in a long time, he was enjoying the 'hand' life was 'dealing' him! Doubtless something was up that would see him on his way back to finish his prison sentence! Complying, he helped himself to the refreshments and took a chair opposite the young executive!

David steepled his fingers, regarding them briefly, before addressing him!

"Warren, I called you in to give you a heads up that Gray and Brenna Prescott, are on their way here!"

Warren studied the floor, his usual posture during conversations. "Prescott! Sounds funny with Brenna! Glad she survived her ordeal~" He paused. Small talk wasn't his long suit!

"Yeah," David agreed. "One of the adjustments you've been dealing with! I know it was tough for you to sign away your rights to Jacob and Emily!"

"So that's what this talk's about? Jacob, and Emily? You're giving me a warning that they're coming~that's all?"

Still no eye contact, which David tried not to resent! "That's all! I haven't decided if it's a good idea, or not! I'm pretty sure there needs to be a resolution of the emotions, for both you and the kids! I don't have a clue if this is too soon, or if it's the right way to go about it~"

"Yeah, me neither! If I keep from popping the guy, can I stay on here awhile?"

David fought panic at the response. "That's what concerns me. I want you to be able to stay here, and I sure don't want to do anything to provoke an incident of any kind~I thought it might ease your mind to see your kids doing well, and see how Gray and Brenna~I think the kids can adjust and have very profitable and happy lives! But they need to know you love them, and you acted out of~"

Warren sprang up, clenched hands grasping the desk top! "My assignment today's to repair the shower building! Maybe I should go get started swinging my hammer!"

David laughed suddenly. "A man after my own heart! Nothing like driving nails to help deal with frustration! Get after it, man!"

⚔ ⚔

David snorted with amusement as he studied the newly arrived family from the deck of his ranch house.

"What's funny?"

He whirled, embarrassed at Mallory's appearance.

"Uh, just watching Alexander Grayson Prescott, trying to show off a cria to Misty"!

"Well, *Honey* is protective!"

"Yeah; but still! He has that Great Dane, Chauncey, and he's not scared of him! Pretty sure a mama alpaca isn't any serious threat to his safety!"

Mallory studied the scenario! "Yeah, harmless or not, their pasture poses a serious threat to Italian leather loafers!"

"Yeah, I should have told them to bring grungy clothes and boots!"

She chuckled. "Yeah, well it would probably be about like telling Diana that! Now, Brenna's more practical!"

She flushed as David gave her a searching look. "What?"

"Well, over-dresser, or not, Diana's mind-set has helped fill our coffers! I'm glad you're excited about having Brenna here! But remember the little song:

> *Make new friends, but keep the old.*
> *One is silver and the other, gold!*

She flushed, genuinely rebuked by his words! "Well, I didn't mean it like that!"

He sighed. "I know! I'm sorry! I fall into the old habit worse than you do, of knocking people just for the sake of knocking people! I know sometimes I grieve you, and you don't preach to me!"

"Well, it's a good reminder to keep the law of kindness in our speech! Especially about Diana~ You're sure you don't mind Brenna and my mission I've planned for this afternoon?"

"Not at all! I have lots to do here! My concern is~if Lilly will mind!"

"It's just a little harmless exploration!"

He laughed at the light that infused her with the thrill of searching and finding!

"Well, it should be 'harmless'! But the whole Diamond world follows what you're doing!"

She laughed. "You give me too much credit! I'm not even a player!"

"Well, I hope I'm right about your whole theory's being wrong! That your dad was driving randomly that day, to make his object lesson point! And that you and Brenna will simply have a fruitless drive through Arkansas back roads!"

☙ ❧

Jacob Prescott glanced up as the chow hall door protested noisily, followed by a triangle of sunlight on the textured concrete floor! Overhead lights switched on, spotlighting the beautiful Mallory Anderson.

Though surprised by Jacob's presence, she smiled a greeting. "Hey, Jacob! Sitting here by yourself, in the dark?"

He rose sullenly, heading for the sunlight of the wrap-around porch.

"Have the Faulkner kids taught you the vagaries of the espresso machine?"

Her voice stopped him, and he turned. "Does anyone speak plain old English around here?"

She laughed. "You'll get used to us! Come over here, and I'll show you how to work this! Then you can show your siblings how to make hot chocolate! The main thing is not to let the steam~"

She smiled, though he continued to glare! "Actually, I'm glad you're here!"

Profanity erupted from the youth, and she frowned. "Hey, I'm sure you've had a tough couple~"

"Just so you know; I hate you!" He tried to brush past her.

To her own surprise she blocked his exit physically! "For endangering Brenna? Yeah, I get that! I hate myself! Look, let me show you how to brew coffees, and then let's have a talk!"

"You won't change my mind! And you can say what you want, but you're sending her right back again! Soon as your dumb boat gets patched up"!

"So, you get the milk here~" She showed him the process despite sullen rudeness. "What do you like? Caramel? Mocha? Latte?"

"I don't know what none of that fancy stuff is!"

"Hot chocolate, then! The sun's shining, but it's pretty chilly out! What did you think of the tree house?"

He shoved his hands into low-hanging jean pockets! Them snooty kids ain't leading me around by the nose! Seemed kinda cheesy~"

She finished the hot beverages, and heaped whip onto the chocolate. "Join me! I won't take long~" Seated across from him, she plunged in. "David told me it didn't go too well with your real dad!"

My only dad! 'Bout like always! He took one look at me, turned, and walked off! And Prescott's interest in me is because of Brenna!" He proceeded with a vulgar opinion of Gray's motives!

"Well, I had an idea that I thought might give you some space for sorting it all out!"

"I always sorted stuff out for myself before you came along!"

Undeterred Mallory pushed forward! "Hear me out! Some of our company execs hire their kids! A lady in DC that reps our fashions hired her daughter, Madeleine. And before Alexandra purchased her silver mine, she was Diana's assistant! And, although I haven't had a chance to bounce this off of Brenna, I'm thinking she should hire you! She and I are taking a drive together this afternoon! Geology stuff-maybe you can even accompany us on our jaunt! You're big and strong, and I see in your background, you're not a bad street fighter-Jacob, I'm not sending Brenna back! She wants to go! She can hardly wait, except it does give her a chance to be with Gray and all of you, and take care of some business details! When she goes back down to Chile, maybe you can go! You can both look out for each other-"

Mallory watched as the desperate bravado crumbled! "Okay, since you said you can help make sense of this, who is Brenna now? Is she my mom? Do I call her, 'Mom'?"

Mallory sighed. "I wouldn't think so! She's still your sister, although in the eyes of the courts, she's become your legal guardian! None of it will matter for very long, because you're about to come of age, anyway! And you had a mom! From what Brenna has told me, no one can take her place! I think Brenna would be the last person to demand that you call her Mom! And, I'm pretty sure Gray will give you space to come to grips with where he fits into your life-you don't have to figure it all out and accept it at once!"

⊰ ⊱

David frowned! Trying to follow up on Captain McKenzie proved challenging! No one in the Chilean port authority could supply any information, either. He texted Daniel Faulkner:

Would it be okay if I stop down there for a couple of minutes?

Receiving permission, he jogged along the asphalt to the neighboring cabin. In spite of the chill, Daniel met him on the back porch. "Hey, what do you need?"

"Well, I'm curious about whether you and Diana kept in touch with Captain McKenzie! He mentioned that he might be on the hot seat with his company for attempting to rescue Brenna rather than continuing on course for the Canal! And, Diana didn't think he was well enough to go back to work, but he seemed worried~"

"I haven't heard anything! If Diana has stayed in touch, she hasn't mentioned anything to me! She's taking a nap, but when she wakes up~"

David forced a smile! "Okay, thanks!" Turning, he jogged back to the main ranch house! Diana Faulkner never took naps. He sighed with concern! In the sanctuary of his office, he tried to concentrate! Hard! Because he was worried about Mallory and her latest mission! And although, he didn't think Diana should be totally possessive of Mallory and her friendship, he hated to think her feelings were hurt!

He sent Mallory a text:

Hey, what do you think about inviting the Faulkners and the Prescotts down for a steak dinner?

He figured she would be fine with the plan! He and Jeff and the camp men would do all the work involved in entertaining. And maybe Diana and Brenna could become friends, too! When there was no response, he resent the text!

Chapter 9: DISCOVERY

Brenna rode in silence, taking in the Arkansas back-roads, fascinated! Jacob pouted in the back because she wouldn't turn the radio to the station he demanded! Brenna mulled over Mallory's proposition, that she should hire her step-brother! She wished Mallory could have discussed it with her before mentioning it to him! Mallory concentrated on following a crudely hand-drawn treasure map!

"Why didn't you pay more attention the day he brought you here?"

Mallory grinned! "Because, the cagey little Irishman tricked me! I thought we were randomly lost, to prove the point of his lecture!"

"What was the lecture?" Brenna was curious about Mallory and her relationship to her father. She used caution with her line of questions, because the last thing she wanted was for Mallory to ask her about hers! Evidently, some guy named, Hamilton! That was the extent of what she knew about her father!

"Well, it was on the ninth day of the month because I smarted off about not liking Proverbs Nine as much as some of the other chapters! It's about the two paths: the right one, or the wrong one! I was pretty proud in my assessment that I had things figured out; that I was on the right path, and so was David! But I wasn't-or I wouldn't have been rebellious about my Dad's cautions! And David truly was in a time of rebellion and crisis!"

"Puh-lease! Some music! I don't want to listen to this!"

"Okay, well, let her finish the high points," Brenna begged.

"I thought my dad was seriously taking me to Little Rock to shop! I could not imagine why he left the freeway at the second exit beyond Hope! I thought he knew a way with less traffic-uh-so, I didn't ask why-And then

I believed that we were really lost! Although, when he had shot the whole day, we made it back to Murfreesboro within forty minutes!"

"We've been driving an hour," Jacob piped up!

"Yes, if I can retrace the way we went, I'll be doing well! I really have even fewer clues about his route back! You know~" she changed the subject, "Before y'all return to Tulsa you should visit The Crater of Diamonds State Park! You might even find a Diamond or two! Entry to the park isn't very much, and I have the screens and equipment; you're welcome to borrow them!"

"Have you ever found any there?" Brenna's curiosity was piqued.

"I haven't," Mallory admitted. "My dad always forbad my going there! The reason why, is a long story; but you should go, if only to see the Strawn-Wagner that's on display in the museum! It weighs in at a little over a carat, but it's the most perfect Diamond on display anywhere! Most jewelers never have opportunity to see anything comparable!"

When Brenna's response was non-committal, she returned her attention worriedly to the roads! She and David had actually tried this several times before! His reason for losing enthusiasm for the quest! But in spending hours combing through piles of fading receipts, she thought the new 'clues' would lead her to the spot!

"The place where he finally turned around~a really ugly, wintry~mud everywhere, and this huge~I couldn't decide that day, if it was a small pond or a big puddle~"

Brenna shrugged. "But in hindsight, you think you were at another Diamond dike!"

Mallory nodded, "Exactly! The craters erode away, leaving depressions." Then as she caught sight of a frame building, she yelped in excitement and relief! "Look! It's out of business now!"

"Okaaayyy~"

"A receipt from Darvy's Bait Shop, for night crawlers!" Mallory's volume rose with her excitement! "But if my dad ever fished one day in his life, I never knew about it!"

Brenna frowned. "So, your dad went around the countryside buying stuff he didn't want, to get receipts to guide you to treasure? What made him so sure they wouldn't get thrown out?"

Mallory's gaze met the other woman's as the wonder dawned. "Maybe he prayed they wouldn't! Maybe he gave me more credit that I'd figure things out faster! I don't think it would be an exaggeration to say, that it's pretty miraculous~" her voice trailed off as she remembered her own emotional blowup at well-meaning friends and relatives who had attempted to clean out the rat's nest of his room following his funeral! Well, even prior to that, his demands that Suzanne and Mallory stay out of his room! The facts were hard for her to fathom, let alone try to explain!

"Brenna, what do you think? Can I go with you when you go? Like Mallory said, I can help look out for you?"

Brenna sighed. "Usually, I end up looking out for you! If Mallory wants me to be able to concentrate on the job, maybe she shouldn't try to send me back to South America with a major distraction!"

Seeing his resentment, she softened her response. "I'll talk it over with Gray!"

"Hmmmph, he'll just go along with whatever you want~"

The argument was cut short by a sudden right turn from the road, and the engine's being turned off. Mallory's voice barely carried. "This is it; I'm pretty sure~" She stared forlornly! There was fencing now, and a gate barred access. No Trespassing signs gave warning that 'Violators would be prosecuted to the fullest extent of the law'!

"So, where was the depression? Looks like we came out here for nothing~"

Impulsively, Mallory released her seat belt and made her way to the gate! Padlocked with a rusting chain, she hesitated only briefly before climbing over! Impishly, she motioned for her companions to join her!

"She shouldn't do that~" Brenna warned~

"We're millions of miles from nowhere~" Jacob launched himself into the dare whole-heartedly! "Come on! Don't be a chicken!"

⚞ ⚟

David wasn't sure whether to be alarmed or aggravated! His real aversion to Mallory's plan was the time they had already devoted to it, with no success! When the second text didn't get a response, he called!

⚞ ⚟

"Maybe this isn't even the same spot," Brenna worried as she lagged behind Mallory and Jacob! "If there wasn't a gate when you were with your dad, maybe it's still farther up the road!"

Triumphant, Mallory paused with a flourish of her hand! This was the spot! And it looked like a Diamond Geologist's dream come true!

Brenna's professional eye took the scene in quickly. "Okay, so you're right! You finally found the place, but someone has beaten you to it! Let's get~"

Her voice died in her throat; and Jacob screamed in terror!

⊰ ⊱

Captain McKenzie strolled the beach in Iquique, oblivious to the scenery, or the scattered sun-bathers! At last, he sank down near the high tide line, running hands and feet absentmindedly through the sand! He sighed as his eyes traveled to the melding point of sky and sea! Not a bad place to be stranded! He could adjust to worse places than this! He had before!

⊰ ⊱

Jacob and Brenna broke and ran, leaving Mallory face to face with a terrifyingly huge and advancing Yeti! Fragments of thoughts ran through her shocked mind! There was no such thing as these mythical monsters! And it just didn't look or sound quite right! Her pistol in the car, she held only her cell phone! On a whim, she punched speed dial for her Diamond mining foreman, Tad Crenshaw! To her amazement, the threatening Yeti paused to feel for his vibrating phone!

"Give it up, Tad," she ordered! "You're not fooling anyone!"

The monster slumped, moving forward dejectedly. "How'd you know it was me?"

"Uh, I don't have any real Yetis in my speed dial! I figured it was you trying to scare us! On whose orders, though? Michael's?"

Crenshaw's tone took a sharp edge! "I'm not really at liberty to say! It would probably be wise for you to head back to your cozy ranch!"

Mallory nodded slowly. "I'm sure you're right!" Turning slowly, she made her way back up the tracks and over the gate!

At the car, she squinted narrowly at Jacob. "What are you up to?"

"Man that was too cool! I'm putting it on~" He named social sites!

"Don't do it!" she ordered! "It was a hoax, and not a very good one, at that!"

"You're not my boss!"

"Jacob!" Brenna's voice halted his intended action! "Part of your job in my corporation will be keeping things quiet! Confidential Disclosure Agreements! Mallory told you not to do it, and this is her exploration! Posting on there, gives everyone these coordinates! If you want a serious job, start growing up!"

Flushing with embarrassment, he slid his phone into his pocket!

"No! Delete the video and or pictures! Do it! Let me see you do it!" Mallory's sharp order brooked no argument!

⚔ ⚔

David studied his silent phone, willing it to ring with a call from his wife! He raked his hands through thick dark hair and down his face, praying one more desperate prayer before he sounded the all too familiar alarm to Bransom and Faulkner! When it buzzed, he nearly jumped out of his skin!

"Mallory, you okay, Babe?"

"Yeah; why?"

"I've been texting and calling–everything's–what's 'the duress word'"?

"Jalapeño I–um–I'm not showing any missed calls, but–I think Lilly–"

David sighed. "That's what I was afraid of–the only reason I haven't called Faulkner or Erik to sound an alarm! Are you–"

"On the way back!" she finished, "Yeah, as fast as is legally possible!"–

"Okay, well you're going back the same way you came, though, right?" His question was agonized!

"Well, I guess! Even the nav system doesn't show that back way from where we–David–it looked good–"

"I know, Mallory! Everything always looks good to you!"

Chapter 10: WARNING

Gray took in Brenna's pallor as she stepped into the cabin they occupied in conjunction with the RV!

Not wishing to alarm him and upset her plans for continuing her contract with *DiaMo*, she planted a kiss on his cheek! "I'll fill you in on everything later!"

He frowned, sensing he should pursue it! Before he could argue, Jacob plunged into an exciting and embellished narrative about the exploit!

"Okay-Jacob! That's enough, Son! I've asked you to watch your choice of words, and I actually wasn't asking you! Dinner's on in the chow hall! Why don't you take your brothers and sisters over there, and get them started! Brenna and I-"

"I'm not you son! And they aren't my brothers and sisters! I wanna go back to Boston!"

"To foster care"? Gray clarified drolly, smiling sympathetically at Jacob's poorly thought out words. "You are practically eighteen! And, you are my son! Because I adopted you! Did you know that biological fathers can disown their children and disinherit them? But adoptive parents cannot? And I knew that when I adopted you! When you turn eighteen, I'll allow you a trip to Boston."

He smiled gently when Brenna cringed. "Or, you can invite some of the friends you miss to come visit you in Tulsa! My aim in life is to bring you happiness; not see how miserable I can make you! And you're correct about the other children! Why don't you go start on some dinner? Summer can help the younger ones!"

⊰ ⊱

"You're sure you didn't just ignore my texts and calls?" David's gaze penetrated her.

"Why would I do that? I would never needlessly cause you to worry, or send out an alarm, just because I didn't feel like answering! I'm wondering if Lilly had anything to do with it! So it wouldn't divulge our location!"

He stepped closer and clasped her upper arms, his face more earnest than ever. "I hope it didn't have anything to do with Lilly! That's what I was afraid of! You can't push the limits like this with the Israelis forever!"

"David, I don't! It isn't about the Diamonds with me! It's about the game! It's like following the clues~"

"Maybe, to you! But with the Israelis, it's about the Diamonds! That's part of the life blood of their economy! And they don't care about your 'game'! If they consider you a threat~"

"Well, I think Lilly 'gets it'!"

He released her with a sigh! "You think Lilly *gets* it! I'm not so sure, but assuming she does, her position in the Diamond Council isn't unassailable! Plenty of people in their government aren't happy at all about her and Benjamin's conversion! Especially not if they can prove she's too soft to do what she needs to do on her job! You put her at risk, too! I'm pretty sure she won't tolerate that for long! What happened besides your phone not getting through?"

"Well, I found the spot!" Her face lit, and he shook his head!

"Goody for you! And~?"

"Well, it hadn't changed too much, except that it's fenced in now!"

"And you could see what you needed to from outside the fence line?"

"Well, the spot's out there miles from anywhere! Even the bait shop's gone out of business! The road's hardly even maintained~"

"What are you telling me?" He was suddenly afraid to hear the rest of the story. "Let me guess; the gate was slightly ajar!"

Her voice came out small. "Well, not exactly! Uh~I climbed over it~ Uh, I shouldn't have! There were even trespassing signs!"

"With all the trouble we have with illegal trespassers~and~"

Tears filled her eyes at his displeasure. "I~I shouldn't have~"

He stared with disbelief! Her admission was more because of being caught than any real regret for her actions.

"Okay, so you climbed the gate! What did Brenna and Jacob do? I guess if your phones were blocked, they couldn't call the sheriff on you!"

"Yeah; no~uh~they followed me~"

"That's just great! Mallory, what you did was criminal! And you led them astray! We're supposed to be the adult, Christian examples here!"

She shook her head. "David, it wasn't any big deal! Anyway, Tad Crenshaw, dressed up in a ratty-looking Yeti costume, came barreling toward us! Trying to scare us off~"

He scoffed, "What?" Hand on the master suite door, he addressed her again! "Okay, Mallory, that does it! Only Lilly could have known your plans~and arranged for Crenshaw to get over there! I'm ordering you to drop this whole thing right now! Maybe you should learn to knit, or something!"

She nodded desperately. "Okay, but I just want to make one inquiry to county records! To find out who owns~"

Their cell phones rang simultaneously!

~≒ ≓~

"Whatrya doin'"? David frowned as he set his tray down across the table from Jacob Prescott!

The answer included plenty of profanity, the gist of which was that he was trying to get his social media accounts reopened.

Despite the place's filling up, David reached across the table and grasped the dumb kid's t-shirt at the throat! "I've told you to watch your verbiage! No one refers to my wife in those terms! You give her too much credit, anyway! She couldn't get your sites closed down if she wanted to! What did she tell you not to post? What's your version of the story?"

David listened. Nothing new except the lies added in by the narrator, and yet more filthy epithets! He was still shaken by the conversation with Lilly Cowan! To whom he felt Mallory still showed a certain unwise defiance~

"I knew it was a hoax! Both the girls ran like rabbits, but~"

Annoyed, David cut in, "Stick to the truth! You're sure all footage is deleted? Permanently? You need to make sure it's so far gone that all of Israel's top tech people can't find a whisper that you ever had it!"

"Well, I sent it to a buddy! And I'll never tell who!"

"Hope not! Because, if you did, you and your buddy might find yourselves in a world of hurt!"

He stalked away without eating, to run into Daniel Faulkner! Guilt hit him like an avalanche! The steaks!

⊰ ⊱

Mallory moved to her laptop when it alerted her to a new email! With the realization dawning on her, of the serious consequences she could have faced, she opened it hesitantly! From Lilly with three attachments! The instructions were terse! Print copies, hide them securely, and delete the email! Quickly she did as bidden! County records on the land acreage, an engineering study of the land, and a copy of her father's will in its entirety! She stared in wonder! From the email's contents, it was obvious Lilly didn't want her making any further inquiries; at all! She smiled through tears of shame! Now she wouldn't have to!

David reappeared and she moved into his arms. "You were right! I'm sorry~"

He smiled. "I know! I mean, just that fast, you can make a decision~anyway, I forgot that one of my texts to you was that I was afraid Diana's feelings were still hurt about your taking off with Brenna! So, I texted you about having the Faulkners and the Prescotts come join us for steaks! Then, in the midst of being dressed down by Lilly Cowan, it slipped my mind until I ran into Daniel! Do you think you can pull yourself together?"

She reached for a tissue. "I guess I don't have much choice! Should I apologize to Brenna and Jacob in front of everyone? No, no point in that, since everyone isn't aware of it! I'll fix my makeup and go talk to Brenna and Jacob first! Where are the girls?"

"Over playing with the Faulkner kids! Go ahead! I'll ask Jeff who's available to get the steaks started!"

"Is this a bad time?" The expression on Gray Prescott's face wasn't its jovial norm as he opened the RV door to admit Mallory!

He stepped aside so she could enter! "Come in, Mallory; we're having a heavy discussion, and it's to do with you~"

Horrified, she felt hot color of shame flood over her. "That's what I came over for! I owe Brenna and Jacob~"

His frown stopped her rush of words.

"You~you~don't trust me~now~"

He motioned with expressive hands. "I must admit I'm shaken by such a serious lapse in judgment~"

"Yes Sir! I could have gotten us all arrested for tres~I was a horrible example ~I~I've ~just~wanted to~locate that spot~for a couple of~years~or more!"

His solid gaze pinned her, and tears flowed in spite of her efforts to quell them.

"Hrrrmph! I'm pretty sure there's more here than the trespassing!"

"Uh, no, Sir, but I just acted impulsively when the land was fenced! I wasn't expecting that!"

"You are not telling me the truth!"

Mallory's eyes flashed. "I am, and I apologized! And I can see that you're reconsidering your decision about letting Brenna finish out the contract down in Chile~"

"I'm beyond reconsidering! She isn't going!"

Mallory was nonplussed! Desperately, she shot a glance at Brenna!

"Brenna sighed sadly, "I have to admit he's right! Jacob's social accounts didn't get shut down because we all hopped over a gate! Are you guys on the radar of the NSA or something?"

"No! Our operations are all legal! They're beyond legal; they're Scriptural! We try always to take the high road~ask Daniel and Diana! But~um~this afternoon, I really slipped up~"

"You were frightened, and you scared Brenna and my son! Why should he not be able to post a silly video?"

"Well, since I own interests in Diamonds, the Israelis wouldn't have liked it~"

"Ah! There's the truth then! The Israelis wouldn't have like it! And when they don't 'like' something, what is their response? You tell my son about CDA's and keeping things confidential, who has never learned to keep a secret in his life, and you fail to warn him that it's a life-and-death issue?"

"Well, that's dramatic!"

"No, Mrs. Anderson! It is not! You may think you can manipulate Lilly Cowan and the Israeli government! Quite naïve! You led my wife and my son into danger! The incident in Chile, with the mutiny of the drillers~I was willing to overlook that! I'm not overlooking this! Jacob's scared now, because he sent a photo to his friend~why should he be afraid of sharing a picture on a social site?"

"You're right! He shouldn't be!"

※ ※

Brenna watched Mallory disappear toward the main ranch house before meeting her husband's stony gaze! "Well, I agree with you! Meanwhile, my fledgling company doesn't have any business looming on its horizon! Alexandra may even cancel me for when the snow melts at her mine!"

Gray extended his arms! "Come Brenna, Love, let's pray about it! First, we will be okay-but I know your Geology and owning your company have great importance to you! I am so proud of you for graduating with a career, in spite of daunting obstacles! You have what it takes-with or without David and Mallory Anderson!"

He led with a humble prayer, and Brenna added hers!

※ ※

"Jacob, you did mail out my letters?" Brenna attempted to keep from whining as she phrased the question bluntly!

Jacob consulted his calendar! "Yes'm, immediately after you signed them. Remember what Father said about being patient! I mailed them first class, but if anyone other than a secretary glanced at them-why don't you send a follow-up-you know, keep your name in the forefront? Everything's about brand recognition these days! Are you sure you don't resent Gray not letting you stay on the Chile job?"

"He loves us, Jacob, and he considers it his duty before God to keep us safe and cared for! The amazing thing to me is that David and Mallory are paying out the rest of the contract for 'Breach of trust' on their part! It keeps your and my salaries paid, and the equipment leased! Al's mine just got another foot of snow; a little unusual for so late in the year!"

Jacob brought up a question with fear and trembling. "Yeah, and she hasn't actually said another word to you about entering into a contract; has she?"

※ ※

Daniel frowned at his phone! Caller ID showed a local Tulsa number that wasn't in his contacts. "Daniel Faulkner! How may I help you?"

He listened in wonder, fighting a wellspring of emotions! "Well, I'm speechless! I-I would consider it a tremendous honor-I-" He broke off to listen to details from the *Tulsa Symphony Orchestra* business office!

"Thank you so much for your call! Yes, I have the dates jotted down! No, they don't conflict with my schedule! Yes, Ma'am, the rehearsal times are great! Sure, I'll keep an eye out for the confirmation letter, and I'll sign the contract and get it back to you as quickly as possible! Again, thank you for the call!"

Placing his phone on his desktop, he sat there, fingers steepled thoughtfully! "Wow! Thank You, Lord! I'm-a-absolutely overwhelmed-but-uh- if You remember-I was asking You to do-something special-for Diana!" He laughed giddily! "Of course, what could be more special to her than my being invited to solo in a summer concert with the Symphony?" He laughed at his own humor! Sobering, he doodled. An extra ten grand! And he didn't care about the money! The recognition of his talent and the invitation were enough! Deducting the tithe from the coming check, he considered what he could buy for nine thousand dollars, to help comfort her in the loss of Mallory's friendship! She already had a couple of guns; they never used the boat they owned; she owned a Sable coat, good cars, beautiful home! Elegant, extravagant jewelry, designed and executed by the *Herbert Carlton Jewelry House*, was at her disposal!

He roamed through the house, searching for her, and found her busily drawing fashion illustrations in her design studio!

She glanced up with a bright smile! "What's up? You're grinning like the cat that swallowed the canary!"

"I just got a call from the Tulsa Symphony, inviting me to be featured violinist at one of the summer concerts! Did you already know?"

"Well, I think it's about time! How would I already know?"

He grinned. "Well, just strikes me a little odd, that someone at the Symphony suddenly thinks of me-anyway, I've been praying for God to do something really special for you-"

Her smile lit beautiful features. "That's how the Lord is! He rewards us for even trying to be nice to others! Especially our spouses! He always does special things for me."

He nodded. "But I know you're hurt by Mallory's silence!"

She sighed. "Well, that night when Gray was so hard on her, and I unloaded on her, too-it's my fault-"

"Well, you apologized!"

"As we both know, that doesn't always fix things! Anyway, tell me more about the concert!"

"Well, for two rehearsals and the performance, they're sending us ten thousand dollars! With the tithe deducted~I want you to have the rest of the money~"

"Well, what about the taxes?"

He frowned. "I knew it was too good to be true! How could I forget anything that constant?"

She brightened yet more! "Well, we'll have to put it into *DiaMal*! That's what I would want to do with it anyway! Invest it into my company! Maybe we should wait until the check actually arrives, or even until you've completed your obligation!"

He reached for her, and she moved into his embrace. "No, we're covered, if the check never comes! But with an opportunity like this, I won't miss it! Unless I'm dead! Which, I hope I won't be!" He swung her around jubilantly!

⊣ ⊢

Gray found Brenna in her office. "Any word yet?"

"Not by email! The snail mail hasn't come yet! Jacob suggested sending another follow-up letter to everyone, so we just finished that task! I'm not sure if I'm doing busy work to justify paying him a salary~"

Gray laughed exultantly! "Actually, Love, you were quite brilliant to come up with the idea! Of hiring him as your assistant! He has so much more feeling of worth and importance, and it's helping him see that his studies are important! And the salary is a reward for his huge strides~"

She nodded, feeling guilty at taking the praise for the idea, when Mallory had actually roped her into it! She tried to avoid mentioning Mallory!

"What about you?" she changed the subject. "Have you been able to get any of the items done on your bucket list?"

"Yes, quite so! My sister phoned me up~"

"Which one? You have six!"

"My older sister, who denies being the eldest, phoned me up to brag to me about Daniel's being invited to perform~"

Brenna took a step backwards, guilt written plainly in her expressive, tawny eyes.

"Well played, my Love, Bravo! Bravo!"

"You're not mad?"

"Only that it never occurred to me! Your idea was stellar about joining the Symphony Association and buying the season tickets and becoming involved in our fair city! You are credited with quite the coup! My brother-in-law's name has come up before, to be dropped because everyone assumed he would refuse!"

She grinned. "So, he did accept?"

"Thrilled to no end! So thrilled that he offered the fee, after tithe, to Diana for her business"!

Her delight faded into a forced smile, and he drew her near! "I know Diana is slow in accepting you! It's~she's usually top-side! Like you can't imagine! And I'm only putting my own supposition on what her problem is! He grinned! I think she is quite envious and bothered by my catching up to her!"

"Your catching up to her~uh~what do you mean?"

"Well, you know! She has seven children, but that hasn't been without its heartaches! Miscarriages and such! And I find you, the love of my life! And I suddenly have seven children, too!"

Brenna shook her head wonderingly. "I have a hard time believing that would bother her! Hers are showcase kids, and yours are~just~kids~"

"Ah, be very careful, Brenna, my love! I won't be tolerating any criticism of my family!"

She stared in confusion as he continued, "Well, you have been a remarkably good sport about my request for you not to complete the contract with *DiaMo*. Like you, I am impressed that the contract has been paid out for the breach of trust! I do feel like they breached my trust, and I'm impressed that we didn't have to sue to prove it!" He shook his head as she tried to interrupt! "Let me finish first, Brenna! I want you to take nine thousand dollars also, to invest in your company!"

She stared. "Gray, it's only a paper company~"

"Of course, you may use the money in your company in any way that you please, but have you considered beginning on an advanced degree? If you return to school, you'll meet more contacts in your field! There may be a bulletin board that announces jobs~I think you won't miss your friendship with Mallory as much, if there are other people you can talk rocks to!"

Chapter 11: FORTITUDE

Mallory stood on the dock, inventorying sample cases as they offloaded in the Iquique port. Hot, tired, and discouraged, were extreme understatements for her mood! A truck emblazoned with an international shipping logo pulled up. She handed over the paperwork and watched until the hopefully valuable cargo was loaded and on its way! Wearily, she headed up toward town and a small, recently purchased bungalow.

Another stressful day aboard *The Rock Scientist*! Some parts on the main drilling rig had flown apart! Even through her exhaustion, she breathed another prayer of gratitude that none of the crew members were injured! The necessary repairs would take a couple of days! She sighed. The ordered parts must arrive from Santiago, and then time for the actual repair work! She should be glad for a break in the exhausting workload! But at this point in time, she wanted to finish her grid and head home to Dallas!

The original plan was to keep their entire family onboard! A plan that had seemed ideal, from the vantage point of the Dallas offices. The reality was altogether different! Despite many added safety and medical features, the vessel was no place for three little girls! Between the dangerous equipment and the ship's rails not designed for corralling children, it was nerve wracking. And then, to either complicate the situation or clarify it, David couldn't tolerate the motion! Being onboard, even briefly, brought on excruciating headaches and nausea! Another reason to get back home! David to see his neurosurgeon in Phoenix, and she was overdue to see her Ob/Gyn.!

She glanced around, uncertain whether someone had called her name! To her horror, David and Nanci Higgins waved eagerly! Through her exhaustion, they seemed surreal! 'What were they doing here? This wasn't a port of call for any mainstream cruises!' She tried futilely to remember where they were supposed to be. Even though she looked worse than she felt, there was no escaping them! Plastering on a 'game face' she was far from feeling, she greeted them warmly.

"What brings y'all to this little corner of the world?"

Professor Higgins made no effort to conceal his profound shock! "Are you okay? You're not actually the only Geologist attached to this project, are you?"

She forced a smile, determined to remain congenial. She wanted to snap out, 'Well, who else is there? You're on a prolonged honeymoon, waiting for a chance to get back in the classroom! And your buddy, Del, can't control his alcohol use!'

Of course, there was no sense in blaming them! She was the dumb boss that enabled them to do their thing, while she worked enough for all three of them. Numbly she repeated her question about why they were in Iquique.

"Where are you headed?" Nanci's response, "Do you mind if we all take a taxi? It's hot out here. Then 'Iggy can tell you why we came!"

⧉ ⧉

David felt frazzled! His attempts at being both dad and mom to the girls while Mallory was at sea seemed futile! Although, he had an office setup, and could conduct quite a bit of business, it wasn't easy with the girls fussing, whining, and fighting constantly! The call about the breakdown and the crews' coming ashore for a couple of days came as a huge relief!

"Mommy's coming! Amelia, pick up the blocks! I'm going to start some laundry!"

"Daddy, I didn't spill the blocks out! Av'y did!"

"Okay, Avery Estee! Come help Sissy pick up these blocks! Mommy's coming! We need to clear a pathway so she can get in the door!" He moved past, collecting week old cereal bowls and dropping banana peels in the garbage!

Screeches erupted, and he whirled around! "Stop fighting! And do what you were tol~"

His voice died and profound embarrassment reddened his face! There in the doorway stood a bedraggled Mallory and a smartly dressed couple from the promenade!

He forced a smile and pecked Mallory on the cheek! "Wow! You made it quick!"

She laughed. "Yeah, we cheated and took a cab! Glad to see that everything's under control here!"

He grinned in response! "Does that mean I get a raise?"

"Y'all, come in," She urged the visitors. "I'll shower and change real quick; and we can all go out to eat together! Seafood here is sensational!"

David blocked the doorway to their room apologetically, "There's just one small problem!"

"Let me guess! I don't have any clean clothes!" She turned to the Higgins! "In that case, let me wash up a little, and I'm ready to go now!"

⇄ ⇆

Diana took her Bible and cup of coffee to the back patio! A chilly day, but nice enough that the little kids could play in the yard! With a deadline screaming toward her for completion of the Holiday line, her inspiration tank was empty! She focused on a picture on her phone's home screen, making her miss the Andersons more than ever!

She allowed the tears to flow freely. "Lord, please bring them back, and restore our friendship! I didn't know any of that about the episode with the fake Yeti, or the trespassing, when I lashed out at Mallory! She must have felt like it was 'pick on Mallory night'! Lord, You know that we have been making strides for You and Your kingdom, and the devil wants to throw a monkey wrench in it! I hate that I played into his hands, though!"

⇄ ⇆

Mallory relaxed into David's arms! It felt good to be home! Home's being, wherever he was! "You can't imagine how horrified I was to see anyone I knew!" she confessed. "I was totally exhausted and out of sorts! And all this week, I had particularly been praying-well, you know the verses:

Psalm 40:1 I waited patiently for the LORD; and he inclined unto me, and heard my cry.

So, I've been trying to be patient through all of this, but then, I've just been ready for the trial to end, so I dropped down to the last verse of *Psalm 40:*-verse *17.*

> *But I am poor and needy; yet the LORD thinketh upon me: thou art my help and deliverer; make no tarrying, O my God.*

So, I was praying that my patience couldn't endure much more, and asking for deliverance, and I was still just furious to see the Higgins there like they just stepped off an elegant cruise liner!"

David laughed. "Yeah, they were actually your help and deliverer! And they did show up just as I was at the end of my rope, too! Thanks for not being upset that the clothes were all dirty! I mean, how hard is it, to just start up a load a day, when I'm here all the time?"

"Oh, well! The fares home, on short notice, are sky-high, but at this point in time, I hardly care!"

⚐ ⚑

Brenna felt a strange poise as she took a seat opposite Dr. James Carr!

He frowned. "Your GPA is quite low for you to qualify for the Graduate Program here at TU!"

She nodded without speaking! He was right, and her excuses, though having some validity, would simply sound whiny! "I agree! I'm here to petition you as the head of the department, to give me a chance!"

He frowned again, and regarded her through pinched lips! "How committed are you to our science? It seems that, not only are your grades poor, but you've received some disciplinary action!"

"I have voiced unsolicited opinions in the classroom! For that, I apologize! My actions were out of line!"

His response was a sharp look! "Explain, 'Out of line'!"

"Well, Sir, as a Christian, I'm, not a believer in Evolution! And I must admit, sometimes it strikes me as dishonest, that other views are barely tolerated, much less presented! Now I realize that it is what it is! And that the professors have paid their dues to have their classrooms and platforms for teaching their views! And I've been an insolent upstart-it isn't my place to try to make changes-the way I approached it! You have my word that I'll be the most respectful student in the department!"

He studied her for long moments! Cute; actually striking! Tall and slender, groomed and well-dressed! Big sparkly wedding set! A tan leather attaché case he would nearly kill to own! At last, he relaxed and she responded slightly in kind!

"Okay, we'll put you to committee! I'll be in touch!" He rose, and she offered a business card! Reaching for it, he stood in the doorway, watching until she disappeared around a corner!

⚔ ⚔

Mallory mopped tears as she cradled her sonogram! "Well, that's a relief; that he's doing okay! Now when you see the doctor–"

"Well, I haven't had any headaches or nausea since I gave up my life at sea! I'm glad I never joined the Navy! Or the Marine Corps"!

She smiled agreement! "Well, maybe, unless your sensitivity to motion is related to your brain injury! David, are you sure–"

His steady gaze eased her panic. "I'm sure! Trust me, I have no desire to try to tough anything out and be brave, after that last incident. And I didn't know you were doing such hard physical work that you were worried about the baby! Dr. Higgins' appearance was timely, that's for sure!" When she didn't respond, he shot a sideways glance. "What?"

"He needs Waverly, David! What do you think? I mean, maybe you could escort him down there from The Ranch–so he won't be tempted by the drinks on the flight–"

"Okay, I'm not escorting Waverly anywhere! He's a grown man! He can either step up and stay sober and do what he's paid for, or we cut him loose! I'm for helping our employees when they're committed to us and their jobs, but I'm not going to enable– And drinks aren't just available on flights, that once I get him past that, he'll be fine! All of the ship's crew and the drillers drink; in case you didn't know! Higgins may struggle again!"

⚔ ⚔

Gray looked up from his monitor as Brenna appeared at the doorway. "Brenna, Luv! How was your appointment?"

She punched a button to brew a strong cup of coffee. "As well as could be expected! I'm thankful again, that my assault charge has been expunged! As it was, I only had to answer for sounding off in classes a few times! Of course, my GPA didn't swing the door wide open for me, either!"

"My brother-in-law could say the word, and–"

She nodded, not foolish enough to insist that she could make it without family favors! "Dr. Carr at least agreed to present me before the committee! I was prepared to drop Daniel's name, but–" she finished with a shrug and an adorable facial expression!

Gray sighed. "Sometimes the thought of sending you back into the classroom with handsome, young, single guys–!"

"What? Spoiled party boys that goof around on their parents' money? I managed to resist the type in Boston while I finished my undergrad! And, whom I served on my job"! She laughed. "I was actually developing into quite the man-hater! And then, you–"

His steady gaze met hers. "And, then I–what?"

"You–were so much–different! A Christian! And a gentleman–Every day, I struggle with why God brought me such an incredible–man– Uh, where are the kids?"

"They've gone out to the new house with David and Jeff! There's more room for them on the acreage, and the weather is quite pleasant! When the furniture arrives, David wants the crew to set up the bedrooms like the children want!"

Brenna grimaced! "That should be interesting! Better to just set it up, and tell them to like it! Sometimes democracy and giving everyone a vote, just plain doesn't work! It's amazing, actually, that the US Government's been as cohesive as it has! If that doesn't sound treasonous! I hope it doesn't!"

⚜ ⚜

Brad Maxwell sat at a popular coffee house, shaking his leg impatiently in his characteristic manner. He threw back an espresso! Sleepless night! His mind wandered back to the previous night's class! Surreal! He massaged his temples as he absently watched cars maneuver into the cramped lot. 'Just plain weird'!

He was a senior Geology major, with a nearly impeccable GPA; but his job inquiries were bringing an alarming lack of response! Desperate, he met with his faculty advisor, who simply deepened his panic! Consequently, he was pursuing graduate studies, registering for a three week intense course with the toughest prof in the department! His preference was daytime classes, hopefully not eight am, because evenings were party times at his frat house! And this prof was known for never giving A's, Dr. Clifford Stone!

But enough about Prof Stone! With a grin, he let his thoughts wander to the only girl in the class! A low wolf whistle escaped, and he glanced around sheepishly! Wow! Gorgeous! The few female Earth Science majors who had crossed his path-well, they looked like they should crawl back underneath the rocks they were studying-

Possessed of a bright, analytical mind, Brad usually sized situations up quickly and filed them away in his memory bank! But last night didn't make sense!

Well, the girl, there early, was the only student to choose the front row! Gorgeous in every aspect! Every aspect! A huge set of Diamond rings screamed 'Married', and yet in Stone's hours of haranguing her, he referred to her as Miss Hamilton! Maybe the rings were her defense against constant hustling; or maybe she was a widow- Afghanistan casualty- But Brad, who could usually figure things out and discard them, couldn't figure this one out! And it troubled him on more levels than he realized he had!

"Sorry I'm late, man!" Tim Alvaredo slung his backpack onto a chair and pulled his wallet free.

Brad frowned. "Mommy set up your parameters for today?"

Alvaredo flushed. "Actually, her tire was flat-I would've phoned but I didn't get your number-"

Brad flinched, not sure he wanted to buddy up with this guy that much!

"You want something else? I'm buying!"

Brad grinned, "In that case, I'll have a large cappuccino and a slice of pound cake."

Placing the drinks and pound cake as he slid into place, Alvaredo thought with relief that since he couldn't afford a pastry for himself, saying grace wouldn't be necessary!

"What happened last night?" Brad's thick dark brows drew together. "I was warned 'to hang onto my hat because this course was going to be intense-yada-yada-hit the ground running'-and Dr. Stone spent the night on a rampage at Miss Hamilton! So what's your take? Is she single or married? You think she and the prof have a history together-I didn't have a clue what he was talking about-"

Tim stirred sugar packets into his drink. "Well, he was blasting her because she believes in Creationism~"

Brad's handsome features registered impatience! "Yeah, I got that part, but what in the _____ is that?

Tim blushed. "Well, you know, the other school of thought, than Evolution! That things didn't evolve over eons of time, but that God created everything~and the earth is relatively young!"

"You're kidding, right? Do you think that there's even such a thing as 'God'?"

Cornered, Tim answered, "Well, yeah, I believe there's a God, or some Force! But science has proven that everything in the universe wasn't created by God in six days like the Bible says!"

Brad's skeptical frown deepened. "So, what's with you, that you have an eleven o'clock curfew and you wouldn't go for a drink with me? I couldn't sleep at all last night! That was so weird, how he picked on her in front of the whole class, and wasted all of our time~it doesn't make sense! And then, he practically ordered her to go with him to the faculty lounge once class dismissed! I mean, if the chick digs this Creationism stuff, so what? And why not start the course; we're all behind now~what was he so scared of?"

⚐ ⚑

Daniel and his father, Jerry, met Gray and Brenna at a coffee shop near TU's Campus. Brenna still appeared shaken, but was composed.

"I'm not sure there's any point in skewing your schedules any worse than I already have." She looked to Gray for confirmation, but he was silent.

"Did you get any sleep?" Jerry's voice was a growl. "I just feel like the Board of Regents should look into Dr. Stone's actions! We know we all have rocks in our noggins, but he left himself and the University open to all kinds of questions when he isolated you in the faculty lounge with him alone!"

Daniel laughed. "Speak for yourself, Dad!" He turned to his sister-in-law. "Dr. Stone didn't actually~"

"No, I'm used to warding off passes! He spent the class time reasserting the basic tenets of Evolution! When he led me to the lounge, I figured he was going to go on in the same vein! I was so determined that I wasn't going to argue the Evolution/Creation issue with him! I'm probationary in the Graduate program as it is!" She paused with a sigh! "But once we were alone in the lounge, he changed tone~and the subject! To Mallory! He just wanted information on where she is, and what she's doing, and how she operates! He knew all about my corporation and my not fulfilling the contract! He demanded of me what she did that broke the contract, and that made her still pay it out! And I couldn't say the right thing! I was trying not to say anything that would violate my CDA or reflect badly on her, or me, or any of us! If I refused to answer, he jumped to conclusions~like he wondered how you discovered the oil field~" The last addressed to Daniel.

Jerry spoke up. "Look, I think we need to file a complaint! None of that's any of his business~and he kept you late and put us all into a panic~ It's ludicrous in this day and time for him to be careless in dealing with a coed~"

Daniel nodded, "Well, I agree! But our alma mater is still blaming us for the loss of Higgins! And Brenna wants to continue her studies here~without exacerbating the animosity!"

Gray spoke softly for the first time. "That's my major concern! I don't want to make waves that will impede her basic objectives! Perhaps I'll go have a word with the gentleman."

Brenna's head snapped up. "No, I can handle it!"

Looking beyond them, Daniel rose with an outstretched hand. "Good morning, Cliff! Thank you for joining us!"

⧋ ⧊

Jacob tried not to be nervous! His first time to drive to the airport, and he was at the wheel of his step-dad's BMW. Pulling in at the curb for passenger pickup, he watched nervously for cops! Just a phobia holding over from his upbringing! Using his new cell phone, an eighteenth birthday gift, he rechecked the arrival information! Gray and Brenna, true to their word, were paying for his best friend from Massachusetts to come visit!

⧋ ⧊

Mallory barely contained her excitement! "There!" she pointed excitedly! "There's Daniel's car and Gray's van!"

David grinned at her as he fit their SUV into the only space in the lot, a tight fit. He slid his pistol into his shoulder holster. "Okay, I know you're excited, but we don't want the whole world to know~"

She nodded. "Mum's the word! But, David, can you believe it?"

He shook his head wonderingly! "Quite the coups! Even for you! But just remember that there are people who kill for lots less than this!"

⌥ ⌤

Dr. Clifford Stone shook hands with Daniel and his father before acknowledging the introduction to Gray Prescott!

"I'm not sure why you summoned me here!" His attitude hotly hostile toward the two alumni! "I'm already under review by the university!" He turned his gaze toward Brenna, "I don't suppose there would be any point in apologizing~"

Gray interrupted softly. "Well, there's always a point in an apology when you've injured someone! Whether it will stop the course of action you find yourself caught up in, I'm not certain."

Red-faced, the professor mumbled a gruff, "Sorry".

"Well, we haven't complained to the University~"

"You didn't need to! A couple of upstart students already went to Carr to complain about my not addressing the subject matter immediately! And you two made such a scene about getting on campus~"

Daniel frowned. "We didn't make a scene. When Jacob couldn't find Brenna after class, and she didn't answer her phone, naturally, Gray worried about her! He called me, and I came down to help him find her! But my alumni card was expired, and~the little power-thirsty gal running security told me I would need to go through proper channels Monday through Friday, blah~blah, to get it renewed; but in the interim, I'm not allowed on campus! That didn't set too well, so I called my dad! He's an alum too, and good friends with a couple of the guys on the Board~"

Stone crossed his arms. "Like I said; 'a scene'!"

Daniel laughed. "I'm getting another coffee; can I get you something, Cliff? And then you can explain why the cross-examination about Mallory Anderson!" Rising, he nearly knocked Mallory down!

"Did I just hear my name?"

With a nervous laugh, he shook her hand, and then David's! "What are y'all doing in town?"

Despite David's warning glance, Mallory bubbled over! "We're so excited! We have something to show you! So we called your office, but they said your were here, and~"

She paused to say hello to Gray and Brenna before addressing Professor Stone! "It's so great to meet you in person! I've enjoyed your lectures in some of my course work!"

Stone took the beautiful woman in with wonder, gratified by the praise.

⚑ ⚑

Mallory settled the girls in while Daniel joined David to order coffees. Still uneasy around Gray and Brenna, she engaged the professor. "I'm sure David Higgins would want me to tell you, 'hello'! I'm not sure, did you ever know Delton Waverly?"

"Yeah, can't believe Higgins landed the wife he did! I've met Waverly; don't know much about him. I hear you're drilling all over the world!"

Mallory laughed. "Typical rumor-mill! *DiaMo* has drilled some sites in the US~and now off the coast of Chili! Hardly world-wide"!

"I've seen your E-zine!"

Mallory looked pleased, "Really? I'm flattered!"

⚑ ⚑

Brad nudged Alvaredo to make him aware of the two guys standing in line! Tim nodded. Daniel Faulkner was his role model, and he wanted to hide rather than stand out!

As if aware of the attention, David noticed the students and waved. "I've seen you around; you sing tenor in the Honey Grove choir!"

Daniel turned, too, "Yeah, Alveredo; isn't it? I guess I didn't realize you were a student at TU!"

Tim's voice squeaked. "Yes sir, I've been studying online, but spring semester I started graduate work here on campus~" He responded to his idol's friendly handshake, trying to avoid the searching question in his eyes!

Laden with a drink holder, David paused beside them. "What's your field?"

"Earth Science! I'm sorry, let me introduce Brad Maxwell!"

115

Hands full, David nodded acknowledgment! "You Earth Sciences, too? Do you have time to join us? My wife's a Geologist, and Dr. Stone is over there~"

Daniel nodded eagerly, "And my sister-in-law, Brenna Prescott! She just started her graduate studies here last night!"

"Yeah," Brad muttered. "We were in the class! She okay?"

Chapter 12: GIG

Brenna fielded phone calls! True, she was the Geologist of note for the core sample; just barely! Questions assaulted her from sister Universities' Geological Departments across the country! They were the ones requesting scholarly reports. Other inquiries came from media, ranging between mainstream networks, to the most obscure! She was unprepared for the limelight!

Laughingly, but tactfully, Gray suggested they order her a wardrobe from Diana, more suitable for her new academic status!

Wide, luminous eyes met his at the suggestion! "I'm sure you're right, but she intimidates me! And I don't have a clue how to put stuff together!"

"I think her designs come in coordinate groupings that eliminate guesswork! They're very fine quality-"

She laughed. "You're talking to the thrift store girl about *DiaMal* quality? I'm sure it's up there, which brings me to the question-" She broke off, troubled.

"What it will cost?"

She nodded miserably, and his gaze searched her troubled features.

"Listen, I know that's part of the bill of goods they sell you! About going to college! That you pay the money and complete the courses, and all financial considerations will become a thing of the past!"

She sighed. "Well, I have more of a grasp on reality than that! Still-" She fought tears.

"You thought your Bachelor's degree-"

"Well, I knew it wasn't the be-all and end-all, but I thought-"

"Things would get easier once you got past that part-" he supplied!

"Yes, I guess so!"

His features twisted. "Oh, Brenna, how I wish I could wave my little wand for you~"

Her face set in determination! "I don't want a magic wand waved! I want to do it!"

His laughter was gentle agreement! "And so you are! But, Brenna, life never gets easy! You win one battle, and here comes another! Rather much, I should think, as the waves pummeling your raft! Without letup! I do want us to weather the storms together!"

"I know, but you've done so much~"

He laughed. "What are you referencing, my Love? That I'm taking care of my children?"

She shook her head wonderingly. "They aren't really your children! They're not really my brothers and sisters~"

"And yet wonderfully and miraculously, God has merged us into a family! He gave us favor with the family court, and it's incredible, quite actually!

She nodded, suddenly unable to speak!

"If you're so determined not to allow me to provide you with a new wardrobe, perhaps you can put the squeeze on Jacob!"

"On Jacob! He doesn't have any money! I'm just relieved that he didn't wreck your car!"

"Brenna, it's our car! And my concern about a wreck would be for him and his friend, more than damage to the car! And he may find himself in possession of quite a sum! Maybe we should pray it won't be his destruction!"

"Jacob? Where would he get money from? Do you mean his salary as my corporate assistant?"

"Not primarily, that! Although the notoriety of your recent find can't hurt your professional reputation! And consequently, his position within your company! But, no! Jacob and his friend Millard have devised quite a clever video game! But back to my original subject! I've been hoping my big sister would invite you to be one of her model/reps, in which she provides the ensembles in exchange for the exposure for her designs! Sadly, her response to my suggestion, broached by our mother, was for me not to be so cheap! That was before every news agency in the company was clamoring for an interview with you!"

Brenna sat processing all of the new information! Jacob and Millard? And their computer geeky stuff? Might have a payoff? And that she,

Brenna, might gain enough notoriety to bring attention to Mallory and Diana's clothing designs? And the treasure coming to light from the sample! Enough to steal her breath away! Nor just for the intrinsic value of the gold coins and the emerald chunk, but the Geological insights being gleaned!

⤡ ⤢

Clint Hammond, long time Faulkner family attorney, sat huddled with Sam Whitmore over the newly designed video game! Both video game aficionados, they were thrilled at the prospects, while nervous about piracy! Not actually a copyright and patent attorney, Hammond wanted to make the concept as protected as possible before passing it along to a colleague who specialized in copyrights!

Hammond straightened up to meet Whitmore's gaze. "Your nieces and nephews are growing up!"

Sam laughed, "That they are, and with Gray's marriage to Brenna, they have also multiplied!"

The attorney nodded seriously! "Yes, I guess everything's working out with Gray's sudden move on the chessboard! When I first heard about it, I thought he was nuts! To marry a girl he really didn't know! And then~without a pre-nup! And then to take on the whole odd assortment of kids~ Who would guess that Jacob, and a friend who's more socially inept than he is, could~" His hand swept toward the game concept! "Do you think Gray knew this was in the works?"

Sam regarded the other man through his thick lenses, considering carefully! Hammond should take his confidentiality with his clients more seriously. This was tending toward gossip~in the computer genius's mind! At length, he responded.

"Well, I don't want loose lips to sink ships, but you'd have to know Gray! He has the first penny he ever socked away, but he's been wise and frugal; not greedy! He didn't have a clue that this game and its proceeds would emerge as a by-product of his kindness! I mean, I know you don't agree with our Christianity, but this is just another example of how God works on the behalf of Christians!"

Hammond bristled. "For your information, I'm a Christian!"

Sam squirmed. He should be the last guy to debate with an experienced attorney. But not seeing anyone else in the room to take on the task, he plunged in. "Let me guess! You were 'baptized' as a baby!"

"What? You have a problem with that?"

Sam laughed, deciding to back off. After all, 'A brother offended was harder to be won than a strong city'! The verse in Proverbs warned of that. "I apologize for sounding offensive, but let me ask you this; have you been back to church since then?"

"To get married! That's the thing, nothing good has ever happened to me in church!" He chuckled at his own joke.

Sam smiled miserably, knowing Hammond was okay with his wife, just liked to participate in the chronic, good-ole-boys-club grumble! Sam wanted to be more loyal than that to Niqui, and he prized his little daughter and soon-to-be-arriving-son!

Hammond pushed his reading glasses onto his head! "So explain to me the way to get on this, 'Magic carpet ride'!"

More speechless than ever, the computer wizard frowned contemplatively!

Hammond pulled the papers toward him and began placing them into his attaché. "That's what's wrong with you Bible-thumping brand of Christians! You have no sense of humor!"

"We do when things are funny! Maybe you should polish up your act! Marrying my wife was one of the most special things that ever happened to me in church, but every service, I learn something new about the Lord and my salvation! But it isn't a 'Magic carpet ride'! There are still heartaches and hurdles! It's just that the Lord helps with those things!"

‡   ‡

Brenna appeared, stunning and amazingly relaxed, to meet a bevy of microphones. Diana had chosen an ensemble of black and honey for the occasion! A houndstooth slender skirt was topped with a honey cashmere turtleneck sweater and double faced wool jacket in black; with lapels, belt and pocket flaps of the contrast color! A swirl brooch of black pearls and diamonds adorned the lapel, and heavy gold hoop earrings repeated the theme of a cuff bracelet!

Maxwell watched with curious interest as she fielded questions! Quite the emerging professional! Seeing Gray Prescott, he moved toward him, offering his hand silently! They both hung on every word the spokeswoman said!

Gray frowned. The tenor of the questions seemed less about extracting honest expertise, than about attacking the credibility of the interviewee! Still, Brenna calmly clarified and reaffirmed her statements! She was the perfect combination of toughness and heart! At the moment her crisp responses reflected more toughness! Gray applauded her inwardly, his heart filled with pride!

As the interview closed, Gray turned to the grad student, "Mr. Maxwell, is it not?"

"Yes Sir, that's right! Your wife did a great job up there!"

A guarded smile, "I thought so! I beg your pardon, but where are Drs. Carr and Stone?"

"I wondered the same thing! I'm sure their intellectual egos are bruised~"

Gray shot him a shrewd glance. "Maybe, but it's not a time for licking psychological wounds! It is their department! They could step up and take ownership over both my wife and the sample! They're still so bent on~" he hesitated!

"Excluding her!" Maxwell finished the thought! "I can't figure out what they're so afraid of!"

Gray tipped impeccable fedora as he sent a parting remark! "The Truth!"

᚛ ᚜

Alexandra scanned across the email from Clint Hammond! The contract for Brenna's company, at last! She fought fear and frustration! The money she agreed to pay seemed gargantuan, and yet, with Brenna's recent prominence~maybe she should forget it. Manicured index finger hit the intercom buzzer and her dad answered, "What's up, Al?"

Summoning a lilt to her voice she was far from feeling, she breezed back. "Not much! Just wondered if I can treat my favorite father to lunch!"

Echoing her tone, he responded jovially, "I can't think of anything I'd rather do than meet my favorite eldest daughter for lunch! As soon as you've sent the document and gotten it back signed! I always try to make it a practice to get my major items of business completed before lunch! Oh, and Al, get the check off to Clint before lunch, too! What time will work for you? Are we talking meeting in the Bistro?"

Staying upbeat required her best effort! So much for her plan; blowing up in her face! Maybe she wouldn't even need any dynamite for the mine, the way things habitually backfired for her! Now, she was still out the attorney's fee, the commitment of Brenna's contract, and buying lunch for two in the pricey Bistro! Her dad would hold her to it, too!

⊰ ⊱

"What do you guys need?" Brenna shut the door behind her as she made her way into the guest room where Millard had stuff strewn hither, thither, and yon! I guess it's really coming together for your game~"

"Duh, yeah, Bren!" Millard's hostility took Brenna off-guard!

"We're giving you a word of warning!" Jacob's shrewd expression accompanied his words.

She laughed. "Okay, thanks! Warning about what?"

"About not blowing this gig!" Millard's wheelchair advanced toward her slightly.

"I'm sorry! What 'Gig' exactly do you mean?"

"Keep your voice down! You know what we mean! And you can't do crazy stuff that can blow things for the rest of us!"

Millard sat nodding sagely! "You don't really think you fooled him, do you? Listen, Brenna, we men are not naïve about stunts like that!"

"Oh, I get it; you obviously think you're men! Did you want to talk about something, or not? Maybe you should straighten up this room~"

"You don't get it, Bren!" Jacob's voice took a harder edge! "That other night when you went to 'your class' and you didn't come back on time, and 'the professor took your jacket with your phone in the pocket, and wouldn't give it back'~"

"Look, when Gray and Daniel found me, that's what was going on~that's why he believes me! Because I told the truth!"

"Right! Since when? He's probably just going along with the story while he meets with his attorneys for the best way to get shed of us all! Brenna, none of us are that stupid! There's more at stake here than you getting in bed with the professors, metaphorically speaking, of course~" Jacob coughed sarcastically behind his hand! After he raised a couple of even lewder suppositions, she recovered her poise.

"Listen, guys, I know you're more worldly-wise than you should be! Our upbringing was pretty~uh~raw~but my marriage to Gray~we're

122

committed! It's a Christian thing, and I don't appreciate you referencing what he and I have, as a 'gig'!" Making her way across the minefield of strewn belongings she gained the hallway! And there stood Gray!

⊰ ⊱

As Alexandra awaited a response from Brenna, a thought occurred to her! Maybe the Geologist was now in a position of being able to decline the contract! Hoping for an out, she drummed nervously on the edge of her desk! An email alert came, indicating another missive from the attorney! With misgivings, she accessed it, hoping it wouldn't be any additional fees!

A delighted smile sent the worry into retreat! The email was a thanks for prompt payment! 'But why would he expect less of a Faulkner?' And then, somehow he had gotten wind of Jeremiah's competing with a prize steer! The email explained that the attorney was buying a country place, and was inquiring about purchasing a steer so he and his son could engage in the project together!

Her laughter bubbled delightedly! "Wow, thanks, Lord! I didn't see that one coming!" She stared at the agreement, but before she could accept and complete the transaction, the response came from Brenna! She was onboard!

She buzzed Daniel's office. "I got my major business completed, so I'm free to meet whenever you are!"

⊰ ⊱

Brenna dropped her gaze at Gray's perplexed expression and moved past him without a word! Shame and worry congealed like metamorphic stones where her heart just was! She scurried to her office and checked emails! Numb, she agreed to the terms of Alexandra's contract!

'How much did Gray hear? Were the boys right in their assessment?' Their observations about her and Grays' intimate relationship flushed her cheeks with searing humiliation! Traveling to Colorado might not be far enough! Grudgingly she admitted they had a sordid point! Gray's passionate desire for her had seemed to evaporate in the past several days! She scrunched her eyes hard, trying to block his strange expression-hurt-disgust? Bowing her head into folded arms, she sobbed brokenly as the tears coursed!

⚜ ⚜

Grayson moved to the elegant space of their shared master suite! David's retrofit was so nice that he sometimes questioned his decision to build from scratch on a larger acreage! Brenna's jacket, handbag, and shoes were discarded neatly on a decorative bench at the foot of the queen sized bed. He sighed, fingering the sumptuous woolen jacket and running a hand over the smooth butter that was the leather of the two-toned handbag! The honey-color chosen by his sister made Brenna positively elegant, highlighting the honey tones of her hair and eyes! He sighed again, then moved where he could study his reflection in an intricately framed, full length mirror! A smile played at the corners of his eyes before spreading down his face into a wide grin! "A 'Gig'!" Jacob's words! A wonderful 'Gig', that Gray didn't want to see marred! If Jacob wasn't learning to love him, he was at least developing an appreciation for the good things! Gray would take it as a triumph, of sorts! And he held no animosity for Jacob's biological father!

And his beautiful love, Brenna! His expression sobered as his thoughts traveled to his wife! Wow! If Jacob felt like he and the children were on eggshells, not to end the 'Gig', not to upset the apple cart, Gray felt it in an even greater way! "It's the best 'Gig', I've ever had, too, Lord! Thank You, and strengthen our love, so we all feel more secure!"

⚜ ⚜

Daniel studied the copy of the signed contract! "She has a lot of character not to cancel or renegotiate! You really stalled around, Al! If no one was beating a path to her door initially, they will be now!"

"Yes, Sir," Alexandra met his gaze unflinchingly! "It is a miracle I didn't miss out! Can you get me on campus to see the sample? Oh, and guess what? I sent the check for the attorney fees and got a response back immediately from Mr. Hammond that he wants to buy a steer! I mean, this steer thing is mind-boggling! It's like they're just little gifts from God that you don't pay for; and then you can sell them for a lot!"

Daniel placed his order before he dissolved into laughter at her observation.

Still elevated by her infusion of wealth, she waited patiently for a chance to ask, "Okay, what stupid thing did I say now?"

He wiped his eyes on the napkin. "I prefer the term naïve! Yes, the reproduction process ordained by God is miraculous, and yet your calves have cost you quite a bit!"

"Oh, well, of course; insurance, hired help, feed, the vet fees, security; uh-how do you sort that all out? I'm sure the IRS has a formula! Like all that depreciation and stuff like that, I don't get it!"

He patted her hand affectionately. "You will; it'll come! Just don't treat this inflow of cash like it's net-"

"A good reminder, but at least it's black ink!"

At length, he picked up the tab-

⊰ ⊱

Brenna raised her head and dabbed at her eyes, focusing her forlorn gaze on the door. Probably Jacob back to offer more of his unsolicited advice! She moved to the door, cracked it open, and was distressed to see Gray standing there!

"Hey, hey; he made you cry? I shall speak to him!"

"No, it's my fault!" she sobbed harder in spite of valiant attempts at control! "I'm used to him-and Millard-too! They've always been that way- What one doesn't think of-to say mean-the other one does!"

He pulled her against him! Kissing her hair and crooning softly, he held her while the sobs erupted. "There, Brenna, love; that's it, then! They just like to tease and make you upset with them! The pattern will change! Well, I'll see that it does-but Rome wasn't built in a day, after all-"

The old saying struck her funny! Surely Rome was built more quickly than changes would come to this family dynamic! So she stood there in the circle of his arms, laughing and crying and trembling and hiccupping!

In the privacy of their suite she met Gray's eyes while she searched for words. "Their opinion of me-is mostly my fault! I made stuff up-to impress them-and other kids-in the neighborhood-um-stuff I never really-did! I don't know-I guess-even before-I found-Christ, He was protecting me-from myself-from everyone- It's no wonder Jacob assumed-what he did-you know-about Professor Stone- It isn't true, though! I swear to you, Gray! And I love you, so much! When Millard leaves-uh-I'll try again to explain-the sanctity of marriage-and that it isn't some-'Gig'!"

A tender smile crinkled at the corners of slate blue eyes! "Call it whatever you will, we have something very special! I've been a good bit worried about blowing the 'Gig', myself! Come now, let's ask the children to join us for a scone and a spot o' tea!"

Chapter 13: EXCELLING

Herb Carlton, master jeweler, bent over his workbench, working intently on the finishing touches of a masterpiece of craftsmanship! He clapped his hands together gleefully! How could a man possibly be more blessed? He sent a text message to Linda, his wife:

Come and see what you think! To me, it turned out rather well!

While he waited for her to make the short walk to his workroom, he burnished and polished the project once more! Then, pressing the button to admit her, he placed the glistening jewel on black velvet beneath a display light! It caught the rays, reflecting dazzlingly so that he gasped with wonder in spite of himself! He turned away momentarily to greet his spouse, smiling a welcome!

She surveyed the object in wonder for long moments before meeting his eyes! "The piece David commissioned for Mallory? Herbert, you have absolutely~" her words trailed off as emotion choked her.

"Yes, the smaller piece that was cleaved from *Radiant Dawn* when I crafted Mallory's engagement ring! This concept was David's! Rather grand; do you not agree?"

"It's an exact miniature replica of Britain's Imperial State Crown, isn't it? The one with the huge diamond on the front that was cleaved from the famed Cullinan?"

Herb nodded, "Yes, the 317.4 carat Cullinan II! Very good, remembering the details from our visit to the Tower of London!"

She nodded, "Thanks, but I flip through our souvenir booklet every so often! You really did a stunning job!"

"Yes, I argued with David that it should have purple velvet inserted, but he wanted the velvet represented in pavé of purple stones! Very small of purple sapphires and purple spinel!"

"I see; very nicely done! What's the weight of the diamond, if I might ask?"

"3.1714 carats!"

"And it's a slide she can wear on any 6mm Omega chain?"

"Yes, that is the plan!" His expression infused with excitement!"

"Let me guess! You have an improvement in mind on the basic Omega!"

A rich laugh rolled from the jeweler. "Yes, but it is such fun!" He turned his attention to his bench where the Omega lay! Texturing in the 14 karat yellow gold caught the light, making the piece glow more enticingly. Tiny diamonds and purple sapphires sprinkled along the surface, lit it further!

"Oh, that's beautiful alone," Linda breathed. "Is there more so I can faint completely?"

"Yes, I make also bracelet! Yet smaller Imperial Crown, and then also copies of Princess of Wales' tiaras and diadems! Except where blue sapphire were in original of diadem, I take liberty of keeping with the purple of the set!"

"So, I suppose David is having Diana design some purple ensembles to show it off to perfection?" Linda strove to curb the envy she felt.

"He didn't say, one way or the other! Mallory, she have already so much in beautiful winter white!"

⚔ ⚔

Brenna carefully hung the new ensemble! She recalled the sense of assurance it lent to her interviews, amazed at the difference it made! Maybe with some of the money from her contract with Alexandra, she could purchase another. She pulled on pajamas and robe and sank in front of the bathroom vanity!

> *I Samuel 16:7 But the LORD said unto Samuel, Look not on his countenance, or on the height of his stature; because I have refused him: for the LORD seeth not as man seeth; for man looketh on the outward appearance, but the LORD looketh on the heart.*

She studied her reflection as she considered the verse. Silly, to be thinking of another expensive outfit! A waste of money and energy! She prayed for the Lord to cleanse her heart; after all, it was her heart that He was concerned with! She sighed! Of course, her heart had to stay right-that was most important, and then the judgment of people was inconsequential! Whether your clothes and everything measured up the way other people thought they should!

She glanced up with a smile as Gray appeared.

"Oh, you're already in your pajamas! I thought it might be jolly-good to go out for a nice celebra'try dinner! Your first big exposure to the media handled with élan, and then signing your contract!"

She sighed, "I told Summer she can wear my jeans! I've kept putting her off, but since I got a new outfit, she was kind of miffed! So as soon as the dryer stops, she's wearing them. I hope she doesn't stain them all up! They were the last pair in the world!"

Gray strove to stay serious. "Well, that's nice, Dear; your sharing! I guess you must wear the ensemble you were wearing earlier! You looked extremely fetching, and all-"

Something about her pensive expression pulled him in. "Is something heavy on your mind? You aren't still fretting about Jacob and Millard; I hope!"

"Um-no-I'm feeling torn about-do you know I Samuel 16:7?"

"Ah, yes, about men seeing what's on the outside, but the fact that God always sees our hearts; what about it?"

"Well, what's in your heart; that's all that's really important; right?"

"Hmmm-good question! It's of course, what's of primary importance; our relationship with God. But of course since people can't look on our hearts, all they really have to go on is our outward appearance! It should be a reflection of being right inwardly! Peace and joy, a clear conscience! How we present ourselves to the world is how we present the Savior!"

He sank down on the edge of the tub, taking both of her hands in his! "The same idea is in:

I Peter 3:3 & 4 Whose adorning let it not be that outward adorning of plaiting the hair, and of wearing of gold, or of putting on of apparel:

But let it be the hidden man of the heart, in that which is not corruptible, even the ornament of a meek and quiet spirit, which is in the sight of God of great price.

This verse does not forbid women to style their hair or wear nice jewelry! In that case, the way the sentence is structured, it would seem to say women shouldn't put on apparel either! We know that isn't the meaning! This means that the care of the inner spirit is more crucial than outward clothing and adornment! Why is it on your mind?"

Her lashes fluttered down, casting ruffled shadows on flushed cheeks. "No reason!" really~"

A shadow flitted across his face, to be replaced quickly with his jovial smile. "Would you prefer to go to dinner another time?"

⊰ ⊱

ARKANSAS DIAMOND MINE FOREMAN KILLED IN ONE-CAR ACCIDENT!

A stunned Mallory took in the headline and scanned quickly down the article! Strange, she hadn't been officially notified! 'Alcohol involved; icy road!' Both probable, knowing Tad Crenshaw! Still, there was the possibility that the foreman's death wasn't an accident!

She looked up as David presented her with a mug of coffee! Without comment, he pulled the newspaper free and threw it in the trash! Their gazes met and she sighed! No sense in making suppositions! Still, her thoughts traveled back to the absurd event of Tad and the Yeti costume, his attempt to scare her and Brenna and Jacob away from the depression that was certainly an eroded diamond dike! Her thoughts were that, not only had he failed in his mission to scare them, but then had also stopped to pick up a valuable stone! But did that mark him for execution? Had he ignored warnings? Maybe it was really an accident! She shivered!

⊰ ⊱

Alexandra tried to ignore her dad's new hire as he settled busily into his area! He was good-looking, but he made her uneasy! There seemed to be something a little off about a guy who owned a thousand exotic plants! Maybe they would at least purify the air in the sealed office space. She opened a site on her computer and scanned the course offerings! Tom

Haynes' company didn't offer anything Ag based! She hesitated about calling him, and his site didn't offer an option for asking questions!

"Hello, I'm Brad," the newcomer offered as he peeked into her space! "How about a Boston Fern?"

"Mmmm. Thanks, but I don't think so! It's already so crowded in here I can't turn around!"

"Well, how about putting it in a hanging planter?"

"I'm not going to be around much longer! Maybe you can offer it to the next person who inherits this space!"

"Really? The snow's that melted? Avalanches have been a serious threat this year, too! The high elevations in Colorado-"

She nodded, "Thanks, Brad!"

He stood uncertainly. "Can I ask you a question?"

She rolled her eyes! Did this clown not know who she was?

"Yeah, you're the boss's daughter! I get it! I'm just curious, though, if you know if Brenna Prescott is coming back to Stone's class."

"I really haven't heard! She's under contract to my mining company, but it doesn't start for a month! That gives her time to complete the course! If that's what she plans to do! I guess the professor didn't cover much subject matter the other night! That's kinda odd, isn't it, for these abbreviated courses?"

His brows drew together and he stepped in further. "Yeah, it's crazy! Usually they talk a mile a minute, and load you down with reading and projects! Your head spins! He spent the entire time berating your, uh-what-she's your aunt?"

"Well, let's say she's married to my uncle and leave it at that! Why was he berating her?"

"I don't know for sure! That's what I'm trying to find out! Something weird that has the department scared of her!"

"The Earth Science department is scared of Brenna? She's a little weird; grew up real poor! Sad home life!"

"Snobbish observations from the girl who has it all! It was something about Evolution! Dr. Stone kept reasserting that it's the truth, irrefutable! There's no room for fairy stories in the world of science! Since everyone pretty much knows that, it seemed like a real crazy waste of time, that he kept blasting her-"

"Yeah, and then, after class, my dad and uncle had to go find her! Professor Stone was grilling her about Mallory Anderson and her geological exploration!"

"He was? Hey, have you seen that core~"

"I wish! I tried to bug my dad about it, but the buzz has grown until security's only allowing really limited access! You saw it; didn't you?"

"Yeah, but I guess the significance of it was lost on me! Hey, I'd better get the rest of my stuff moved in!"

⊰ ⊱

"Gray, where did all this stuff come from?" Brenna stood at the entrance of the walk-in closet, taking the contents in dumbly!

He was beside her immediately, eyes twinkling with mischief! "Must have been an angel put it all there! To give you peace in your heart that it's okay to adorn the outside once you've devoted some daily time to inward beauty!"

"Gray, I don't know what to say; it must have all cost a fortune!"

"Not totally! My sister is not altogether heartless; so she gave me a 'favorite brother' discount! Anyway, they are all quite lovely, actually! Very good quality at a price she works at keeping to a minimum for the value received! I love you, Brenna, and these are things you need! God is launching you beyond your wildest dreams, but you can't meet the professional world day after day in the same pair of purple jeans! By the way, I had quite a fracas with Summer over them! They were indecently tight on her!"

Brenna sighed. "She told me! She was pretty ticked! Thanks, though! I was afraid she might split them out! But back to the subject at hand!" She moved dazedly into the space, running her hand across each hanger! "How do people decide? I've never had choices before! Just wear what little you have that's clean; or cleaner~"

"Okay, this is what I like best!" He held up a collection created in Honey and Robin's egg blue! A circular skirt in Honey that also coordinated with her original outfit, paired with a shirt in the delicate blue, topped by a three quarter length jacket of brushed mohair plaid that combined the two hues! Solid Honey pumps and leather bag finished the look!

"I think that's my favorite, too! Although it's hard to say! But it's too dressy! I should save it~"

"No, Brenna, dear! Go ahead and wear it! You're still having meetings with myriads of people!"

132

"Well, I know that! But they're interested in what I have to say, not what I'm wearing!"

"Well very true! That's why it's good to be knowledgeable in your field~" he hesitated.

She met his eyes in the mirrored reflection, then turned to face him earnestly! "But, it really isn't wrong~to look as nice as possible~the Bible says not to care about what you put on~"

"No, it says that the One Who created the beauties of nature is able to clothe you more gorgeously than you can clothe yourself! If you choose to live for Him, then He adds all of the things to you, which you willingly surrender for His sake!" Still overwhelmed, she dressed carefully. As she pulled wads of paper from the new handbag, a silk drawstring bag, materialized! Shaking the contents out onto the bed, she gasped in wonder! A brooch featuring a small golden bird's nest cradled three little eggs carved of soft blue stone, while a mother robin hovered, wings spread!

"How exquisite," Gray gasped. "I may owe my sister an increased sum! That might have been inadvertent~"

Relinquishing it longingly, Brenna whispered wistfully, "No, we should just give it back to her!"

"Nonsense! And it will coordinate beautifully with the gold hoops and bracelet you have!" He pinned the brooch on the jacket lapel and stood back to survey her! "You are very beautiful! Have I told you that? See also, the pin can be worn on one of those plain gold necklaces that are so popular! We must get you one!"

⊰ ⊱

On a whim, Bransom barked a couple of orders! Nate Halsey and Gabe Pritchard! Strange, their continuous reappearances at Mallory's doorstep! They were the type of executive that now raised red flags in his mind!

"Those two already have criminal charges levied against them," Caroline Hillman observed! "They have slick attorneys, and they've posted bail~" She stopped herself with a rueful chuckle! "Yeah, they fit the profile, alright! I'll see if I can connect them to any of the others! And~I'll go through our film archive and see if either of them shows up~"

⊰ ⊱

Diana gasped in wonder! "Okay, Lord, help me not to envy Mallory!" She enlarged the photo to better view the shimmering design! The request was for a new collection for Mallory in purple. She dubbed the new color, 'Amethyst'! Why not feature the color prominently in her coming line? She went to work illustrating new designs, then glanced up as Daniel's shadow fell across her notebook!

"Wow, I guess I lost track of time!"

He laughed at her guilty expression. "Well, everything seemed under control as I came through! May I see?"

Flushing, she handed him her work.

A whistle escaped! "Wow! Strictly nice! Stuff like this just comes into your mind?"

"In a sense!" She turned her laptop toward him and opened up the picture. "David asked Herb to make a piece of jewelry for Mallory, using a 'leftover chunk of diamond' from *Radiant Dawn* and her engagement ring! Herb came up with the idea of copying the Imperial Crown!"

He chuckled, "Quite a process in the inspiration cycle!" A strange expression flickered in his brown eyes as he handed it back. "Very elegant! Let's go back into the city and have a steak! "I'll go pick up some pizza for the kids; be ready to go when I come back!"

She watched his retreating form, puzzled. 'Sure, no problem!'

⚔ ⚔

Gray blinked mildly behind his glasses as a stranger approached them about the Geological sample! He didn't mind! After Brenna's hard work and yielding herself to the Lord, she deserved the recognition!

She disagreed! Her argument, that the expedition was planned and funded by *DiaMo, Inc*! She had barely arrived on site in Chile to secure the sample case before setting herself adrift on the raft! All the same, she had nearly died, and Gray was unhappy about Halsey and Pritchard's being out on bail, continuing business as usual!

David and Mallory didn't want any additional notoriety, and the attention for Brenna could only boost her up the ladder.

"I understand that the coins are gold, and they're from ancient Greece?" The inquirer arched a brow. "That seems rather far-fetched."

Brenna nodded candidly. "That's everyone's take who has viewed the coins! I'm not a historian or a coin expert! I'm a Geologist, and to me, the interesting thing is that we drilled through volcanic matter to reach the wreck and its treasures. Which would indicate that a volcano engulfed it after it sank! Whenever that might have been!"

"How would coins from ancient Greece end up in the Western Hemisphere, in the Pacific?"

"I can't tell you how, all I can say is, that's what appears to have happened!"

"Well, it smells of a hoax to me!"

Brenna shrugged! "Well, if so, it's an expensive one! And to what purpose? And who would be able to figure out when and where to sink a craft and a fortune, where a volcano would cover it up? It's very odd, as you say! The Greeks were known mariners; maybe they ventured farther- Or, perhaps another civilization from another time and place, pillaged the coins and were bringing them home! We can't rule out pirates~"

Gray laughed as he nudged Brenna gently by her elbow. "As you can tell, there are many intriguing theories floating about! Here's my wife's business card. Good day to you, Sir!"

⚔ ⚔

"Well, this is an unexpected treat!" Diana glowed across a small intimate table in a premier steak restaurant. "What's the occasion?"

Intense eyes met hers! "You are, Diana! You're absolutely incredible! Did you not feel even a little twinge of jealousy about that jewelry suite?"

She laughed. "I can honestly say I didn't! I didn't feel a, 'little twinge'; I felt a 'big surge'! But then I confessed it, and just started on the project; which was fun, and actually gave me much-needed inspiration! Do you think I overdo using the 'print in the lining' thing?"

"Not at all! If anything, it's kind of your signature! And that handbag was the most incredible you've ever designed! Which is saying a lot! And you know the scarf will bring in sales! They always do! People who can't afford an entire outfit see the possibilities your scarves provide for updating things they already have!"

"Oh, thank you! You're so nice! Let's talk about the wonderful world of rocks now!"

He laughed. "Let's don't, except that the wells are still producing! That's another thing that somewhat mystifies me!"

She smiled. "Let me guess! How Mallory nailed it, when oil exploration isn't her primary interest!"

"Yeah; I feel jealous of her and David sometimes. But then, I don't know if I was jealous, or just hit by guilt, that David was doing something special for her, and I've been-I don't know, taking you for-'Granite'!"

"No, you haven't! You're always Gneiss!"

"Well, not as Gneiss as I should be, but thanks, Honey! Di-uh-we have so much, and I don't know if I really even take time to disclose everything to you the way I should! Everything we have is just so incredible! I know it's all the Lord's doing, but you've been amazing! Like even your trust-to agree to help with Mallory in the event of Patrick's death! I'm not sure many wives would have agreed to that!"

"Well, in all honesty, I didn't realize how beautiful she was! And I certainly couldn't have foreseen all the myriads of blessings that would flow our way for opening our hearts to her! And you helped me, too! You always kept the appropriate demeanor and arm's length in dealing with her!"

His anxious features relaxed, "Well, I've certainly tried to! I've gotten plenty of weird comments from guys over the years!"

"I know! I've gotten a few remarks, too! Some people really have defiled minds, while others simply work at trying to get underneath your skin! I try to steer clear of them."

※ ※

"Millard, you're insane with that thing!" Brenna's voice followed the speeding, motorized wheel chair! "The Andersons didn't give you that so you could kill yourself!"

Jacob's friend whirled the device, giving a mischievous thumbs up as he spun past her!

She sighed in defeat at the sheer exuberance! Who would have guessed? That the Lord would have done all of this for her? She softly quoted a favorite verse:

Psalms 37:4 Delight thyself also in the LORD; and he shall give thee the desires of thine heart.

The desires of her heart, yes, to overflowing! And the desire of her heart was to get a good job as an entry level Geologist and stay in contact with, and exercise some influence over, her 'family'! But to be married to Gray, and for him to adopt the 'kids', and provide so astonishingly~

The chair did a couple more loops before racing back up the hill toward her!

She jumped aside before the maliciously evil grin and approaching chair! "Millard!"

Gray caught her and planted a kiss on her cheek! "Those two do love antagonizing you!"

She laughed in response! "Yes, but it's hard to be too mad at them! It's just amazing that everyone's so~"

His gaze met hers. "Yes! So happy!"

"Still, Jacob's nervous to see Warren." Her candid observation!

"Well, he needn't be, because of me! I would naturally expect him to have feelings for his real father!"

A marble hardness froze beautiful features! "Well, let me assure you, that you're more of a 'real' father to him than Warren ever thought of being! I don't understand Jacob's feeling any sense of bond or loyalty to him! It's a one-way street! That's for sure!"

Gray's eyes searched hers. "Warren~uh~he's not~"

Aloof hardness turned to pain! "What, my father too? Uh~no~no, he isn't~" She spun away and dashed the opposite direction!

"What's up with her?" Jacob frowned in annoyance! "Millard was just messing around! He wouldn't really run her down!"

"No! No! It isn't that! Come along now! Jeff said your father is waiting for you in the chow hall! She's happy to see Millard have fun!"

〜 ⧓ 〜

Warren sat indifferently as Jacob and Millard tried explaining the concept of their new game to him! That is, until Jacob mentioned the size of the check that was coming their way! Back ramrod straight, and dark eyes glittering behind narrow slits, appeared positively fiendish! Gray shivered involuntarily!

"Y'know, Son! When that happens, maybe we can get an apartment together! Us three!" His gesture included the incapacitated kid he had always held in revulsion! He hadn't ever had much more use for his son! "Maybe we can get in the same complex!"

"What same complex?" Jacob frowned! "You mean in Somerville? I don't care if I never go back there!"

"What do you mean? That's where your roots are! We have good friends there!"

Jacob stared, "Millard's the only friend I had there, and he isn't going back! Your so-called friends left you to take the fall for them!"

"I just got caught! I'll be smarter next time! When~when are you expecting your money to come? Remember Agnes? The landlady?"

Jacob paused sadly before responding. "Yeah, I remember her! I remember all of it!" Still hopeful, he tried again, "Listen, there's this guy, Sam Whitmore, he told us we're absolute geniuses! The game is complex, and yet doable! It should really get the attention of the gaming public! He~he thinks I'm smart~"

"You are smart, Jacob!" Brenna's voice as she approached angrily! "But, if you're trying to make Warren proud of you, you're wasting time and energy!"

The convict leered evilly and emitted a wolf whistle before releasing a string of epithets~ "Whooo, is that you, Bren? You clean up real nice! Anyone ever tell you that?" With a look of pure disdain, he made some highly offensive comments about her mother!

Trembling with rage, she turned on her heel and walked away!

≒ ⊨

Caroline Hillman sprang from her computer with a shocked screech! Grabbing her extension she contacted tech!

"Please tell me you can enhance this image even more!"

A bitter chuckle, "You guys never want much, do you? Sorry to say, that what you have is the best we can do! Except, would it help to view it on a large monitor?"

Disconnecting, the agent sent the image to the large screen, not certain if it lent clarity or increased the graininess! Still, her breath caught~she went in search of Bransom!

Chapter 14: ENIGMAS

Brenna disconnected from the owner of *The Deep Ocean Salvage, Corporation*, insistent that the coordinates for the core sample were quite exact! The GPS system on the *Rock Scientist* was state-of-the-art, and Brenna didn't see how *Deep Ocean* could insist that the valuable sample unearthed was related to their quest! There were no records of a Spanish Galleon having ever transported ancient Greek coins! But retrieving any ship wreck from an encasement of volcanic material seemed problematic! She shrugged. Just one of a bevy of crazy calls! She wouldn't call them prank, so much as misinformed! With a sigh, she gathered keys and an armload of books and headed for the door.

"I'm going!" She paused for a kiss from Gray. "Pray that it'll be better than last week! Still, it's amazing the changes a week can make! I groaned inwardly when Professor Stone announced that the course would dwell largely on Vulcanology! Volcanoes haven't been my favorites, until this week! Well, still not my favorite, but the seafloor volcano covering the wreck has my interest piqued! It seems like an anomaly, but maybe it isn't! Just, no one has ever drilled into one before! Did you know that the UN estimates that there are in excess of three million shipwrecks of one kind or another in the worlds' seas and oceans? That figure doesn't include lakes and rivers!"

He grinned, "I had no idea! Be careful, Brenna, Love; and don't leave yourself open for any problems! Just because you were forced to learn to deal with advances when you waited tables, doesn't mean you can always keep the upper hand! Yell, 'Fire!' and then run like crazy if you have to! I mean it!"

"Okay, Gray! These aren't exactly running shoes, so I'm praying it won't come to that! I love you! And my phone will stay right in my hand!" With a lingering hint of fragrance, she was gone!

෴ ෴

David's finger paused on the scroll button! 'Hmmm; activity in the Diamond account again.' He studied it, less surprised than in times past! It didn't mean Mallory was holding out on him! It meant that Lilly and company were paying for Diamonds coming from outside the normal allotment! His thoughts were that it somehow related to Tad Crenshaw, the late *DiaMo* mining foreman!

It was possible that, providing that the accident was really an accident, Lilly's spies could get into the deceased's accounts and safety deposit boxes! And restore the purloined gems to their rightful owner! Scary though! He sent Mallory a carefully phrased email!

෴ ෴

Brenna tried to focus her attention on the lecture! It was charts and graphs of crust movements and magma hot spots! And then suddenly the data proved 'the fact that the universe was four billion years old!' No matter how hard she tried, her logic couldn't make the leap! She rubbed her temples and realized the professor was frowning at her body language-and any other indication that she disagreed with him! She straightened in her seat and forced a smile! When he backed away from the brash statement and resumed the lecture, she kept her head bent and her hand racing across her notebook! At last the monotony interrupted itself as handouts made their way around the handful of grad students! There was the usual grumbling about required projects! Brenna stifled her own moan! The class was to form into three different teams to work on 'group' projects! She fought tears! As the new kid on the block, she figured no one would want to team with her! Why couldn't they accomplish the same material working individually? She scooped all of her possession into her arms and headed for the door! Maybe she should drop this for now and try again later! She thought she heard a sarcastic 'Class dismissed' as she made the freedom of the corridor! Like since she had fled, he had little choice but releasing the others!

140

"Mrs. Prescott! Mrs. Prescott!"

Finally she slowed in response to the urgent voice at her heels!

⊰ ⊱

Cade and Catrina Holman watched a clip from an interview with Brenna Prescott! "Wow, she's sharp," Cat acknowledged. "I love the outfit! I wonder if it's one of Diana's designs~"

Cade frowned, trying to make sense of the edited segment. "So, from what I could gather, David and Mallory aren't drilling for any more of the ancient loot! Yeah, it would make sense that she's wearing~" He paused frustrated. "Why wouldn't Mallory go after more of the coins? Ancient Greek? Gold? They're worth a fortune! Why don't you go to *DiaMal's* website and order some of their stuff?"

"Well, I can't imagine how expensive it must be!"

He grinned broadly! "Well, we're not doing too badly, you know! You don't have to buy out their store, but check it out if you want to! And it sounds like you want to~"

She uncurled from the sofa, "Maybe I will! And it looks like the Andersons are focusing on the Danube project! *The Rock Scientist* is currently docked."

⊰ ⊱

Brenna turned to face Brad Maxwell and Tim Alvaredo, "What do you guys need?"

The men exchanged glances and then Tim spoke up diffidently. "We wondered if you'd like to be on our team for the project!"

"Yeah, about that~I don't know what to do! I think I need to discuss it with my husband!"

"Hmmpf! Sorry!" Brad's smile turned to scorn! "Guess your family has enough clout around here that you can get out of it!"

Brenna flushed. "I doubt that! It's not even that I want out~I don't know! Working and playing well together with others has never been my long suit! Prof Stone doesn't like me, and I'm sure that will affect my grade! No use you guys risking the association with me~"

"Good point!" Maxwell turned on his heel, striding away while Alvaredo stood staring at the polished cement floor!

"Thanks anyway!" Brenna readjusted her tote on her shoulder and headed toward the nearest exit! She stood gulping in the cool freshness of the night!

⚔ ⚔

"The coordinates are correct!" Mallory repeated her statement for the sixth time! "I don't know why *Deep Ocean Salvage* hasn't been able to locate it! They're actually a salvage operation and not equipped for drilling; or perhaps the ocean floor has shifted and the wreck isn't where it was a month or six weeks ago!"

She listened to harried questions, more grateful than ever that Brenna was fielding most of these calls for her! "No, Sir! I don't know why the lava was hot enough to melt the coins on the outer edges and not melt all the way through! No, I don't know anything about the volcano except that our lab analysis indicates that's what the rock is that encapsulated our find! No, I'm not interested in studying the volcano further! No, I'm not interested in redrilling the site for more from the wreck! No, I'm not a marine archeologist or a historian! That's right! I'm actually not that worried about which ancient sailors sailed where and when! I'm a Geologist."

She listened, trying not to be aggravated as the caller insisted she had a moral obligation to explore further-

She interrupted. "I'm not sure that there is even a way to calculate what you're asking! The universe is full of unexplained mysteries! But if there's a way to make the calculations you're asking, it's outside my area of expertise! Yeah, I don't know if the wreck has moved! I guess it's possible with plate movement! Right, and I have no idea where the volcano's crater might be in comparison with our core sample's location! Experts who are examining the coins are pretty sure they're genuine- Yes it's true that the government of Greece is laying claim to them! I'm not sure their claim is valid, but I guess I would as soon see them go to an Athens museum as anywhere!"

Mercifully, David grasped her phone. "Thank you for your call; we appreciate your interest!"

Mallory gasped, but he smiled disarmingly, "The Greek claim isn't valid! And if the Greeks want some, they can buy them from us!"

Mallory flushed. "Well, morally-"

"Exactly! Morally, the sample belongs to us! Coins, emerald, and all! We brought them up with our drill rig on our ship in international

142

waters! If the wrecked ship was wooden, which it must have been since there's no trace of Iron, it has long since decayed or disintegrated in the lava! There's nothing to prove that it's the Spanish boat that *Deep Ocean's* been searching for! It's probably more ancient than that! Mallory, I know your primary interest is Geological finds, but God has dumped this into our laps!"

She stared at him, lips parted slightly, gasping as his words sank in; before emitting a whoop of joy that made him jump!

⚔ ⚔

Brad sat on the 'hot seat' in Daniel Faulkner's private office! Even as he listened to the searing words, his mind wandered to the awesome persona of the man seated across from him! He was absolutely the pinnacle!

"Are you paying attention to me?"

Brad recoiled involuntarily as the papa bear sprang from his polished leather chair to loom across the desk.

"Yes, Sir! You're mad that I talked to your daughter! Sorry! It won't happen again!" Aggravated at the whole thing, he tried not to sound like a smart aleck! Setting his sights on wooing the beautiful, stuck up heiress-apparent, had never entered his mind! Faulkner could relax!

"Okay, good! That's all!" Faulkner strode across thick sculpted carpet and swung his door open more forcefully than necessary!

⚔ ⚔

Alexandra hugged Norma affectionately as the older woman met her at the Durango, Colorado airport! "How are your sales going, Norma?"

Norma's face creased into a million wrinkles! "I'm the top rep in the state!"

Alexandra chuckled with delight! "Good for you! Thanks for coming for me!"

"Glad to do it! What sped up the plan? Thought you weren't coming for at least another three weeks?"

Thoughtful gray eyes met the older woman's. "Well, I guess the Lord's will, precipitated by my Dad's hiring this grad student he doesn't like or need! Really strange! So this grad student, Brad, moved into a cubicle adjoining mine, offered me a Boston fern, and then proceeded to pump me for information about my uncle's wife, Brenna! I'm not sure what his interest is in her! She is married, after all! So, when my dad found out about it, he shipped me here early!"

Norma laughed at Alexandra's obvious annoyance! "So, this grad student! Tell me more about him!"

Al blushed! "There's nothing to tell! Except I guess he's a wannabe Geologist masquerading as a Botanist! I mean, Norma, come on; what Geologist raises plants?"

Norma's hoarse laugh filled the interior of the old car, "Yeah, this guy sounds pretty suspicious all right!"

☙ ❧

Daniel Faulkner emerged from a storage closet with an armload of Geological maps! Still exasperated, he headed toward Maxwell's cubicle, plunking the maps unceremoniously on the undersized desk! The rolling tubes did something crazy, seemingly violating all laws of physics, and a couple of plants hit the carpet! Too aggravated to apologize or help clean the mess, he withdrew to his private office! That kind of thing never happened to him!

He flopped dejectedly. "Okay, Lord, what am I doing with this guy? Why did I ship Al early instead of firing him? Well, because he's barely hired, and firing can lead to all kinds of ramifications! And there's plenty she can take care of at the mine. I guess I overreacted to his conversation with her, but-what's the deal with all those plants?" A sigh escaped! Diana wasn't really happy with him, either, about the sudden plan to send Al away ahead of schedule!

☙ ❧

Brad threw the plants and planters in the trash and went in search of a vacuum cleaner! At least so far, Faulkner wasn't firing him! He reflected miserably on the morning. Getting called on the carpet was his first experience with seeing Faulkner's executive office! Some kind of space! He studied his tiny cubicle; 'lame bringing plants in to lay claim to the turf'! He needed a wall full of neatly framed sheepskins, and Geological samples sparkling beneath just the perfect lighting! With maybe one big Peace Lilly! Every office had a Peace Lilly! Or the ubiquitous Devil's Ivy!

Guessing Faulkner wasn't coming back to explain the assignment, he unrolled one of the maps!

⚏ ⚎

Brenna ran a hand over the delicate page of her Bible! Everything was slightly 'off', and she tried to push the worry away so she could concentrate! Forsaking the daily passage in her plan, she fled to the Psalms! Tears started.

⚏ ⚎

Just as Daniel reached toward his extension to phone Diana, it buzzed, making him jerk involuntarily! "Yes, Amy; what is it?" In spite of his best efforts, his voice had an edge!

"Mr. Grayson Prescott on line one for you, Mr. Faulkner!"

Without his usual thanks to the receptionist, he punched the button. "Hey, Gray, what's up? How can I help you?"

He listened, glancing out his window at weak sunlight! "Golf! It isn't that warm! But since it's the first half-way decent day in months, the courses will be packed!" His annoyance level shot up as his brother-in-law systematically shot down all of his excuses! "Okay," it was more of a defeated sigh than an actual word! "Meet you out there in forty minutes!"

True to his word, Gray used some kind of clout to get their twosome on the country club course, complete with caddy and cart! The wind was piercing, but Gray was impervious! Daniel eyed the other golfer's Irish woolen Fisherman's pullover enviously! And this was proving to be the worst round he'd played in years! Bogeys where he usually shot under par! And he had too much going on for this, anyway.

When Gray shot two under par on the fifth hole, Daniel spoke up! "I concede defeat! Let's call it a game at nine!"

Gray nodded. "Yes, quite right, then! Let's have a bite of breakfast!"

There was no escape! Although guys milled around and there was a line at the clubhouse café, Gray seemed to pull a low-key rank, and they were ushered to an ideal table overlooking the eighteenth hole!

Daniel stared moodily across the wintery brown course! At least the coffee was hot and good!

Gray brewed tea fastidiously and when his eggs Benedict arrived, he wielded utensils in his usual fashion, shoving bites up onto the wrong side of his fork, like he was European royalty or something! None of the other members of Diana's family ate that way! After a couple of mouthfuls, he carefully placed the knife and fork on his plate.

"I wondered if I might not get a word or two of advice from you!"

Concern and dread flooded Daniel, "Well, I'm not sure how much it will be worth, but~"

"Right! Quite so! Let me lay a bit of a groundwork!"

Daniel groaned inwardly! "Maybe it's something you can share with Diana! She always has good advice!"

Gray laughed softly before reverting to his usual serious persona! "Actually, I've been quite aware that you've never liked me, and I must admit, you haven't topped my list~"

Daniel reached for the coffee pot; not because he wanted a refill, so much as something to stall his angry retort! What a crazy day!

The server pounced on him! Evidently, when you were here with Mr. Alexander Grayson Prescott, you didn't pour your own coffee! And he couldn't figure out why every little thing grated on him!

"Okay, enough laying groundwork then; we don't like each other! Talk to Diana! She adores you!"

Mild blue-gray eyes lit up behind his glasses. "Quite right! You know, I've sensed it; my not being married making you and Diana both suspicious of me! To be around your children! I mean, that's one of the bogey-men they caution against! The weird, single uncle!"

Daniel flushed. "Listen, it's nothing personal! It's just like the world's gotten so crazy~and that has happened."

"I suppose perhaps! But not with me! But that is not the reason for this conversation!"

"Look, we've never meant to hurt your feelings!"

"Well, do you think I wanted to remain unmarried for so long? But Father and Mother always said I couldn't go wrong by waiting for the mate of God's choosing!"

"True; that's what Diana and I want our kids to do!" Daniel was perplexed. 'So, Gray got tired of waiting for God's choice? And made a mistake blundering in with Brenna Hamilton?'

"So I was returning recently from Nigeria as you know, and I had felt Parker and Callie felt the same fears about me; the suspect, unmarried uncle! I-well, never mind about that, but I sensed they were so relieved to see me go!"

"Well, they're on the run! Diana can hardly ever pin them down to Skype-"

"Quite so," Gray's voice was barely audible! "But when I finally boarded, I felt such pangs of loneliness, and I asked the Father if He indeed had someone in mind for me, or if I should start traipsing about from church to church where there are more 'singles', or if I should shop on line!" Tears rolled copiously from behind fogged lenses. "I told Him I had tried to be quite patient! Quite patient! But my soul cried from the depths! O, not aloud, of course, in the first class cabin!"

Daniel sat, subdued and sympathetic, still curious as to where Brenna came in!

"And I never doubted; never doubted for one second, that God could give me a very pleasant and adequate lady-"

Daniel laughed through his tears. "Interesting 'ground work'! Get on with the story, man!"

"Yes, when it was permissible on the flight, I opened my iPad to read my Bible, and the background check request from *GeoHy* popped up!"

Daniel eyed the perfect melding of egg yolk and Hollandaise sauce, ruing the fact that the perfectly executed dish was growing cold! Diana steered him away from eggs, for the most part, allowing for egg white omelets crammed with spinach!

"The background check you requested on Brenna-"

Gray's repeating of his phrase jarred Daniel back to the conversation! "Yeah sorry, go on!"

"Are you quite sure you won't have something, then?"

"Pretty sure! Go on! You checked out Brenna when you should have stuck to your plan to read your Bible?"

Gray regained knife and fork and shoved another mouthful onto the fork's back, then released it onto the plate with a clatter! "You know; I find you not the least bit funny!"

Daniel couldn't help grinning anyway! He thought it was funny! He took a swig of coffee, and when the ubiquitous server appeared to refill his cup, his resistance crumbled!

≒ ⊭

Brenna sank breathlessly onto a banquette in the Sullivan Building Bistro! Brad and Tim were already there! She wasn't sure why they couldn't meet on campus to work on the project!

Brad looked her over with a lazy indolence, and she frowned. She knew she was overdressed! But that was her option these days! Wear what Gray ordered from Diana, or try to find the jeans when they were either clean, or off of Summer! The jeans thing never seemed to happen!

"Wow, this is pretty expensive!" Alvaredo closed the menu uneasily! "I guess I'll just stick with coffee! And it's four dollars!"

"Well, our teammate here looks like she's pretty flush!" Brad grinned impishly.

"Well, looks can be deceiving! You're the one who has a job at a prestigious firm in this building!"

"Yeah, that's right!" Tim Alvaredo's voice conveyed yearning! "I've known Mr. Faulkner from church for ten years, and he hires you! Wh-what does he have you doing?"

"Can't tell you! CDA!" Brad held his finger to his lips mysteriously!

Brenna scoffed. "It's probably just such penny-ante stuff that you won't admit it!"

⚎ ⚎

Gray didn't continue his narrative until two orders of eggs Benedict were carefully placed! The staff solicitously noticing that the original order had grown cold!

Daniel took a bite, ignoring the injured air of the other man! The flavors of the perfectly executed dish needed his full attention! He bit hungrily into more! Like a starving man! Maybe hunger was making his nerves raw!

"Okay, I apologize!"

"As you should! Apology accepted!" Gray leaned in, disregarding the hot plate of food before him! "I opened the file, and there was this mug shot-"

Daniel paused with fork to mouth to frown inquisitively. "Mug shot? Of-"

"Of Brenna! Even in the poor pose, she was gloriously beautiful-"

"Okay, so you gave me a scrubbed background check? That woman's going to be at a mine recovering valuable minerals, with my daughter, and I didn't know she has a criminal background?"

"Will you please just feed your face, and allow me to talk? As I was trying to say, I couldn't pull my eyes away! I was hopelessly captured! I began devouring every word there was, of the details provided in the initial report! She was made to sound quite the little scalawag!" He chuckled indulgently, remembering!

Daniel shifted uncomfortably! 'Scalawag?' "Well, what exactly was she charged with?"

She assaulted a man, but it was because he came into the-er-restaurant where-she worked! He created a substantial tab and walked on it! But as I delved into my dossier, I was quite more taken with her than ever! I learned that she was a stout believer, having even taken on some of her professors; taking them to task on the various untruths they were disseminating! She was just barely graduating, you know, by the skin of the teeth, and appearing before a judge, trying to get custody of her siblings, and I thought, 'How I wish I could help!' And it was as if the Holy Spirit whispered in my ear, 'Yes, exactly, Grayson! I have you in the very proper place-' My eyes filled with tears as I tried to grasp the wonder!" A sudden exuberant chuckle escaped. "One minute, I'm asking the Lord, please, show me who my wife will be! And he showed me, and I immediately, am arguing with Him! In the very words of the Disciple, Peter, 'Not so, Lord'!"

Daniel smiled, pulled into the narrative in spite of his reservations.

"I was telling the Lord, 'Oh, I don't need anyone that beautiful, that young, that shapely, that perfect! Or also that devoted! It was quite a lovely thing, her love for and responsibility for the other children! In short-" He choked up-

Daniel finished softly, "...exceeding abundantly above all that we ask or think... So, is there a problem?"

"Well no,-er-I guess not! I'm just quite new to all of this! And I try to treat Brenna as my wife and not as one of the other children-and mostly-it's this- The children all equally adore Brenna's late mother! I guess biologically speaking the children are not all even related! And Brenna adores the memory-"

"Let me guess," Daniel leaned in. "She doesn't know anything about her father-"

Gray nodded. "Yes, quite right! And, I don't know-"

"Will she talk about it?" Daniel's concern was genuine now! "You know, the stuff I take for granted! It sure makes me appreciate my parents more! I mean, they didn't know the Lord, and they were far from perfect-"

"But absolutely idyllic compared to Brenna's situation! As was my own childhood! I guess perhaps we're off to a lopsided start!"

Daniel smothered the urge to laugh, "Maybe so, but it'll balance out! Give her permission and means to search for information about her father! Offer to send her to a Christian counselor if she needs to get resolution! You both the love the Lord, and you're committed! I hope she is, too!"

⇥ ⇤

Brenna frowned. "Well, I guess that would be a good project! Ambitious! I don't have access to the sample, or authority to get you guys in again! And our studying the sample won't find the data you're referencing! You're talking about seismic activity, and a volcano that's hundreds of feet underwater! The *Rock Scientist* isn't still out there, but if she were right on site, every drilling operation burns through money!"

Brad leaned forward, animated. "People want to know this! There aren't already a thousand papers on it!"

"People in the media are asking! It's their job to think up thousands of irrelevant questions! I'm not sure anyone in the field of Geology cares! Probably the origination of the Emerald is the most relevant question; and it definitely didn't originate where it was found! And we three don't have any clout to request the Emerald centers of the world to send us samples to compare!"

"Well, why don't the Anderson's care?"

Brenna frowned, then smiled at the server, ordering a house specialty sandwich!

"Yeah, that's what we'll both have, too," Brad gave Brenna a pointed look as he ordered!

"Okay, the Andersons!" Brenna took up the challenge. "Do you mean David? He's an Architect! And Mallory is a Geologist who views her approach as that of, 'Applied Science', and not a, 'Pure' Scientist'!"

Brad scowled so Tim explained, "'Pure Science' is like the Academics! They want to understand things for the sake of understanding them! They feel superior to scientists who take their knowledge and use it for money-making schemes! That's what, 'Applied Science', is!"

"Hello, like seventh grade general science, Alvaredo! So, what's up with you, Prescott? Are you interested in finding answers to the deep mysteries of the universe? Or just making money?"

Brenna toyed with the end of her straw! "Well, I like to think that there's some middle ground! I mean, staff scientists doing research for the biggest money-making companies discover mind-boggling truths! Funding has to come from some place, so you can take your idealistic head out of the clouds! And I already know the answers to many deep secrets of the universe, from studying my Bible!"

Tim flushed and dropped his gaze, but Brenna's tawny eyes held the gaze of the other grad student!

Maxwell backed down. "Whatever floats your boat, I guess!"

᎒ ᎒

Bransom studied the fuzzy image barely discernable in the background of a photo previously studied and studied, before meeting Hillman's gaze, seeking clarity:

"So, your thinking is that this could be-maybe you're right- George Whittier, aka, The Ghost-blurry because he was trying to move out of camera range without calling attention to himself! Have you checked all the other frames?"

"Requested from archive! This one showed Halsey, Pritchard, and Dietrich the best, so we isolated and have held onto it! I've also sent for all agencies' files on Whittier! Nothing has poured into my inbox though! So, his moniker, is it from his being albino?"

᎒ ᎒

Brenna stared dazedly at her reflection, then smiled as Gray appeared behind her! He circled his arms around her waist and she relaxed back into his embrace! "Okay, the flight's on time! It's cold in Boston, but flights are arriving without any problems. You have your ticket and credit cards, and Summer has hers. I want you to know, Brenna, Love, that whatever you learn won't change my love for you!"

Anxiety flitted in wide, expressive eyes, "I'm nervous!"

"Nerves are a part of life! You'll be all right! Don't forget Who is on your side!" His lips brushed her hair, and he released her to disappear momentarily! "A little something to help keep you warm in my absence!"

She gasped in amazement! She was actually too stupid to know for sure, but she thought the coat he held for her might be real mink! It was cute, sculpted in at the waist, and worked in a chevron pattern of golden pelt shades crafted skillfully into white!

He turned her toward him, his eyes alight with adoration as he hooked the closures! "I love you incredibly much, you know! Just relax and have a lark with Summer! And if you can find what you seek, all the better! Treat Mrs. O'Shaughnessy and Shay and Emma to a lovely dinner! I shall miss you terribly! Keep in touch!"

Grasping her suitcase, he led the way to a cab waiting at the curb. "Come along, Summer! The taxi meter is running!"

Chapter 15:   MISERY

Alexandra wrapped a shawl around her shoulders before settling into her office! A powerful north wind swept across the foothills, rocking the little village of modular homes! David said they were all tied down securely; she hoped so! Morosely, her thoughts turned to the Haynes family! It was strange, the way she felt so released from Tommy! No point in visiting Mr. Haynes' website for courses she needed! Inhaling sharply, she scrolled for online courses offered by Colorado State University! Odd, the strange turns, life could take! Who would have guessed that she would end up being a cattle rancher? She grinned! To be sure, she was every inch a Geologist, and the minerals she sat atop made her blood race with excitement! She sensed what drove Mallory! Not the value of the finds, as much as the thrill of discovery! Well, the value of the finds was nothing to sneeze at! The truly amazing thing was how much she loved her cattle operation, as well!

She scrolled the course offerings, wishing she could start with some of the more advanced levels! With a sigh, she selected a couple of courses! 'Welcome to the world of freshmen,' she moaned.

⚎ ⚎

Gray frowned when the children's Tylenol didn't take Misty's fever down! He hated to worry Brenna when she was off in Boston with other things on her mind! And, he didn't see how he could leave the others to their own devices if he was forced to take her to the doctor! As much as he adored his new little clan, he was somewhat at a loss! He supposed he wouldn't mind leaving Jacob in charge of the younger ones, if his friend Millard were not here! The two of them together, except for their developing the electronic game, seemed to be a bad combination! They required more oversight than the small children! Still, the whole development filled him with a strange sense of pride and delight!

"Dear Father, if You could see fit, to simply take the fever~"

⚔ ⚔

Brenna tried not to resent Summer's bristling resentment! First it was non-stop grief about how many minks had to die to create a coat for one vain woman! And now she was on a diatribe about the high cab fare when they both knew the Boston area rapid transit system as well as they knew their names!

"Look, you promised Gray, too!" she shot back!

Summer shrugged, bringing her hands up in her characteristic sarcastic gesture, "So, how will he even know? We should take the subway and shop with the difference!"

"Okay, well, it's important to keep your word, and we can shop anyway!"

"Let's get some lunch; I'm starved!"

"I know; I'm hungry too! Here's an apple! I want to start on my search before these offices close for the day!"

"I don't want an apple! And there's no use finding out who your old man is first thing! Let's drag it out to a whole week! We can go home, and you can go see Jill and everyone from your old job! Maybe you should call the college and offer to come do your thing about the Greek coins!"

Brenna shivered from the wind in spite of luxurious clothing beneath the fur coat, but also from the oppression she felt at being back! The places mentioned by her step-sister were the last places she cared about re-visiting! She wouldn't mind seeing Candy and some of the people from church! She sighed; maybe she just wanted to flaunt her new possessions and position! 'Lord, thank You for where You have brought me from! Please prosper my search and help the other kids to see and want You through my life.' When she glanced around, Summer was gone! With a glance at her watch, she dashed up the marble stairs of the stately building!

An hour later she settled into a booth at a busy downtown diner! Her hands shook with the printout she clasped, and she fought tears!

Her phone jingled and it was Gray! Reluctantly, she accepted the call!

154

"Brenna, Love!" his hearty voice ordinarily evoked a delighted response in her, but at the moment she felt profound guilt and failure!

"Hey, how's everyone there?" Hopefully she sounded more upbeat than she felt!

"Well, not too badly! Misty came down with a bit of a fever, and then Lindsay and Emily were quite blue with you gone away, too! I was quite in a quandary, and then, I hope you will be okay with this, but when Sam came to work some with the lads on the game's details, he brought Niqui with him! Well, Niqui was taking little Deidre to the doctor for an inoculation, so she insisted on taking Misty along as well! And then as rather an afterthought, she suggested taking the other girls along with her! They were going to a nail salon, and then for a treat at some doll store that has a tea house! Their spirits all lifted immeasurably! And don't be concerned with Summer! When she swiped her credit card for the city bus fare, I phoned her and demanded what she was up to!"

"I should have gone looking for her~"

"No, the offices were closing! You did quite the right thing! And it's not like Summer is out of her element there! Although she knows her way about, I expressed my wishes for her to exit at the next stop and go straight to the hotel! She is awaiting you there with an apology!" His tone changed, "So, now what, Brenna, my Love; what are you going to do with your newfound information?"

"Nothing for tonight! I can't decide, so I thought, until I have a chance to get alone with the Lord for some clear guidance~" She stared at the name on the printout: Alex Devon Hamilton. "Gray, can I change my mind? Here's his name! Would you please see what you can find out about him?" She struggled with raging emotions! ~And, do you~suppose maybe~you can cross-reference him~"

Gray listened, perplexed, as Brenna couldn't force the words out! "Cross-reference with whom, Love?" Then the answer struck him! "Ah, with your mother~where they met~the particulars of their relationship at the time? You~you don't know too much~about your mother's family~either~do you?"

"She was wonderful!" Brenna's defenses rose and then crumbled~"But you're right~when I'd ask anything about family, except our weird little tribe, I hit a wall!"

⇥ ⇤

Shock! Brenna stared in disbelief as the O'Shaughnessys followed the maître d' toward the table where she and Summer waited. She rose for hugs all around, but Shay looked decidedly unwell! She assumed the shadows on Delia's countenance and tense lines around Emma's mouth were caused by concern for him!

"You must be Summer!" Delia extended a bejeweled hand as she introduced herself!

"I'm sorry!" Brenna felt herself flushing, at not knowing what to say to Shay, and the forgotten introduction! The social niceties were new to her, and she was trying to do a fast study!

"Never mind, Dear! You look positively stunning! You wear marriage well! Ah, the bread tray! I adore eating down here! Shay, why do we so stick to home?"

Shay shrugged, green eyes standing out in red rims in a thin face! "I guess I just prefer sticking close to home these days! Like even now, I hate leaving the baby!"

"She's fine, Shay!" Emma's tension spilled over. "Good grief! Margaret has six kids and two grandkids! She knows how to look after her!"

"Okay, please don't quarrel!" Delia turned again to Brenna as she situated herself in the indicated chair! "You have had quite an afternoon, yourself, Dear! Thank you for not asking, but we have taken Shay to doctor after doctor! They can't find a problem but he continues to lose weight!"

"Yeah, and he refuses to see a shrink, even though he has all these phobias~"

Surprisingly, Summer was the one to take the bitter young wife to task! "He went through a lot of stress~"

"Well, so did I~" Emma bristled!

Summer graced the table with her annoying shrug! "Yes, and no! Although they held you, too, you guys were separated! So his experience was not identical to yours! And even if you had been kept together, everyone has different responses to the same stimulus!"

Brenna scoffed softly, "Oh so you're a shrink now! The doctor is in, if you have your nickel ready!"

Summer laughed at her sister's ridicule as she continued speaking to Emma, "And maybe your background just provided you with more mental toughness!" Her brows drew together thoughtfully! "It's okay not to be tough, Shay! Lighten up with yourself!"

Subdued, Brenna placed a dinner roll on her bread plate!

⇥ ⇤

A gasp of surprised delight escaped from Mallory as she checked an incoming call! "Hey, Shay! Long time, no~ Grandmother? Is she~"

"Okay, easy does it! Grandmother's doing great, as always! Sorry for not calling~much~"

"What's going on, Shay? Did you guys meet Brenna for dinner?"

Shay expelled a long breath! "Yes, and it was something I really needed! I guess I can't quite~figure out~how~I got shorted~"

"Shorted?" Mallory was perplexed.

"Yeah, on mental toughness! Emotional stamina! My dad had it in great measure! And so does Shannon! So does Grandmother, you, Emma~everybody but me! I'm falling apart~"

Tears flooded Mallory's eyes! "I don't have toughness, Shay! Well, in some ways I do! But the abductions, and the nightmares~David holds me together! Amelia~sometimes~ Sometimes you have to force yourself out the door~"

"That's just it! I can't! I think Emma's ready to leave me~and I can't change~I want to~"

"Okay, Shay, what does your pastor say?"

Silence!

"So, you're not going to church? Okay, you told me you can't force yourself out the door! I quote this verse to myself a lot, and when I'm overwhelmed, David quotes it to me! And sometimes I don't much appreciate him doing it!

> *II Timothy 2:7 For God hath not given us a spirit of fear; but of power, and of love, and of a sound mind!*

Be glad you're tenderhearted and not like your father was! Do you mind if I call David's dad and we arrange an electronic prayer circle?"

"That might be a good thing!"

⇥ ⇤

Gray answered his cell, concerned! His sister! Hoping Missy's condition wasn't worse, or the girls weren't giving her too much grief, he answered!

"Hi, Gray, we just finished watching chick flicks together; now I think the girls are a little homesick for you! I told them they could talk to you on face time! You push this icon-"

"Yes, I know how it's done!" He connected, and Misty's little face filled his screen.

"See my toes!" Sparkly embellished toenails appeared and he chuckled at her excitement!

He responded, Very beautiful! Was it fun?"

"Oh, yes, ever so much! And the doctor was real nice! He gave me pink medicine and it tastes good! And then we watched two Barbie movies and I want some pink wings!" Her wistful face was back in his screen, and happiness flooded across him! Patience repaid, with a family exceeding abundantly beyond his dreams!

"We're having little chocolate donuts and milk for a snack before we go to bed! I love you, Daddy! Misty wants a turn! Bye!"

John Anderson assembled a close circle of men to share the confidence about Shay's struggles and request their participation in the prayer meeting! Not certain if Roger Sanders was aware of his son-in-law's struggle, he passed up his name. He smiled as he quoted *Matthew 18:20* to himself:

> *For where two or three are gathered together in my name, there am I in the midst of them.*

An amazing age, to be able to gather in His name, though separated by thousands of miles! United in heart and spirit being the more important issue, anyway! More than physical proximity! He considered again the mystery of his electronic church! Nothing he had sought! Something he would have thundered out against, except that God in His greater wisdom, had thrust it upon him! "Lord, You do work in mysterious ways! Now please work to unbind Shay!" They all connected for the conference call!

Irene Annette Williamson! Gray stared as the picture popped up! Pretty high school girl! Not as beautiful as her daughter! But it was her, all right!

Brenna's deceased mother! Gone before age fifty! He expanded the search, frowning as her parents and siblings popped to life on the screen before him! 'H-m-mm!' He was actually shocked to be doing this search, shocked that Brenna knew nothing of her biological father, and not much more about the mother she adored! With a sigh, he printed the documents before forwarding them to her!

Within fifteen minutes she called him. "What did I do, Gray? I should have let things lie! If her parents were alive, why didn't-"

"I can't imagine, unless they disowned her for something-which, that thought boggles my mind! Your children are your children after all! God never disowns His children, no matter how we make mistakes and grieve Him! Do you want to fly down there and contact them? I think you should! I mean you have aunts and uncles and cousins-"

She spoke thoughtfully! "Yes, I'm having a hard time getting my mind wrapped around it all! How can I just show up on a stranger's doorstep and say, 'Hello, I believe I'm your granddaughter! If they disowned her-it was probably-because of-"

"Not because of you, personally! Perhaps because of an unwed pregnancy-"

"Yeah-me-"

"Well, that wouldn't have been your fault! Unless you just like taking all the blame of the whole world upon your slim shoulders! I should think you couldn't hold up long, though, beneath it all!"

She liked the tone of his gentle teasing, his love, but she didn't laugh! She knew more now, but what to do with the knowledge? She knew she couldn't handle the rejection! From either her real father, or her maternal grandparents! Nobody wanted her; only her mother! And she had done the best she could!

"Brenna, Love, you grew very quiet! I know it's a lot to sort out! You and Summer go out and have a coffee together! Be sure and hire a taxi! If I understand correctly, you don't have the same father-"

"But we share the grandparents-Okay, coffee sounds like fun! You're so wonderful! And she did apologize for taking off earlier!"

"Yes, Love! Phone me when you get back in! Even if it's late! Take your time! It's an adventure, Brenna, discovering! Don't be a little 'Much-Afraid'! I think you should introduce yourself to your mother's family! If they don't receive you, the loss is theirs! But, it's up to you, and I know I can't begin to fathom your feelings!"

⚔ ⚔

Jeremiah sent an email, complete with photos of his steer, to Clay Hammond! He enjoyed having a friend who shared the same hobby! He smiled when he received a response! Clay's picture looked practically identical to his! Jeremiah's *Blizzard* and Clay's *Crème* looked like twins! Satisfied, he posted about his relief that *Crème* would be entered in Oklahoma, while *Blizzard* would represent Arkansas!

⚔ ⚔

Brad pored over the Geological maps, not certain what exactly he was supposed to be looking for! Anything of value, was his guess! Even as he searched, his mind struggled with new developments he was aware of! Not only was the development of bio-fuels a threat to oil exploration, but a new study had emerged about scientists formulating crude from algae within a short time period! In that case~why continue searching the world for depleting supplies? With that in mind, he turned his attention to Bauxite, Iron, Copper, Titanium, as well as the noble metals! With a sigh, he straightened. He scrunched his eyes closed, massaging his temples, then rose for another trip to the coffee pot! It all seemed so locked down tight, and the vague thought troubled him that he might have chosen the wrong field! Like the thirty percent of the earth that wasn't under water, was daunting! The average thickness of the earth's crust was nine miles, but that was averaging the thinner crust beneath the oceans! The crust beneath the Himalayas was a daunting fifty-six miles, and the average continental crust, twenty-two miles! Finding wealth seemed more daunting than finding the proverbial needle in the haystack! No wonder Mallory Anderson held to the theory that most of the world's wealth was yet to be discovered! But how? Drilling operations were mere pinpricks! The deepest borehole ever drilled was less than seven miles deep, where heat caused the drilling to cease!

He jumped as Faulkner burst from his office. "Ah, Maxwell, hurry down to the Bistro and grab a table for eight, would you please? David and Mallory are in town and Diana's joining us! Whenever the coffee pot goes dry, by the way, feel free to brew more!"

"Yes, Sir!"

꘎ ꘎

"What did you just say?" Mallory paused from preparing her children's plates to address the grad student!

"Word is that some scientists have created petroleum from algae in the lab!"

"First I've heard of it!" Daniel didn't seem particularly impressed either way!"

"Well, how long did it take?"

Brad's eyes met hers! "That's the thing! Not millions of years! You know, I can't help thinking about Stone's blasting Brenna Prescott! But, what if she's right? I mean; what–" he caught himself from using his normal peppering of profanity–"what if she's right? Crude oil formation was one of the criteria for dating the earth at millions of years! Although some authors say billions! Like, do they not know what a vast difference there is between a million and a billion?"

"Well, actually, the entire evolutionary theory is so preposterous, that the powers that propagate it, incorporate a time warp! That even the implausible might happen, given enough time!" David's thoughtful response!

Brad gulped on too hot coffee and curbed a retort! This was his chance to socialize with this group of peers, and he didn't want to wreck it! Still, his mind was blown, and the thought occurred to him once more, that in spite of time invested and dollars spent, a career change might still be in order!

Mallory pulled her phone free, placing a call to Gina in her Dallas office! "Yes, could you research this, and get back to me with details as soon as possible?" She gave a brief synopsis of Brad's words.

"Does that make you nervous?" Maxwell felt shaken to his core!

"What? The crude synthesis?" Mallory seemed surprised by the question! "No! Why should it? Known deposits are being depleted as most of the third world is industrializing and buying cars! Well, motorcycles, and scooters, at any rate!" She laughed! "If it can be synthesized as you describe, I want to get in on the ground floor!" She shot a glance at David! "I need to get with Cade and Cat!"

"Well, don't put my wells out of business!" Daniel's tone was upbeat, sure that it would take a while to affect drillers! By the way–how–"

"Did I know about the deposits up there? I thought you'd never ask!" Mallory's countenance glowed!

"Well, I haven't wanted to look a gift horse in the mouth, but oil exploration isn't your field of expertise!"

Mallory laughed. "Yes, actually, I didn't find it! You did! The day my dad first visited you at *GeoHy*, the eastern Canada map was spread on your conference table~"

Puzzlement showed on handsome features! "I was trying to determine the feasibility! And then, since I didn't have a crystal ball~or capital for exploration of that scope~I rolled the map back up and forgot about it! Do you really think that your dad saw and remembered that?"

David's turn! "Not much ever got past him! He's the one who left us a clue, that when followed up on~"

Brad sat silently, aware that his main purpose for being included was his ability to sprint down to secure a table in the popular establishment! At last he asked, "I'm a Geological graduate student, and I've been trying to derive meaning from the Geological maps! How could your father have possibly zoned in on the petroleum, with no education?"

Mallory winced! "Well, I guess you mean no formal education! My father was an avid reader, and he noticed things! His learning was practical, and not burdened down with conjecture!"

"And, wasn't he into the religion thing?"

"Christianity and the Bible," Mallory clarified. "He had *Job 8* memorized! I don't think any Geologist is educated who isn't aware of what it says!"

"So, how long is your boat going to be docked?"

David and Mallory exchanged significant glances, and Daniel laughed uneasily. "If it's none of my business, just say so!"

"No," David's response came slowly and with thought! "We found some noteworthy information, but nearly from the get-go, Mallory wished we had started on the Atlantic side of South America! Notably, at the mouth of the Amazon!"

Daniel dipped a fry in ketchup, pausing to ask, "Why? What do you think is there?"

Mallory laughed. "What wouldn't be there, is the better question! The force of the river scours out a cross section from the continent, a continent proven to be a treasure-trove! However, fighting both water and overburden have become somewhat daunting! David gets so motion sick, and keeping track of the girls on-board is terrifying! I'm not sure if we'll ever do underwater exploration again! Our attorney is working on paperwork so we can lease out *The Rock Scientist!*"

Daniel's expression registered both surprise and interest!

Mallory helped Avery with her drink before responding to the unasked question. "So what are we land-lubbers going to be up to next? We still have plenty of projects on our plates! Brad, you were shocked that my father found treasure when he wasn't a Geologist, but actually, most great finds have not been made by Earth Scientists! A little boy started the South African diamond rush, and John Huddleston, a farmer, discovered diamonds in Arkansas! The Columbian emerald rush was precipitated by a farmer digging a stock pond! Sutter started the California gold rush, and he was a rancher! Our immediate plans include starting another Alpaca operation, but in the higher altitudes of Colorado! The colder the winters, the more luxurious the fleece! And we have also started a gravestone business!"

"Gravestones? That's kind of morbid!" Diana shuddered at the macabre thought!

"Well, you know the saying, that nothing's more certain then death and taxes! We love some of the beautiful pieces of granite and marble, or travertine and limestone! It's actually another idea from:

Job 28:3b...the stones of darkness and the shadow of death.

We're not entirely sure what the passage means, but we don't feel like we're misinterpreting it! We emphasize Christian themes: Scriptures and testimonies! And David's using his architecture to design some amazing mausoleums!"

David nodded, "Then, the same passage talks about dried up river beds, and we know those are prime targets for prospecting! We're starting some sand, gravel, and concrete operations, most of which will be overseas! Many of the developing nations are in the midst of building booms! Infrastructure, apartment complexes, and high-rises! I'm not as interested in drawing the designs as I am in supplying the materials! Whatever properties we acquire, we'll drill to see what else we might find!"

Diana frowned. "Hmmm; you're not planning to start anywhere dangerous, are you?"

"Everyplace can present danger! I mean, Shay thought that his Bolivia trip would be pretty safe, and yet he's still struggling with PTSS from his ordeal! We were just at a Major League Baseball game~"

Amelia's head shot up, "Yeah, and then there were those mean men~"

Diana nodded sympathetically!

⚯ ⚯

"Maxwell, you've been making yourself scarce! You still chasing after that married chick?" Brad frowned as a Frat brother flung a jacket toward him.

"Not chasing any chicks! Just lots going on with my job and the intense course! Big project!"

"Well, we're all headed out drinking! Time for you to take a break and join us! You missed a great party at the frat house!"

With a lot to think about, he didn't really want to join them, but in an effort to avoid their jeering remarks, he fell into step!

Chapter 16: *VULNERABILITY*

Following a couple of hours of tossing and turning, Brenna gave up! No worries of bothering Summer in the palatial suite! She moved to the kitchen and brewed coffee! Caffeine wasn't the cause for her sleeplessness, anyway! With the coffee brewed and a microwave pastry, she settled at the table with her Bible and the sheaf of documents she and Gray had cobbled together about her unknown family members! She couldn't decide. Gray thought she should sail boldly into the lives of people, who had either rejected her from the outset, or who at least had no idea she existed! Well, not exactly his words; he felt that as long as she was there, that she should at least do a little recon work! She cringed at the thought of spying, but Gray's idea of hiring a PI scared her, too!

She bent her head over the printouts, sending tears plopping onto the pages!

"Lord, I've always done just fine-without knowing-Mother-didn't want me-to know! She wouldn't-talk about-" She sniffled into a paper napkin. "Okay, the truth is, I'm terrified! I can't decide if I should try, or if I do, shall I take Summer? She can be so hateful! But at least she might be some moral support-"

Her eyes rested on a Monet reproduction of the *Lady with a Parasol* and the artful way the decorator had used the soft blend of colors to pull the rooms together! The purply-blue color of the sky and the iridescent glow of pink-tinged clouds! With a sigh, she returned her attention to a photo of the attractive home now occupied by her maternal grandfather and his second wife! Brenna lacked information about the demise of her grandmother! She was unsure if Gray was pursuing information about her paternal grandparents, the Hamiltons!

In the silence of the elegant suite, she pled with God! "Lord, if You want me, and You promise that You do; and You have given me Gray, and he loves and accepts me; do I really need these other people?"

The answer came, more softly and subtly than the gentle wash of colors surrounding her! 'They need you! You are the one to show them the way to Me~'

Even as she sensed the answer, a confusing swirl of portions of Scripture whirled in her mind! It wouldn't be easy! She would suffer rejection! But not such rejection as her Savior had suffered! And He would comfort her and give her wisdom to be strong for His sake!

⚜ ⚜

Alexandra paused to take in her surroundings once more! The temperature was capricious; causing her to pull off her sweatshirt when the sun smiled warmly, only to regain it quickly when a wind gust hit her and sent clouds swirling across the source of the warmth! She inhaled the fresh, thin air, drinking in tranquility of brilliant Aspens against deep, rich, green-blue tones of the firs. Pink and yellow wildflowers spilled down a meadow where a sparkling stream carried snowmelt from the higher elevations! The peaks beyond soared, glistening, against nearly flawless cerulean! Colorado in springtime had to be the most beautiful place on earth! She sank against a lichen-covered boulder to pull out a snack bar and bottle of water! Jared and his father were busy with the tasks of getting the mining operation underway, while she had enjoyed a prosperous outing herself! She castigated herself for contracting with Brenna, not certain it would pay off! She frowned, scuffing at stones and gravel with the toe of her boot! Startled, she knelt down for a closer look, and straightened with a sizeable gold nugget in hand!

'Hmmm, the boulder she rested against was beyond the current streambed, but doubtless, when melt-off picked up steam~

She surveyed the glowing stone with wonder: 'There's gold in them thar hills!'

⚜ ⚜

Summer panicked! "Seriously, you want to just show up on his doorstep and announce that we're the missing grandkids he always wanted?" Tears streamed as she paced frenziedly! "Okay, I thought this was your mission! To find the man who fathered you and then dropped out! Why you care-"

"Okay, Sum, calm down!" Brenna's lifetime of experience comforting and calming the others, was being called seriously into play! "Since I was letting my curiosity reign, I grew curious about mother, too! Gray gathered some information-"

Summer spun on her-"Why?!"

Brenna stepped away, refilling her coffee cup! "Listen, I love her so much, like you do-her memory! Nothing I find out about her can change that! She was a-free-spirit-defying convention-she paid for it-we're paying for it! Although, she never meant that to happen-"

"If you hadn't told her your religious stuff!" Summer's voice rose in a shriek of rage and pain!

"S-sshhh, Summer! You'll bring hotel security! I-I've apologized and apologized to all of you, but-the truth is-no one knows if it was suicide-or accidental-"

"It doesn't matter! She's gone!"

Brenna watched miserably as her younger sister succumbed afresh to grief!

"She's gone, and you have this weird husband who thinks he owns us and can order us around! I hate Tulsa! I hate you! I hate him!"

Peace flowed over Brenna; this was part of what the Holy Spirit had just whispered in her ear! She didn't need the family members! Christ was everything, and His gift to her of Gray! But the family members needed her, and her witness!

"Okay, okay, Sum! Hey! Stop crying! I'll fly down to Providence by myself! You get ready to go, and take the train to Somerville! I'll make sure it's okay with Gray! You can go get a visitor pass at the high school and hang out with some of your friends!"

Summer whimpered, "He won't let me-"

"Well, he probably will if you promise to take the train back in tonight and be at the hotel by the time I get back!"

"Does that mean I have to talk to him?"

Brenna sighed. "I know he's the first authority you've ever had over you! But by the same token, he's also an incredible umbrella of protection! But promise me, and I'll talk to him!"

Summer stared pointedly around the richly appointed suite! "No problem! I could get used to living like this!"

☙ ❧

Daniel stared at the number on his caller ID, unsure who was calling! "Daniel Faulkner," he answered.

Diana smiled, equally puzzled! Puzzlement changed quickly to panic as Daniel paled and ran for his study, closing the door behind him!

"What do you mean, she hasn't showed up?" He sank woozily onto the polished wood of his desk, pushing the phone more tightly to his ear, struggling to breathe!

"Well, my dad and I and a few guys who are assembling here to start mining, spent the day up at the mine site! Abby spent most of the day in Silverton giving lessons, and Norma was out delivering her cosmetic orders! When we all met in the chow hall~Alexandra didn't show for chow! Her car's here~"

"Okay~" Daniel forced his voice out, striving for calm and logic~"What were her plans for today? She was at breakfast? Did she say anything then?"

"Uh~Abby and I usually just have coffee and juice and toast at the house~Ordinarily Alexandra doesn't get breakfast either! Do you think we should call the sheriff? We've been trying not to panic! We thought she might show up before we had to call and scare you!"

Daniel's tone rose in both pitch and volume, despite his efforts to hold emotion in check! "Yeah, call the sheriff! Call the church! Do everything you can to get a search party out there!" The room spun, but he clenched his teeth as he scrolled quickly through his contacts for Trent Morrison's number! Usually the last man on earth he wanted to call, but with Al out there~somewhere, this was no time to nurture manly pride!

Flinging the door open, he nearly mowed Diana over! "You heard?"

She nodded, panic showing in expressive features! "I guess we should pray!"

☙ ❧

Brenna rushed through Logan for the short domestic flight to Providence, Rhode Island! Heads turned as she reached her gate and paused to purchase a coffee beverage to enjoy on the flight! She wore a creamy worsted dress topped by a three quarter length jacket of windowpane plaid, creamy white with the honey-tone Diana favored for her! The shoes and bag in matching honey, completed the ensemble. Yellow gold jewelry shone softly!

Hailing a cab at ground transportation she breathlessly announced the address of an unsuspecting grandfather! What would be her welcome?

Chapter 17: BRILLIANCE

Dismay filled Brenna at news of Alexandra's disappearance! At the end of a day filled with heartbreak following contact with her grandfather, it was nearly one thing too much! Not that she felt a heart full of love for Alexandra, or even a thimbleful of Christian charity! It was just that now her contract seemed in jeopardy! Even if Alexandra showed up, which Brenna figured she would, Gray would decide it was too dangerous!

"Lord," she whispered, "I don't even know how to pray-well, for them to find her safe and sound, of course; but if Gray thought Mallory's character is dubious-" She sighed, with Alexandra's being Gray's niece-

She hurried out of the crowded airport and found the taxi queue for a ride back to the hotel! She was praying Summer would be there already, keeping her word! The last thing she needed was for Summer to be among the missing, too!

⚊ ⚊

Concern etched itself into Trent Morrison's handsome features! Without mentioning the disappearance to his wife, Sonia, he headed for his home office, "Couple of calls to make-"

With the door firmly latched, the head of the United States Forestry Department's Law Enforcement and Investigations Division made a call to James Buford, Rocky Mountain Division head who resided in Golden, Colorado.

Buford listened patiently, although the girl wasn't assumed to be lost in his actual jurisdiction! His boss was known, and even lauded, for rushing to the rescue of those in need of help, whether they were in national forests and grasslands, or not!

"Thanks for calling, Trent; I'll call my guys in San Isabel to respond immediately with everything they've got at their disposal! I'll head over there myself in the morning, unless she's been found before then! I hope that's the case! It's still really cold up there at night!"

With a few closing pleasantries, Trent disconnected, shivering involuntarily!

☙ ❧

Diana was inconsolable! Their gracious home teemed with both her parents and Daniel's, and several of her siblings:David and Mallory were en route from Dallas, and David had contacted friends in the Civil Air Patrol to call in members from the Rocky Mountain Wing to aid in the search!

☙ ❧

Brad pulled up in front of the Alvaredo home, scorning its tumble-down, built onto appearance! He wasn't crazy about Tim, but none of the frat brothers appealed to him for his mission, either! Frustrated, he jabbed the radio button off! Usually, loud enough music could drown the voices that plagued him~

☙ ❧

Alexandra dragged herself painfully to a position where rocks towered behind her! Now, hopefully, her adversaries couldn't sneak up from behind! With pistol in hand, she resolutely scanned open spaces to her right and in front of her! Heavy forest to her left provided cover to her stalkers! If one emerged from there, she would have little time to aim and shoot! She shivered, aware of sunset colors, deepening twilight, and definite knife-edge to the wind! For the hundredth time she uttered a desperate prayer! Gone was her excitement about the gold nugget and its significance!

☙ ❧

Brenna was too drained to cry~or worry, when the suite was still dark! Summer was tough enough to fend for herself, and she'd show up when it suited her! Wearily, she kicked free of her shoes and started coffee! Maybe she would enjoy a hot Jacuzzi and then order dinner from room service! Something she had long dreamed of doing~ She was lonely for Gray, but he was immersed in the drama surrounding Alexandra's disappearance! Just as well, no use worrying him about Summer, too!

Taking a hot cup of coffee and a handful of cookies, she disappeared into the bathroom! Emerging from the relaxing tub, she was surprised to see her sister slumped forlornly on the sofa!

"Bad day?" She made a beeline for a coffee refill, not really wanting Summer's woebegone details! Turning on a table lamp, she stretched out on the love seat opposite!

"We~uh~got in~trouble~"

Brenna moaned. "With the police? Sum~!"

"Okay, well, it wasn't our fault~"

Brenna sat with crocodile tears dropping into the sculpted carpet as Summer spouted the vivid details of a day's outing gone bad! Misdemeanor, but Summer would have to appear! No way to hide it from Gray! Buying cigarettes when they were underage, and Amy and Julie were charged with truancy! Summer's truancy charge would go away, once they proved that she was indeed, a home-schooler in Tulsa!

"Wh~why didn't you just get a visitor's pass to the school and attend classes with them?"

"I~uh~know!" Sullenness! "It just sounded more fun~to go hang out at the mall! How did your meeting go with our Grandpa? Did he hand over all the birthday money he's missed out on sending us?"

A lost little voice came from Brenna's lips. "No~uh~he disowned~Mother~ He wants nothing to do~with any~of us~"

Rage burned in Summer's eyes! "Told you you were asking for a bashing! That's why I didn't want to go! You think it will be better when you show up on your old man's doorstep? Let's go drinking!"

"You have got to be kidding me! If you're not old enough to buy smokes, you're sure not old enough~do you have a fake ID?"

"None of yours~if I do or if I don't!" Summer hopped up in a rage and slammed out of the suite!

⚑ ⚐

Rhonna Abbott spoke softly to Mallory! No flights, and Rhonna was the group's travel logistics expert! No charter jets were available! Business was good, and though sorry about the emergency, business sense was against bumping steady customers to help out! Only so many planes, so much staff! No way! Commercial was cobbled together, but Rhonna nailed down the flights and emailed the itinerary!

David took charge, "Rhonna has a flight booked for y'all, but it doesn't depart until 6:05 in the morning! One just took off for Denver, but there's no connection into Grand Junction until 9:00 in the morning anyway! We'll make sure the other kids are cared for! Maybe there'll be some word by the time~" his voice trailed off, and they convened another prayer meeting!

⊰ ⊱

"It's starting to snow again, and it's nearly impossible to do a ground-search at night! Even in good weather!" Sheriff Bill Cassidy was frankly concerned for a female lost alone in the high country! His confidence in her ability to survive was shaky, based on what Norma and the mining foreman related!

"Well, Bill, ya gotta do something!" Norma's weathered face was in his! "At least assemble mounts and dogs for first light! Can a chopper go up? Maybe she managed a fire! I hope, because it's gonna be cold~"

"Okay, just simmer down, Norma! Can you two ladies keep lots of hot coffee going?"

"Better'n that!" Another local chimed in! "I'll open the chow hall and get plenty of flapjacks and bacon goin' on the griddle!"

The sheriff nodded approval, "Thanks, Francine!" He addressed the growing group, "Forestry just sent word that they're bringing a search party in! Crazy time of year to search! Not enough snow for snowmobiles, but enough mud to hinder ATV's!" He spread a topographical area map for Jared to view! "What's your take on where she might be?"

⊰ ⊱

Brad slung his carryon into the overhead and shoved Alvaredo in next to the window, keeping the aisle seat for himself!

"Tell me, do you always have to answer that many questions before your dad and mom let you out of the house?"

"Well, they care what happens to me," Tim defended!

"They're OC if you ask me!"

173

Alvaredo mumbled under his breath, something about that he hadn't asked! Aloud, he asked, "What do you think we can accomplish that the professional search and rescue teams can't? My dad knows Daniel Faulkner, and that man can move mountains! That's why my dad thought your story was nuts! They don't feel like you're a good influence on me!"

Brad's features twisted sardonically! "Whatever, Alvaredo!" He unrolled a map across both of their laps! "I think I do have some expertise to offer the other experts, because Al's a Geologist! And so are we! We have to assume she's not just another cute, loony girl out for a walk, who got lost! We can figure out where she would have gone, and why!"

Tim frowned uneasily, not convinced! Why did Maxwell presume to call Alexandra by her nickname, or mention her cuteness? If he thought he was in a league to win Daniel Faulkner's approval for Alexandra, he had more rocks in his noggin than the average Geologist!

Maxwell pulled out a Sharpie importantly and made a neat black X! "That's the mining village!" With the Sharpie cap back in place, he pointed, "Road, mine site, original ranch house and sheds and barn! Here's the flood plain for the spring snow melt! My guess is she was tracking up stream for the Platinum source!"

Tim frowned again, "Without waiting for Brenna to get up there? You think Brenna's husband will let her go now?"

Brad's face took on a frustrated hardness! "Well, that'll be a moot point if anything happens~" Emotion choked him! "Come on! Come on! We have to get there~"

Tim slumped into the corner next to the window, directing his gaze at blackness punctuated occasionally with lights of hamlets and cities! Plane could only fly so fast! Maxwell seemed gone on Alexandra, smart or not!

⚐ ⚑

Alexandra panted; pain like she had never experienced shot up her calf and down into her foot from the break at her ankle! Her leg continued to swell, although she tried to twist in such a manner that it was elevated slightly with a gentle rise in the ground! Every attempt to get more comfortable intensified the pain! She bit her lip! Someone was still out here, or her screams would escape to the throne!

⚐ ⚑

Daniel faced Diana miserably! No chance of either of them napping! This was his fault! Di was kind to hold her feelings in, but-"

"Let's go; we can get there faster if we drive!" Blue eyes, filled with indescribable pain, pled for agreement! "Sitting here, just waiting, when Alexandra-"

"David and I already discussed that, it's just so far!-Honey, why did I-let her go-so-far?"

"Because that's where the minerals are! You've been right! This whole thing has thrilled her to the core! And I mean, 'The whole thing!' She loves the church up there, and they love her!" She struggled to go on, "I can't bear-the thought-of- losing her-"

He nodded, relieved in spite of the vise clamped on his heart! "We would have lost her, trying too hard to hold on-"

Diana nodded, "I agree! I'm going to make-some coffee-

਼ ਇ

Alexandra shivered violently! In possession of a book of matches and surrounded by material that looked like it would be good tinder, she resisted the idea of starting a fire! Of course, if any good guys were out looking for her, a fire would- But, sadly, it would bring the bad guys to her location first! Scared, she swept her view across her surroundings again!

਼ ਇ

Noë Keller! The name that greeted Trent when he landed in Denver! Known among law enforcement agencies as, *Noah the Killer*! Jaw set, he darted toward the next departure gate! 'Keller in San Isabel?' Trent's mind returned to an event the previous year! Miraculous that he was still in the world! In his mind's eye, he could see a large cobweb alerting him to a tripwire across his path! Every time the incident occurred to him, he was more struck by the Lord's miraculous intervention on his behalf! And then, his youngest daughter, Megan-he had nearly lost her to a severe asthma attack!

Brown eyes and freckles stood out against gaunt pallor as he found a seat at his gate. "Lord, I need another miracle! Please, protect Alexandra!"

਼ ਇ

Brenna ordered a hamburger and fries from room service and fixed a glass of ice water! She was aggravated with Summer as all get-out, but what else was new? Her mind traveled to Gray! "Lord, how can our marital relationship weather stress like-what Summer's adding? Gray's from this perfect functional family! None of them ever dreamed of smoking a cigarette, let alone breaking the law, having a fake ID! You know I never even asked You for a husband, and You brought him to my life! Now I feel like the whole dream is going to crash and burn-And I should be worried about Alexandra, and not just my own, neat, little world-"

Hearing someone outside the door, she rose to check it out! Fast service! To her surprise, Summer was back! And spoiling for a fight!

"He wants you to have his babies; doesn't he?" Summer's unmodulated voice made Brenna cringe!

"Okay, that's really none of your business-"

"Like_____!" Summer screeched profanities!

"Calm down! You're going to get us thrown out of here!" Brenna couldn't imagine how Summer knew about a recent tension between herself and Gray! The baby issue! She didn't feel like she owed her sister more info that she seemed to have already! Why did Summer care? It was Brenna's Geological career that a baby-thing would jeopardize!

Angry tears poured forth as Summer stood just inside the door, fists clenched in rage! "He told us he loves us! We thought **we** were his children now; that finally, **we're** good enough for somebody!"

Taken totally aback, Brenna responded, "Well, you are! He does love you! You better hope so, after the shenanigans you pulled today! You guys try to put pressure on me to keep him happy; where's your responsibility?"

Summer shook her head violently! "I'm telling you, he takes one look at a kid of his own, and we won't be fit company-like we're not to the rest of his family!"

"Well, in all fairness to them, you guys could work a little harder on being 'fit company'! We're trying to teach you better manners; and the profanity-you don't have to talk the way you do, Sum!"

"I can't help it! It's how I talk! Just because you could turn yourself around, doesn't mean the rest of us can-or even want to! We just all think he'll change his mind and turn us out if-"

Brenna scoffed softly! "He won't, Sum! You still don't realize what kind of a man he is! He has character and commitment! Something new to us in light of the sleaze balls Mother drug home!"

Summer whirled away! "Don't!"

"Okay, I'm sorry!" Brenna reached for the hurting younger girl, but Summer wrenched away, defensive!

Brenna folded her arms, exasperated now, herself! "So the seven of you have held discussions about what might happen if Gray and I decide to add to the family? That's frankly-do you have any idea how tough it is for Gray and me to have a relationship when you guys have eyes and ears to the keyholes 24/7? I can't guarantee how Gray might see you guys in comparison to a new baby! He pretty much is crazy about babies! Something I'm just finding out myself! The truth is, Summer, if he decides he despises you all, he's legally bound to see you through! If you catch up your academics, you can go away to college- It won't be up to you to tend our babies in exchange for room and board!"

Enraged visage softened notably as a light tap came on the door!

"Ah, dinner! We'll order another and share!"

She stood back to allow access for an elegant, linen-draped cart! As one who once depended on the life-blood of tips, she carefully added an appropriate amount!

With the door closed, they gobbled the entrée hungrily, laughing and talking, relaxed! Like real sisters! When another order arrived, they made equally short work of it!

Suddenly sobered with the weight of the day's action settling on her, Summer changed tone!

"Seriously, Bren, I've tried to change, and be like you!" Her features twisted as she strove to stem tears from flowing.

Praying for wisdom, Brenna responded gently! "Well, as you know, I chased down the people who came to the apartment, the ones who wanted to give you kids a bus ride to Sunday School! And not long after I received Christ and started going to church, there was this preacher we heard about! He was a meth addict, and God delivered him from it; so he has a ministry helping addicted people, or those struggling with different sins! I've heard him say this several times, and it speaks powerfully to me:

[1]*God loves you just the way you are, but He loves you too much to leave you that way!*

---

[1]   Pastor Richard Wallace, Jr., Senior Pastor, Life Change Church, Dallas, TX

⚔ ⚔

Alexandra struggled to keep her bearings! Between pain, shock, and the falling temperature, she realizeded her extreme vulnerability! Terrified, she kept her finger locked onto the trigger of her pistol! The darkness engulfed!

⚔ ⚔

Brad was on his feet before the seatbelt sign chimed off, struggling thoughtlessly past other passengers who felt equally eager to deplane! The flight attendant regarded him haughtily as he shuffled his boots restlessly, waiting for the hatch to swing open! Freed from the confines of the jet, he raced down the jet way! Alvaredo could catch up or get left behind! With the car rented and a restroom break squeezed in, he took the wheel of a rent car! He turned on the radio as they raced westward! "Find a news station!" With no news of the girl reported missing on the Western Slope, he slung his phone at the passenger, "Call your dad and see what he's heard!"

"He's probably asleep!"

"I don't care! He didn't believe this was what we're really doing; let him know it is! Call him!"

⚔ ⚔

Alexandra panted in pain and panic! Even the heavy hardness of the nugget brought no elation!

Underbrush snapped, and she forced back a scream as she raised her pistol! This was it!

Chapter 18: BRAVERY

Trent slung his bag into the overhead and slouched down into the aisle seat of the small regional jet! Bumpy ride over the fourteen fourteeners, if this flight was as usual! He checked his phone hopefully for messages! Frustrating! The search just barely being pulled together! Well, word of Noah's presence in the environs, and reports of gunshots! No wonder the searchers wouldn't head out in the dead of night! The thought of Alexandra Faulkner in the clutches of Keller turned his blood cold! Idly, he wondered if any ransom demands had been made! He started guiltily as Daniel and Diana appeared in the hatch, to be greeted by the flight attendant!

⊰ ⊱

"Wish Rhonna had routed us through Durango!" Daniel's frustration boiled over! "What was wrong with me? Leaving this up to her? Now we have a three hour drive if the roads are good! I should have called one of the charter companies personally~"

Diana nodded numbly! "I wonder if Trent would like to ride with us; no use getting two rent cars~"

"He'll have a Forestry vehicle; I think he's already gone! You okay? I'd like to make the drive with no stops~"

He broke off as Trent Morrison rushed toward them. Fear swept him from head to foot as the question refused to utter itself! He crushed down on Diana's hand, unable to decipher the other man's expression!

"I just got word from my Division Head! A couple of searchers found her! I guess she was in pretty serious shape! A broken ankle and hypothermic! They're preparing to fly her to St. Mary's here! It's actually the nearest good trauma center!"

"Th-they found her?" Diana's tears of relief burst forth! "Oh, thank You, Lord!"

⚔ ⚔

Tim Alvaredo sank dizzily onto the rickety porch of the ranch house! What a crazy few hours! He was ready to be rid of the frenzied Brad Maxwell, but Brad was the one with the funds! He raised his head, still feeling sick, as Brad approached. "Now what?"

Brad lit next to him! "I'm trying to decide! The Forestry service law enforcement people are heading back up to bring down the body! I'm not sure if we should go with them and show them where-! I need to talk to the head guy; Buford, I think they were calling him."

"Yeah, Buford! You think Alexandra will be in trouble for shooting that guy?"

Brad scowled! "She better not be! Nothing makes sense about those guys!"

"Why, whadaya mean?"

Brad shrugged impatiently. "Never mind! It's what I need to talk to Buford about!"

⚔ ⚔

Daniel took charge. "Man, that's the best news I've ever heard, Trent! You said the flight will take a couple of hours?"

"My guess, by the time they transport her to Durango by ambulance, get her loaded, and she makes the flight! You guys should get a room and get something to eat before you head over to the hospital!"

"Care to join us?"

"I would love to another time! I need to get up there!"

"Why? They found her-" Daniel was puzzled. 'Mystery solved,' as far as he was concerned!

Trent frowned. "Yeah, from what I can cobble together, a couple of college kids showed up, dressed the searchers down for waiting for daylight, and took off on foot to conduct their own search! The one kid, name's Maxwell-okay-well, let me back up-a local resident received a confusing radio message-thought it was a girl's voice-but then the radio-well, tracing the radio brought up the name of a really bad hombre! Noë Keller! This Maxwell kid's contention is that Alexandra was actually forced up into the higher elevations by some guys heavily armed, primarily with cross bows! One of which was Keller! Alexandra shot him in self-defense! My men went to retrieve the body, but my bets are that they won't find it!"

Daniel stared at the other man unbelievingly, feeling suddenly sick!

Trent nodded sympathetically, "Has it gotten easier to deal with?" He referenced a former incident when Faulkner had been forced to shoot and kill a felon attempting to rob Trent!

Daniel's voice came clipped! "Maybe! I finally came to grips with the fact that I had no other valid choice! And I'll do it again, if needs be! Keep me posted on your investigation! You said, Maxwell?"

"Sure did! The kid carried her a couple of miles down from the high country! From what I understand, it's a really, really good thing that they arrived when they did!"

⊣ ⊢

Daniel's voice was brusque as he responded to Gray's earnest inquiries about Alexandra's state! "Hopeful! Listen, the reason for my call is that I need you to do a background check on someone for me, stat!"

Gray tried not to resent the high-handed order! Chalk it up to the stress of the last harried hours! "Okay, who are we investigating?"

"That grad student! Brad Maxwell!" Daniel's voice was a growl! "Find out everything you can!"

"Okay, why? It's interesting to me that you hire him first, and then-"

"Well, you've met him! Can you honestly say that you like him?"

"I can honestly say that I do not!" Gray's retort! "He reminds me rather much of you with the BMOC persona! The rich frat brat! And all that!"

Diana's features reflected puzzlement! If Brad Maxwell was the hero of the hour finding Alexandra, what was the problem? Why a background check? And what was with Gray's sudden attitude toward Daniel?

"Just find out what he's up to? If you can't dig up much, put Sam on it, too!"

"You want laws broken?"

Daniel's voice rose slightly! "You know we're talking about a huge gray area, here! I can't tell if he's after Al, or if he's just sniffing around the ranch and mineral deposits! To undercut her- I intend to find out what he's up to! Like I said, you don't like him much, either!"

"Jury's still out on that one!" Gray disconnected, relieved! His wariness of the handsome grad student had to do with his friendliness toward Brenna!

⚜ ⚜

"Have you tattled on me to Gray?" Summer's challenge at breakfast!

"No; not yet! He has too much on his mind with Alexandra! The search party found her, I guess just barely in time! I'll probably wait to tell him about your scrape until we get home tomorrow! So, we have today to kind of kill! Let's go to the mall and find a place to get our nails done; and then eat lunch! Tonight we can have one more elegant meal in the hotel restaurant! It's been fun! I enjoyed our talk last night!"

Summer's laconic grimace was her response! "Guess you chickened out about hunting down good ole Alex! He's still pretty handsome for an old geezer! Bet he was a hunk when he and mom had their thing! She could really pick 'em!"

Brenna bit her tongue at the idol-worship-tone Summer held for their mother! 'She could 'pick 'em', all right! Pick ones to love her and leave her! Using her up, enabling her drug usage, and casting her aside like so much garbage!'

⚜ ⚜

A preoccupied Daniel Faulkner headed the rental car in the direction of the hospital, to be brought up short by an ambulance screaming past!

Diana's nails clamped into his thigh! "It's headed out to the airport! To meet Alexandra's air ambulance! Follow-"

Without argument he complied, pulling close as a small plane taxied to a stop and the ambulance bounced toward it! Without waiting for him to shift into park, Diana launched herself toward the EMT's and the gurney they awaited! She stopped short, startled!

"Ma'am, you need to step aside!" The order came from a female medic and Diana complied! There was no time to waste in argument! Back in the passenger seat, she turned concerned eyes toward her husband!

"She's in serious shape!"

182

Gray frowned as he worked on the assignment from his brother-in-law! Relieved to realize that Brenna wasn't the object of Brad's quest, he was forced to agree with Daniel; that he wouldn't do at all for Alexandra, either!

'Must have made jolly good tracks getting out to Colorado to play the part of the dashing hero! Was he indeed that taken with Alexandra? Were they even acquaintances? Ah, yes, the *GeoHy* office! Maybe that explained Alexandra's decision to return to Colorado earlier than planned! Or Daniel's decision to send her!"

He sighed. Brenna was heart-set on working her contract at the Colorado mine! Now who knew if Daniel would permit Alexandra to return? Or if she would even wish to do so! Now he felt some level of regret for forbidding Brenna to complete her contract with Mallory and *DiaMo*! Brenna longed to test her wings as a Geologist-before taking on the responsibilities of motherhood! His eyes scanned across financials regarding Maxwell! Hmmm! No surprise that the kid was well-funded! Gray whistled softly! 'Very well-funded!'

James Buford studied the terrain, his face clouded with gloom! "Spread out and check every inch again! There's gotta be something–"

That there had been echoing gunfire up here, lots of guys could attest to! And the lost girl and her two rescuers all shared a harrowing tale of pursuers, and then one of the three of them had shot someone dead! And the name of the infamous Noë Keller had been bandied about! Buford questioned whether either of the college boys could get the drop on a guy like Keller! Maybe they were just aware of the bounty, and trying to cash in! Still, what other explanation could there be for the girl's being covered with blood? Her sole injury was the broken ankle, and that not a compound fracture! Hmm-mm! That was a thought! He placed a call to the Grand Junction police department and explained his mystery to one of the detectives!

"Wondered if you can get to the hospital and take those clothes into evidence! Maybe we can figure out if someone really was shot, and if so, who?"

Chapter 19: CREDIT

A cry of alarm escaped from Diana as the ambulance they trailed pulled up at the ER entrance behind two others! Diana's heart sank! Having worked ER Triage, she was aware that the critical car accident victims would precede Alexandra's treatment! In anguish she wished her daughter had simply been taken to the Durango hospital! Doubtless, someone's decision to transport her to the superior facility was well-intentioned!

᷂   ᷂

Trent Morrison listened, white-lipped to Buford! "But Keller was a huge guy! How could anyone make his body disappear?"

Buford's broad gesture indicated the immensity of the search area! Trent nodded understanding! But still-the Forestry and county guys conducting the search weren't novices! No signs of ATV's or any other vehicles, or any beasts of burden! He started to ask Buford to go over the stories again, relayed by Alexandra and her two young rescuers!

"Where did the two witnesses go? I'd like to visit with them! The story I've heard was that three heavily armed men surprised Alexandra above her ranch; that she managed to evade them for hours, and finally shot Keller!"

"Well, one of them shot him! My bets are on Maxwell!" Buford clarified.

"No, it was Alexandra! Didn't you say that the weapon was found on the Alvaredo kid; that he toted it from the rescue site down to the ranch with the safety off? Because the other kid had to carry Alexandra? That means the two grad students didn't know enough about guns and safety to own one, let alone shoot! Faulkner has all his kids indoctrinated into the world of weapons! It's Alexandra's gun, and she was the one who was forced to use it!" Of that Morrison was certain!

"Well, Maxwell claims it was him, and by now all three of their prints are on the gun! Why would he say that?"

Trent frowned, "Not sure! Either in a misguided attempt to protect Alexandra from any legal ramifications! Or, he knew about the bounty on Keller and wants to collect!"

Agent Buford eyed his boss with new respect! Word around the division was that the DC bureaucrat was too far removed from the National Forests and Grasslands to have a grasp of what the boots on the ground agents went through! Instead, the other man's expertise shed a lot of light on the developing case! "Okay, that all makes sense! Look, here comes the wimpy kid; maybe he knows where his friend went!"

⚑ ⚐

Agonized, Daniel endured the process of presenting insurance information and waiting, while Diana completed the medical background of allergies and immunizations for their first-born! Handing the clipboard to the ER charge nurse, she announced that they would be in the waiting room!

Dazed, Daniel followed her, "Can't you do anything? Did you even tell them that you're a nurse? Why didn't you ask them if we can see her?"

She clasped his hand! "As a nurse, I know this; sometimes family members are in the way! Thankfully, they are fully staffed and seem to have earned the top rating for their trauma center! It seems to me that Alexandra would have been better off if they had simply transported her to the ER at Durango, Mercy; we need to trust the Lord, that He is having His way, in spite of some judgment lapses!"

His terrified eyes sought hers, "What do you mean?"

"Well, she was severely dehydrated before they put her in a small aircraft that bounced all over the skies! I think her flight must have been as rough as ours was from Denver! The nausea was sure something she didn't need! I couldn't tell why she's covered in blood! Hopefully, it isn't hers!"

⚑ ⚐

Trent felt unaccountably put off by the charming and debonair graduate student!

185

"I have a case to get to the bottom of! So, if you could stick to the truth, we might be able to get some hard facts!"

"That was the truth!"

"I can bring you up on federal charges for obstruction of justice! The weapon in question belonged to Miss Faulkner! The victim was dead before you and Alvaredo arrived on the scene! You probably followed the gunshots to find Miss Faulkner's position! Can you add any important details? Or are you just going to keep on totally wasting my time?"

Maxwell shifted uneasily, "Did you find the body? It was gone; wasn't it?"

Trent frowned. "Why don't I ask the questions, and then you give me truthful responses?"

There was an awkward pause, and then the words fell over themselves as they tumbled forth!

"Well, Alexandra isn't foolish enough to head into the high country, alone, late in the day, with no supplies! She has a good head on her shoulders! She was still within site of the barn-she thought someone was watching her-then there were three of them, spread out across the meadow-"

"Blocking her from returning to the ranch," Trent supplied!

"Yeah-unh-yes, Sir! Her only escape route took her farther and farther from home! By the time we reached her, she was in so much pain from her ankle; I just wanted to get her to medical help; but she still told us more! The three men, they weren't just hunters; well, this time of years, they would've been poachers-but they were all armed to the teeth! Toting really heavy packs! She said that was the reason she was able to climb faster than they could! Evidently, they didn't want to risk leaving their supplies while they hunted her down! And there was this radio-"

Trent's head shot up! "What about it?"

"Well, on the dead guy-uh-I'm fascinated by radios-I've never seen-it was gone, wasn't it? By the time the searchers got up there?"

"Tell me more about the radio!"

"Well, just guessing-an impression-because Al was in bad shape-mobile ham, but encoded? My thoughts were something serious anti-government! If there are any unregistered patents on it, when you find it, I'm claiming them for Alexandra!"

Trent shrugged; the kid had a lot of nerve! "Well relax, we haven't found it!"

"It's underground! They got the body, the dead guy's pack, the radio~how else could~I've been studying this Geological map, and there are some caves~"

Trent slammed his fist on the desk! "Why did you waste so much time lying?"

⊣ ⊢

Summer stared through wide glass windows as snow filtered lazily downward! "Well, I like snow, and I've had a great time, but I hope it doesn't snow enough that we can't get home tomorrow!"

Brenna nodded vacantly, surprised by every word uttered by her sister! Personally, she dreaded facing Gray with her failure to keep her sister in line! "I've had fun, too! I'm with you, eager to get home! I'm going to close my eyes for a few minutes before I dress for dinner!"

Summer snorted! "What do you mean; dress for dinner? You're already dressed to the nines! I'm wearing this!" She pirouetted in front of a full length mirror, proud of a cute outfit purchased on their shopping spree!

Brenna nodded. "It's adorable, Sum! Hmmm-mm, it looks like they found Alexandra; but~she broke her ankle and she's in serious condition!"

In her room with the door closed, she pulled her Bible from its place! She made a guess that Daniel Faulkner would never allow Alexandra to return to her ranching and mining operation! But even if the unthinkable happened, and he did; what would Gray say about her fulfilling her contract? If the contracted work didn't happen, she was quite certain that Alexandra wouldn't pay out the contract as Mallory had done! With Jacob's devoting himself to his game, her assistant was gone! It looked as if she were a one-woman Geological company with nothing to do~and no revenue! Opening her Bible she found a verse that resonated with her:

Psalm 27:10 When my father and my mother forsake me, then the LORD will take me up.

"Lord," she breathed softly. "I've never known my father, and my mother is gone now! Locating my grandfather was a fiasco~and I don't know what to do about reaching out~to~anyone~else! Lord, You know I've been dying to go to Colorado~and put my education to the test in the real world! And Summer and I have blown so much money this week~"

187

☙ ❧

Daniel sat miserably, watching Alexandra's restless sleep punctuated by moans of pain! He could barely stand to watch-or listen! Still, he was grateful that the outcome wasn't more disastrous than it was!

Delicate blond hair fanned across the pillowcase and her pallid, drawn face made her look small and helpless!

Diana appeared with a couple of coffees! Relief and vibrancy reflected on her face! "Trent's here with some details to fill you in on! I'll sit with her! I'm dying to know the latest, too!"

He accepted the coffee gratefully! "She still seems to be in a lot of pain! I'm not sure she's using the pump at all!"

☙ ❧

Brad finished checking in at a Grand Junction hotel! Exhausted from his frenzied previous twenty-four hours, he planned to go out just long enough to bring back a sack of tacos! Alvaredo had served his purpose, and Brad was ready to be rid of him! He waited impatiently for the elevator, and then recoiled in dismay as a guest stepped off!

Recovering slightly he gasped, "Stephen; what a surprise!" He didn't even try to add any after-thought pleasantries, like 'a nice surprise'!

The other man stepped forward, looking him over pointedly head to toe! The ordinarily natty Brad couldn't imagine how awful he looked! To make things even worse, Tim appeared at his elbow!

"Stephen Maxwell, my friend, Timothy Alvaredo! Timothy, my grandfather, Stephen!"

Tim snapped to attention at the sudden show of formality. "It's a pleasure to meet you, Sir!"

He shot out his hand as the older man responded with a disinterested, "Likewise!"

☙ ❧

Brenna studied herself in the array of sparkling mirrors! She liked the results of having her makeup done at an exclusive department store's cosmetic department! She wasn't sure she could master the technique and wished more ardently than ever that Gray were here! She pulled a dress from the closet! She didn't know fabric terminology to know it was silk crepe, but the smooth, cool silk lining felt good as it slid across her! It fit cute with a softly draped neckline and three-quarter sleeves embellished with delicate bows! Matching silk stockings amazed her as she worked to straighten seams! Delicate bows on the hosiery rested above her heels and flirted adorably above the heels of peek-a-boo toe, high-heeled pumps! Her sister-in-law didn't leave any detail to chance! She threw compact, cash, credit card, and lipstick into a tiny leather box bag that repeated the smooth honey leather of her shoes!

"Wow!"

She glanced up to see Summer regarding her from the doorway! "What do you think?"

"Now, that's elegance! It's hard for me to believe you're my same sister! I need to take your picture! Love the way they fixed your eye makeup!"

Brenna posed for the photo before returning her attention to her reflection! "I guess I really like it! But it's like Diana's stuck on this color! I wish someone would tell her I like purple!"

Summer uttered a disgusted sigh! "Maybe that should be your new favorite color! Brenna, you're a sensation!"

⊨ ⊨

Seated in the finest restaurant Grand Junction had to offer, Stephen ordered his usual libation! Fighting exhaustion and the surreal effects of it, Brad opted for coffee, to hear Tim's usual echo of whatever he said! He was annoyed to no end, that his attempt to draw on his trust fund had brought his grandfather out of the woodwork instead!

"Why a ranch? Of all the choices to invest in?"

"It's more than a ranch, Sir! It's the minerals! As a Geologist~"

"I wish you had studied business! There are no minerals left, to speak of, within the continental US! Perhaps this property has been salted to take advantage of your naïveté!"

Alvaredo squirmed before plunging in, "I'm pretty sure it's the real deal, Sir! Mallory Anderson is a Geologist who finds and drills sites she feels have positive markers! Then she makes them known through an ezine called *The Drilling Platform*! The fact that she recommended this ranch would be good enough proof to me that there are viable minerals deposits!

But then, the fact that another respected Geologist, Daniel Faulkner, set his daughter up there~"

Stephen shot the kid a look that indicated he was unaccustomed to contradiction! And Brad had to admit he was shocked at his pal's sudden courage!

"Faulkner, hunh?" Stephen Maxwell studied the two young men for several moments! "That man belongs on the concert stage permanently! Amazing to his devotees that he is at last performing with the Tulsa Symphony! The tickets haven't officially gone on sale yet, but there are none to be had! I even possess a credit card that guarantees~"

"I might be able to get you a ticket!" Again, Alvaredo was exhibiting an unexpected bravado!

Brad frowned, "Surely you don't think you're in that tight with him!"

"Of course not! I've known him for years and you're the one he hired! But Brenna set up the whole concert! I'll bet she can comp a ticket!"

Brad's grandfather frowned at the unassuming graduate student! He had known Daniel Faulkner? For years? And he might have a line on one of the coveted tickets?

～§ ξ～

Daniel listened in amazement to Trent's story! It was tough to sort out! Alexandra, not simply at the mercy of the mountains and their formidable dangers, but hunted down for hours by hardened criminals! Survivalists! How she managed to outwit and escape them, finally shooting the worst of them dead-but now she would be forced to deal emotionally with it for the remainder of her days! His exhausted mind whirled with unasked and unanswered questions! He could ferret out all of the details soon enough! He scoffed at Trent's revelation of Maxwell and Alvaredo's not even having enough sense to engage the safety on Al's gun as they packed it back down to the ranch! A miracle they hadn't accidentally shot her, or themselves!

"Maxwell seems to be a pretty sharp kid," Trent added. "How does he fit into the picture?"

"He doesn't!" the answer gritted out between clenched teeth! "When Al feels better, I plan to get to the bottom of what he was even doing here! He works for me, and I didn't give him any time off!"

Trent regarded the other man steadily! "Well, with the cold and the shock, it's a good thing for Alexandra that~"

"I'm giving God the glory for Al's safe return to us!"

Trent grinned at the testy response and let it go! "Well, he was instrumental in helping us find the body, and an underground militia headquarters! And by underground, I don't just mean out of the mainstream! I'm talking a sophisticated cave/tunnel system! Remember last year when I came with Rob Addington and discovered a tripwire just before I rode into it? We assumed it protected a marijuana patch of some kind, and that by the time we assembled a team, they had cleared it out? It isn't drugs! It's anti-government! Once Alexandra caught sight of those warriors on the slopes above her ranch, she was doomed! They have comm and weapons~like someone in their group is sheer genius! We cleared everything out and Alexandra's mine foreman and his dad are blowing the entire complex up right about now! Alexandra's entitled to a dead or alive bounty on Keller!"

Faulkner's brows rose expressively! "Thanks for the update! Anything else?"

"Well, just that Maxwell noticed the radio~okay~I'll back up a little~the local Civil Air Patrol commander received a weird radio comm! Hardly lasted a few seconds! Sounded like a scared girl! But then it popped up Keller's name on a license! We were all afraid he had abducted her~and~well~his reputation~is that no one~lives to rat him out~ So, to come to my point, Maxwell saw the radio on the body! He is already trying to get the patent rights to some of the state-of-the-art inventions~"

Daniel shrugged, wishing Trent would stop mentioning the would-be hero! "Good for him! You think it might happen?"

"He's trying to get them for your daughter!"

⚑ ⚑

Gray frowned. Young Maxwell was a busy man! A very wealthy and busy young man! Nothing criminal in the background that he could ascertain, but sometimes a family fortune could obliterate such things! He sighed! Nothing about him that indicated any Christian heritage! Alexandra would do well to steer clear of him! He brewed a fresh pot of tea and checked on the boys!

⚑ ⚑

"You look cute the way they did your makeup, Sum! I almost wish I had bought us everything! I'm not sure Gray wants you to wear quite so much for every day! Don't you love the atmosphere of this restaurant?

"I guess! I'm not sure what any of this stuff is!"

Brenna laughed. "Well, any of it's bound to be better than canned ravioli! Did you ever dream of anything like this–" She paused in confusion as her sister's face conveyed sudden recognition and shock–

Automatically, she turned to see the reason for Summer's distress! Both hands flew to her face and she burst into tears!

Chapter 20:   INTRODUCTION

"How's she doing?" Daniel's whisper as he resumed his spot at his daughter's bedside!

Diana shrugged and rose, beckoning him to follow her. "She's doing as well as can be expected, I guess! I pumped a little more pain med into her, but she's still restless! And the more she thrashes, the more she increases her pain! It's like a vicious cycle! I wish she would calm down! I think that would help the nausea to subside! What did Trent say?"

She listened intently to the narrative! "So, Brad and Tim put themselves into real jeopardy! Keller was dead, but the other two were still out there someplace!"

Daniel was startled at her logic! "Yeah, maybe because it was starting to get light, and they had the state-of-the-art top secret stuff to stash in their hideout!"

She surveyed him quizzically, "Why don't you like them? We've known Tim and his family for a long time!"

"Yeah, but the boys shifty-eyed! If you ask me, he's straddling the fence about serving the Lord! It's like, since he's still living at home, he has to comply, at least outwardly, to his parents' belief system! I didn't have much respect for him, even before he started hanging around with Maxwell!"

"Okay, which brings us to-your problem with Brad! You hardly know him! And you did hire him!"

"Yeah, because a man can be a good Geologist without being a good Christian! His putting his moves on my daughter never occurred to me! I purposely put distance between them, and told him in no uncertain terms to leave her alone! So, how he ended up here, hours ahead of us, to become the man of the hour, I have no idea! But, I don't consider him a hero! God brought Al back safely to us!"

Diana shrugged. "They were His instruments!"

He smiled, determined not to give, "Which proves that the Lord moves in mysterious ways, His wonders to perform! Your brother summed up my feeling for Maxwell rather rudely when he pointed out he's a lot like me! Diana, I'm not good enough for you! I hate what the things from my past have forced you to deal with! If Maxwell got saved and served the Lord from now on, with a perfect heart-which I have no reason to expect he'll do, I still want better for our little girl!"

She regarded him steadily. "You're the best Christian man I know; right up there at the top with my dad and brothers! You know the passage about whoever is forgiven the most, loves the Lord the most! You have more passion for Him and His cause than a lot of other Christian men-with what we refer to as-better Christian backgrounds-"

⚏ ⚏

Brenna's hand flew to her mouth to suppress any further alarmed outbursts! Troubled eyes moved from the handsome Alex Devon Hamilton, to the maître d,' and the Captain, who seemed uncertain whether they should summon hotel security! Mustering every ounce of courage, she reassured the restaurant staff before inviting her AWOL father to join her!

Through an emotional fog, she watched, fascinated, as his mouth moved! Slightly crooked teeth, but attractively so! Nice smile, dimples! Making a rehearsed speech that bounced harmlessly off her time-hardened heart! Surely, his appearance here, unbidden, should resonate with her! She was simply numb, while Summer sat there, bawling her eyes out! Brenna couldn't figure out why! Parts of the practiced speech rang hollowly! At times, she wanted to interrupt with a 'That's not true'! Probably just as well that she was struck mute!

"Okay, your turn! Tell me everything about you!" Brenna's eyes shot up to meet ones strangely like her own, although set into mature, masculine creases! Too stunned by the thoughtless demand to answer, she picked up her salad fork and began poking around in 'Field Greens' that resembled the weed patch that crowded out the grass at the old apartment complex!

At last, a frustrated gasp preceded her words, "It's really nice to meet you at last! I appreciate your honesty in coming! I-I actually hadn't decided whether or not to pursue contacting you~it might take more than a few minutes for me to trust you enough to tell you all about me~maybe this is a~start~ My intentions were never of making trouble for you or bringing you embarrassment!"

A long awkward pause, and then he spoke once more! "Richard told me about his response to you! I still don't get it now; any more than I did when he cut Irene off! I mean, he claims to be such a God-lover, but he was a mean-spirited autocrat! He said he told you that the rest of the family wouldn't be interested in being in contact now, after all these years and with so much water under the bridge! Here's a contact list, though! Jerome is your mother's oldest brother; he pastors a little church up in Connecticut! Rachel lives in Providence and she and her three kids stay the closest to Richard and his wife! The Williamsons managed to accumulate enough money to keep the kids at odds with one another! Gaylene lives in New York City, making occasional stabs at gaining theatrical acclaim! Charlie manages a resort down in Costa Rica! His kids have lived in Nevada with their mother, although, they may be out on their own by now~"

Brenna's exhausted brain struggled with the information overload! Aunts, uncles, cousins~that might welcome her with open arms~or cling blindly to the hope that if they eliminated contenders to the family fortune, they'd get more!

As if reading the jumble swirling in her brain, Alex continued in the same vein! Yeah, that's what they say; 'Blood's thicker than water, and money's thicker than anything'!"

Seeing her confusion, he elaborated: "Family ties are stronger than non-blood ties, but money~ Crazy the way money affects people; you know?"

She nodded vaguely. If he thought his, or her maternal grandfather's money, was the object of her quest, he was mistaken! At the moment, she wished she had never embarked on the strange odyssey, whatever her motivation might have been!

"Are you familiar with the story about the last Tsar of Russia?"

Brenna couldn't remember ever feeling so odd! She couldn't feel her hands or feet, and it seemed as though she were being dragged beneath the surface in the grip of a surreal whirlpool!

"I~I'm sorry!" she gasped. "What did you ask me? The story of~uh~what?"

He repeated the question! Kind of what she thought he had asked her! She pressed manicured fingers against her temples, scrunching her eyes tightly! 'Was this a test?'

Opening her eyes again, she grasped both knife and fork in a panicked stall for time! At last, "I-I guess you lost me-"

Summer snickered, but neither of them gave her a glance!

"The last Tsar of Russia! At the close of World War I, and as the Bolsheviks rose to power in Russia, the last reigning Russian monarch and his family were captured and eventually executed!"

Brenna nodded politely at the tutorial, not sure what the sudden history lesson had to do with her, or with his life-long lack of a relationship with her!

He flushed and laughed at himself; not altogether a bad sort, she guessed. "I'm making a point about money and the strange things it can make people do, even to family, where blood-ties are supposed to prevail!"

She nodded, relieved to hear that he had a point and wasn't merely testing her education!

"They killed them all! Or thought they had-"

"The Tsar and his family?" Brenna clarified.

"Yes, the Tsar, his wife, the Tsarina, and their five children were all shot at close range in the basement of a farm house in 1918! However, in 1920, a young woman came forward who claimed to be Anastasia!"

Brenna frowned. "I've heard a little about that; wasn't she a fake?"

Alex leaned back, his long, tapered fingers steepled thoughtfully! "It's an intriguing story! A number of pretenders came forth, but this woman, later known as Anna Anderson, was different! When presented to the Tsar's family members who escaped the revolution and were living large in Europe, their immediate impression, without exception, was that she was the lost granddaughter, niece, or cousin, as the case was! Then, without exception, one by one, they all recanted their early admissions of her legitimacy!"

"Why would they do that?" Brenna was drawn into the story although she couldn't figure out the relevance to this situation.

"Well, prior to the Revolution, the Tsar of Russia was the wealthiest and most powerful man on the face of the earth! Not totally trusting in Russian banks, he had huge assets throughout Europe, and money stashed in European banks! There was a will and ample provision for his five children, assuming of course, that they would survive him! With the story of the mass-murder of the entire family; the Tsar's mother, brothers, and sisters, having fled the Revolution to other European cities, were living as absolute royalty on his money! Imagine the ramifications for all of them-with the appearance of a surviving, legitimate heir! They would become the poor relations, dependent upon staying in her good graces, were she indeed Anastasia! So, in short, the family colluded to deny the legitimacy of her claim!"

Brenna was stunned at the sadness, if the scenario were indeed true; and she knew the Bible warned about what, 'the love of money', could do to people!

"So, you're trying to warn me that my aunts and uncles and cousins won't accept me with open arms? Because of my grandfather's will? They might not, anyway, if they have animosity toward my mother as the 'black sheep'! I'm just going to take things one day at a time!"

"This is a marvelous restaurant, and you've selected a superb entrée! Maybe we could all relax enough to enjoy it!"

With the suggestion, Summer attacked her plate with her usual abandonment! Brenna made a valiant effort, but her writhing belly was less than accommodating!

Brenna tried not to resent it when Alex insisted on coffees and desserts, and then insisted on covering the ticket! She felt empty! Where was he when she had needed him? When her mother had needed him? His story sounded hollow and untrue-about not knowing-

"You'll stay in touch?" His eyes probed her depths as he rose and requested his topcoat!

Brenna's response sounded tinny and childlike. "I-I guess so-if you-want-"

He smiled again, like he was accustomed to everything opening up to him with whatever he wanted-Brenna could see her mother falling for-she halted the anguished thoughts! She really didn't know! It didn't matter, she guessed.

He slid his arm around her waist and drew her toward him to plant a kiss on her cheek. "I'd like that! I-I'm so proud of the way you struggled-and got a-a degree! I'm sorry-" He broke off, pressing something into her hand!

Hot color flooded her face as she opened the check! 'So this was what all his talk meant-about family-and money-and the Tsar-and Anastasia!

"I'm not after your money! Although now your little classroom lecture makes more sense! Yes, I could tell from my search that you've done well for yourself! All people-are not-the same-"

She slapped the check onto the spotless linen tablecloth and fled!

꜠ ꜡

Daniel was trapped! Fleeing from watching his eldest child's suffering, he lit in the small hospital café; empty except for a small knot of hospital personnel! Feeling like one raw nerve, he stared dismally as Alvaredo and a distinguished looking man approached! Trying to mask his disgust at the young man's social ineptness, he extended his hand, introducing himself!

"Stephen Maxwell," came the modulated response of the other gentleman! "I count this as a privilege! Tim, here, just managed to secure me a ticket to your upcoming performance!"

"Ah," beyond the exclamation, Daniel wasn't sure what to say! The concert date was bearing down! He had received the selections to work on independently, prior to a more arduous couple of rehearsals with the orchestra preceding the event! Now, with Al's injury- Aware of publicity in the works, he figured he could never cancel and save his good name! Strange that a wimp like Alvaredo secured a ticket to the event! What did that mean? To his knowledge, the performances never sold out! Especially not the summer ones!

"I trust your daughter is doing well! My grandson is quite the hero!"

Daniel cringed inwardly, "Ah, Brad, yes; so I hear!" He frowned as it dawned on him that while Alvaredo and grandpa were down here delaying him, Maxwell might be sneaking in a visit to Al!

"Pleased to meet you, Sir! I guess I better get back upstairs!"

꜠ ꜡

Gray stood at baggage claim, watching as weary passengers scurried past to retrieve belongings and exit the airport! At last, Brenna and Summer came into sight and he moved forward eagerly! Brenna was extraordinary! Bright welcoming smile, and her body melting into his arms, took him aback! How blessed he was! "Mmmm-mmm!" His lips lingered against hers, and then he relinquished her to welcome Summer, too! "Welcome home!"

Sullen, Summer didn't respond, but Brenna bubbled. "It's great to be back! I missed you so much! How are the other kids? None of them came with you?"

"Actually not! The boys are totally taken in with the new game! It is great fun, actually! And the girls are still with my sister! They've gotten on ever so famously!"

Consternation showed on Brenna's expressive features! She couldn't imagine leaving the boys home alone! And Lindsay, Emily, and Misty didn't seem like long-term fits with Niqui and her little ones! Summer rolled her eyes, indicating she was thinking the same thing!

Chapter 21: PASSION

Anguished screams assaulted Daniel's ears as the elevator doors opened! Panic washed over him! Alexandra wasn't just going to be okay! Just springing back! He thought the nurse was rushing it, pressing to get her up! And Diana took her side! He could still see Al's terrified eyes in a face that grew even paler at the thought of stirring around so much! He bolted into a restroom and heaved up coffee and little else! It brought back searing memories of the last time he had vomited! He moaned weakly!

"Dear God, I know I have to be there for her! But I can't stand this! Please let her get okay!" He regarded his haggard features in the mirror! This was Maxwell's fault! He went charging up there, without a sat phone, or anything! Consequently, when they found Al, they couldn't call in their location and a chopper evac! He must have hurt her something awful, carrying her, making her injury worse! And then there was the trauma for her to deal with, of having shot and killed a man! His own memory flooded back! A memory he usually tried to chase away! But judging from Al's clothing, her experience was even more up close and personal- Tears broke free and he sank down, sobbing!

After a few minutes, he splashed cold water on his face before making his way resolutely back to his daughter's bedside!

⚔ ⚔

"Summer, dear, I'd like to speak to you in my office!" Gray's tone, soft but resolved.

Brenna started guiltily! "This was probably about Summer's taking off the first afternoon! Gray didn't know yet about the police incident!

200

At least, she hadn't sensed a good opportunity to tell him! She looked in on the boys, who were indeed absorbed in the intricacies of Yetis scaring off trespassers who tried to steal their diamonds! Ah, Jeremiah was over, helping keep things in line! Not that he could probably exercise much authority over Jacob and Millard if they decided to get into trouble! She wandered into the master suite and started to unpack! What a trip! The words of her grandfather swirled dizzyingly with those of her new-found father! What were her aunt and uncles' names? Jerome was a pastor; that was interesting! And Alex' accusations about her grandfather-They didn't like each other, but they stayed in touch? Evidently, Richard had phoned Alex to warn him that she would be on his doorstep! And, if her father had really been as much in love with her mother as he claimed, why had he believed Richard? Why hadn't he sought Irene with all his heart? Why hadn't he bothered to learn that he had a baby on the way? Why? Why? Why? And why would aristocratic family members deny the Grand Duchess, Anastasia, the right to who she was? Was that story really true? Could people be that greedy and self-serving?

Her buzzing phone interrupted her troubled thoughts! Niqui!

"This is Brenna! Hi Niqui, thank you for helping entertain-" she tried to sound upbeat, although she was slightly miffed with Gray for handing them off the entire time! She and Summer could have returned home earlier!

"Hi, you made it back, okay, huh?" Niqui's voice sounded as forcedly upbeat as her own did!

"About an hour or so ago! How are the girls?"

"Oh, just fine! I'm nearly there with them now!"

"Oh, that's great! We should have picked them up on our way back from the airport-"

"Yeah, well, bringing them is no problem!" Something in the panicked tone attested to the opposite!

⚔ ⚔

Daniel stepped into the path of a startled florist delivery boy! "I'll take those off your hands!"

Diana watched him, shocked, as he strode down the corridor and stuffed the arrangement into a large trash receptacle! Alexandra was nearly to an age where his autocratic interference might send her into rebellion!

"Figured they were from that Maxwell character! Thing is, I don't like Haynes much better! If someone wants to send her flowers, they can check with me first! Otherwise, he's throwing his money away! Do you know if she and Haynes have been in contact?"

"I don't! Would you calm down? It's all I can do to deal with Alexandra without you acting berserk!"

"I'm not acting! Was that her that was just screaming? I should have spoken up, that I felt it was too soon to make her get up! When does the pain start to ease off? Do you think Maxwell's rough trip down the mountain with her has made it worse?"

"Like I said, Calm down! What are you going to decide about letting her go back?"

He stared blankly! "Okay, that's not something we have to discuss tonight! Let's just get her better! Once the pain gets under control, I'd like to talk to her about the shooting! I know that's foremost on her mind! I'm not sure she's aware yet of what a bad guy he was! She may even get a bounty!"

Diana folded her arms determinedly! "I disagree! I'm sure the shooting will haunt her with some demons, as you well know! But foremost on her mind is whether you'll grant your permission for her to go back and resume her activity! I think she's trying to be brave and not use the pain meds as much as she could, to prove to you~"

He stared; taken aback! His assumption had been that Diana would want him to quash the entire ranching/mining operation!

"Well, she doesn't have to prove anything to me! I just can't stand to see her hurting so much! I'm not sure why she'd want to go back and keep at it, but with Forestry and the Feds discovering and rooting out that operation, it may be the safest place she could be!"

☙ ❧

Gray interrupted family responsibilities to phone Daniel with an update! Concern creased his forehead.

"You asked me to keep you in the loop on Maxwell's activities! He's been working the southwestern Colorado Real Estate powers that be, to notify him immediately if Alexandra's ranch comes on the market! He wants first bid! Of course other wolves have been snapping around at it ever since Alexandra closed! I must hand it to young Maxwell for being savvy legally to try to lock it down! His grandfather came on-scene, too, to see why he's trying to dig into his trust! I'm thinking that anything Brad can't accomplish, his powerful grandpa, can!" His concern for Brenna and her career caused him to plunge forward! "My opinion is that Alexandra's operation is a keeper; although, I certainly understand your protecting her from further danger!"

Daniel frowned at the thinly veiled probe! The jury was still out! None of Maxwell's business! Or Grays!

⇄

Brenna tried to curb annoyance at Gray for shoving the girls off on his sister! Evidently, they had an overall miserable time, especially with Niqui-dealing with their language! She fought tears! In all fairness to them, they didn't know what was appropriate! And helping them sort it out was challenging! She helped them put their carefully laundered and folded clothing away!

"Okay, I'm sorry you had a tough time! I'm back now, and we're all back together!"

Misty swiped at tears with a dirty hand, leaving a pitiful smear across a pudgy cheek! "But you're going on your job to Colorado! Did Mr. Gray change his mind about us? We thought-but he sent us-away- Do we have to go back to foster care?"

"No! No; he hasn't changed his mind! He loves you very much!" Even as she spoke, she prayed she was telling them the truth!

⇄

"Okay, Honey; what's happening?" Additional personnel assembling in Alexandra's room sky-rocketed Daniel's alarm!

"Well, when they tried to get her up earlier, she passed out from the pain! Which ratcheted the nausea up again! Finally, she admitted that her foot feels like it's on fire! And sometimes, though they're not sure why, heat does build up inside a cast! They're going to cut a window in it and see if it's burning her skin!"

He reeled out of the room, anguished that time wasn't making Al more comfortable! He prayed again! Maybe he had been assuming too much, that once she was found and admitted to the hospital, she would be fine!

And he couldn't figure out Brad Maxwell's angle! Was he an admirer? Or did he seek to undercut Al for her silver mine? If he already had a fortune in trust funds, would he have claimed to kill Keller, for the sake of the bounty? He paced, wishing and praying that Alexandra could get lucid enough for him to talk to!

⊣ ⊢

Gray completed a call to David Anderson, and then appeared, summoning everyone to the kitchen for bedtime tea and scones! His good-humored solidity comforted Brenna's doubts! Summer seemed subdued, but not sullen! Jacob and Millard seemed typically like Jacob and Millard! He patted the girls on their heads, suddenly curious about how and when they materialized from the care of his sister! Jeremiah fished his keys free, preparing to go home, but Gray stopped him with a softly voiced invitation!

Then, they were all talking at once, chattering about anything and everything! Evidently, the girls had done a lot with Niqui and her little ones, having a lot of fun! Millard and Jacob overflowed about the game and closing details for its sale; Summer rattled about the luxurious hotel suite and fun shopping! Brenna met Gray's gaze above the happy hubbub and peace flowed over her!

Then, the front doorbell rang!

⊣ ⊢

Alexandra went limp with relief when the window indicated flesh burned black, and the cast was hurriedly sawed in half! With some relief from the burning, she still reacted with a violent case of the shakes! Even so, the nausea subsided once more. When she tearfully expressed her desire for a milkshake, Daniel was on his way, relieved at last to be able to do something for her!

⊣ ⊢

Jeremiah blanched as Gray courteously ushered a man and woman to join the family tea party!

"May I present James Colter and Terri Danville; from the CPS?"

Hands shaking, he fidgeted with the tea pot lid, offering hospitality to the uninvited twosome! Refusing the tea, they took over arrogantly, interviewing each child privately, and demanding access to their rooms to inspect their accommodations!

Brenna sat, shocked! Maybe Oklahoma was more effective than the state of Massachusetts in caring for children in pitiful situations! In all of Brenna's growing-up-in-the-slums-years, no one had ever looked into her well-being! Or that of her siblings, until after her mother's death, and Brenna's inquiries into gaining custody! Then she was deemed too young and underemployed! 'Unreliable', and the kids went to foster care! Now, they were all in an ideal situation! And there came a knock at the door? The kids were all understandably terrified! After an hour and a half ordeal, they returned to where Brenna and Jeremiah still sat in the kitchen!

"Okay, how old are you? What's your name?" Terri seemed pleased with herself for not overlooking one!

"I'm sixteen, and my name's Jeremiah Faulkner! I came over to visit with my Uncle Gray and the kids!"

James cracked a smile for the first time since entering! "No way! Well, I thought you kind of looked familiar! You've~uh~grown a lot!" The government worker relaxed, almost seeming personable! Terri frowned disapprovingly!

"Jeremiah, do you remember that day when I was asking you questions?"

Jeremiah regarded the man silently: 'Did he remember? Could he ever forget?'

"Yes, Sir! Our family attorney showed up just in time!"

James winced, "Uh, yeah, but before that, remember the 'game' you wanted to play, about answering my questions?"

Jeremiah sighed. "Yeah, I remember! I offered to answer your questions if you answered some of mine, too!"

James laughed. "Yeah, you were the cagiest little kid I ever had to interview!"

'Interrogate' was more like it! Jeremiah's pallor proved that he remembered the incident in searing detail!

"So, the question you asked me, was leading, to say the least! You asked me if I died, if I'd go to heaven~"

Jeremiah nodded slowly~

"For two years, I couldn't get your face or your question out of my mind! Then, finally, I started following that Arkansas preacher that your family~"

Jeremiah nodded, "Pastor John Anderson~"

"I guess that's all for tonight!" Terri's authoritative voice cut through her partner's sociability! "We'll be in touch if our investigation reveals any other irregularities!"

⚑ ⚑

The milk shake stayed down, and at last, Al's condition improved! Maybe she would heal enough in a couple of days that she could travel home! For now, the swollen leg with the charred skin still rested on the bottom half of the cast! Once the condition of the skin improved and the danger of infection passed, she would wear a removable cast until the break healed!

"Daddy?"

He paused at the tremulous voice! "What's on your mind? You need to relax and get some rest!"

She nodded through tears, "Yes, Sir~" She dropped her gaze and picked at her blanket with nails that still looked salon fresh!

He pulled a chair near and sank into it, giving her his undivided attention; not pulling his 'looming father' act that usually stood him in pretty good stead!

"Are you this worried that we plan to make you give up the mine?"

Luminous silvery eyes locked his, and her voice held amazing poise! "Yes, Sir! And once they release me to travel, I want to go home, and not back to Tulsa with y'all!"

He was sure his jaw dropped, and his gaze flew to Diana's, which divulged equal shock, before his attention returned to his first-born! That obstinate expression, so like Alexandra the toddler, set in every feature of the grown woman who lay before him!

Al Faulkner was a force to be reckoned with!

⚑ ⚑

A shaken Jeremiah drove home, and Gray and Brenna sprang into action to assure the kids that their new situation was an established fact! They were a family! No one could change that! The fury in Gray's expression and body language reassured Brenna that he hadn't changed his mind from his original decision!

With the children settled down at last, he withdrew to the master suite! "It was my sister, Dominique! She set the Gestapo on me!"

Brenna was shocked at the words, and with the ferocity with which Gray uttered them!

"Come on, Gray; Niqui? She wouldn't do that!"

"Well, who else then?" The usually tranquil gray-blue eyes suddenly reminded Brenna of the tempestuous ocean that had nearly taken her life! She surveyed him wonderingly as he trembled with rage and the after effects of the unpleasant interviews!

'He cares!' The impact of the revelation shocked her! Not that she had doubted his sincerity in his placid solidity! But the fierceness of his emotions spoke to her in a strange new way! So, her grandfather didn't want her; her biological father was questionable! But Gray did! And he wanted her brothers and sisters, too; was ready to fight for them~

When she could speak past the sudden lump in her throat, she averred once more her opinion that Niqui wasn't behind the surprise visit! "It has to be the Massachusetts' legal system following up on the kids, since they allowed us to move them out of state~"

He listened, unconvinced!

"Why do you think it was Niqui?"

"Her name is Dominique! Niqui is my affectionate name for her! My entire family seem to regard me as some type of family eccentric~or worse! Because I remained single, waiting for God's timing to bring you to me!" Tears started at the unfairness of their groundless suspicions.

"What? Gray, no one thinks that!"

"I wasn't certain, when my younger sister rushed to my rescue~or the rescue of my little girls~and so I didn't insist she bring them home~although Misty's fever was gone, and I was afraid they might be overstaying their welcome!"

"Look, let's just cut her some slack and give her the benefit of the doubt that she was trying to help! I think you're amazing how you've gone from your established ways, to accommodating a houseful of crazy kids! I wasn't sure about going off and leaving you with them~not because I don't trust you~but, because they're uh~a~lot!"

He laughed suddenly in agreement, and color washed back into his face! Then his expression grew troubled once more. "What did that woman mean about, 'any further irregularities'?"

Brenna sighed and shivered. "Not sure! Just intimidation talk! Your assessment wasn't far off, when you used the term 'Gestapo'! And I'm familiar with so many 'homes' that are totally dysfunctional, and maybe they could do some good-if they'd charge in there~" she shrugged. "Anyway, with Alexandra's injury and things being so up in the air, it at least doesn't seem like I'll be leaving you to fend with them alone while I go to the Colorado job!"

᳗ ᳘

With Al's declaration of independence, she pumped up the pain med and fell hard asleep! Still, wound up tight, Daniel encouraged Diana to go to the hotel for some much needed sleep! In the comparative silence of the hospital room, he opened his laptop! An email from Mallory popped up, and he smiled at her key verse for her businesses:

Ecclesiastes 11:6 In the morning, sow thy seed, and in the evening withhold not thine hand: for thou knowest not whether shall prosper, either this or that, or whether they shall both be alike good.

The attachment to the email was a thorough and well thought out agreement for leasing *The Rock Scientist*, complete with crew! He gasped involuntarily as he viewed the bottom line! Hardly an inexpensive venture, and *GeoHy* assumed quite a bit of risk if anything befell the expensive vessel while in his governance! Usually, he didn't make such commitments without running them by Diana! For some reason, he felt a sense of urgency! He stepped into the corridor to converse with his newest staff Geologist!

"Maxwell, use your corporate card and head to Panama City!"

"Florida?"

"No! Panama! Tell me you have a passport!"

"Yes, Sir; I do, and I have it with me; what about my course?"

Daniel did a slow count to ten! He was pretty certain that with Alvaredo and Maxwell still here, the course was the farthest thing from their minds! He acquiesced, "Okay, go back to Tulsa to attend the class, and then get out as early in the morning as you can! My meter's running on this boat!"

He disconnected, pleased with himself for finding something constructive for Maxwell to do, while separating him across a broad geographical expanse from Alexandra! 'Nicely played, Faulkner', he chortled.

※ ※

Before Brad and Tim could exit the small regional jet at the Tulsa airport, their phones bonged messages simultaneously!

The University regretted to inform them that with Professor Stone's sudden demise, the course was officially cancelled; money would be refunded, regrets for the interruption of academic pursuits-funeral arrangements pending!

Tim emitted an exuberant whoop, but the missive hit Brad a walloping blow! How could the middle aged man be hale and hearty, in class one week-and then-wham-

"Here's cab fare home, Alvaredo! I'm sticking around to see what arrangements I can make to get right out for Central America!"

Tim stood, staring at him in the jet way! Then, with a wounded look, he turned and bounded off!

Brad stared after him with loathing! Alvaredo just didn't get it! With a sigh, he headed for the ticket counter! Maybe booking a flight and winging off to an exotic destination to do work he had dreamed of doing-would take his mind off-

※ ※

Gray entered their master suite balancing a breakfast tray of coffee and toast! Brenna stared around, shocked at the lateness of the hour!

"Why didn't you-"

"I thought you needed some rest, and I'm afraid I have some distressing news for you. Professor Stone passed away yesterday afternoon! Your course is canceled to be reoffered at a later date!"

She scooted the pillows up behind her, her delicate features registering profound shock! "What? Car wreck?"

"Sadly, my brother-in-law, who is in the Tulsa University loop, feels that the professor took his own life!"

"I should have tried to witness to him!" She spread honey feverishly.

Gray squinted thoughtfully! "That man ran smack into God at every bend in his career! And at every opportunity to embrace truth, he purposely chose the lie! He was aware of your lovely testimony, Brenna Love, before you ever set foot in his classroom! His screams of anger that night, were not at you; well, or course, in a real sense they were!" He chuckled mirthlessly! "His wrath was directed at the God, Whose very existence, he chose to deny!"

Brenna nodded at the clarity of Gray's assessment! She sighed. "Do you think Tim and Brad have heard?"

"Yes, which brings me to some other issues we were too tired to deal with last evening! Daniel has leased *DiaMo's* drilling and exploration ship, and Brad is on his way to oversee the operations on board! He's flying into Panama City to join her before she crosses through the Canal~"

"Hm-m-m, wonder how Tim'll make it without him!"

"Which brings me to my next point~"

She smiled at his droll expression, "Which is?"

He pulled a slip of paper from his wallet and handed it to her, to receive a puzzled frown in return!

"I would ask you how you got it, but I assume Summer must be the culprit!" She sighed! "Actually, maybe there's hope for Summer, that she didn't forge my name and cash it!"

Gray laughed, his jolly, unreserved rolling laughter! "She probably didn't think of it!"

Brenna crossed her arms, frowning! "Oh, trust me, she thought of it, alright! Gray, I don't want his money! That wasn't what I was hoping~" she struggled for composure! When she could speak again, she reached for it. "I'm just going to tear it up!"

He danced back impishly, enjoying his game. "Brenna, Love, he owes you this for not being there with you; for not being there for you-I know your heart questions every word that he uttered! Let him make this good faith gesture!"

She paused, angry retorts on her lips! Shocked that Gray didn't agree with her righteous indignation! "You didn't hear his parting jibe!"

He laughed, "No, but Summer did, and that's almost the same as hearing it for myself!"

She flushed with embarrassment, and filled with sudden confusion, "Do we need the money?"

He laughed again, "Well, let's suffice it to say, that forty thousand dollars can always be put to a good use!"

She hesitated, "Well, it's the principle of the thing~"

He sat next to her and slid his arm around her! "There are no principles violated! Let him ease his conscience! And I'm sure he thought you were hypocritical to be insulted by his offer of money when he truly believes that you married me for mine! I'm sure that's how it must look to many people! Forgive him, Brenna! Now, for my assessment! You should deposit the money into your company, hire Alvaredo, and get to Colorado! And send an email to your father, apologizing for your haste, and telling him you've invested the cash into your company!"

She stared at him, the money issue forgotten with her arguments about the inadvisability of hiring Tim!

"Didn't you tell me that Brad knew where to look for Alexandra, because, as a Geologist, he knew how Alexandra thought as a Geologist, and that led him to a pinpoint location?

Gray nodded mildly. "Yes, according to the recounting of the incident by Trent Morrison!"

"Right, and didn't Tim admit, that he couldn't even figure out what Brad meant, because he doesn't know how Geologists think? How can he have an undergraduate degree in Geology, and not understand something that simple?"

Gray pressed his mouth against hers. "You're so beautiful; have I told you that?"

She laughed at him, wiggling free, "You didn't answer my question!"

"Okay, here's the answer to your question! You're a Geologist, and you know what it is, 'to think like one', whatever mysterious thought process that may be! You're the president of your company! You don't need Alvaredo to do his own thinking! You need someone who can follow your directions!"

She sighed, her eyes widening with wonder! "He is something of a little puppy dog!"

She reached again for the check he still held, and he pulled it away~"No more talk of tearing it up?"

Chapter 22:   OBSTACLES

Brad scanned high-powered field glasses around nearly three hundred sixty degrees:

"Water, water, everywhere,
And not a drop to drink!"

He muttered lines from Samuel Taylor Coleridge's <u>Rime of the Ancient Mariner</u> morosely under his breath! If he could read 'the lay of the land' as an Earth Scientist, he had no clue where to begin probing into the vast expanse of ocean floor! The immensity overwhelmed him! Which brought him to the question; 'Did Faulkner really expect any kind of positive results from this mission? Or was this simply a ploy to send him worlds away from his daughter'? Well, the answer to that was a no-brainer! Too much cash outlay; Faulkner expected results! Big results, just in order to break even! With a shudder, he turned and headed to his cabin!

⚑   ⚐

Even though Norma double-parked for her, hobbling on crutches into the sheriff's office exhausted Alexandra!

Bill Cassidy hopped to his feet to help with the door and pull a chair forward! "Sorry if this is an inconvenience! We just need to hear your side while it's still fresh in your mind!"

Shocked eyes met those of the sheriff! Like the details of killing Noë Keller could ever be anything but seared on her brain in grizzly Technicolor!

"Is Mr. Morrison going to be here?" Alexandra was surprised at her own tinny voice! She strove for more authority, "I guess it doesn't matter! I can make my statement and you can send a transcript to whomever it may concern!" Suddenly frightened, she questioned, "Do I need an attorney to be present?"

"No, Keller had a dead-or-alive bounty on his head, so if you had set out to gun him down, you'd just get the money! I'm not sure your friend Maxwell did you any favors with his conflicting story! I'd like to hear some unvarnished truth! The only info Maxwell shared, that made sense, was that Keller and two other warriors decided to track you down! I guess their policy is to track down anyone who might ever be a witness to their activities! They hemmed you in, pushing you toward the higher elevations, and pinned you down! Good thing you were armed!"

Alexandra nodded agreement!

☙ ❧

Brenna sought Gray, "I contacted Tim and offered him my package! He didn't seem really impressed with it! Do you think I should attend Dr. Stone's funeral?"

Gray paused his activities to address her words. "Well, unless Timothy has a desktop full of better offers, he should jump on yours! A week ago he considered himself an equal, or perhaps superior to a female grad student! Adjusting to thinking of you as boss may be a challenge! As for the funeral; yes, you probably should attend! Your chosen field is important to you, and your respect for the man will be noted in professional circles!"

She nodded, "Then, after that, you think I should still plan to head to Colorado?"

"Yes, your contract hasn't been cancelled! I would go forward as if it's in effect, because it is!"

She nodded, still concerned about going off and leaving him with all the family responsibility; especially now that CPS planned 'unscheduled' visits at their whim!

"What were you doing?" She was suddenly curious about the task he was performing,

Guilt flooded his usually placid features. "We-ll," his slight stammer piqued her interest further, and she laughed.

"Well, what? You act like one of the kids when they're caught!"

He sighed, "You might not like this very much~I mean, I trust you~to be~on your own~"

He regarded her steadily as light dawned for her, "What, you're~you're coming to Colorado?"

He flushed, "I hope you don't mind terribly~"

Joy and relief flashed in her features! "Mind? Nothing could be more perfect! I felt really guilty all last week, besides which, I just missed you and worried about all of you!"

He beamed, nearly overwhelmed that her feelings mirrored his own! "So, I have purchased an RV, and the children and I will leave first thing in the morning! You can fly in to meet us immediately after Dr. Stone's funeral!"

"Wait a minute; what about CPS?"

His expression hardened, "What about them? We aren't criminals, and we haven't done anything wrong, to be summarily ordered not to leave town! To be on the safe side, I've checked with Clint Hammond, our attorney! This is the US, and the Constitution and Amendments are still in effect!"

She nodded, "What about Millard? He hasn't mentioned plans for going home~"

"Hmmm, yes, I hadn't considered Millard; he does get on wondrously well with Jacob!"

Brenna laughed, "I'm surprised that Maureen hasn't called and demanded for him to come back! She~" She cut her words short, not sure how much to divulge to Gray!

He looked up mildly, "You were saying?"

"Maureen, his grandmother. She relies on her Social Security retirement, and his Social Security disability!" She sank onto the edge of the bed sadly. "They fight like everything, but they're both all the other one's got! They're both about to reach their end, and they still resist the Gospel!"

Pain creased Gray's face! "Diana made a comment in the same vein! I accredited it to her nursing experience, which sometimes sees situations as being more dire~"

"I'm afraid, in this case, she isn't making overstatements! It seems to me as though he's gone down, just since he's been here! Don't bond with him, Gray; it's asking for heartache!"

He smiled gently, "And yet, can one embrace life fully while worrying about facing sorrow? I'm afraid your warning has come too late! I've been contemplating adopting him; but then discovered he's nineteen! And I didn't realize about the grandmother, and their codependency! We shall probably have to adopt them as a twosome!"

Tears streamed freely down her face, "Don't ever go visit my old neighborhood! There is so much sorrow and loss! You-you can't rescue the whole world, Gray-"

⧓ ⧓

Alex Hamilton's feet pounded the asphalt trail as he completed a five mile run! He dropped onto a bench, admitting defeat! Even pouring on his best steam, he couldn't outrun thoughts of Brenna, and her younger half-sister, Summer! His thoughts raced, going back to Brenna's terse email, changing her mind about keeping his check! Plowing it into her new Geological company, on the advice of her 'husband'! He tried to push his grown man experiences and intellect aside and become the seventeen year old boy again! If he had it to do over-but, he didn't! Brenna and Summer both resembled his long-lost Irene! A face nearly lost to his memory in the intervening years. Her lighthearted laugh and teasing eyes were the stuff his memories were made of! A rebellious PK and proud of it! Her Devil-may-care attitude and defiant daring made her a lark to be with! At the time, and in his juvenile immaturity, he had thought he was in love! Probably, he was the one who had introduced her to the drugs! Her downfall and the heartache of her daughters! She was just always so eager to reach out and take the elixir that was life! Sadly, he considered, that he himself had dabbled in lots of stuff, kicking free before really getting 'hooked'! He admitted he couldn't comprehend the reasons why! Now it was just his to wrestle with watching his friends and associates, one by one, succumb to the suffocating effects of habits initiated at his teasing insistence!

He rose and once more broke into a run, "I didn't have a gun to any of their, heads, for heaven's sake!" But the mocking accusations in his brain refused to silence!

"Irene!"

To the beat of his footfalls on asphalt, his mind traveled back to that afternoon! To a scheduled tryst with her in neighboring Medford, in a quiet cove by the Mystic River! He had spread the blanket, waiting expectantly, and then Richard was there! In his face! Threatening to throw him in prison-because of his age spread with Irene! Tears burst free as he charged up a dune and hopped a ridge of tall grass! The terror of the long-past event overtook him with fresh panic! At last he fell down, sobbing, into the sand!

⚐ ⚑

Brad Maxwell sat on the stern deck, alone! He had no idea what time it was! Sleep eluded him! Stars shimmered in the ebony canopy that stretched in immensity around him! A cool breeze stirred gently, a contrast to the torrid heat of daytime! 'Stone offed himself! Must be pretty _____ sure of himself on the 'No God' thing!'

Brad's mind replayed for the thousandth time, the professor's furious tirade at the innocent-seeming Brenna Prescott! 'If a few people chose to believe something off the wall from mainstream schools of thought, so what?' Brad's sense that night, was that the innocuous-seeming belief system terrified Stone for some reason! Otherwise, why waste time arguing it so hotly? And it wasn't like Brenna was saying anything contradictory! And if she had a reputation for doing so, why couldn't the prof have warned her privately that her views wouldn't be tolerated, rather than ranting for two hours in a course that didn't allow time for deviation from the prescribed material? He sighed; his thoughts had run these same laps during the previous month! A mental exercise that didn't take him any farther than the physical exertion of running laps!

He rose and paced, trying to lasso the troubling thoughts! Maybe if he thought about Alexandra-her face danced before him as she appeared the afternoon in the cubicle adjoining his, before turning to the macabre; her visage covered in blood and gray matter- He trembled! How was she doing? Where was she? Why couldn't he get her out of his mind?

His grandfather's mocking voice filled the silent air, to forget about her! That women were basically all the same! That his fascination with Alexandra was due to the challenge of her seeming unobtainable! But if he ever managed to win her, her magic would evaporate, and she'd be nothing more than another notch in his belt! The flat cynicism stunned him! Evidently, though, that was the thought process of Maxwell men! Love 'em and leave 'em! None of them matter enough-to keep and cherish and

216

protect! They're money-grabbers, so take what you want from them, and cut them loose! He reflected in the silence; obviously, that was the reason he didn't know his mother! His impression was that she was so silly and self-centered, that she had taken off for the payoff of a tidy divorce settlement to get lost, permanently! Signing over custody of her son without a backward glance! Suddenly, he questioned if that was the truth! His father and grandfather didn't really care about him, particularly! What had brought his grandfather to Colorado post-haste, was concern for the trust money! Still, he was a powerful ally! Cold as they come; but powerful!

⚔ ⚔

Jeremiah's brown eyes registered surprise at the united front his parents presented!

"So, how exactly, did you manage to be at Uncle Gray's?"

"Well, Grandpa let me go~"

Diana frowned. "And then Gray drove clear out here to pick you up?"

"Well, no, Grandpa let me drive!"

"You took advantage, Jeremiah!" Daniel's voice rose! "Your sister was badly hurt, and while your mother and I went to be with her, you took advantage of our absence! You pulled a fast one with my parents!"

Jeremiah countered, "Well, it's a good thing I was at Gray's! I think my former run-in with James made them ease off~"

Daniel's face whitened, and his eyes narrowed. "You tricked your grandfather into thinking your driving out there was okay, but you know we never give you freedom to take off in one of the vehicles on your own! You're barely sixteen, and you've hardly driven! You had no business on the freeways! You could have killed yourself, or someone else! Your mother and I have worked too hard for what we have, for you to go out and risk it all! What if you'd hit a little kid? Your plan was immature and selfish!"

"Okay, can I say something?"

"You can try, but I can't think of any logical defense! Don't put that 'called to preach and being spiritual' on us! It seems rather hypocritical!"

"But I am, and I study my Bible! Look at David and Samuel, and some of the other young men~in the Bible! ~Some of the kings were on the throne by age six~or eight! And the apostle Paul warned Timothy not to let people despise his youth! The Holy Spirit gives me wisdom and discernment and protection!"

"Well, obviously you've deceived yourself, because your actions were fleshly and rebellious! You need to face yourself honestly, Jeremiah! You stole my truck, just like you stole Mom's credit cards last year! We could have reported you as a runaway when you took off to DC to visit Megan in the hospital; and you would have a juvenile record! Your taking off in my vehicle without permission could get you charged with grand theft-auto! I'm talking about some serious character flaws Mom and I see in you, Son! How you can gloss them over by comparing yourself to young men in the Bible is frankly, beyond us!"

Jeremiah hesitated, "Well, I still think I have protection from the Holy Spirit and guardian angels!"

"Yeah, and you're looking at 'em!" Diana's blue eyes snapped! "The safety net you boast of lies solely in your submission to our umbrella of protection over you! God gave you two parents who love you, for a reason! And if you want a fine Biblical example of a Young Man being subject to His parents, consider the boyhood of Jesus! By age twelve, He astonished the learned men of Jerusalem with His wisdom, knowledge and doctrine; and yet at the words of Mary and Joseph, He returned home, and was subject unto them! Did He know more than they did? Undoubtedly! Check Luke chapter two! Actually, from that point, we don't hear any more about His youth! He began His earthly ministry around age thirty!"

"Grandpa said I could go!"

"Jeremiah, go to your room!"

⚐ ⚑

Alex rose at last, making his way back to his condo to clean up! A message from his soon-to-be-ex showed on his phone as he made his way to the elevator! Crazy mistake to marry an attorney and think he could emerge from the union with any semblance of assets! He figured she was miffed about the check to Brenna! He deleted without listening to it!

Sliding into the smooth leather seats of his BMW, he headed toward Cape Cod! He wouldn't drive all the way; just enjoy the smooth ride, stop somewhere for dinner and a couple of drinks! The plan sounded suddenly hollow! His thoughts turned backwards in his time machine, and he was an inexperienced kid facing down an enraged father! Maybe the terror had forced him to suppress the event! Now it seared his consciousness! Richard's words, to the effect that, 'Irene was on her way to Texas, to get straightened out! Not to ever try to contact her again! Unless he wanted to face criminal charges, which Richard wouldn't file, as long as'-

He squinted at himself in the mirror. So, that night, he had relegated the lovely Irene to a pleasant memory and moved on! Evidently, according to Brenna, she had neither gone to Texas, nor gotten straightened out! That he might have fathered a child had never dawned on him! Agonized thoughts turned to the beautiful woman who was his daughter-what had she gone through? What had Irene endured? Because of him? Summer, born of another man, and other brothers and sisters? It all boggled his mind so thoroughly that he couldn't sort it out!

'What did Richard know? Was he aware that his rebellious firstborn had resided practically within a stone's throw of him, destitute and desperate? How could a man who claimed to be so religious-' Yeah, not his to judge! He pressed the accelerator and the high performance engine responded smoothly! The usual thrill wasn't there!

᚛ ᚜

Daniel dealt severely with his oldest son! If Jeremiah had issues, he had to talk about them!

"If you want more practice driving, speak up! If you want privilege, you earn it by building trust!"

"Well, Al-can just do anything she wants-"

"This isn't about her! It's about you! She's three years older than you are-and she hasn't pulled any stunts-"

Jeremiah's defenses crumbled suddenly, and he fought tears!

The wise father felt the tears were a sign of humility, but only a start. He sat regarding his offspring, fighting the desire to weep with him. "What would you do if you were me?"

The words barely forced out as emotion intensified!

"Um-have-me-a-um-pray-and con-fess-"

Daniel kept his countenance hard and unrelenting, his voice holding an edge- "Confess? Confess what?"

"Doing wrong-uh-pride-being phony-Dad, I didn't realize-I was-"

Daniel nodded agreement. "Jeremiah, you can't twist the meaning of Scripture to justify-I know you read it, and study-We're proud-of you-We have trusted you, based on your-call-to preach-"

"I meant it too, Dad! I am called to preach! I didn't mean to violate your trust! I did make it sound to Grandpa like y'all let me just go out and run around~"

Daniel frowned. "Any other jaunts you took that I'm not aware of?"

Jeremiah dug the heels of his hands into his eyes, quelling tears. "No, Sir; that's all!"

"Jeremiah, Grandpa gave me liberty like you dream of! My own Mustang GT on my sixteenth birthday, no curfew, a gas credit card, money~"

Jeremiah hung his head! As appealing as that sounded to his fleshly side, he was aware of the bondage his dad struggled with, from having had too much freedom! At last, he met his father's gaze! "I'm glad you're my dad, and that you're how you are!"

They prayed together, and then the 'judge' passed down sentence! Still not fooled, Daniel didn't take it easy on him!

⋌⋋ ⋌⋋

"Hi, do you have a few minutes to talk?" Al's diffident voice nearly pulled Daniel's heart through his cell phone! Professional, but still weak!

"I always have time for you, Al! What's on your mind?"

"Well, when Norma picked me up, she took me by the sheriff's, to make my statement!" A pause before she could continue, "I know you wanted to find out~what~happened~It was pretty hard to talk about it~but I thought~I should tell you everything, and then~uh~try to put the incident~to bed~"

"Okay, just start from the beginning, and take your time~do you want me to get Mom?"

"No!" Tension in her voice, before she softened slightly. "No, you can tell her~as much as~you think~you~should~ Okay, from the beginning~Why, would Jared have tried to send Brad and Tim the wrong direction looking for me?"

"What are you talking about, Al? You don't trust Jared?"

Silence, before she responded, "Well, I did~ Okay, I told him and Norma both what my plan was! It was the first really nice spring~like day, and I told them I was going to try to trace the source of the Platinum! That means upstream!"

"Hmm~m, well to us it does: so you headed into the country above the ranch?"

"Yes, Sir! I was really just getting started, and I felt kinda-I-don't know-jumpy- I should have waited for Brenna's start, but the weather was nice-and I felt like maybe I should start doing something constructive."

"Okay, I'm glad you had the sense to take your weapon! Keep it handy, Al! Use it again if you have to!"

"See-that's the-problem-"

He was aware of her trying to steady her voice!

"I know what you're going through is tough, Alexandra; but unless you promise me you can shoot again, I'm bringing you home! You did what they forced you to! However morbid it is to deal with-you simply must deal with it and come to the realization that you did what you had to do; and that you can do it again, if it comes down to it! So, you were moving upstream through the meadow; when were you aware-"

"They were stealth! I kept getting this fleeting impression-that someone-that I wasn't out there alone! But when I would stop and look, I couldn't see anyone! It was just flitting-shadows-I told myself I needed to steady my nerves-"

"But, you still moved up, farther from the ranch?"

"Yes, Sir! Not the smartest, in retrospect!"

Daniel laughed and it eased the tension for both of them! "The problem with 'retrospect', Al, is that it kicks in too late to do any good!"

"Yeah, no kiddin'! I mean, Yes, Sir! So, I came to this huge boulder! How it got where it is-anyway, Mallory taught me the hydrology to guess where Platinum nuggets would be deposited around it-I didn't find any Platinum, but there was a big Gold nugget! That's when I realized for sure, that someone was watching me! There were three of them, and-they were like out of a movie-well, not that I watch any of those kinds of movies-but-they were-so-sinister-"

Daniel listened tensely!

"One of them had this cross-bow, Dad! And he shot at me! I took off, zigzagging, and running for ground that provided more cover! I-uh-was faster-to begin with-they were weighted down by their packs! But they just kept coming at me, inexorably! They knew I was in their pincers; like they were toying with me!"

Although fury rose in Daniel's heart, he strove for a calm tone. He couldn't imagine anyone sighting in a young woman, a young woman on her own land, and minding her own business! "Go on!" His voice was hoarse!

Chapter 23: CARNAGE

A startled Lt. Joshua Ogilvie straightened to full attention! His routine mission was suddenly anything but that! He checked his camera and made another sweep! Odd, the charter fishing boat was out again! With identical sports fishermen on deck, as the previous days! Ogilvie frowned! Odd! That none of them changed positions on deck, or seemingly, their clothes, either!

He studied his camera feed as the realization sank in, that the deck was a dummy, set up to fool aerial reconnaissance! Trembling, he reached for his radio to contact his commanding officer!

⚞ ⚟

Brad Maxwell at last went from shell-shocked numb, to a violent trembling reaction!

"It's okay, Kid," Captain McKenzie found his voice! "I think you saved the day with that little pea shooter ya got there!"

Brad's gaze traveled dazedly from the twenty-two pistol, to the Captain's face, and then back to the gun!

"Keep the safety on when you're not firing!" Daniel Faulkner's words rang in his ears! With shaking hands he returned it to safety and moved to the deck railing to release the contents of his rolling stomach!"

"That's the most gruesome scene I ever seen in all my years!"

Brad turned his head toward the speaker, still infinitely shaken!

⚞ ⚟

Brenna flew into the Durango airport where Gray and the ground caravan met her!

"That was a good thing you did, Brenna Love, staying for the funeral!"

She nodded uncertainly as she slid into the captain's chair of the RV! "Yes, I guess. Evidently the professor didn't have many friends, and the few he had seem to be of the mind that he was depressed at whatever course of action the University might take against him, due to his incident with me!"

Gray shrugged. "Fleeing when no man is pursuing! Both Daniel and his father backed down; I don't think any action was to be taken! But if it were, he's the one who went off half-cocked, flying into an unwarranted tirade, and then snooping into Mallory's confidential corporate business! It seems people are always eager to lay blame-at the wrong feet! You look exceptionally fetching, by the way!

Brenna gazed around in wonder as Gray headed the vehicle into the high country! Her eyes glazed over! A Geologist's version of heaven! Enchanted, she swiveled from side to side, trying to take in every sill and dike in each road cut! She didn't know if she wanted Gray to slow down, so she could gawk better, or hurry to their destination! A lengthening string of traffic behind the cautious Gray was the answer! No time to slow down!

☩ ☩

Daniel sat in a lawn chair watching Jeremiah wash vehicles! It was only a beginning of his discipline! His mind traveled to his eldest in Colorado, picturing the horror as she had related it!

With her injured ankle, she had struggled on, finally reaching a rock face to guard her position from the rear! Pistol ready, she waited and waited! But no one came! Cold, hurt, hungry, and frightened, she finally began to relax-to hear a branch crack like a rifle shot! Although her clip was full, she didn't want to waste ammo, waiting until she finally saw a black-clothed figure scrambling almost effortlessly up toward her position! She fired and he fell!

Darkness came, and she could hear the moans and curses of the fallen villain!

Daniel scrunched his eyes closed, but the mental images still danced in his tortured brain! Of Alexandra's desperate prayers for rescuers to come to both of their aid! She remained fearful of the other two, not knowing where they were, or how many others they might summon to track her down! He sighed! She had even called out to the injured predator that Jesus could still save him, like He did the thief on the cross! Talk about loving your enemies!

Keller's response was violent cursing, after which he summoned every bit of strength possible, to close in on her and finish her off! Then, according to Al's account, she bobbled the gun, barely recovering it to fire! To her horror, he collapsed, dead, on top of her!

He opened his eyes to see Jeremiah staring at him strangely. "Get to work, Son!"

⊰ ⊱

"You did what you must!" McKenzie's brusque words to the dazed Brad! "Their plan was to board us and take us hostage! Or worse!"

"Why did a fishing excursion boat fire on us to begin with? We're in international waters, just minding our own business! That was some kind of a big gun! Brenton had just bent over to check on the rig-" Brad couldn't finish!

"What about Brenton?" The Captain frowned. "I thought everyone was present and accounted for!"

"Maybe they didn't intend to hit him!" Brad's voice through teeth clenched to halt their chattering! "Maybe they were trying to fire a warning shot across the bow, and then he straightened up-not much left! That's probably what brought the sharks in in such a frenzy!"

"50 cal, Sir! Must be drug smugglers to possess that kind of fire power! Me thinks the fishing excursion business is a subterfuge!" The first mate trying to make sense of the surprise attack!

McKenzie's scowl deepened! If the attacking ship was drug smugglers, which he questioned, this was out of the way for any drug customer base! This simply wasn't along any smuggling routes! It didn't add up! "Maybe they think we're atop more of those ancient, solid gold, Greek coins! What's the real nature of this mission we're on?" McKenzie faced off belligerently with Brad!

He straightened defensively! He wasn't sure, himself. Random drilling, to see what valuable metals presented themselves beneath the ocean floor, as far as he could ascertain! The drilling log then fed into the *DiaMo, Inc.* offices for initial analysis! And then the core samples were shipped to various places for actual physical testing! If the charter fishing boat was a clever hoax, was Faulkner's mission an equal sham? His analytical mind couldn't make sense of the horrific and jumbled sensations! Text books and the dull classroom routine didn't prepare for anything like this! Strange, Faulkner's insisting on him bringing the pistol along!

⊰ ⊱

Sequestered in the music room, Daniel attacked the concert selections, at last! The concert date loomed, and he wavered between elation at the prospect and irritation at himself for agreeing to perform! It was plenty to master, and he realized he should have started much earlier! But it wasn't exactly like his schedule presented huge gaps for anything extra! Concern for both Al and Jer crowded the edges of his mind! At last, he laid bow and instrument aside and knelt next to the piano bench! Confused, he wasn't sure how exactly to pray! Maybe he should have prayed before he committed! That was a moot point; too late for that! No backing out, with all of the advanced publicity! He prayed for family, business, children, before the Holy Spirit released him to address the concert issue!

"Father, please just let all my efforts that seem stretched so thin, bring honor and glory to Your name! In Christ's Name, Amen!"

Feeling better, he tucked his violin beneath his chin and positioned the bow!

⊰ ⊱

Mallory listened with growing alarm as Captain McKenzie related his macabre tale! Woozy, she sank down at her desk! She wasn't familiar with the victim, Christopher Brenton, the drilling rig foreman-someone Daniel knew! It was Daniel's mission, but her boat; and the incident filled her with dread! A death! The U S Navy was sorting out the details?

"Okay, hold on a second, Captain!" She strove to control herself; she needed details. "What were your coordinates? When the other boat fired on you?" She listened as the orders passed along to gather her requested intel. She moved to a large screen that showed a map of the western coast of South America and the eastern Pacific! "Okay, hang on, Captain! That doesn't even make sense!"

"That's what we're saying! What are this *GeoHy* and *DiaMo* really up to?"

We're up to exactly what we told you we're up to! Could you please have them check the coordinates again? What you gave me is right over Richards Deep!"

"Yeah, that sounds about right! I'm not sure this kid that's in charge knows if he's afoot, or horseback!"

Her mind reeled. Understatement there! She surveyed the map once more! Richards Deep was the deepest spot in the Peru-Chile, or Atacoma, Trench! Why would Brad order the drillers to drill there? At its shallowest points, the ocean depths protected its valuable mineral resources! She frowned! Maybe Brad was even dumber than he acted! But who shot 50 cal. shells? And why? The depths in Richards Deep were far too great for profitable shipwreck salvage, no matter how riches-laden they might seem! Who would feel threatened enough by a dumb Geologist sending a drill bit down-She paused, and her jaw dropped at the possibility!

"They're dumping waste! Illegally dumping waste!" The assurance in her voice startled Captain McKenzie, but the hypothesis did make sense!

"Let's say they have fairly good containers;" Mallory's breathless voice grew more animated, "that can withstand both saltwater corrosion, and the pressure! Maybe they can dump for say, ten or twenty years? By the time it gets discovered, they've pocketed lots of money and moved along! And it seems like a good gig-"

"Ah," Captain McKenzie caught on, "But the last thing they want is a drill bit ripping into the mess- No doubt they fired on us to scare us off! Then, their shot killed a man, and they sent a party to board us and silence all of us?"

Mallory shuddered; sounded like it!

᠃ ᠄

Gray frowned! Snowmelt in Colorado evidently meant rivers of mud everywhere! The little mining village of pre-built homes huddled forlornly in a river of sticky muck! Hmmm, this was something completely unforeseen! He certainly didn't want to get the vehicles stuck! He gazed longingly at his Italian leather loafers and Brenna's trim business pumps! Evidently, they weren't ready for this!

"That's Norma!" Brenna's face brightened visibly as she recognized the aged car that pulled behind them on the county road!

A woman emerged and greeted them with a chuckle that Colorado natives saved for out-of-staters, "I wouldn't try getting in down there right at the moment!"

Gray frowned, a conclusion he had already made!

"Come on up to the house!" Norma waved toward the opposite side of the road where the actual ranch property sloped steeply upwards! With a final chagrined glance down toward his recently purchased modulars, Gray complied! There seemed few other viable options!

⚎ ⚎

Daniel lost himself in the selections, the scores on the pages transporting through sensitive fingers into the resonant instrument! They melded, and his ragged soul took wing! This was what he needed~a diversion~

He fought annoyance as a tap on the door interrupted his moment! Diana popped her head in.

"Phone call~"

Her expression, a mix of perplexity and annoyance, stopped his reminder about fielding his calls. Taking his phone, he moved onto the balcony and slid the door closed.

"What's up, Maxwell?"

He sank dazedly onto a swing, listening, barely able to follow the grad student's overwrought narrative! 'Chris Brenton? Gone? A life obliterated in a blink of the eye? A great guy! Husband! Father! Obliterated by a blitz attack!' He struggled to breathe, too distraught for tears! And with damage to the *Rock Scientist* as Brad described, panic seized him! His name was on the line for the lease agreement~and this was a venture he hadn't yet mentioned to Diana! The entire thing was so implausible! Who fired fifty caliber rounds on ships doing routine research? His theory was, 'environmental crazies'! But still, the vessel was under his oversight! And a wrongful death! How could such a disaster happen?

Disconnecting from the call, he slunk toward his office to access the lease agreement! Sadly, with his photographic memory, he remembered all too well what the legal document spelled out!

His phone chimed again! Mallory!

⚎ ⚎

Gray herded his chattering family into the aged ranch house, taking notice of Alexandra in a derelict recliner with her foot elevated. Curious as to why Daniel and Diana had allowed her to return here, rather than insisting she come home, he greeted her cordially:

"Ah, my favorite eldest niece! How in the world are you managing to get on, what with the mix of crutches and mud?"

She frowned, although she took comfort in his reassuring presence! "I'm not sure what to do; I can't SOS David and Mallory every time I face an issue! Mallory's doctor is probably going to put her on a travel hiatus soon, until after the baby comes! You're right; I can barely maneuver around at all!"

Gray studied her steadily! Not possessing his sister's nursing skills, he still thought she looked wan; more than simply the dejection from the new challenge for getting her mine up and running!

"I noticed on the drive up that most of the ranchers seem to have their own dozers!"

Norma stuck her head in from the kitchen, "Yeah, some years they see more use than others, depending on snowfall and the amount of mud!"

⚔ ⚔

US Navy Commander William Dexter frowned. Both the ship's crew and the drilling crew from the *Rock Scientist* told pretty much the same hair-raising story! He studied the small caliber pistol, taken from Maxwell and bagged as evidence! Lt. Ogilvie's surveillance footage confirmed the story of the surprise attack! The Commander supposed the theory about dumping illegal waste into the depths of the Trench made as much sense as anything!

He directed one more question toward the Geologist in charge of the *Rock Scientist's* expedition, "Are you sure you can't tell me anything further about the men on the raft? Was it your impression that they were Americans?"

The shocked young man sat with tears flowing unchecked down his face! His only impression was their screams! Whether those indicated the English language, or their citizenship, he hadn't a clue! He wanted to cooperate and be a help, but he didn't know!

The Commander was sympathetic, but he needed answers. "Okay, so the pistol belongs to your employer, Daniel Faulkner? How can I contact Mr. Faulkner? He can notify Christopher Brenton's next of kin?"

⚔ ⚔

Brenna moved restlessly from window to window of the ranch house! As eager as she was to get started, there seemed to be too many obstacles! The kids were fidgety, too! If only they could begin unloading their stuff from the RV, they would have something to do, settling in for the next few months! She reminded herself that delays, though chafing, were often from God's hand, and that through delays His purposes were often accomplished. She was under contract with Alexandra, and as awed as she felt around the girl, she supposed she should ask where to start!

Getting her laptop, she made her way purposefully toward the recliner! Startled, Alexandra brushed guiltily at tears.

"Are you still in much pain?" Brenna's soft question showed concern.

"Quite a bit, and then, with all the mud~" a frustrated gesture accompanied the words! "But, I just got some really appalling news!"

Brenna's eyes widened, not sure how much to push for confidences.

"I'm not sure how to tell~my~dad~"

Brenna shrugged, pretty sure that Daniel Faulkner was securely wrapped around Alexandra's little finger.

"Is it something about Brad?"

A shot in the dark that was answered by a puzzled frown, "Brad? Maxwell? Uh~no~what about~him?"

Brenna shrugged noncommittally! "Well, it's probably none of my business~"

Alexandra dabbed gently at her eyes and nose! "Okay, you know about Tommy Haynes~right?"

Brenna grinned. "Not much, but I thought he was relegated to ancient history~"

Alexandra laughed. "Yeah, but it's his dad that has lined up all of our study courses for years and years~"

Brenna nodded, "Yeah, it's amazing how much my siblings are catching up academically!"

Alexandra nodded agreement! "But I checked everything out online that Mr. Haynes offers! He's barely dipping his toes into college curricula!

We all put the thumb screws to him about the Earth Science major, but-I decided to start on an Ag degree, too! From CSU!"

Brenna made a face! "So, I'm assuming it's not working out too well?"

"I paid so much for the courses; and then I knew I was buried, even before getting lost and breaking my ankle!" Fresh tears flowed, "They've just assigned me failing grades! If I retake the courses and make A's, the average will still only be C's!"

Brenna considered thoughtfully! "Are you sure you need such a double major? I mean, you hired a mining engineer! You didn't try to get a degree in mining engineering! Except for King Solomon, nobody has a handle on every discipline that's out there! Maybe you should kiss the money good bye, and hire someone to run the cattle operation and do the accounting!"

⚔ ⚔

Gray studied Tim Alvaredo in astonishment! The kid knew heavy equipment! With a hastily gasped prayer of thanks, Gray completed two major purchases and joined the grad student at the RV! "They'll be delivered first thing in the morning! Now to the lumber yard!"

He laughed as they completed their work several hours later! "Well, not pretty to look at, but at least one can navigate the property without sinking to one's knees!"

Tim glanced around in agreement! Plywood, planks, and large scraps of carpet created paths between the major buildings! Gray Prescott was a more take-charge kind of a guy than he had credited him with being!

⚔ ⚔

Diana looked blankly at the stapled papers in her hand! The scope of the maritime tragedy's going far beyond simply Daniel's not having mentioned the venture to her! Mallory's lease agreement was spelled out to the letter! With ever i dotted, and every t crossed! It looked like *GeoHy* would be liable for all of the damage inflicted on the boat!

"How many children do-did Chris and Wendy-" Her voce faltered. Worries about a wrongful death lawsuit and a genuine sorrow for the victim's family tumbled together in her jumbled thoughts!

Daniel sank down on the corner of his desk and raised his head to meet her questioning gaze! "Four! Like middle schooler down to four year old twins!"

His phone jingled a marimba tone, and he thought dully he should change it to a dirge!

"It's Mallory!"

⧈ ⧈

Norma scrutinized the serving line in the chow hall! She didn't cook, but her responsibilities included placing the grocery order and overseeing the kitchen staff! Jared and Abby appeared, followed by Jared's dad, his head miner, nicknamed, 'Pick', and a couple of other miners! She indicated for them to serve themselves and noticed when Gray and Brenna entered with their family and the scrawny Timothy Alvaredo! Kid needed some meat on his bones!

"Where are you going?" Gray's alarmed tone as Brenna headed toward the door with her tray of food!

"I'm running this up to Alexandra! She hardly moves from that chair! Good job with all of the paths~"

"I'll run it up~" his hand stretched authoritatively toward the food! "The air has taken on a definite chill! You and the children begin eating! I'm fearful that I need to persuade my niece to visit the ER!"

"That's kind of what we've thought!" Jared spoke up for Abby as well as himself!

"I second the motion, too! She refuses to take the pain meds!" Norma onboard!

"Well, I know she's still worried her dad will insist that she come home~" Brenna observed.

"All the more reason why she should show them she has the wisdom to take care of herself! Perhaps the ER staff will send her right back home; she'll be out some money, but our minds will all be eased! More than likely they'll keep her overnight for additional antibiotics and fluids!"

⧈ ⧈

"Hello, Mallory, I~uh~guess you've~gotten the news~?"

"Yes, Sir! I've spoken with Captain McKenzie and Brad! Then I called Kerry Larson! He's checking on claiming damages from the company that fired on my boat! I'm fairly certain that they were dumping waste in the Trench! Who would ever know? Since they were involved in illegal business practices, their assets will be seized for sale at auction! They're the ones who committed murder, and in addition to answering for that, they should pay the wrongful death-"

Daniel sucked in a ragged breath! Mallory was right! Others were actually the culprits! But he still felt weighted with a terrible sense of grief and guilt!

As he talked with Mallory, his phone indicated a second caller! An unknown number!

"We can talk later, Mallory! I believe this is the Navy Commander calling!"

Chapter 24: *ENDURANCE*

Gray and Brenna were shocked at news of the ill-fated ocean exploration! Brenna listened to the craziness of Brad's choosing the deepest part of the ocean to send down the drill bit! Just because the surface of the ocean all looked the same, didn't mean the floor did! Still, he seemed to rise to the surface every time, like cream! Proclaimed a hero again, by foiling a company's illegal waste dumping! Like a cat always landing on his feet!

"I truly apologize, Love~"

She smiled at Gray's apologetic countenance! "Please don't! Just take her down while she's willing to go! The kids and I can unload and I'll head them all toward bed! This is very nice!"

"Very nice, indeed!" He paused to bring the gas fireplace to life! "David has outdone himself once more!"

※ ※

Mallory puffed! This was going about like normal! Or maybe a little worse! As usual, her mother couldn't make it! Bad enough! But then, David's mother could! Mallory wanted to scream! Both from the contractions, and from Lana's repeating the same thing over and over! She clamped down on her lip, but a moan escaped!

"Mom, please~" David's voice from gritted teeth!

"Well, you do have that big blockhead! Just like your father's! And you were my first, and I'm so petite!"

"Yeah, Mom! We get the picture!"

When the doctor softly mentioned the possibility of a C-section, it was Lana who chimed up! "Not yet! If I could do it; she can!"

David groaned inwardly! You didn't throw down a challenge like that to Mallory! He was in favor of anything that would shorten this ordeal! Blessedly, little Adam Essex appeared, and his high-pierced screams filled the delivery suite!

꿩 ꙩ

Commander Dexter frowned. Not any surprise, really, that the outlaw ship escaped capture! Ogilvie's recon photos ended when the vessel reached Chilean waters, and if Chile's Coast Guard even tried to find and apprehend the vessel, evidently it managed to evade! Hundreds of thousands of square miles of ocean! And who knew what subterfuge the crime entity had at its disposal? It wasn't out of the realm of possibility to camouflage the ship with ocean blues to fool aerial searches! Similar to the fake fishing deck! His assumption was that if they had indeed been dumping in the Trench, they wouldn't return any time soon! Maxwell's harried tale put seven victims on the raft! Captain McKenzie thought six! Nothing left from the shark feeding frenzy, except for pieces of the inflatable, salvaged for forensics! Hopefully it would yield some clues!

His call to Daniel Faulkner hadn't raised any red flags! According to the Tulsa-based Geologist, the same exploration vessel had suffered a mutiny several months previously, causing that Expedition Geologist to flee by raft on extremely heavy seas! Arming Maxwell made sense! Especially in light of the prior experience! Scary, the resurgence of piracy and crime on the bounding main!

꿩 ꙩ

Brenna sat up and turned on a bedside lamp. It was nearly midnight! Rising, she peered through slats in the blind! Moonlight bathed the peaks soaring beyond the ranch buildings in luminescence and serenity. Concern for Alexandra deepened. Maybe the ER was just backed up! Even as she stood transfixed by the other-worldly beauty, the RV purred into view! She moved to the front entrance and stood in the chill as Gray approached.

"You needn't have waited up! However, I just recently made the realization that I quite forgot to add a key to my new home~"

"Well, I didn't actually wait up! We got a lot accomplished, and then the kids were worn out! I went to bed a little before eleven, but then, something-I have this queasiness-maybe something in the Sloppy Joes-If you were locked out, I'm glad I was awake!"

"Yes, well, I could have rested quite comfortably in the RV, so it wouldn't have been so bad-"

She nodded before asking the obvious, "They must have kept Alexandra?"

"Yes, quite so! Infection was starting in the burn wounds; so IV antibiotics were the order of the day! And fluids as well! She phoned her parents on the way to town!"

Brenna held her breath, and he laughed before continuing, "This is a strange thing, but our friend, Brad Maxwell, is chomping at the bit to own this property! That, in and of itself, has Daniel quite determined not to let it go!"

Brenna frowned, not sure why Brad would want it! He wasn't a good enough Geologist to take one look around and know if rich veins of ore crisscrossed the acreage! No one was that good! He didn't even have access to the article in *The Drilling Platform*, Mallory's ezine! Well, whatever his motivation, it seemed to be working in Alexandra's favor for her parents to let her stay, in spite of her injury!

Suddenly overcome with nausea, she bolted toward the bathroom!

⊰ ⊱

"Oh, Daddy, he looks like a little bitty you!" Amelia cooed approval of her baby brother, reaching for him authoritatively!

"I can hold him! I know how!"

"Okay, well, let Daddy help you!" The lip shot out defiantly, but she reluctantly accepted his assistance! She was pretty much Mallie made over! Outspoken and independent!

Avery and Alexis took the newcomer in with bored indifference.

Avery set herself in his line of vision. "Now can Mommy play ball with me? You said not until the baby comes!"

David laughed. If Amelia looked like Mallory, Avery was the one with the baseball gene!

"Well, let's give it a few days," he hedged!

Amelia's blue eyes met his, challenging! "Well, then there'll be another baby on the way! There's always babies on the way!"

"Well, yeah, so you can have brothers and sisters!"

Big blue eyes, more eloquent than words, swept across little sisters! With a resigned sigh, she indicated she was done holding her new brother!

∗ ∗

Diana forced herself to concentrate! Yes, no telling what their liability might be in the loss of Christopher Brenton! She paused again, to pray for the widow and children whose lives changed drastically, forever, in a split second of time! She shuddered! Not even a body to help with closure! And what dollar amount in damages to the *Rock Scientist*, might hit *GeoHy's* insurance company? And concern for Alexandra remained real! Still, life must go on! She paused, caught up short! A smile spread across her lovely features!

∗ ∗

Sequestered again in the music room, Daniel practiced with an intensity not experienced in a very long time! If he was going to do this thing, and he was, he needed to do it heartily, as unto the Lord! Visions of crucifying reviews danced before him, and he shoved them away! They were as inevitable as pain accompanying a decayed tooth! Sadly, the critics' remarks always hurt his mother the most! With that in mind, he bore down even harder! At last, he turned his attention to the composition which was newest and least familiar! This was the one for which he possessed the entire musical score, meaning that as guest violinist, he might also be privileged to conduct the piece! After studying it for forty minutes, he moved to his office and accessed the Vienna Symphony Orchestra's performance of it! Nothing like using another of the senses in the learning process! Music filled the house, and Diana appeared at the doorway!

"Too loud?" Brown eyes were apologetic.

"No, it's amazing! That gives me the inspiration I've been needing! Did Mallory ever tell you about the time Amelia tried to make Avery play Sunday School, singing *Deep and Wide*? And that gave Mallory the idea to tell Higgins to drill wider and deeper on site where he was?"

He shook his head in wonder as he paused the concerto. "No, I always wonder what the secrets are to her success! What was your inspiration?"

"Well, you know how much I love leather accessories? Shoes and handbags, especially!"

"Pretty sure that's why we already need to expand the closet!" He laughed at his teasing, but she didn't! "What about it, Honey?"

"Well, so many other handbag designers and manufacturers have seen the possibilities presented by other materials, especially, the coated canvas!"

"Mmmmm, yeah, like Deborah's rowboat line based on your drawings!"

"Exactly, but she brings out darling bag after bag; because she isn't so tied into leather! I mean, her trim is always quality leather, with sharp and innovative hardware!"

"And you basically taught her everything she knows!"

A lilting laugh, "Maybe so, but she's a smart girl, and she has taken everything and run with it! Anyway, I'm going to introduce a new line of handbags, travel themed!" She flipped proudly through a few preliminary sketches!

"Wow! Those look exquisite, Di!" He backed through the sketch book slowly! "I helped you come up with these?"

༇ ༈

Gray peeked groggily at the alarm clock! Sunlight filled the small bedroom, but the house was quiet! Even after arriving late, he and Brenna had stayed up talking, waiting for her nausea to subside! After which she was starved, raiding the chow hall for more of the Sloppy Joe's she had lost! Bit of a strange thing! Shoving feet into worn slippers, he padded out into the family area! Like a cyclone had struck, leaving the space devoid of life! Nothing like a suddenly obtained family to turn a starchy bachelor's existence downside up! He started his ever present tea kettle and returned to the bathroom to shave!

The sound of big rigs delivering his heavy equipment brought him to the back door! Now he was faced with the challenge of finding operators for them! Still, he considered the sudden purchases a good investment! Colorado! With a history of booms and busts, was now on what Alexander Grayson Prescott figured was the beginning of a boom cycle! With the rumors generated by Alexandra's mine, fueled by her disappearance and rescue; more would-be, rags-to-riches, fortune seekers would be arriving daily! He smiled smugly at the face in the bathroom mirror! Sipping tea and humming softly, he pursued his mental strategy! Mining booms! Inevitably brought in fortunes! Not necessarily for the prospectors and miners, as much as those who moved in to provide the population influx with trade goods and services!

⚞ ⚟

With plastic grocery bags secured protectively around her tennis shoes, Brenna trudged up beyond the ranch buildings! With the winds calm, the air was crisp; exertion caused her to pause and shed a layer! Making it a short distance farther, she halted, puffing! Thin air like she was totally unaccustomed to! Still, the beauty of the soft morning filled her with delight! She traversed rivulets that splayed across the meadow from the main stream bed, bogging down, but struggling free until she reached Alexandra's boulder! Not sure she would find another such sizeable Gold nugget, she nevertheless dug her pan into the gurgling water eddying behind the solid obstacle! Her first attempt at panning! She suddenly felt like a genuine Geologist! It was fun, although she wasn't certain she had the hang of it! Her second scoop didn't require panning! Several small nuggets winked in the morning light!

With the discerning eye of a true scientist she squinted up the sparkling water course!

I will lift up mine eyes unto the hills, from whence cometh my help.
Psalms 121:1

She quoted the verse softly to herself! Aware of the verse's primary meaning, of looking upward to the Father for divine aid, He often supplied with matter wisely supplied by Him at creation!

⚞ ⚟

A small private jet taxied down the tarmac and halted a short distance from the main terminal! David and the flight attendant helped Mallory and the kids deplane! A convoy awaited them! With Mallory, Amelia, and Adam Essex settled into the luxurious RV, David secured car seats in the back seat of a new quad pickup and secured Avery and Alexis! With a nod at long-time employee, Waylon, they headed out toward Silverton!

"What do you think?" David phoned Mallory as they neared the small tourist town, "You want to stop in town for a bite to eat? We may get to the ranch too late for lunch in the chow hall!"

She considered, "Probably so! I'm surprised the girls haven't already needed to stop! Besides, a funnel cake is calling my name!"

⫞ ⫟

Relief flooded Gray's face as he pulled up at the front entrance of the hospital! Alexandra was checked out and raring to go! Color infused her cheeks and she looked like a different girl from the wan one sprawled in Norma's recliner the previous day!

"I'm sorry for you having to make the drive—"

"Nonsense! Now I think you are finally on the mend! Even so, why don't you rest up a bit on the drive—do you have need of anything while we're in town?"

"Maybe a Starbucks? I'll treat!"

"Starbucks it is then!"

⫞ ⫟

Brad paused in shock as he raced through the Panama City airport! His grandfather? Here? He plastered what he hoped looked like a delighted smile on his exhausted countenance!

"What a surprise," he gasped!

"You look like _____!" The word choice wasn't flattering.

"I can't say I feel much better," Brad admitted. "I do think I'm a big enough boy to get home by myself, though!"

"Okay, well hold on! Let's get a libation! I'm here to find out what happened! Faulkner set you up?"

Brad turned tired eyes toward his irate grandfather! "Pretty sure he didn't do that! The drilling foreman he hired was a really nice guy; Faulkner's liable for damage to the ship, according to the lease agreement! Thanks for the offer, but I have a connection to make!"

"Well, get something as soon as you board! You look like you could use a bracer! Don't forget I have two tickets for the symphony!"

239

"Yeah, count me in for that–" his face brightened in spite of horrified exhaustion! Alexandra would surely be present for her father's performance!

⚐　⚑

Alexandra stretched in the back seat; scrunching her hand opened and closed to restore circulation! Almost home! She sipped at the cold coffee beverage, untouched in the drink holder! She stared in awe at the amazing improvements! Securing her orthopedic boot, she tried to take it all in!

"Wow, Uncle Gray!"

His baritone chuckle reflected her amazement! "'Wow', is right! It looks as if David has arrived! What a transformation!" He paused at the entry to the village: His plywood and other lumber purchases weren't money thrown away! It was just that David's crew knew how to utilize the materials more skillfully! Bringing in a truckload of gravel was a great idea, too; as well as sod going down!

Al's voice held soft wonder! "He's made my house and the chow hall, wheel chair accessible, even though there's a sea of mud! I've been grateful that I could hobble in at Norma's and collapse into her recliner! But; did you call David and Mallory?"

Gray flushed guiltily! "Well, not recently! I phoned him about where I could get the best deal on modular housing here for Brenna and the children and myself, and where I could hire a crew to get everything installed and hooked up! He suggested himself, so since he was amenable, I hired his crew! He brought them in earlier and accomplished most of it before you got here, and before the baby was due! I didn't know they planned to return right away! How fortuitous!"

⚐　⚑

Brad asked for coffee; which, at the moment, sounded like as 'bracing' a beverage as was offered! Forlornly and too late, he accessed diagrams of the ocean floor! What a knucklehead he was! Shame spread up handsome features, but he was isolated in the crowded plane, as usual! Strange how you could be jammed shoulder to shoulder with a mass of humanity and still be terrifyingly alone! Though his gaze rested on the charts, his brain played different images!

240

Sheer force of will pulled him from the brink of that insanity! To Brenna Prescott, and the late Professor Stone! What was that about; really? And Tim Alvaredo knew! Yet hanging with the annoying guy didn't pull it out of him! Some kind of initiation, secret knowledge? He was forbidden to tell? Afraid?

His errant thoughts continued taking him on a journey! As long as it wasn't back to the *Rock Scientist*-But ugly images refused to be pushed aside! He could see Keller, sprawled dead as a hammer, atop Alexandra Faulkner; remember his and Alvaredo's horror of pulling her free, covered with gore! Ah there was the elegant Alexandra Faulkner again, who seemed to have taken up permanent residence somewhere deep inside him-Could he really see her, if he attended the symphony with his grandfather? Would Faulkner have security alerted to bar him from the concert hall?

The charts on his monitor caught his eye again, and he flushed with embarrassment! What a no-brainer! To the ire of Captain McKenzie and the drillers, he had wasted a day and a half, with no clue as to where to drill! Well, in his defense, he was inexperienced, barely out of the classroom! And the two colleagues he should have been able to call on-Brenna Prescott and Mallory Anderson-he had blown the opportunity for a professional bond with them, by trying to come across as such a lady killer! A persona which had set poorly with both husbands! Yeah, for a guy who usually thought he was pretty brilliant, he had some boners racked up to his account!

☙ ❧

Brenna picked up her pace! She didn't realize how far she had managed to wander, and although she headed steadily downhill; darkness approached swiftly, and with the shadows, came cold! Although her watch said it wasn't yet four o'clock, Gray might be starting to worry! Topping a low crest, she sighed with relief as lights winked at her from the cattle barn! Elation overtook her! What a profitable outing!

Making it past the ranch house, she dropped to undo the hampering, make-shift galoshes.

To her amazement, the sea of mud was tamed to neat boardwalks, gravel paths, and ramps! Sod created yards in front of the different temp buildings!

Watching for traffic, she crossed the county road that separated the properties, softly humming, and misappropriating, the song, *What a*

Difference a Day Makes! Suddenly hungry she hurried to join a group of people heading toward the chow hall! She stopped short, both hands flying to her face in alarm! 'Oh no! What was HE doing here?'

♯ ♭

"I feel great," at last Alexandra's tone matched her words as she spoke, happy and relaxed, to her parents! "I was starting to worry about myself a little bit-but I hate to ask anyone to drive me all the way down to the hospital! I was relieved when Uncle Gray insisted! And the endless mud has been almost as much of a problem as the snow was! Using the chair was impossible, and the crutches-wow, that's an effort that creates new kinds of pain! Did you get the pictures? I'm sorry I don't have any 'before' shots, so you can see what a difference there is! So, I'm actually settled into my own house, and Janni Anderson's staying with me a few days, just to help me with whatever! David and Mallory hired both her and Melodye for the summer! Melodye's helping David and Mallory with the kids while they work! Adam's adorable, by the way!"

She listened to her parents and their updates before answering her dad's questions eagerly! "Well, Brenna's amazing! She wandered up above where I made it before, and she brought back really promising samples! She's hired Tim Alvaredo, not because she's impressed with him as a Geology major, but because he follows orders! So, today, he worked, helping David and Uncle Gray! Tim has a lot of family experience with heavy equipment, so he helped Uncle Gray buy a dozer and some other large, mysterious, yellow contraptions! Uncle Gray figures that as word spreads about my finds, that prospectors and mining companies will show up! That's why he's investing in heavy equipment!"

Daniel's eyes met Diana's! That news was a huge relief to both of them! That Gray was there, keeping his firm hand on Brenna, and starting a timely business venture that would definitely add a level of protection to Alexandra, as well!

Daniel smiled to himself as he disconnected! On the ground floor with heavy equipment- Not a bad business concept at all!

♯ ♭

Brenna faced off angrily with her husband! "What do you mean, you invited him here? Why would you do that?"

242

Gray stood just inside the front door, hands in pockets! "Because you still need him in your life! He showed up voluntarily at the hotel in Boston! I think your grandfather tried to give him a warning, so that he could steer clear of your search! Instead, he rather moved toward you, embracing the truth of your existence! The check he offered you was his admission of having not been present in your life!"

"You don't know what he said about you!" Brenna wasn't quick-tempered, but once stirred up, she had a hard time turning issues loose!

Gray laughed. "Yes, I do; thanks to Summer and her penchant for repeating everything! When he offered you the check, you told him you weren't for sale! You refused the check and walked away! So, hurt, he took a shot at you! Although there's never a call to be unkind, I think he simply responded to what he felt was your rejection of him!"

She swiped at nose and tears with one motion! "He said not to give myself airs about what I'm willing to do for money! He accused me of marrying you for your money! And he likened me to what mother felt compelled~" Hot color flamed up her cheeks! "I feel like that's what people think of us, anyway! That I just married you for~"

He surveyed her steadily as sobs racked her.

"Gray, it's not true~"

He stood smiling that gentle smile! "I know it's not true, Love! But we can't waste our time trying to correct what we think people think of us!"

"But he went past thinking it! He said it!"

"Well, once it's said, one can take the speaker to task~if one wishes! But it won't resolve anything! Leave it alone! Let him in, Brenna! It's true, people are largely motivated by money and having more! It's no surprise that he superimposes ordinary motives onto the actions you've taken! You need him. You didn't marry me for my money, nor to get a father-figure! I think you said 'Yes,' to me; I hope you said, 'Yes,' to me, because you could see Christ in me! And that's the reason I asked you to honor me by being my wife! You are beautiful beyond belief, and I can't say I'm sorry that you are! But your beauty~there's so much more to it~than people see~who don't care to see it~ Remember, the words of Jesus in:

Matthew 7:6 Give not that which is holy unto dogs, neither cast ye your pearls before the swine, lest they trample them under their feet, and turn again and rend you.

There's no point sharing your heart and feelings with those determined to drag them in their dirt!"

He approached and pulled her near! "We have something amazingly beautiful! The children don't grasp it; they make it what they're familiar with! They are still vulgar because that is how they've been allowed to be! They know things far beyond their years, but not with a holy light shone upon it! We can't demand that they be different and be something beyond their capacity of the moment! We must show more than saying~" His eyes riveted hers to his own! "And you don't have to convince me! I'm happy to provide some of the material things you have been denied! Please, wipe away the tears and join us all for dinner~"

Chapter 25: PERFORMANCE

Daniel sat back-stage in the guest dressing room! With tuning and warming up behind him, he sat waiting his cue to come on-stage! He felt strangely calm! So calm that he worried about not being more nervous! What was wrong with him? He had practiced! He knew the material; the rehearsals with the orchestra had gone smoothly! Now the moment was nearly here! To face his diminutive fan club, and a whole slew of critics! Not sure if it was the peace of God or sheer stupidity, he surveyed his reflection calmly! Past due for a haircut; but a fresh one would have looked worse! Flecks of gray showed decidedly at his temples! The new tuxedo supplied by *DiaMal* was a dream! Flattering fit, but free range of motion! He thought he might have picked up a couple of Tux orders for the company: one from one of the civic leaders who presided over the symphony association, and another from one of the musicians! A light tap at the door, and it was curtain time!

彐 彑

Brad poured coffee into a Styrofoam cup and slunk to his cubicle! The closed door of Faulkner's inner sanctum let him know the boss was in! Bright and early, without taking time to savor taking the Tulsa musical world by storm the previous night! How could one man have it so much together? He stared at his favorite fern! Drooping pathetically! Evidently no one showed mercy to it in his absence at sea! He was debating with himself whether or not to sally forth for some water-or pronounce it dead!

The office door opened, and he bent his head over his attaché case.

"Maxwell!"

"Sir?" The response barely scraped out! Mouth drier than the potting soil, he rose, "Yes, Sir! Good morning!"

Brown eyes flicked across him, not missing a thing! "You have a report for me?"

Brad's hands fumbled with the thick document, and he thrust it toward his employer!

⚑ ⚑

Alexandra greeted everyone as they showed up for breakfast! With the worst of her injury behind her, she made the best of the time remaining until she could give the boot, the boot, once and for all! Although she was able to balance a tray on her lap and select her own breakfast, she allowed Janni to help her! Janni was a blessing, as was the motorized chair, and the paths and ramps that made her able to negotiate her mining village! She attacked a stack of bacon and syrup-laden French toast hungrily!

She smiled as Gray passed her, carrying glasses of milk for Emily and Misty! Brenna's absence must mean she was fighting morning sickness! Al had no problem with that, because her contracted Geologist spent every minute on the job she could! And she was good!

Jared appeared, with Pick and several of the other miners! "Finally ready to start blasting!"

She nodded, surveying her domain blissfully! Finally! And her dad had helped her understand why the mining engineer didn't have any kind of bead on her location the day of her disappearance! She smiled, remembering his words.

"Mining Engineers aren't Geologists, Al! They can't find a vein of ore any better than the three blind mice can!"

She laughed, thinking about it! "Geologists read the rocks and find the deposits! Then they lead the Mining Engineers to the cliff face and say, 'Blast here!' And then they're put in charge of the mining operation! Blasting, heavy equipment, logistics of transporting ore, processing-establishing and running the mine, itself!"

She roused from her thoughts. A totally different discipline! Like the Agriculture course she had started and failed in- Brenna didn't think she needed to tell her daddy about the fiasco, but she wasn't convinced! The tuition left a good chunk of change unaccounted for!

꙳ ꙳

Brad stiffened involuntarily when his intercom buzzed. The boss!

"Yes, Sir?"

Across the desk, he cringed as Faulkner raised his attention from the report! "What is all this? That a tree sacrificed its life over? And a waste of your time and mine! I knew the details of the shooting incident! I want a log of where you drilled and what you found prior to this point in time! This has not one word of a Geological report, whatsoever!"

"Well, Sir, there wasn't any prior drilling- We were, Brenton and I, were on deck, getting ready to send the bit down for the first time! It-uh-seems as if everyone on board knew we were over the Trench, but me!"

"Okay, so you're telling me that you were on site a day and a half-"

Brad nodded miserably! "Yes, Sir! I had no clue that there are charts of the ocean floor! I didn't know that was what Mallory Anderson went by with her exploration-"

Daniel couldn't believe it! "Did it not occur to you to call someone, if you were that lost in the sauce?"

"It did, but-Dr. Stone was my faculty advisor! My mind's still blown at him offing himself! And I considered contacting either Mallory or Brenna-but I didn't think their husbands would be real crazy about me calling them! So, finally, I figured one place must be as good as another-"

Daniel sat staring in disbelief!

Brad plunged ahead. "I know anything I say will sound lame, but my studies have been pretty concentrated on the thirty percent of the earth's surface that's not covered by oceans! Listen, I'm not sure when I started wanting to be a Geologist, but I did! Both my father and grandfather disapproved of my plans! It's their automatic response to me! They said all the valuable stuff's been discovered, and I should major in business, because manipulating paperwork is the only way to make money anymore!"

Daniel's frown deepened! He was still irked, for one thing, about the kid's showing up with his grandfather at the symphony! A sure way to see Al, and be noticed by her!

Figuring he was buried anyway, Brad continued. "So, I have a passion about being a Geologist, and being a good one! I wanted to get on with a big firm someplace, as field Geologist! I wasn't sure about starting my own company! I'm not sure I'm that much of a ground-breaker–if you'll excuse the pun!"

When there was no answering smile, Brad cringed. Evidently Faulkner was in no mood for excusing anything!

"Anyway, I always heard that when companies get ready to hire, they look at more than academics! Things like tardiness and absenteeism! I never cut any classes and I never slept through any of them! For those reasons, I know I didn't just skip class the day they addressed the oceans! I'm a grad student, but as I look back, I see just how much of my academic time was monopolized by the same rant Stone was on at Prescott that night! I mean, everyone believes in Evolution already– what was he so scared of?"

But, everyone doesn't believe it!" Faulkner spoke softly, "You're right about how the same thing is drummed into people's heads, constantly! And it isn't education; it's indoctrination! Propaganda that brooks no contradiction! And it has wasted your time, as well as making you seriously misinformed!"

"Well, surely, you don't believe in the Creationism myths!" Brad's amazement brought forth the quick retort!

"No, I believe in Creation! It's not a myth; Evolutionism's the myth! And in answer to your question, what they are afraid of, is The TRUTH!"

Brad sat, at a loss for words as Faulkner shoved the thick file across the desk toward him!

⊰ ⊱

With the preliminary forensic report in on the tatters of the raft, FBI Agent, Erik Bransom picked up his phone! Circumstantial! He hated the fact that Halsey and Pritchard were free on bond while they awaited trial for corporate espionage, and their endangering Brenna Prescott in the earlier incident with the *Rock Scientist*! Now, they were also on the board of directors for the shell company owning the ship that fired on *The Rock Scientist*– Investigation unearthed records of *The Porpoise Paradise*, registered in the Bahamas as a deep-sea fishing, day excursion boat! With no sign of her appearing at any port of call since the incident, Eric wondered if she had been scuttled! Wherever Halsey and Pritchard's names appeared, bad stuff seemed to follow! He didn't believe it was coincidental! Those two should be behind bars, permanently!

⇥ ⇤

Brenna sat with Alexandra following breakfast, where they plotted their recent discoveries. Gray and David had worked out a vehicle that could traverse the mud, modifying it to comfortably accommodate the orthopedic boot! The two Geologists discussed their target for today's exploration! Brenna tried to mask her frustration when Alex asked if he could join them! Like he could make up for a lifetime of absenteeism by forcing his presence on her this week! Sure enough, Al excused herself, leaving Brenna awkwardly alone with the man!

"Sorry; didn't mean to interrupt your conference! It's a beautiful day! Are you going on the Narrow Gauge Train ride?"

"I'm not! I have too much to do here! The kids are excited at the prospect, though! What about you? Did Gray ask you along?" She hoped he planned to accompany everyone else on the outing.

"He asked me! I thought I might be able to make myself useful to you girls!"

"Well, that's nice, but our findings are quite confidential!" She realized she sounded terse, but it was true! She waved as Mallory appeared with her three daughters. Melodye appeared a couple of minutes later, pushing the baby in a stroller! With plates for everyone in hand, Mallory asked to join them! With practiced ease, she settled the kids in with their food before pausing and praying!

"You're all out and dressed up bright and early!" Alex was a personable man! "Are you going down to take the train ride?"

"I wish! It sounds like fun! I definitely want to work that in sometime before the season ends! We're going over to Marble today! It's kind of a slow drive, so we're taking the chopper! What about you? Are you joining the tourist crowd?"

"I haven't decided; I'm trying to convince Brenna to let me tag along!"

Mallory hesitated. "I guess it's Alexandra that you'd have to convince! And she's not the push-over you might assume! Why don't you join us? There's room in the chopper! We're going to check on the marble quarry, get lunch there, and be back mid-afternoon!"

To Brenna's immense relief, he accepted the offer eagerly!

⇥ ⇤

Brad scowled! Accessing a Bible on his computer was easy, and locating the book called Romans didn't take too long! He reread the first chapter, feeling more disturbed and confused than ever! He backed up to verse eighteen and read to the end again!

Romans 1:18-32 For the wrath of God is revealed from heaven against all ungodliness and unrighteousness of men, who hold the truth in unrighteousness;

Because that which may be known of God is manifest in them; for God hath shewed it unto them.

For the invisible things of him from the creation of the world are clearly seen, being understood by the things that are made, even his eternal power and Godhead; so that they are without excuse:

Because that, when they knew God, they glorified him not as God, neither were thankful; but became vain in their imaginations, and their foolish heart was darkened.

Professing themselves to be wise, they became fools,

And changed the glory of the uncorruptible God into an image made like to corruptible man, and to birds, and fourfooted beasts, and creeping things.

Wherefore, God also gave them up to uncleanness through the lusts of their own hearts, to dishonour their bodies between themselves:

Who changed the truth of God into a lie, and worshipped and served the creature more than the Creator, who is blessed for ever. Amen.

For this cause God gave them up unto vile affections: for even their women did change the natural use into that which is against nature:

And likewise also the men, leaving the natural use of the woman, burned in their lust one toward another; men working with men that which is unseemly, and receiving in themselves that recompense of their error which was meet.

And even as they did not like to retain God in their knowledge, God gave them over to a reprobate mind, to do those things which are not convenient;

Being filled with all unrighteousness, fornication, wickedness, covetousness, maliciousness; full of envy, murder, debate, deceit, malignity; whisperers,

Backbiters, haters of God, despiteful, proud, boasters, inventors of evil things, disobedient to parents,

Without understanding, covenant breakers, without natural affection, implacable, unmerciful:

Who knowing the judgment of God, that they which commit such things are worthy of death, not only do the same, but have pleasure in them that do them.

Rage rippled across him! 'What? Faulkner thinks I'm gay? In that case, he wouldn't need to keep me away from his daughter! But the context of their conversation had been about Evolutionism vs. Creationism!' He stared, still mostly baffled. So what was it saying? That Creation was obvious and people tried to explain it away? Purposely turned from facts to build their own construct? One they liked better; that enabled them to do whatever they pleased? And the wrath of God was against all unrighteousness, and people who turned from the truth! *The wrath of God!* That had always just been an expression to him! But there were so many other religions, with the books they espoused. Who could say one was any more right than another? And religious people were just weaklings who needed a crutch! Right?

A presence, suddenly at the entrance of his cubicle, brought a smiling mask down over raging emotions! Not fast enough though!

"Are you okay?" The lilting question sounded more Continental than Oklahoman! He knew the vivacious girl from the symphony!

He found his voice! "Wonderful~uh~er~performance~"

"Thank you! You changed the subject! I asked if you're okay!"

"Yeah, I'm fine! Well, are you ever scared~uh~like~of~dying?"

With an impish smile she responded, "Only when my sister drives me through the mountains! Then I'm extra-grateful for my salvation! You must be Brad! The sharks~did they really~"

He felt alarm when she entered his small space! Faulkner wouldn't like it!

"Yeah, they really did," he muttered!

She perched on the opposite corner of his desk and pulled his laptop around so she could view his work! Definitely not shy!

Suddenly, Faulkner stood there, frowning!

"Cassandra, what are you doing?"

She straightened, easing from her perch! "I came down town to get my hair cut, but then I wondered if you have time for lunch! And I asked if you were busy, and they said you were on a call~" her lilting voice trailed off before his stern expression!

Totally shocked and off-guard, Daniel wasn't sure exactly what to do!

"There are chairs over there for you to sit in; you don't have to disturb people who are working! Go in my office!"

His wrath turned on the hapless grad student! "My father told me he had to run you out of the conference room~"

"Well, Amy said it's not scheduled for anything, and I needed room to spread out the map~"

Fury shot through the executive! This kid wasn't happy with his cubicle? He needed to take the whole place over? And what was his attraction to both Al and Cass'?

"Okay, why don't you start focusing on someplace other than Colorado? I hear you're interested in purchasing property there?"

"Not seriously. It's just that I talked to Tim this morning!"

Daniel's jaw muscles tightened.

"Well, Sir, I'm kind of worried about what their plans were! David and Gray got hold of an all-terrain vehicle so Alexandra doesn't have to be left behind! So, she, Brenna, and Tim are headed into the higher elevations. But it's suddenly warmer in the mountains, speeding the snow melt, and there are flash flood alerts! And Brenna and Tim might be able to make it to high ground-if-but Alexandra-with her ankle and needing to stay on the ATV-"

Daniel's wrath gave way to alarm!

※ ※

David disconnected and signaled a course reversal to the chopper pilot! "Possibility of flash floods!" he explained to a startled Mallory. "There was so much snow this winter, and now, with the warming trend- That was Faulkner! He wants us to get Alexandra evacuated! Well, I'm sure he meant everyone-"

※ ※

Brad pulled up at the Tulsa Performing Arts Center. Having checked the Symphony's web-site, he knew he could hear the entire concert again on one of the local stations! Curious, though, he wondered if DVD's might be available!

His thoughts were jumbled! His employer had taken Cassandra in tow and made a hasty exit! Hopefully, he had changed Alexandra's plans, and ordered her to safety, first!

As Brad entered the Mathews Building, he focused his thoughts on the symphony performance! Never too much for classical music before, he figured it was time to change! And Daniel Faulkner was good! Even to Brad's unpracticed ear! And his grandfather, cynical and not moved by much, had sat enraptured throughout every note and nuance! A smile crossed the young man's face fleetingly as he remembered the guest violinist's being granted the honor of directing the entire orchestra! He could still see Faulkner, poised, waiting-if he were directing-which violinist was on cue to perform the solo? Practically unflappable, he had recovered smoothly when Cassandra stepped into the spotlight! And the crowd went wild!

His thoughts traveled to Alexandra in her motorized chair! She was improving, thankfully! So beautiful in a peach colored lace suit! Although he and his grandfather had attended the Post-Concert Reception, Brad had kept his distance. Cassandra was cute; amazing talent and poise for her young age! There it was again! He was back in his cubicle reading the agonizing words from the Bible-whatever they meant, he tried to escape from them! He cursed his photographic memory! *Worshipped and served the creature,* and what did it mean *that the invisible things of him from the creation are clearly seen*...How on earth could something invisible be clearly seen! If things are invisible, you can't see them! And if they are 'clearly seen' then they're not invisible! It was an oxymoron at best! Silliness! He should shake it off! *The wrath of God! The wrath of God!*

And Americans don't worship and serve creatures! Most of us are anti-religious! We don't worship cows as the people of India reportedly do! So, maybe we don't worship the Creator as we should–we're pretty sure there isn't one...

Professing themselves to be wise, they became fools, 'Was that Dr. Stone, with his mad-man ranting'?

Gaining his car, he bore down on the accelerator out of Tulsa!

⚔ ⚔

The miners were slow to move, almost mocking David's desperate attempts to evacuate at the very real possibility of wide-spread flooding!

⚔ ⚔

Alarm shot through Gray as the train station PA announced that the train was canceled due to flooding of the tracks! Panicked, he placed a call to Brenna. Relief left him limp when she told him they were en route to Durango!

⚔ ⚔

Daniel sat moodily in his home office! He shoved aside a stack of newspapers! He knew Diana had put them there, so she could clip the reviews of his concert performance! Well, his and Cass's! How she had taken the crowd by storm! Was that what happened to her? Too much adoration went straight to her head? He wasn't even upset at Maxwell for this one! It was all Cass, invading the cubicle, sitting on the small desk-top, basically cornering the man! He thought she was too young and naïve to really know what she was doing–but–she wouldn't be returning to Israel for a while! Obviously, she needed more restraint than she received from Lilly!

So, she wouldn't be sitting comfortably on desktops, or anywhere else for that matter, any time soon! And she was losing some privileges! Of course, then, her special bond with her younger brother, Xavier, meant that he basically sided with her!

He nearly laughed when he perused the top review! Faulkner was great, pretty much as expected! And then, since adding *Amazing Grace* to the repertoire had enhanced a certain European director's popularity, the Tulsa orchestra had encouraged Faulkner to perform one of his favorite gospel songs! His choice: *It Takes a Storm*! The reviewer went on to mock the song and the pathos infused by the gifted violinist!

> *Although Jeremiah Daniel Faulkner III, born to a socialite Tulsa family, with the proverbial silver spoon in his mouth, surely has never faced any storms~*

He slid to his knees! "Lord, you know I've faced storms! You know I'm facing them now! I have a drilling foreman dead, because of my actions! I'm not sure how much that liability and the damage to the *Rock Scientist* will be~ And I'm at my wit's end about Maxwell~ Thank you that most people don't know I'm going through storms! That I bring them to You~and try not to blab~my problems around to anybody and everybody! Thank You, for the good reviews, and the not-so-good-ones, too! Thank You for the gifts You have given me! You know I want to honor and glorify You! I need so much help and wisdom with my kids, Lord! Thank you for giving Brad Maxwell the sense to foresee the flood danger!"

Chapter 26: DISASTER

Trent Morrison stared, horrified, at the raging water below the Forestry Service helicopter! Barely able to evacuate a campground in the path of the torrent, he felt deep responsibility for any solitary hikers or fishermen!

A cry escaped! Suddenly disoriented, he strove to get his bearings! It couldn't be!

"Wow, that old ranch is totally gone!" One of the Rangers speaking, "Doesn't it now belong to that girl that was lost up here a few weeks back? Hope the county got everyone warned in time!"

Trent leaned back, dazed, skin white behind sunglasses! He freed his cell phone! His voice wouldn't come when Daniel Faulkner's voice answered his call!

"Hey, Trent; what's up?"

Daniel was afraid of the call's ominous portent! He thought that David had time to halt the planned excursion and find a safe place for everyone on high ground! Now the strange timing of Trent's call left him waiting breathlessly for word he might never be able to bear!

"Trent! Trent!" Panic filled Daniel's voice! Maybe the call was one of those unintentional-

At last Trent found his voice! "Hey, I'm back in Colorado, finishing with the criminal investigation! Uh, there's some sudden, severe flooding-have you heard from Alexan-"

"Not for a while! I got word that there might be some flash flooding, so I was able to get in touch with David! They-they're all supposed to evacuate! What does it look like up there?"

Trent's tone, soft and somber, came with heart-rending slowness! "Doesn't look good! All of the infrastructure's gone! County Road's washed out! If-if they all made it to safety, it doesn't look good for mining any time soon!"

Daniel rocked back on his heels in shock! "Well, the ranch buildings were kind of old-"

"Yeah, uh-their entire new mining village-is-gone-too! You just can't believe-the force of-Why don't you call-and then get back with me-let me know if we need a-search and rescue-"

Trent cut off, suddenly infuriated! "What's that guy doing up here? Contact him on the radio and tell him to put down! Unless he's part of a coordinated search and rescue, he shouldn't be up today!"

The pilot met his gaze, equally disgusted! "You are absolutely right! Looks like an aerial scout for looters! People never cease to amaze me!"

⁂

"Hi, Daddy! We made it to Durango and got some rooms; just in time! I think every room in town is taken! We're all okay, though! We're kind of crowding into the rooms we got, and Uncle Gray came in his RV and David and Mallory are in theirs! Stuff on TV looks pretty scary: I hope I don't have too much-damage-"

"Well, if everyone's safe, that's the main thing!" Diana's relief-filled voice inserted itself!

Daniel stared at her like she was an alien! Good point, but beyond that, Al's mining opportunities were shot! The devastating news would hit her like a thunderbolt! Idly, he handled the newspaper section that still lay on his desk! 'Oh, yes,' he reminded himself sulkily, 'I'm the *silver spoon* guy who's never known a day of adversity! What do I know about storms; right?'

⁂

David and Gray sprang into action! "Okay, you girls and the kids, stay inside the hotel!"

David noted the panic in Mallory's eyes! "We think the hotel is safer for the time being than the RV's! I'll haul in whatever you need me to!"

"I need to do some laundry-"

He kissed her firmly! "It'll have to wait! We'll probably be until past dark! Promise us you'll just stay put!"

Brenna spoke up, "Okay, but promise us you'll be careful! It's not just the high water, but if there really are looters~"

"Yeah," David's dark eyes, intense as he spoke. "Trent located some of our stuff downstream, deposited by the water! Alexandra's office safe, for one thing! Actually still seems to be sealed up tight! And some of Gray's heavy equipment, a little worse for the wear~Whatever we can find and salvage, the better off we'll be! Especially if we can get the equipment operational! It'll be more in demand than ever for cleaning up!"

Mallory nodded agreement! Maybe the outlook for the mining season wouldn't be as dismal as Trent's original assessment! If they all got busy right away! "Okay, I'll call the insurance company~"

⚐ ⚑

Brenna and Mallory scoured the piles of refuse left behind by the raging flood waters! Wielding metal detectors, they found small and large appliances, parts ripped from vehicles, electronics! Plenty of salvageable materials! The item they sought was a small jewelry safe from the Anderson's modular home containing the *Imperial Crown* set recently crafted by Herb Carlton, and which Mallory had worn for the Tulsa Symphony performance! Since she always wore her wedding set and the spectacular Diamond solitaire ring from her father, those items were still in her possession! Everything was insured~whatever that might mean! Hopefully they could recover the jewelry!

Brenna moved cheerfully, despite forbidding mud and huge heaps of debris! With as much tragedy as nature's events could bring, there was always that thrilling flip side! She recalled the example of Hurricane Mitch, which had hit Central America in 1998! A devastating level five category, but the flooding and resulting mud slides in Guatemala later revealed a fabulous jadeite find! And more recently, raging forest fires in the area surrounding Mesa Verde, Colorado exposed previously unknown cliff dwellings! She was certain that these receding waters were leaving untold riches scoured from the higher elevations!

And David saw treasure in every item he encountered! Well, the ruined electronics would be on their way to the plant down in Durango that mined gold from the discarded gadgets and also recycled plastic and other components! In addition to the jobs it created! The lumber, some of which was smashed and broken, still found its way onto a 'keep' pile!

Gray cleaned up long enough to meet with FEMA officials about how much priority the washed out county road would have! The answer was a laugh; not surprisingly! Hardly deterred, he returned to his RV! How fortuitous that he had overlooked Alex Hamilton's facetious remarks-that Gray was an old maid type of guy, so consequently, the only reason Brenna might have consented to marry him was his money! Yeah- Money! And it was on the line now-Not like he was totally made of the stuff! This mining season must be salvaged-at all costs! And everyone seemed to be in agreement about the urgency! So, back to his consideration of his newly-found father-in-law, Alex! A civil engineer! They would simply have to rebuild the washed out road, themselves!

Back in Colorado, Trent marveled at the progress the miners were making in recovery and rebuilding of their village!

With the loss of her herd, her cattle barn, and her fiasco into studying agriculture, Alexandra decided it was a sign from the Lord to pursue her original intention of Geological exploration and mining! Her dad's response when she had confessed the attempted classes, was that he would prefer she gain a working knowledge of accounting! Still, he gave her a break on that, allowing her a hiatus from course work until snowfall, when the mine would face some slowdowns!

Within three weeks, the village was restored with new and improved pre-builts! Sod and flowers took hold, and security fences surrounded both the upper and lower properties! As soon as the road was completed, trucks should begin hauling ore! A makeshift store in Silverton displayed some salvaged items! One of the neighbors met Norma's gaze sadly!

"I'm pretty sure that's my Remington! But if I had my bill of sale on it, it washed away with everything else! I don't have any proof!"

"Yeah, you clean it up, it'll be okay," Norma agreed! "If you think it's yours, it probably is!"

Happy, the local went on his way, his prized gun in hand, deciding the newcomers were okay!

Gray and Tim patiently listed salvaged car parts on their web site! From engines, transmissions, differentials, lots and lots of tires in different sizes! Fifty percent of the sales of car parts went into a community fund to assist those hit the hardest, and who had the least ability for recovering! Of the remaining half, Gray tithed before reinvesting the remainder! His heavy equipment, dried out and restored, was in demand constantly by other landholders cleaning up from the disaster! He sent Tim to Grand Junction, the largest city on the Western Slope, in search of more machinery to purchase! He was still hoping for a prospecting boom, once the emergency passed!

With everyone reassembled in the chow hall for the first time, emotions ran high! Brenna sat proudly next to Gray, and even managed a smile when her father entered! She could tell he was trying, but somehow it seemed like too little, too late! Besides which, every time she saw him, she was reminded again of the sad story of the last Imperial Tsar of Russia~ had Anna Anderson really been the long-lost princess? Or a clever trickster? She tried not to think about it! How even your own family might sell you out for money~

Gray's expression turned from beaming smile to worry. "Feeling sick again?"

Strange, she wasn't! Until his question! With the power of suggestion, she bolted!

Back in place, she loaded her plate: cheeseburger with everything, fries, and pork n beans!

Gray shook his head wonderingly!

"I know!" she laughed. "If it seems weird to you, you should experience it from my side! Um~uh~to change the subject~have you ever heard of this lady named Anna Anderson?"

His quizzical eyes met hers! "Strange you should ask me that! From my short time of schooling in jolly old England, I grew captivated by European royalty! Although the denials of the woman still continue decades after her death, I find her story entirely plausible! And Rasputin! There's a controversial man!"

She frowned. "I guess you lost me~"

She listened, captivated, as Gray filled her in with hair raising tales!

"I actually never liked history that much," she admitted, "But you make it interesting!"

He laughed. "Really! Well, it might surprise you to know that there's a whole world out there besides your preoccupation with rocks!"

She smiled and rolled her eyes! "So, what's your assessment of Rasputin? I mean, I guess preachers getting caught up in the lust of the flesh isn't anything new! Where do you think his mystical powers came from? I mean, surely not from God!"

Humor-filled eyes held hers!

"It's a strange bit of a conundrum; is it not? Firstly, God has no perfect men to engage in His work! We are, the lot of us, weak and prone to the flesh! I notice a verse from the Pentateuch each time I read my Bible through, about the Princes of Israel, digging a well! Using their staves! Seriously, if one needs a well dug, Princes wouldn't be considered typical hard workers, who put their backs into the digging! And one would hope for a high-powered bore; but if not that, at least a good shovel or spade! A walking staff is a poor tool, and a prince is a poor one to do manual labor! And yet in the verse I reference, God caused the waters to spring up! It's a beautiful picture of how God uses, blesses, and magnifies our poor efforts! As for Rasputin, it's hard to say! His power might have come from God, although, Satan specializes in counterfeits! It's plausible that he was satanically granted some very limited power! There's also the possibility, that the Mystic was a talented con man!"

"But he made the Tsarevich better; isn't that what you said?"

"That's how the story goes, and of course we believe in the power of prayer! And there's no denying the man was vilified, as was the entire royal court, in order to overthrow the monarchy and bring the Bolsheviks to power!"

She sighed. "You know, I bought in with Socialistic thought, hook, line and sinker! We were so poor, and I thought it totally unfair for anyone to have great wealth in the face of such need!"

"I didn't tell you about an episode of Daniel and my meddling one day, with the Tulsa city government! We were on a mission! That we were convinced would be hailed as the greatest to come along! We went down to try to get that extended stay place shut down!"

"Sounds good to me! What happened?"

"Well, we met first with the PD chief of detectives, to try to find out how often the PD is forced to respond! The answer! They maintain a presence there! They know everything we know about the place-a thousand times over-"

"So, why don't they do something-"

"That's just it! They do! And the detective couldn't help making a jibe at Daniel! That they manage to maintain relative order down there, without having to shoot anyone dead! Several years ago, when the property was a low end hotel, Daniel drove Trent Morrison out there! When a threesome approached Morrison with a hustle, Daniel ended up shooting the man! It was arguably a necessary move. To prevent a robbery-" He broke off with a perplexed shrug- "Next, we approached the Health department! Maybe at least the plumbing issues would condemn the place!"

Brenna's indignation flared. "Yes, you would think-"

"The spokesperson for the health department told us our option was to report the business to the BBB! Which, good luck with that, you can't even get through their phone menu to make a report!"

"So, that's it? They can just keep doing business as usual?"

Gray laughed. "Yeah, basically! Finally the city manager called Daniel and met with us! See, we want to close down places that are eyesores that offend us in our lofty perches! But rundown apartment complexes, aging trailer parks, high crime areas, low-income places like that, are the last ditch effort for thousands to avoid homelessness! We both kind of slunk out of city hall with our proverbial tails tucked between our legs!"

So, really there's no solution?"

"Of course; Jesus is still the answer! As surely as restoring of sight is a remedy for blindness; so also, is the preaching of the Gospel to the poor the remedy for poverty! The church is failing sadly, in its mandate!"

Brenna frowned as Tim entered and took a place near Alexandra!

Gray picked up on it, "What, you don't think those two would be fitting for each other?"

"Okay, you know your niece! She wouldn't give Tim Alvaredo the time of day-"

"They seem quite cozy enough!"

"She's using him!" Brenna's impatience surfaced! "She's stuck on Brad Maxwell, unless I totally miss my guess! Since Daniel warned her about Brad, I think she at least pretends to be towing the line! I think she pumps Tim about Brad, and he's so dumb, he just enjoys having something to say to her that she finds interesting!"

"What's your take on Mr. Maxwell? I had a concern the night of your class, that you fancied him!"

Her beautiful face broke into a pleased smile! "Did you really? Uh-No- of course he tried to use his lady-killer lines on me, but I've heard them all before! He reminded me of the Boston University grad students I used to wait on! Between those guys and their phony personas, and the men my mother paraded through our lives, I determined to steer clear of men forever! I mean, my father seems to have been the best of the lot-"

Gray nodded understanding!

"Thank you for contacting him and inviting him here~" She paused, fighting emotion!

"So, you were determined to be a man-hater?" Gray prodded humorously, although he felt a sudden vulnerability.

She laughed! "Not exactly! Just a man-avoider; steering clear of emotional entanglements! Even after I received the Lord and started going to church; I sensed that even some of the 'happily married' family men~uh~sent out vibes~"

"You are incredibly beautiful~"

"So, it's my fault?"

He shrugged, and she continued, "That morning you chased me down; uh~I seriously believed you just wanted to talk to me about the packet! And apply sales pressure to me~so I had my defenses up as to why I couldn't hire your financial services~I was blind-sided when you asked me to marry you instead!"

"Ah, so I very cleverly made you deploy your defenses in one area, and then I slid right into the undefended position! I had no realization I'm so remarkably clever!"

"You were so honest and straight-forward, and different! Not different like odd, but different like refreshingly so! And you were mature, both as a Christian, and a well-educated man! I thought I was learning to trust God, but I guess I still didn't credit Him with being able to provide~so exceeding abundantly above all~"

⌟ ⌞

Alexandra gave up on sleep! Scooting up, she turned on her bedside lamp! According to Tim Alvaredo, Brad was really interested in her! When he tried to focus on tasks; her smile played in his mind?! He could hardly think of anything else~She ran his image through the motion picture screen of her mind! Thick, dark hair, dark long lashes rimming incredibly blue eyes! Nice build! A little bit taller wouldn't hurt! He probably measured in at just under six fecaet! She sighed dreamily! Nice, high-dollar, ivy league style in clothing~probably didn't own a suit, but her mom could take care of that! She sighed! He had to get saved! Or her dad and mom would never agree~already her dad was trying to put space between them~lots and lots of space! She reran the short mental video of seeing Brad and his grandfather at the post-symphony reception! Frowning, she recalled her mom's pulling her gently toward Mallory to view the gorgeous jewelry suite! (One that thankfully, had been recovered!) A diversion tactic! 'Nicely played, you guys,' she whispered into the silence of her room! 'I'm not a little kid anymore~' closing her eyes, she went back to the night when Brad had rescued her! She could still feel strong and warm arms enfolding her as he carried her down toward the ranch. Her arms twined about his neck; his occasional soft kisses falling along her hairline! She was in love! And so was Brad!

⚔ ⚔

David sat at the short kitchen counter in the small modular home! Early, he poured himself a cup of coffee! Moving softly, he retrieved his Bible from the cramped office he shared with Mallory! He had relapsed to reading sporadically, trying to excuse his oversight by explaining to the Lord that he had too much going on! And there wasn't anybody else quite as smart, talented, or capable, for him to entrust the endless tasks to! With a frustrated sigh, he allowed the volume to fall open! Smirking to himself, he knew his dad would never approve the haphazardness! But his dad wasn't here, and he didn't have to tell him! He winced: this was the reason he should have made an orderly choice! The book of Job! He never read it! Probably, he had waded through the entirety of the other sixty-five books, but the thought of reading this particular book scared him!

Job! Even before he scanned the first lines of the first chapter, he knew the crux of the story! Job was a great Christian man, full of wisdom, and greatly blessed in all of the material realms~until the devil challenged God about Job's sincerity! That if Job lost everything, he would curse God and stop following Him! David couldn't bear the thought of losing everything he and Mallory were working so hard at building up! Just the losses from the flood were terrible! He paused to pray for favorable insurance settlements! With a wry grin, he wondered how Job made it without insurance claims!

'Yeah, Lord,' he admitted inwardly! 'There really isn't any insurance; no guarantees of anything outside of Your promises' He willed himself to read, speed reading, skipping through~most of it he was familiar with~from sermons delivered by men who seemed to like the narrative better than he did! He resisted tiptoeing to his sleeping children's bedsides because he didn't want them awake this early! He couldn't imagine the horror of losing one of them! Much less all of them in one swoop! He thanked God again, that Brad Maxwell had foreseen the possibility of mountain flooding, in time to mention it to Faulkner, in time to call him, and all of them reach safety in Durango! A string of coincidences? Definitely not, but this was his first time to consider the miraculous nature of their deliverance! He paused as lines jumped from the delicate paper and seared into his brain:

Job 33:27 & 28 He looketh upon men, and if any say, I have sinned, and perverted that which was right and it profited me not;

He will deliver his soul from going into the pit, and his life shall see the light.

He sat, considering the words. Of course, he had sinned! According to the Bible, all people were sinners by sin nature! Then, even after receiving Christ, God's children still sinned! Even Christians who tried hardest to please Him, failed; needing daily confession and restoration of fellowship!

"But, Lord, this is really true of me! When I started to rebel against You in high school, nothing from that time period was profitable at all! I'm just ashamed of being such a moron! Thank You for deliverance from the pit, and for giving the light You readily shine on those receptive to it! Forgive me for being careless in my walk with You, and for taking Mallory so for granted! Please safeguard and protect what You have given to us-"

꒿ ꒦

Brenna handed Gray a stack of mail. "It looks like Millard and his grandmother are settled into their new place!"

Smiling, he reached for the letter and photographs. "Yes, the initial payment for the game concept should fund this month, too!" Concern wiped away the smile crinkles. "Have you an idea what Jacob plans, once he becomes independently wealthy? Legally of age, I hold no recourse-"

She sighed, afraid her well-intentioned spouse was about to really get hurt in return for his kindness! "I'm not sure! He may want to go back to Somerville, so he and Millard can live it up together! He's just been on his own course for so long-"

"Quite right! Quite right!" Gray rose, pushing the troublesome thoughts aside! "You look positively splendid this morning!" He patted her tummy affectionately. "Don't worry for me, Love! God has given me a family to love! Whether I receive love or gratitude in response, is quite beside the point! The important thing, though~" he broke off~

"Is their getting saved," she finished. "It's like everything I've tried to explain since I got saved, has fallen on deaf ears! And Alex isn't interested, either! He's totally put off about religion~due in part, to my grandfather's disowning my mother! I guess, it basically killed my grandmother, when Richard forbade her to contact~how can good Christians disown their own flesh and blood?"

Gray debated with himself before answering. Not wishing to air his family's dirty laundry, but seeking an honest relationship with his beautiful wife, he plunged in~

"My father~er~disowned~Diana~"

"Diana? Whatever for~are you~kidding~"

"No, Love, totally serious!"

"A~about Daniel?" Brenna recalled Gray's enthralling family saga related to her on that first day~

"He was the worst sort!" The words spewed forcefully! "But Diana couldn't see it! Reason was gone, and just stars in the eyes; you know?"

"And~and, your father just disowned her~like that?" Brenna's shock echoed in their small room.

"Well, 'not, just like that'! It rocked on for a while~because Daniel made a profession of faith~and because she wouldn't listen~ They married and he stole her away to Tulsa! Where he continued with his old tricks! Her, thousands of miles from we who loved her~she~uh~miscarried their first child! But he didn't care! Living for himself! That's why he's no use for Maxwell, now, to come sniffing about at Alexandra!"

Brenna sank sympathetically next to him! "So then what?" her question was soft.

He sat quietly, lost in memories. At last he resumed the narrative, "Then, Diana completed a successful pregnancy, and Alexandra was born! Eager to show her off, they came to Africa to visit us! That's when Daniel got that fever and hemorrhaging the second time! Once again, he nearly died! We hoped God had his attention after the first bout! Father held little hope that, 'the leopard could change his spots'! He and mother pled with Diana to stay with the baby; and not to go back with him! But Diana nursed him through the illness again, with no thought for her own exposure; and as soon as he was strong enough to travel~ Mother~Mother's heart was broken; what made Father's reaction so strong!"

Tears flowed down both their cheeks, and he patted her hand! "My father and mother are the finest Christians I've ever known! Did they handle it correctly? I've never ascertained! Don't make your grandfather out into too much of a villain! If he strove with all he had within him, to rear obedient Christian children, to be dealt rebellion~" A deep sigh~ "I don't know, Brenna! Your memory wants to keep your love for your mother intact, and blame Richard for your life! And your father! Things just are not that simple! We'll pray for your Alex to see beyond the faulty Christians he has known, and see the Savior!"

Chapter 27: *ANNOUNCEMENT*

Gray stood in the middle of the living room, his family seated around him! Absently, he noticed the cheap carpeting, totally ruined by heavy traffic and mud! The place already looked well lived in! Of course, Chauncey was also responsible for damage! From Jacob down to Misty, the children sat with heads lowered, intent with electronic devices~or whatever else they could find to focus on!

"Children, Brenna and I have an announcement to make!" Not one eye raised his direction, but he was accustomed to addressing the crowns of their heads! "Brenna and I are with child!"

The only response was a snicker!

"Yes," Gray continued, undeterred, "I'm sure you have all been aware from the get-go! Not much escapes you! You are all very intelligent, and of course with the nausea~Still, we felt it would be well to have a discussion~ I guess every family faces challenges when a newcomer is on the way! Some parents start something like this with the siblings! 'We love you so much, and it's so great being parents, that you've made us want to have another child'!" He chuckled before continuing! "Not a bad approach, I don't suppose, but then someone likened that to a husband telling his wife, he loves being married to her so much, that he's decided to take more wives!'"

The total lack of response made Brenna squirm, but his serious eyes meeting hers quieted her spirit! He had the situation in hand! She smiled confidently, and he continued.

"I guess I should begin at the beginning! I didn't get custody of you children as part of a 'deal' to get Brenna! One of the things I fell in love with about your sister was her love for, and determination to, watch out for all of you! Of course, I fell in love with her beauty! Recently, though, she has confided your concerns to me about where you will be when we produce children from our union! I mean, let's face it honestly; we're an odd sort of a lot~"

Jacob's gaze lifted, filled with pain, before he returned attention to his tablet!

"And I don't mean you children! I reference myself! A stodgy old bachelor with a horse of a dog; what do I know~ Of course, my parents hardly knew how to respond to my sudden move! And my sister, who holds the family monopoly for producing their grandchildren, was more than slightly miffed~ But the other day, my parents made an admission to Diana regarding us! They said, 'When Gray found a wife, he found himself!' And they are right, absolutely! But it wasn't Brenna alone, who filled my life with joy and vitality! Who helped me find myself and gave new purpose to my existence! It's every one of you! Each of you has a lodging place in my heart that's difficult for me to express! Your positions are~unassailable! You needn't fear one another, nor the baby on the way~"

Another mocking snort, this time from Terry~

"I know you think this is easy for me to say, and that only time will tell! Can any of you children see that I generally keep my word? If not yet, I understand!"

"Yes, you do!" The words burst forth from Summer. "I don't know anything about my biological dad, but as far as I'm concerned, you're my dad now! And I don't care how much you love the new baby! If you'll just keep keeping us together, and helping us turn into real people~"

"You were already real people! Very uniquely created and molded~just exactly what I needed, and important members of our family! I cherish you all! You're not simply a bad lot I was forced to accept to win Brenna's hand!"

⊰ ⊱

Summer joined Brenna at a table in the chow hall, brimming with pride and excitement!

"It looks as if you managed to sell your idea?" Brenna knew her guess was on-target!

"Yes, everyone I've spoken to has jumped at it! But, then, Alex suggested I prepare a contract! Not hiring a lawyer, but just spelling things out in order to avoid misunderstandings!"

Brenna stirred sweetener into iced tea, fighting uneasy feelings about why her father should take such interest in Summer! He was wayyyy too old for her, and he was having trouble getting his attorney-soon-to-be-ex-wife to settle in the divorce! As if her thoughts had conjuring powers, he appeared!

"Do you two beautiful ladies mind if I join you?"

"Not at all!" Brenna sort of did, but what could she say? "You can fill us in on how the road work's progressing! Taking that long detour up, in order to get down the mountain, is getting old, fast!"

He fixed a tray and returned. "It's going slowly! It always does; I'm sorry to say! The weather's supposed to be clear tomorrow, so Anderson plans to meet his chopper in Grand Junction to lift in some of the depleting supplies! Maybe you should make a list-I guess Summer told you that everyone in the village is interested in hiring her!"

"Mmm-hmmm; I'm proud of her idea; and she's really pretty talented at cleaning and organizing!"

"Yes, and when the mud goes, the dust will start! I was the first to hire her!"

Brenna frowned, at which he laughed. "You're wondering, hire her for what? I've purchased an RV, scheduled for delivery Wednesday! My-uh-wife-has seen some of our Facebook posts; she wants to come see the mountains, and work on hammering out our issues face to face! We will neither one be interested in cleaning our own space-"

"Brenna, can you front me, so I can buy a good vacuum, and other cleaning supplies?" Summer's eager expression was hard to resist!

"I'm not so sure you need to do that!" Alex addressed his response to Brenna's pleading sister. "It's really a bad idea to take a vacuum and mop from one house to another! Doing so can spread germs, fleas, whatever! You need to require your customers to have their own supplies, and you won't be culpable for someone getting a flea infestation who doesn't even own a pet!"

"Well, how can I look like I'm in business?"

"Go online and shop for polo shirts imprinted with your logo! Or an apron and matching dew rag?"

Brenna laughed at her sister's puzzled expression! "A Logo is your exclusive design that you use to advertise your business! Have you thought of a name for it?"

"Well, I thought I might just call it *Summer Prescott's Maid and Laundry Service!*"

"Whoa, you never said anything about doing laundry, but that's brilliant! I'm pretty sure the miners hardly bother-"

Alex smiled as he stepped in front of her steamrolling venture, "Summer, before you get ahead of yourself with that one, maybe you should check with David, what the septic system can handle! I mean, I guess it doesn't make much difference, whether you run your washing machine more, or if the miners-"

Brenna cut in, "I think their only option right now, is the coin laundry down in town! Which now takes an hour and a half to get to! Your idea is timely, Summer; but Alex is right; we should run it past David!"

Alex smiled sympathetically at the young girl! "I'll talk to him about it if you want! The way our little village is blossoming, maybe we should upgrade the sewer system! You girls stay out of trouble!" He rose with the food on his tray practically untouched, then turned back toward Brenna. "Are you heading uphill this afternoon?"

She sighed, "I wish, but Al has to go down for a checkup with the orthopedist, and Tim's working for Gray, driving one of the dozers!"

"Well, I'll find David and discuss Summer's ideas; then, I'll hike up that way with you! I know Gray doesn't want you to venture up alone, but you're chomping at the bit-"

⊰ ⊱

Mallory's eyes sparkled with delight! "A real sewer system? A real town? Incorporated? And Alex Hamilton referred to it as, 'our' little village? And his wife's coming, too?"

David laughed, "Whoa there! Although, I must admit my imagination started running away with me, too! Hey, if he's interested in putting down roots, and being our 'civil engineer' gratis-I mean, we can even name our town Hamiltonville- And she's his estranged wife!"

"Maybe Hamilton Village! I've liked referencing it as a village! It sounds New Englandish! And you're serious about Summer, too? Wanting to do cleaning, organizing, and laundry? My prayers have been answered! I hope she doesn't fill up all her slots too fast!"

David laughed. "She's really shy around us! I'll go find her and tell her we want her services twice a week!"

Mallory planted a kiss on his lips! "Cleaning! That's practically as propitious as having a chow hall!"

⊶ ⊷

Brenna strove to control emotions as she headed across the road and onto the leveled ranch acreage! Walking side by side with the man she had always dreamed about-why couldn't she just be normal around him; rather than tongue-tied and suspicious?

"Whoa, slow down a second-you're obviously more accustomed to the thin atmosphere!"

She paused. Her being twenty years younger was in her favor as well!

"Either, that, or I'm getting old!" Sometimes he seemed to read her thoughts! "Why are we not using this thing?" He tapped the metal detector she carried over her shoulder.

"The batteries don't last real long; but why not?" Pulling the earphones from her backpack, she started to attach them.

"I need to talk to you-"

Her hand froze and her heart lurched, "What about?"

He settled down onto a piece of foundation, the only remnant of the ranch house! "About Summer," His pronounced pallor and mentioning her sister, redoubled her alarm.

"Wh-what about her?"

"Well, she figured that since you found me, and I'm not a *Simon Legree*, she's more interested in finding out who-"

"Her father is!" Brenna sank suddenly beside him, simply because her knees gave way! "Uh-she just told Gray-that to her thinking, he's her father."

"Yeah, I know! Listen, if you're worried; the last thing I want is an entanglement with a little girl! I wish you were as taken with me as she is!"

Brenna laughed, although tears tried to escape. "We don't know as much about him-"

"Yeah, she told me she once wore your mother down-that she thought your mother admitted his name was Simon-"

"Uh-huh, but not as in *Legree*! Just as in, that we don't know any more-than that-Do you think Richard would know? When exactly did he disown-my-mother-"

He frowned, "I'm not sure about that! Listen, Richard and I are by no means, buddies! I'm surprised he contacted me to let me know you were searching-I'm glad he did! Especially since you nearly decided to let it go-"

Honey-brown eyes widened and met his! "Are you really?"

"Yes, and then I'm doubly glad that Gray-helped me get another chance-this-the mountains-and distance from the East Coast-Brenna, I-think-I might know-who Simon-I mean-I'm not sure-"

"Is-is he a good guy-I mean, she's about to let it go, and just accept Gray-"

"She does accept him! If you noticed, she plans to use her adopted name for her company-but she'll still always-"

"Wonder!" Brenna finished sadly, "So, tell me about Simon!"

⚔ ⚔

Alexandra frowned! Good news! And bad! Although her ankle was healing nicely, she panicked at the PT regimen the nurse scheduled! With the section of the road out, it was a worse pain to come down than ever! And she still wasn't allowed to drive! For thirty minute sessions! Three times a week! Part of her considered going to Tulsa! Her mom would gladly take her back and forth for sessions at any PT facility there-and she might get to see Brad! As much as the ease of the plan tempted, thoughts of her mine and the short remaining days in the mining season, made her relinquish the idea! Brad would have to wait until snow forced mining to a slow down! Forcing Brad from her mind, she reviewed a wish list of equipment she planned to acquire! She needed more capital! If things worked out with Brad-and if he inherited his trust-

⚔ ⚔

Incredulous, Brenna listened to Alex's reluctantly related story!

"So, you're pretty sure it might be the same Simon-"

He shrugged sadly. "I've never known there to be that many Simons! I mean, aside from him, I'm not sure I've ever known another guy named that!"

Brenna nodded pessimistically. The logic was sound, but for Summer's sake, she shrank from the idea-Except-that it sounded so plausible-like her mother's MO!

"Okay, well-please don't say anything to Sum-until I finish mulling it over-is it okay-"

"To talk to Gray about it? Sure!"

She shuddered. Why did they finish each other's sentences? Uncanny and weird! Idly, she jabbed at a large stone with the toe of her boot! With Alex's troubling revelation forgotten, she knelt, grabbing a branch to push topsoil aside! Excitement mounted, and she plugged the earphone into the detector and switched it on! Rocking back on her heels, she met his gaze again at last! "Quartz!" Barely above a whisper. "And although I can't see any flecks of gold, it-uh-sounds-encouraging! I need to get down and find Al-"

※ ※

Gray studied Brenna keenly as they prepared for bed! With the excitement of announcing her mineral find ebbing away, she seemed troubled! Not sure how much to probe, he pulled her close, "Are you ready for a prayer, Love?"

She nodded tensely, "Yes, and for an unspoken request!"

He began by praising the Lord for safety for all the group through their efforts of the day, and for allowing Brenna to discover traces of gold! Then he switched tones, imploring the Lord's help in making Brenna trust him enough to confide-

With the 'Amen' said, she swatted him playfully. "And I do trust you, Gray! It's just that everything I find out-"

He waited for her to continue!

She rose and paced, frustrated and asking herself, 'Why can't Gray figure it out, and finish the sentence for me? So I don't have to say it?'

"Yes, everything you find out-" he prodded.

"Nothing! I'm tired! Let's go to bed!"

He grinned impishly, *"As you wish-"*

She glared in mock-anger-or maybe he was really getting her goat! He used the line from *The Princess Bride* they were both familiar with! Often! But sometimes, he used it to get what 'he wished'; more than what 'she wished'.

Surprisingly, he grew annoyed, too! "Why you insist on trying to paint your mother as a saint, when obviously, she was not-"

She burst into tears and lunged for the bathroom to lose her dinner!

⚔ ⚔

David pulled Mallory close! "You're sure you and the kids will be okay while I go for supplies tomorrow?"

She laughed. "I'm sure! I can manage them, you know! And knowing that Summer will be cleaning-and Melodye is so great-do you suppose your parents would agree to us keeping her indefinitely-like forever?"

He laughed. "Maybe; why? What are you thinking?"

"Well, she said something the other day about Frances' having a dream job-"

"Okay, you lost me! Who's Frances?"

"The Faulkner's nanny! Well, she doesn't live in, but she comes every week day and teaches the kids- She has for years! So, that started me thinking-What about hiring Melodye full-time? We can provide room and board and pay tuition for her college courses! Not surprisingly, she wants to be a school teacher! She's already mentioned that our girls' minds are like sponges-"

He nodded! All very good points! Mallory was smart! There was no questioning that! "Let's give it some thought," he evaded. "At least she'll be around tomorrow when I'm out of pocket all day! And I want to educate the children, of course; but they also need a chance to just be kids! To play and be outside! And of course, life is a learning curve-"

⚔ ⚔

As Brenna emerged, Gray appeared with a tray of tea and scones, "I apologize, Love! Your blind loyalty is one of your most endearing traits, among thousands of them! I assume you're troubled about Summer's considering searching for her father-and that he is deceased!"

She blinked back tears! "Did you find that out in the records when you adopted?"

"Well, Sam and I continue our search for background information! The children will be tormented more, by not knowing, than by finding out the truth! None of them are under any rosy illusions about the details of their births!"

Taking a deep breath, Brenna met his gaze and phrased the question, the possible answer to which, she found terrifying! "So, my mother-was even-worse-than what we knew about?"

"Well, perhaps not worse than you've realized; more that she's worse than you can bring yourself to admit! Again, your loving and loyal disposition makes you tend to gloss over some details! You know plenty-that you refuse to admit-even to yourself-"

"Is it a wrong thing, Gray, if I choose to filter my memories and dwell on what was good?" She struggled for composure.

Gray poured the tea, his hand trembling slightly as he considered his response! "Okay, you're the oldest, and so you may have good memories of your mother, before she grew more and more addicted and desperate! Before so many men, and before the crushing weight of more and more children whom she was less and less capable of providing for-or dealing with!"

"I'm still just so puzzled by the pieces that I'm pulling together! The thought that she grew up in a Christian home and knew what was right-She never breathed a word to any of us about anything religious! And when I got saved and started trying to go to church when I could, she didn't seem to care, one way or another! And when Candy and I witnessed to her, and she made her profession of faith-"

"She still never mentioned that she knew it all-before! Who knows what damage the drugs and alcohol abuse had wreaked on her mind?"

"So, Simon, was he really Summer's father? Is that all true?"

"It would seem so! Simon O'Connell! A young man in the church youth group that was dating your mother! They were 'going out', as the expression of the day was! Of course, your grandfather wasn't particularly pleased with the situation! Neither your mother nor Simon seemed to have much interest in spiritual things!"

"Yeah, and they both snuck off to a party they should have never attended-Where they both met Alex, who introduced them to the big wide world of drugs and under-age drinking!" Her tremulous, enraged voice barely in check!

"Happens multiplied thousands upon thousands of times a day in our nation, I'm afraid! Curious, dissatisfied children, lured by one of Satan's best-used tricks: 'that Christian or conservative parents only aim to spoil their fun and their youth'! Of course, your father's role, though proving fatal eventually, wasn't intentionally malignant! He was a youthful fool, as well! You must forgive his role and failure of you, as generously as you have-"

"My mother! At least she stuck and raised me!"

"Yes, but give Alex the benefit of the doubt! He says he didn't know-"

Gray returned to his narrative, "Then, after your grandfather threatened him, and he moved on, Simon came back into play! He and your mother stayed in an on-and-off again relationship for a couple of years, during which time, Jacob was born, and then Summer!"

"But Warren is Jacob's father!" Summer asserted. "After which, Warren disappeared for a few years!"

"That's right!" Gray's steady demeanor comforted her.

"So then, Mom had Luke- sleeping with her dealer-for a few fixes-his name was Raul Juarez, who never admitted- fathering a child-"

Gray nodded sympathetically! "He's in prison for life for killing a police officer! And then, in the meantime, Warren shacked up with a Menda Wilkinson! From which relationship came Lindsey and Terrance! I'm not sure how, but he managed to keep his kids when he moved back in with your mother!"

"Yes, that's just how she was! She loved kids-"

He nodded, "Maybe because she was one herself-so determined, like Peter Pan, to never grow up-"

Brenna shrugged. Yes and no! Her mother had been such a strange mixture of vulnerable appeal and sin-hardened addict!

"Yes, Brenna, you are correct! Your mother put a roof over the heads of children not her own-and you accept them as siblings and sense such responsibility-"

"When we're not actually blood brothers and sisters! But we have such a common bond-that I think it's stronger than blood ties! Well, I felt such a bond! They mostly resented me trying to take over following mother's-death-if you hadn't come along when-"

Gray nodded agreement about the Lord's timing bringing him into the equation, before continuing, "So, then, Emily is the greatest mystery of all! Some woman at an opium den handed baby Emily to your mother and asked her to look after her-And then your mother never saw the woman again-they assumed she OD'd! The reason I have a little black daughter! And you credit your mother with having a kind heart-but you're actually the one who shouldered each extra responsibility! The little mother of the clan when your mother was checked out!"

"Well, I did what I had to! And then Misty came along after mother and Warren got back together!"

Gray sat silently for long moments, studying her with fresh wonder! She flushed with embarrassment, "What?"

"What do you mean, 'What'? You are so incredibly remarkable! Not just to have survived all of that-but to have-bobbed to the top! I mean, even before you actually met our Lord as your Savior-He-He had his hand upon you-The things you bragged to have done, and yet you actually never did-"

"I was just scared of getting pregnant-and there were already more in our apartment than the legal number-and we could barely make rent-without getting a bigger place-"

"A good healthy fear! You broke free of an environment-not only finishing high school, but with a scholarship to advance further-"

"Yes, but I had a heated argument with Mama on that one-I still feel guilty-she thought my high school diploma was good enough-"

"Yes, that you could get a minimum wage job, stay home, and add financial support as well as caring for the domicile-"

"You make her sound self-centered-"

He smiled suddenly! "I sorrow with you for having lost her! I credit much of your loving and caring nature to her! I wish she could still be alive, growing in grace! That I could actually know her, and not just what I know to be true of her! Her essence as a personality carries on through you! You haven't forgiven her for saddling you with her load; you have lovingly overlooked it! As though it never happened! I pray you can extend that much grace to the parent you still have with you!"

She chewed a bite of the scone reflectively before responding, "Should we talk to Summer now?"

Chapter 28: MOURNING

Alexandra's concern deepened as the evening meal drew to a close in her chow hall! Usually, Norma showed up around four! But with her house and meager possessions washed away in the spring flooding, she seemed to have grown more distant and out-of-touch! Al couldn't figure out why! The older woman still held all of the proceeds from selling the ranch; and she did surprisingly well as a cosmetics rep! She needed to ask Norma about driving her back and forth for the PT sessions! Everyone else was even busier than she was! And none of them could keep from giving their opinions, either vaguely or openly, about Brad! Norma understood!

⊰ ⊱

She frowned as her Uncle Gray and his odd little entourage settled in at their usual table! Aware of their ongoing drama, she knew that Gray was springing to exhume the remains of a guy they thought might be Summer's biological dad-like, why dig him up? What difference did it make? And Summer went around crying like she had lost a real dad! Brenna was AWOL! Probably sick again! Longingly, Alexandra wished she could trade Brenna to her dad and get Brad instead-She glared as Janni appeared with a dinner tray!

"I had to wait for them to bring out more food," she apologized! "That's what happens if the miners beat us in line!"

"Yeah, I was kinda waiting for Norma to come-no problem!" Disdainfully, Alexandra pressed the chicken fried steak between napkins, shuddering daintily at the greasy deposits!

Janni tried to ignore it! Al was the one who approved the menus! The chow was actually pretty good. She returned to the line for her own tray! Maybe Jared and Abby would join Alexandra so she could eat with Melodye!

⚔ ⚔

David leaned back with a sigh, not sure when he had known so many things to go wrong in one day!! 'The best laid plans of mice and men', he mumbled! In spite of advances made by civilization, mountain living was still fraught with challenges! Maybe it was exhaustion, but suddenly the idea of forging a new town seemed impossible~as well as totally undesirable! Like just a trip for groceries~well, groceries to feed a small army! And the formidable terrain made everything extra-expensive! No wonder early Americans were forced to be self-sustaining! Dallas looked better to him every day! Too bad it didn't have more exposed rocks for Mallory to look at! Thoughts of his beautiful wife brought a smile, though, and he pulled his phone free!

Before he could call her, an incoming call jingled! 'Ray Meeker? What could Ray want?' Tensing, he answered, "Hi Ray; this is David! What's up?"

He listened pensively, asking for a few details before disconnecting!

Norma Engels! Gone! Massive stroke! He fought tears! Salty old gal; never would try to watch her language in front of Mallory and his kids! Still, maybe he should have left that alone and witnessed to her clearly! Not that she allowed any openings~refused to go to church with any of them~still, she was a person you couldn't help liking~ Sighing, he turned up his Gospel music! Really not the kind of news to break to Mallory over the phone!

⚔ ⚔

Mallory was barely surprised that Alexandra went to pieces when they broke the news to her about Norma! Alexandra, always aloof, seemed colder with every day that passed, to people who loved her! Like if any of them died, she couldn't care less! But now, Norma? And it was the end of the world?

Well, Mallory had sort of liked Norma! She was just what she was, without pretense! Which also meant that she didn't pretend to be a Christian, or act like one!

She gave Alexandra another sympathetic hug, to be shrugged off impatiently! Mallory knew that David was disgusted! They had invested a ton of money, coming to Alexandra's aid-before the calamitous flooding! Losses since were still being tallied! Wearily, she moved to join David and Gray and Brenna!

"They can't locate any surviving family members, at all!" Gray's sympathy-filled eyes!

Mallory sighed! "And Alexandra's the main one who's bonded, but she doesn't have any money for final expenses! David hates it that Norma drove off the road and totaled her antique car when she had the stroke!"

"It was an awesome piece of Americana," Gray agreed! "As for burial, Norma had money! I can find out about any other insurance or burial policies-" he paused awkwardly. "Brenna's contract is up, and Alexandra hasn't mentioned renewing it-I'm considering selling the equipment! It will bring a good price right now, with so much area-wide damage still needing repair and rebuilding-"

David's fatigued visage registered relief at Gray's implications! "You mean, you guys are out of here?"

His eyes met Mallory's, and she nodded. "David and I haven't had a chance to discuss it, but I think we share the sentiment! I'm not sure what we're accomplishing here!"

Gray flushed, "I've been disappointed by my niece's callousness toward-"

"Basically everything-" Mallory cut in with an uncharacteristically tart tone! "I'm pretty sure her affection for Norma was that she was facilitating communication with Brad behind Daniel and Diana's backs! And she won't listen to any of us about him!"

"He's such a creep! I mean, maybe it isn't his fault!" Brenna's concern boiled over, "When Gray did his background check the most troubling thing to us was that Brad never seems to have had any nurturing! His dad is big in the French wine business-just had Brad sent away to this school and that-And his grandfather, Stephen! He has to be the lewdest old guy ever to stalk the earth! And he has suddenly decided to step in with the promised trust fund, and pull Brad's strings with it like a puppet!"

⚔ ⚔

Brad cashed his *GeoHy* paycheck! Pathetic! The paycheck details indicated that he was in an apprentice program, and subsequently receiving credits toward his Master's degree! Still, Faulkner could show some gratitude! After all, he had rescued Alexandra, not once, but twice! As well as everyone else going about their business the day of the flooding, with no inkling of pending doom! Plus, Faulkner had sent him into danger down off the coast of Chile!

His phone jingled! Stephen! Coincidentally in town, and offering dinner at Tulsa's best steak place! Brad was hardly in the mood, but his grandfather wasn't one to be shunned! Accepting, he drove slowly to the frat house to change! Back in the car, he frowned at a text message! From Alexandra, directly! Informing him that Norma, their go-between, wouldn't be going between anymore! He smirked! The lovely Alexandra was probably one of Stephen's key topics for the evening! It seemed Faulkner wasn't the only one determined to come between them!

'Old people should nose out,' he muttered! 'Still, if Steven plans to disinherit me over this, I can skip Faulkner's kid! Who needs trouble? Like they say, there are women everywhere, who are ready and willing!'

⚔ ⚔

"Thanks for the jobs," Brenna enthused to David and Mallory at breakfast!

"No problem; they aren't much, but they'll be bread and butter for your company for another month or six weeks! We're going a few more places in state before we head home! To our Arizona home!"

We're trying again, to check out the quarry at Marble; then to a source of beautiful Rhodochrosite, and then Grand Junction! From there we may go see Dinosaur National Park"

"Well, the jobs <u>are</u> something!" Brenna disagreed gratefully, referencing the requests *DiaMo* received almost daily from adjacent landholders, realizing their properties might yet hold stores of wealth! Land owners begged *DiaMo* to come take a few core samples, just in case~

Mallory smiled, "We'll be back through for Norma's funeral, and we're leaving our home away from home set up here! Alexandra can use it to

282

house more workers for her mine! Maybe she'll agree to leasing it-if not, she can just use it-"

"Yes, quite a great attitude! Perhaps we shall do the same!" Gray broke his troubled silence! "I am showing the equipment tomorrow to a bloke who may take the whole lot off of my hands! At a price where I shall pocket a handsome profit! God blesses our efforts on His behalf! And I need not lose sight of that fact! Tim can help Brenna with the drilling, and by the end of next week, we shall all be one our way home to Tulsa!"

⊣ ⊢

Abby faced Jared squarely! "Why is everyone leaving? I thought there were all these big plans-"

"I don't know, Abby! They've all done a lot! Before the flood happened! And then it all needed doing over-But while they've been here, they've advanced Alexandra and the mine immeasurably! It would have taken us five years, to accomplish here what's been done in a summer!"

"Us, Jared? You and Alexandra, you mean?"

"Come on Abigail! She's the mine owner, and I'm her mining engineer! Yeah, the Andersons and Prescotts helped *us* with *our* mine! I own a small percentage, which goes into our, your and my, pockets! Listen, in case you've missed the major gossip topic, Alexandra is totally interested in someone!"

"Yeah, and in case you haven't figured out the obvious! It's kinda one-sided! And with Norma gone, Alexandra's going to rely more and more on you! I'm tired of her, Jared! I'm tired of our dirty cracker box of a house! I'm tired of chili dogs and corndogs!"

"You knew it was going to be like this, Abby! You told me you didn't want or need the accoutrements of your dad's wealth!"

"And you told me you wanted to serve the Lord and start a family! And you've done a complete one eighty on me! How dare you suggest this is about my dad and what he has? Yeah, the prospect of having Summer come do cleaning, and having David and Gray being here to be her slaves, has made things more tolerable! She's a witch, and she has her hooks in you!"

"Abby, listen to yourself! She gave me this job when everyone else laughed at me, and there're still so many valuable mineral deposits! We're right on the cusp! She's been under pressure! We all have! You're mostly mad that the church doesn't ask you to sing more solos!"

"Why would they invite me to be a vocalist? When we're never there? Remember how we used to resent church members who showed up to shine? But then they weren't just faithful and steadfast in the shadows? I get bored out of my mind up here! Let's start a family~"

He gazed into troubled eyes! "We will~just~not yet~"

≒ ⇌

"Gray, are you sure we're doing the right thing? About leaving here?"

"Well, Love, if you still have doubts, we can talk it over further! Are you certain you're well enough to do this? We can send Tim to direct the drill operators!"

She smiled. "He is getting savvier, but he's not there yet! More time on this learning curve, though~"

"Yes, I regret needing his services with all of the heavy equipment~"

"Well, his familiarity and expertise with the equipment were Godsends! But there's also hope for him as a Geologist! Summer isn't happy about accompanying us~"

He pulled her close and kissed her lingeringly, before gazing deeply into her eyes.

"Yes, not much makes her happy at the moment! Let's be patient with her! Surely she has clung to that little girl dream, of one day, finding a daddy~one who somehow would love her! Her dream crashed hard with meeting reality!"

Brenna sighed, "Okay, so you don't think she's just carrying on so much, in order to get attention?"

He laughed. "I definitely think she is! But I think the hurt and disappointment are also very real!"

"Well honestly, all her histrionics just annoy me! We all came up hard~"

"Well, perhaps Jacob would like to go~rather than your sister~"

"No! Everything's all worked out about who's doing what today! I'll be nice to her!"

≒ ⇌

"Morning, Boss! What's first on the agenda for today?" A still annoyed mining engineer answered Alexandra's summons!

284

"Well, I'm supposed to somehow make it down into Durango three times a week for PT sessions on my ankle! I thought it might not be too much of an imposition on one person, if everyone took turns! Like Norma one day, and Mallory, and then~"

He sighed. "So basically Mallory and Norma spelling each other off! And now they're both out of play-you're-you're not thinking about-Abby?"

Alexandra shrugged, "Why not? What else does she have going on? Besides yodeling to the mountains all day?"

"What about Janni? Or is she leaving with the Andersons, too?"

Alexandra frowned, "What did you mean about Mallory being out of play? Where are the Andersons going?"

Trapped, he was forced to be the bearer of bad news! And it didn't make her a happy camper!

⊣ ⊢

Brad drove slowly, leaving the city behind! Realizing traffic was backing up, he moved to the left lane and increased speed, setting cruise control!

The steak was good, but the rest of the dining incident left him feeling like he might lose it!

He rubbed his belly, swallowing hard! Alexandra was definitely out, if he planned to inherit the family fortune! Stephen's scathing report on the Faulkner family still rang in his ears! They were paupers, barely eking out a standard of living by slave labor at a number of pitiful enterprises! Working so hard for so little was simply gauche! He needed to avoid the little gold digger, at all costs! She would never do as a Maxwell wife!

A statement at which he now dared scoff! Evidently, no one made it as a Maxwell wife! The reason why there were none! No grandmother! No mother! Just a patriarchy of selfish men who used women and bragged about it!

He frowned. What was it that Steven had said? Brad had missed the significance of the comment at the time! Something-that his mother-a pitiful, mousy, little thing, had thought she could take them on~

He exited and pulled over in time to lose the fifty dollar steak! A few miles later, slouched in a truck stop booth, he swigged cold, strong coffee! Surely a truck stop should keep good coffee brewed. He swore at the waitress and she scurried to start another pot!

He was losing his mind! On one track, that crazy Bible chapter played endlessly- *worshipped and served the creature more than the creator-fornication-without excuse-covetousness-* And with another track, he attempted to pull up recent words from his grandfather, and reconcile them with long ago defenses from his father-

According to Stephen's revelation earlier this evening, the woman who had birthed him was pitiful and mousy! But she tried to stand against the combined powers of Brad's father and grandfather-to get custody-

But, according to long-past answers from his father, his mother was a beauty who ran around with other men, and never wanted him-simply walked away from him for another man-and a lot of alimony! No mention of fighting for him! Which way was it?

A sardonic smile split his face! Why would she not have walked away? Surely any man would have been better than his father!

He fought tears. 'Did she really try to fight for me? That would take courage! Could she have loved me? Why would my father have lied? Was there a God, a Creator? Surely not! And Faulkner could be far richer and more respected if he gave up on holding with all that garbage-and *creature* and *Creator*, And Brenna Prescott sitting there taking grief-and Al-

⇥ ⇤

FBI Agent Erik Bransom studied his screen! Information reached him in bits and pieces, usually accidentally! Well, he didn't use the Bureau to sleuth for his personal agenda! But sometimes the official lines of investigation crossed paths with looking out for his friends! As in now! Strange that Alexandra Faulkner's elderly friend, Norma Engels had died suddenly at the wheel, before crashing over a precipice on a mountain road! 'Hypertension/stroke?' Certainly plausible! Still, this fresh death reminded him eerily of another 'natural causes' death in a previous case! Suddenly curious, he opened a search to locate an exhumation and autopsy report! He studied the data reflectively! The law suit was still pending in the wrongful death of a Louisiana Gulf ship's captain! That must mean that the insurance company for the pharmaceutical company was quite certain they couldn't be pinned with culpability! They could probably beat the case without settling!

Sighing, he raked both hands up and down his face, before tapping pencil eraser on blotter and rising to refill his coffee! That case was suspicious because the captain was an important federal witness! Who conveniently, after a long history of high BP, stroked out and died! Leading Erik to believe that somehow, the criminal entity he continued to chip away at, had hacked the online pharmacy the sea captain purchased his generic meds from, and substituted a medication to raise BP! He sat considering nosing into a death declared natural by a county morgue, with no solid reason for trying to make it federal!

Dawson, his superior, wouldn't like it! With financial pressure on, he was willing to allow lower level LEI's to handle and pay for as many cases as possible! Erik grinned! Strange, how Dawson had forbidden him to investigate the other suspicious death! But after praying about the situation, the victim's daughter had called him! His concerns about the 'natural death' had then caused her to hire a private investigator, and consequently facilitate the lawsuit! Her contention was that the online pharmacy made a mistake! Bransom held with his theory: a deliberate medication switch to opportunely eliminate an important witness!

He rubbed his face again, digging into tired eyes with his knuckles! "Who would stand to benefit from Norma Engel's death? The only player he could finger at all was the Geology grad student, Brad Maxwell! But, how would Norma's death help him? If she were really facilitating his getting with Alexandra contrary to her parents' wishes, she was his ally! Right? But maybe–something about Brad raised a flag– Perhaps, that was the reason Erik had no use for him! Didn't mean he was a murderer!

He closed his computer. Maybe he should go home and consider his approach to this one on his own time! Already, he considered avenues to investigate! The report from the Navy might be illuminating! But there was no way he could access that information without bringing official pressure to bear! Probably, Dawson couldn't get it; even if he wanted to! 'Okay, so forgetting that for the moment! I can still see what else I can dig up on young Maxwell!'

⊰ ⊱

Myrna Diane Johnson Maxwell stared in consternation at the mess left at one of her round tops! A tough and demanding family to wait on had finally complained about her to her manager and refused to pay for two entrées; insisting she got them wrong! And now, not surprisingly, no tip! She was tired! Her feet hurt like everything, but waiting tables was all she knew! Getting the little floor sweeper, she attacked piles of crumbs and shredded paper!

She looked up as a customer entered and paused to allow his eyes to adjust! Her hands flew to her mouth to throttle a cry of recognition! Her ex? No! Too young! Like him when they had first met–could it be? She stood dumbly as intense blue eyes adjusted and he swept his gaze across her contemptuously! Before she could speak, the young man spun and was gone!

Numbly, she sank into the nearest booth and wiped tears with the rag she used for cleaning tables!

≒ ≓

"That was foolish! What did you expect to find?"

Brad recoiled, trying to force his mind to accept the incongruous fact, that his grandfather was personally following him everywhere! The old guy didn't have anything better to do with his time? Why couldn't he keep busy parlaying the family fortune into more, and butt out of Brad's business?

He shrugged, filled with ire, yet afraid to risk his inheritance! "You're the one who brought her up! And then your story didn't gee haw with the official line I always got from my dear old dad! His story was that my beautiful mother was too busy sleeping around to care about me, and that she turned her back on me without a second thought!"

"Well, you saw for yourself what she looks like 'She was rode hard, and put up wet!' He cackled at his own witty observation!

Brad forced an exhausted smile! Obviously not beautiful now! Hard to tell if she ever might have been! "Night before last, you told me that she stood up to the two of you and fought for custody!"

Stephen's turn to shrug! "Obviously, she didn't try very hard!"

Brad considered sagely, 'It wouldn't be wise to stand up to either of them, let alone their joint muscle!' Capitulating, he agreed, "Yeah, I saw enough! I'm done here!"

≒ ≓

Erik studied a terse text! Strange! Usually his superior, Jed Dawson, didn't text! And Erik never met him at cafés, like the FBI did in movies! Even as it occurred to him that this could be an ambush, he hurried to the location!

Cautious, he stared around the half-filled eatery. Sure enough, Dawson sat partially concealed behind a newspaper at one of the back booths! Erik slid in, ordering coffee!

"Mornin', Bransom! What's up with your poking into financials of a gazillionaire named Stephen Maxwell?"

Erik frowned. "A hunch!"

Dawson swirled his mug of dregs meaningfully at a waitress; then with privacy restored, he pressed his issue! "If my department's taking heat, I'd like to know what kind of 'hunch'!"

Erik shrugged indifferently before countering with a question of his own! "Who's squawking, if I may ask?"

"Treasury!"

Erik laughed. "That's a big Department! Come on, Jedediah; how can a family have what the Maxwell family has, and not pay a penny in taxes?"

"I don't know! That's why I'm a Democrat!"

"I didn't ask you for your political views! I thought we're not supposed to discuss politics! But, Republicans aren't in favor of the wealthy paying no taxes at all! They just shouldn't be overtaxed to support bleeding-heart government giveaways!"

Dawson opened his mouth to speak, then closed it again! His bad for opening the door on the topic!

Erik tried not to snicker when the little diner featured neither egg substitutes, nor egg-white omelets! The place didn't look like a health food spa! He ordered biscuits and gravy, at which Dawson capitulated to a greasy selection, also!

With the food before them, Dawson leaned forward intently! "Giving you a heads-up; Eastern Division picked Sharon Saxon up early this morning!"

"She was privy to what her husband and son were up to!" Erik's voice rang with conviction!

"More than privy; complicit! Heavily involved for at least the past ten years~" Dawson lipped the words soundlessly!

"And keeping the empire rolling, even after Robert and Bobby's deaths! I should have kept a closer eye on her! After the Merrill Adams incident, I thought I learned a lesson about family members of felons!"

"Well, here's the thing, besides that she's talking better in custody than most of them have; both the Saxon and the Maxwell families were big buddies with the late Undersecretary Coakley in his DC social circle!"

Erik stared in shock! Evidently his queries were pulling someone's chain! "Do you mind stirring up the Department of the Navy, too?"

Dawson couldn't help guffawing! "I have the Navy transcript, but the Maxwell kid's story, that your friend Faulkner sent him out there, has been corroborated by Faulkner! Surely you don't suspect him of wrongdoing~"

The agent sighed, "It's true, that Daniel sent Brad Maxwell as a Geologist to oversee the expedition! And it's true that the ship that fired on *the Rock Scientist* was guilty of illegal dumping! It's true that their fifty cal shot, took the life of the drilling foreman, and that Brad's shooting the threats in the raft saved the lives of both crews on *the Rock Scientist~*"

"But?" Dawson prompted.

"I'm afraid Maxwell's a sociopath~or he became one during that episode~I think he changed quickly from horror at the shark's~"

"To getting a thrill at the carnage? The navy transcript doesn't indicate anything like that~"

Erik agreed before adding, "But it doesn't paint him glowingly as the hero! I have concerns about him~growing up with no mother! No nurturing, no values~just a rich and warped paternal grandfather calling all the shots~Young Maxwell's handsome, loves attention, and~"

"May be a menace to society?" Dawson finished doubtfully! "Do you have any evidence tying him to any cases~"

"Not a case, exactly! A death from 'Natural Causes'! That should be a case~"

Chapter 29: DEPOSITS

Brenna didn't need to drill to see the glowing possibilities on a high country ranch! Still, with ranchers paying for drilling, she gave the order! Instinctively, she knew the sample was rich before the first readings were logged! So much for folklore suggesting the wealth was all mined out! Still, she was aware of futures-trading in precious metals and other commodities, and the questionable way a few players could manipulate prices! Well, her responsibility was drilling as contracted, for which her company was earning revenue!

That caused her to appreciate afresh, the fact that Mallory had turned the projects over to her company! Mallory's business model was different, and she knew firmly which direction she was going, not sidetracked with gobbling up every penny for herself!

Brenna shot a glance toward Summer, who sat in the truck fiddling with her phone! Her sister had spent the morning being particularly uncommunicative, and she sighed! She prayed once more for salvation for her siblings! It seemed the more she prayed, the more their resistance grew! Which took her thoughts back full-circle to Alex Hamilton! Since she couldn't come to grips with her feelings about him, she tried to shove him from her consciousness! She fought sudden tears!

"Lord, I'm trying so hard, to bring them to You~"

The trill of a bird and a whispering, pine-scented breeze caused her to pause in her oft-repeated prayer. The gentleness of the Holy Spirit swept over her ravaged spirit!

John 12:32 And I, if I be lifted up from the earth, will draw all men unto me.

The memorized verse flooded her with new revelation! That was the problem: she was trying! Trying too hard! She needed to cast her care upon the Lord; He was able to draw the ones she loved, inevitably, to Himself! She needed to relax and reflect the joy of the Lord, all that He had done for her!

Taking Tim Alvaredo in tow, she interpreted to him what the rocks indicated! He stared at her in amazement before confiding, "Now that you point things out-I don't know-I've been relieved to help with the heavy equipment rather than trying to fake it as a Geologist-"

She laughed, a natural joyous sound that shocked even her! "You haven't been faking it, Tim! It's just that you have the book knowledge, and now you need experience in the field! Don't be so hard on yourself!"

Even as she voiced the last sentence of encouragement, she smiled at herself! She didn't have to be hard on herself, or on her delinquent father, or on her struggling siblings! Just relax! Lean back in Jesus' arms, and enjoy!

"Do you know what Jacob wants to do? Once his money funds for the game?" Tim's sudden question nearly threw her from her new-found equilibrium! Just when she was turning people over to the Lord, Tim was going to divulge news to panic her afresh. "I have no idea, and I'm afraid to find out!"

Alvaredo nodded understanding! "Yeah; I'm not violating a confidence! He wants me to tell you, so that you can tell Mr. Prescott-"

She sank down suddenly on a boulder for support! "He's afraid to talk to us?"

"Yeah, I guess so! He doesn't want to go back to Tulsa!"

Brenna fought tears! Not for herself, but for Gray! He didn't deserve this! If Jacob returned to Somerville, Summer would doubtless go with him! And Jacob, being legally of age, and with the frightening freedom of a huge influx of cash-cash he didn't know the first thing about managing-Gray couldn't stop him! A scudding cloud cast a shadow over them as surely as the report cast one across her new, sunny spirit!

"He wants to stay here-"

Brenna was so engrossed in her own thoughts that she had to ask Tim to repeat his sentence!

"He wants to stay here, and so do I! He's been praying for his money to fund before Mr. Prescott sells his equipment to the bloke! What's a bloke?"

For the second time in as many minutes, Brenna posed the same intelligent-sounding question! "Hunh?"

Then with the joyous shriek, "Never mind! I heard you! It's just- what's a 'bloke'? It's a 'guy'! One of Gray's British expressions-Jacob said he's been praying? Tim, why didn't you already tell me this? Why couldn't Jacob-? Never mind! I need to call Gray!"

⊰ ⊱

Brenna relaxed in Gray's arms in the semi-private sleeping area of the RV! "Wow! Busy day!"

His laugh came softly against her ear, "Yes, indeed, but a very good and productive day! How miraculously it all came together!"

"It did, except that now we really need to pray for no snafu's in Jakey and Millard's getting the money-and that then he'll keep his word-Listen to me! I'm trying to relax more and be joyful in the Lord, but I still keep letting my mind run way ahead! To cause me to fret!"

"Yes, a difficult habit to break!" He agreed. "We barely allow ourselves to enjoy our blessings, for worrying they will all blow up in our faces!"

"Another way we let Satan win! If we're as miserable and nervous as the unsaved, why should they listen to us? So, it is incredible that you got the lease on that store! Although, it seems like Norma should still be there-but it's perfect, because there's still room to display the flood salvaged items for the owners to claim, with enough space to run the equipment business! And the store happens to be at the end of the street, adjacent to that big lot so they can park the equipment close by!"

"Yes, Brenna Love, an amazing series of coincidences; what?"

She laughed as his lips sought hers, "Yes, more 'amazing' than 'coincidence'!"

⊰ ⊱

David and Mallory toured the Yule Marble Quarry, both equally fascinated! As a Geologist, Mallory realized the white, fine grained marble ranked with the finest in the world! And the quarry was once again operational, with acres remaining of untapped material! David admired it from his Architectural and building standpoint, as well as for their burgeoning headstone and mausoleum division!

He noted with interest that the Tomb of the Unknowns at Arlington National Cemetery utilized the largest single block of marble ever quarried from any source! A fifty-seven ton block! A long litany of other impressive structures around the nation also boasted the Yule Marble Quarry as their source!

Picking up a business card for future contact, they rejoined Melodye and their kids for the drive back to a restaurant and campground!

David took notice of Alexis' lingering after their late lunch, to snuggle extra with Mallory!

"She doesn't feel feverish!" Anxious green eyes met his across the table!

"She's fine! I guess she just missed you this morning while we were on our outing!" He paused; no use telling her that her favoritism toward their infant son was obvious to the girls!

Still, perceptive to the significance of his silence, Mallory engaged on purpose with their youngest daughter! She wanted to be a good mother! To all of the kids! Diana was such a great mother, a natural at it, and Mallory cared about her opinion, nearly as much as she treasured being in good regard with David! There were just so many demands! Still, she prayed silently for a better balance! Remembering an affirmation from Mr. Tom Haynes, her school principal, she quoted it inwardly; 'Duties never conflict'!

David winked at her, and as always, she melted inside!

⊰ ⊱

Brenna couldn't read Gray! She thought his emotions were mixed about Jacob! Extremely proud of his decisions up to this point, but worried about him~and also missing him~ Surprisingly, Summer seemed eager to return to Tulsa! With her earlier legal scrape in Somerville cleared up, she seemed more mature! Her heart still torn about discovering her father's identity at last, to learn of his early demise; she clung more desperately to Alex! And Alex seemed to revel in it! At first, reserved about the situation, Brenna decided not to torture herself! Evidently, it was Summer's yearning for a father figure, which aligned with Alex's late-budding need to nurture! Brenna envied the affection for Gray's sake~but Gray was so easygoing~

With everyone settled in, Gray headed downtown to his office, while Brenna moved to her home office to accomplish some tasks! To her amazement, several proposals awaited her little corporation! Then, to her absolute shock, TU offered her a teaching position while she worked toward her Master's Degree. Wow, this was a lot to talk to Gray about over tea!

She paused dreamily-in her wildest imagination, she couldn't have planned a life like she was now living! A wonderful man like Gray, to discuss her hopes and plans with! Owning a corporation that was slowly making headway! An offer to teach her passion in the hallowed halls! Yet, even as she weighed that option, she felt a certainty that it would never work! She could keep her world view to herself, out of respect for a professor! (Albeit, a hard-learned lesson!) She couldn't stand before a classroom of eager young minds, and purposely parrot the lies, accepted and propounded by, Academia! She grinned. 'Okay, so everything didn't have to be run past Gray'! Still, the offer was gratifying! That anyone could believe little Brenna Hamilton could have anything to offer- The offer was a gift from God, to fill some yearning deep in her psyche, for recognition and confirmation as a professional-

᛭ ᛭

Steve Elwood looked over his shoulder as he slung his bag into the trunk of his rent car! The afternoon was steamy, and he mopped his face. Time for something nice and cold! Following the nav system, he pulled in front of a particularly elegant-looking establishment! A few drinks, and he would be braced to do it!

᛭ ᛭

Tim hustled back toward the equipment company with a couple of cans of cold soda! While saving money to reinvest in the business, he and Jacob carried brown-bag lunches! Still, buying the individual cans of soda, made them expensive! They really needed a refrigerator-which would be expensive-not an immediate savings-He frowned as a yellow Dodge Charger drove past, turning to follow the state highway! He didn't like it, but was hardly surprised when Maxwell pulled over and lowered his window to gloat!

"Giving it up as an Earth Scientist, are you?"

Alvaredo shrugged, "Let's just say I have several irons in the fire right now! Surprised to see you here! Are you still interning with *GeoHy*?"

"Eat your heart out!"

Tim tried to mask his aggravation! Brad was right! He would give anything for an opportunity to work for Daniel Faulkner! To have the man hold him in any regard! And Brad had it and was squandering it!

"How's my little Alexandra?" A sick, fakey-sweet tone with equally sarcastic sneer!

Tim would give anything for Alexandra's favor, too! Brad was a moron who didn't deserve~Tone cold and steeled, he responded, "I haven't seen her in several days! I'm assuming she's fine~"

Brad winked knowingly, "Oh, yeah; she's fine, all right!"

"So," Tim's heart sank into his boots, "does Faulkner know you're out here?"

Brad frowned, fighting sudden irritation. "He didn't ask me my weekend plans, and I didn't tell him! And, I don't need for you to pass along any information but what I tell you to!"

"Whatever, Brad! I'm done being your go-between!"

Sheer rage shot upward, twisting handsome features to gargoyle! "You're done when I say you're done, Tim! You're done! Your services are no longer needed! Ciao!" The window shot up and gravel spurted!

☙ ❧

Steve Elwood threw back a couple more expensive shots before heading back to the men's room! Now was the time! Twice before, he had come to town, only to learn that his quarry was gone! Now, she was back! This time, she would pay! Returning to his barstool, he faked answering his cell! Then, moving out the front door under the guise of hearing better, he made it to his car!

"ATF! Put your hands up!"

A stunned Steve Elwood complied! Aggravated at the surreal series of events, he couldn't believe that anyone could be on to his cleverly laid plan! He was in the process of being unceremoniously thrust into the back seat of the government SUV when the cocktail waitress approached, screaming obscenities!

The agent chuckled, "Nice to see that you have enemies in low places, Elwood! Maybe we should let her take a couple of swings at you! I'd make you settle your tab, but your credit cards are no good!"

☙ ❧

David sprinted to the RV to do a quick check on his family! Seeing that his sister had the situation well in hand, he backed off! If his kids saw him, it would make it tougher for her to get them back to order! He grinned as he headed back to meet Mallory! She was right about Melodye, of course! The perfect fit! One of Mallory's particularly strong suits was matching people with positions! Probably one of the main reasons their companies were as successful as they were! David's parents were totally onboard with the plan, and to calm his worries, Mallory was engaging with the kids, all four of them, more, and not less!

They strolled around, taking the self-guided tour of Dinosaur National Park! Never having been intrigued with fossils, Mallory was forced to admit the displays were stunning!

"The earth is full of His riches!" Her tone awed to match the light in expressive eyes! "I mean, you know me and gemstones! But to fossil collectors~and I am awed by the size!"

He nodded, "I think the kids would be interested in a quick tour! I know their attention spans are short, but this is really incredible!"

⩳ ⩵

"Steve Elwood!" The ATF agent booking the alleged criminal scoffed! "A sobriquet the Boston PD should have caught! The culprit's real identity was Carl Burgard, and he was wanted on several state and federal warrants! Well, the dumbbell had come to the end of the line! His fake ID's were impressive; practically of more interest than the felon himself! Why would anyone run up a tab and skip on it, when a criminal empire hinged on his not being apprehended~for even running a stop sign? Whatever! Authorities now had a major thread to pull in the unraveling of a smuggling ring! How could Boston have missed Burgard and brought charges against the girl?" He accessed the police report, and smiled as several more suspects came to his attention!

⩳ ⩵

"Alex thinks you don't need him because Gray is like a father-figure to you now!"

Brenna frowned. Summer was definitely a gossip, and she could keep the pot stirred with her, 'he said, and then she said', tidbits! But rebuking her for gossiping wasn't the answer! Summer needed to meet the Lord, and then the Holy Spirit could take over her refining.

"He really didn't know about you! Why don't you give him a chance?"

Brenna strove for patience, "I am giving him a chance! And Gray doesn't treat me like a child! I see him as a wise Christian husband, and I value his guidance and input! We laugh because our family came together in a highly unorthodox fashion! And so we're still sorting out our roles and relationships! With suddenly having some nearly grown kids to parent, he's worked hard not to see me in the same light!" She laughed, "That I'm not quite as clueless as the rest of you!"

Summer glared sternly, even as a dimple gave her away! "Well, I think you keep hurting Alex's feelings!"

"Really? Well, I don't want to do that! I never try to hurt anyone's feelings! I guess I have ambivalent feelings, and I need his understanding! First, he surmised that I married Gray for his money, and now he's decided I was looking for a dad? I don't need him sending you to me with little messages he can't say for himself! Okay, that wasn't fair! He's finding his way, too! You can tell he's been in the business world long enough to use the grapevine to his advantage! I guess there'll always be the grapevine, so why let it work against you? Would you print labels and stuff these letters and mail them for me? And bear in mind your CDA!"

"Yes, Ma'am!" She snapped a mocking salute. "You may not believe it, but I'm trying not to talk too much!"

Brenna bit back on her own response!

⇥ ⇤

"Pleased as punch," was Erik Bransom's response when Dawson gave him the interagency report about Burgard, AKA Elwood's, apprehension, with its corresponding flow of fresh intel! "I'll lay you odds, though, that he dies in custody!"

Slightly taken aback, Dawson agreed. "I'd give them a heads up, but they won't appreciate it!"

"Probably not," Bransom's agreement! "And things like that save taxpayers the expense of multiple trials the perpetrators usually manage to beat! Maybe they'll think of isolating him on their own! Not that it does that much good!"

Dawson commiserated before asking, "What's the story on your Colorado woman and the 'natural causes'? I'm giving you some leeway, because I'm hoping it connects cases as vitally as you suspect!"

"Let's go out for coffee!"

"Come on! FBI buildings aren't bugged!"

Erik sighed, not sure of that, but aware that every computer search he made could be tracked by those in high places.

Lowering his voice, he began, "Stephen Maxwell, past-his-prime, multi-millionaire, has Washington ties that went all the way up to the late Undersecretary Coakley! Maybe higher, but we don't know that for sure! Which, you told me that! Now it seems that Stephen Maxwell is implicated in Norma Engel's demise! I was kinda hoping it was Brad! Granddad orchestrated the crime, so as not to get his hands dirty! He seems to be working harder at keeping his grandson clear of Alexandra than Daniel Faulkner is~"

"Holy Bat Cave, Bransom! Not here!"

Settled at an outdoor table at a coffee shop, Dawson leaned in, paranoid! "Why would Maxwell be so against Brad's interest in Alexandra, that he'd arrange Norma Engel's death? That's an excessive way to play anti-Cupid! Alexandra isn't your typical 'gold-digger'! Her mine's actually a viable entity~A grandson with a social circle to entertain could do worse!"

Erik regarded his superior in wonder; he really didn't 'get it'!

"It's Alexandra's Chrisianity; and her family's Christian associates in law enforcement! Trent and myself, mostly!"

Dawson studied him blankly!

"There's a huge gulf there! Daniel's fighting to keep Alexandra from it; and on the opposite side, Stephen Maxwell is fighting for the same thing!

Proverbs 28:4 They that forsake the law praise the wicked: but such as keep the law contend with them.

And

Proverbs 29:10 The bloodthirsty hate the upright: but the just seek his soul.

Stephen's insatiable appetite for young girls is as bad as the criminals that supply the demand! What he's been doing is against the law; and then he crossed another line, in having Engels eliminated! The last thing he wants in his world, is a bunch of Christian do-gooders who condemn his actions! Who refuse to look the other way because of money or social standing"!

Jed sighed, "What gets me, is how high up these tentacles~"

Erik nodded, sensing an opening, but afraid to push:

Ephesians 6:12 For we wrestle not against flesh and blood, but against principalities, against powers, against the rulers of the darkness of this world, against spiritual wickedness in high places.

Dawson laughed suddenly, holding his hands in classic 'time out'! "Okay, enough Bible verses! I've started following John Anderson's online flock; verses are his job! Yours is to pin this murderer~"

※ ※

David took the airport exit off Interstate 70 for Grand Junction! He was mildly surprised at the difference in terrain! Mountains looming above the interstate were imposing, but totally void of vegetation! Coming in from the south on Highway 50, they had emerged from forests to scrubby juniper terrain, before finally coming through desert foothills, white with alkali! He figured it was a Geologist's dream, while he found the drive monotonous! Personally, he was intrigued with Mesa Verde and the cliff dwellings left behind by early Meso-Americans! Mallory's response to his suggestion that they visit there: "Maybe next time!"

"Let's check in at the Holiday Inn!" his proposal made tenuously!

"Great idea! Maybe we can get adjoining rooms to spread out with Melodye and the kids! David, I'm sorry! I didn't mean to cut you off about the tourist trap back there!"

He shook his head wonderingly as he grinned at her good-naturedly! "Yeah, wonder if an ancient civilization realized they were building a tourist trap!"

She frowned as he loosened his seat belt and opened his door! Anyway, they were here! At last! Maybe touring the candy factory would cheer him up! Plus, with his big frame on the small, thin RV mattress, they neither one got much rest! A hotel room was a good idea!

Checked in and unloaded, they took a table in the empty café! David reached for the baby and bottle! The job of feeding Adam was one Mallory and Melodye preferred over the hassle of managing the girls! He didn't mind managing the girls! He could do it all at once! He was the dad! He remembered how he and his siblings had always paid attention to their dad's edicts, while running over the top of their gentle-natured mom! He surveyed Mallory covertly! She was lovely! Positively stunning! And eager as she was to head up the Big Thompson Canyon to commence drilling operations, she seemed happy and relaxed to pause for a lunch that was destined to be slow! At the moment she was engaged with Amelia and a game on her phone!

"Look at you, 'Mea," she marveled! "You're really good!" Luminous eyes met his across the table, and he smiled as little thumbs manipulated whoever the monsters were! Or to whatever baked goods~ He had given up on games after being whipped by a bunch of green pigs that didn't die, even when you injured them mortally!

"It's Jake and Millard's game!" she explained. "It went live yesterday! And the ap wasn't free!" she laughed. "It is fun, though! I guess Lilly felt it was harmless enough to let it pass!"

He nodded, then relieved at a server's finally making an entrance, he placed their orders!

The food was slow but actually very good! Or being starved might have made sawdust taste good! After a wait to sign the meal to their room, they headed toward the lobby.

"What's next on the agenda?" He figured he knew, but was pleasantly surprised by a totally unexpected response!

"Well, the place is nearly deserted! Why don't we let the girls swim? You can start teaching them! They've been cooped up a lot in the RV!"

He nodded, 'Cooped up' being a relative term! Cooped up was when he was a kid and their family of seven made car trips in a sedan! That was cooped up! After the morning's drive from the dinosaur place, he didn't mind the diversion. Still he ventured, "You're not getting sick on me, are you?"

"Actually, I've never been better! The drill rig is in place and ready to go! I don't have to be there! Although, I thought that we can start tomorrow touring Enstrom's, then have lunch and drive up there to make my presence known~"

He nodded, pretty sure she made her presence known whether she was on-site, or not!

"So what do you think you'll find?"

"A cross-section of everything the Colorado River erodes out, on its course from its headwaters, to where it slows and broadens out here! It should be a cross-section representation of the Colorado Rockies! I wouldn't mind eventually drilling the river's mouth down in the Gulf of Mexico!

"Hmm-mm. thought you wanted to drill the Mississippi Delta!"

She agreed soberly, "It's also one of the big X's on Daddy's radar! He was certain diamonds would turn up! You know his route: Little Missouri, to the Ouachita, to the Red River, before ultimately the Mississippi, and the delta! I'm not sure an operation like that would be sanctioned by Lilly! Because she and I both know Diamonds would be targets for my search, at least, in part!

Chapter 30: *ADDICT*

Brenna raced across campus! Excitement shone! Gray was right! Response to her posts on the Earth Science Department's bulletin board had finally brought an unexpected call for her to meet with an editor of a prominent professional magazine! Of course, his main interest was in the marine sample brought to light by *The Rock Scientist's* earlier expedition! No surprise there! It was still central to a lot of controversial buzz! But the article would accomplish three things: getting her name and picture out there, free exposure for her corporation, and plaudits for the university! Reaching her car and placing a call to Gray, she was puzzled when he didn't answer! He always wanted to hear from her, regardless of whatever else might be going on! She fought alarm! One of the kids? Maybe he was hurt, or ill? After several more unsuccessful calls, she started the car and headed for home!

No one there, and still no answer to her frantic calls! She debated whether to call his office! His parents seemed to like her well enough–She maneuvered toward the freeway and downtown!

꙳ ꙳

"You're kidding!" Mallory moved from the pool enclosure and the joyous shrieks of her daughters to a quiet spot in the lobby!

"That's just great! You didn't have a clue?"

Deborah Rodriguez' distressed voice, "Well, maybe I did, but–not that it was so out-of-control!"

Mallory sank down, dazed! "Well, this could suck you under! And it won't help any of us, either! I don't think we have any choice but to all go down to Miami, find out exactly how bad it is, and bail you out! I'll find David and see how quick we can get there! I'm thinking we should try for the first of next week! The weekend we can't get with the bank~"

Stunned, she disconnected and went in search of David!

He glanced across the pool at her approach; something was up! And not something good! Placing his protesting daughters into the shallower spa, he pulled himself up and pulled a deck chair near for her! "What now?"

"It's Deborah's Aunt Rose! She's in over her head with gambling debts! Deborah just now put two and two together! But nearly too late! First, Rose borrowed against the equity in her business to stay afloat; but then, she tried even more drastic measures! So, a thug already roughed Deborah up~ Deborah and her parents have been scrambling to keep things going without letting any of us know~" Her face clouded with dejection! "It's a total mess! And I'm the one whose idea it was to launch Deborah~So if her production dies, it kind of pulls a rug from under *DiaMal*!"

David listened calmly! "Okay, don't be so hard on yourself! Your instincts about Deborah were your usual brilliance! She's the one who gave her aunt a chance!" He paused thoughtfully! "So, you need to call Diana!"

"No, could you call Daniel? I'm sure Diana's scrambling to increase production at the Philippines factory! Just when things are going so well!"

He laughed. "Things are generally going well! The surprise is that we actually have so few meltdowns to deal with! I hope this means a trip to Miami! I've been craving blintzes from Reuben's! See, there's always a silver lining!"

She smiled in spite of disastrous implications! "Well, I wouldn't mind seeing Bryce and Lisette! I can't imagine how much Mark has grown!"

"Mmmm-hmm; the rub will come when we show up with Daniel and Diana to confront Rose! She has family loyalty; as well as the Latino bond~with the other workers who aren't family!" His frown deepened! "Well, it must be dealt with! Do you think my dad can help with an intervention? I mean, it's a business problem, but it stems from a spiritual issue!"

"Maybe you should call him and see what he thinks! He can at least start praying about it! Diana should do the same with Mr. Prescott! He can pray, too, and his involvement with obtaining *Honduran* work visas, as well as his experience with different cultures as a missionary, might make him a valuable ally!" She smiled, "I'm feeling better just formulating a plan of action!"

"Should we get the girls out?" His assumption was that she would want to speed up the schedule!

"Only if you're tired of it! Do you mind if I go check on flights? I told Deborah there's no use in our getting down there over the week end when the banks are closed! But maybe we should have Gray get on top of putting together some liquid cash! Here we go again with someone's lack of consideration creating an emergency for us! Well, the main thing we need to pray, is that Rose sees her need for the Savior! They're all so religious, but~"

⊰ ⊱

Gray opened his office door apologetically to admit Brenna! "Forgive me, Love!" He landed a quick peck and retreated behind his desk! "All of this talk about the benefits of the state lotteries! They are actually curses in disguise! We received news earlier today that has sent shock waves through all of our combined endeavors! Rose Reynosa has buried herself in the bog of legalized gambling, and her puny efforts to free herself are like the proverbial struggles in quicksand~"

Not certain whether to advance or retreat, Brenna settled uneasily across from him. "I'm sorry; I'm not sure I've met Rose! Well, I met so many people at the beginning~"

He shot her a quick grin before total concentration overtook him!

Rising, she went to the outer office, returning with cups of tea!

"Ah, saving the day, as always! To answer your question, a few years back, David and Mallory began hiring young graduates from their alma mater, Murfreesboro High School! A move that has worked out brilliantly for them! One such young lady was a second generation Latin American! Well, *DiaMal* was working closely, and still is, with a family-owned leather company in Spain! Deborah's command of the Spanish language couldn't have been more opportune! And yet, Mallory soon recognized that Deborah's abilities and contributions, went far beyond her linguistic ability! Mallory and Diana helped her incorporate and form her own garment production company! Well-Mallory's idea! Diana held deep reservations! Because, although *Rodriguez* could help fill a good number of orders for *DiaMal*, they could also compete! Deborah is a talented designer and her mother, an accomplished seamstress and tailor!"

Brenna nodded. "Ah, I've seen the *Rodriguez* logo in the catalogs and been curious!"

He sipped slowly before beaming a smile at her!

She laughed. "Tea calls for a scone! Be right back!"

After several minutes of concentration on his screen and keyboard commands, he resumed his narrative.

"So, *Rodriguez* was a great concept, and Juanita, or 'Nita, Deborah's mother, still had family members who also happened to be competent garment industry workers-the problem! Most of them still lived in Central America! So my father and I have included helping obtain work visas and settling the émigrés as one of the services we offer! Overall, it has worked quite well! I guess one should expect the occasional hiccup!"

Pausing, he devoured the scone hungrily! "So overall, Deborah's family members are far better off than they ever were before! Still, one day, one of Deborah's aunts began badgering her for a raise! Although Rose was earning more than she could ever have dreamed, she was envious that Deborah, as the CEO, was making so much more! Making money off of her, Rose's, hard work! Classic management-labor misunderstanding! So, Rose wanted more money for less work! Instead of making an entire garment from start to finish, as was the *Rodriguez'* system, she only wanted to cut out the garment pieces! To everyone's amazement, Deborah single-handedly helped her start a companion corporation to specialize in the cutting aspect! She helped with the business loan available to minority women! I wouldn't say they have soared, but both corporations have been doing remarkably well! As CEO of her own burgeoning business, evidently Rose still wanted to get richer quicker! Hence her quagmire of debt as a result of the insidious sin of covetousness-leading to gambling!"

He returned full attention to the task at hand while Brenna considered his words! As a poor kid coming up hard, poisoned with Warren's bitter diatribes against the wealthy at every news story, Gray's mind-set was a strange thing for her to grasp! She was glad his attention was riveted on his monitor!

She wrestled with a new moral dilemma! Who was right? Was she right in accepting and reveling in wearing expensive clothing and exquisite jewelry, if it required the 'poor joe average' to make them, while they and their children did without? The disparity between the rich and poor troubled her, since she had been one clenched in poverty's grasp! Was Rose Reynosa so terribly wrong? What was the difference between that and what Gray did every day? What David and Mallory did? Were they all just greedy for more? Was it okay to have a closet full of expensive clothing, when it was more than she needed? Was it really that bad to play the lottery? Wasn't there something to be said for 'hope'? What if hope of winning the lottery kept someone going? Rising unsteadily, she retrieved her bag, "I'm heading home! Can I stop down in the Bistro and have a sandwich sent up to you?"

Bringing his screen saver across his work, he rose! "That's a terribly kind idea! I'm sure more nutrition will shed light on the subject! But my backing off and focusing on something else for a while may bring even greater clarity! Let's grab a late luncheon together! I've been so terribly focused on this, that I haven't asked you about your news!"

Seated across from him, she dribbled soup from her soup spoon back into the bowl, before stirring listlessly and repeating the actions! It didn't take long to share her news! It seemed to have lost its luster!

Gray didn't need a psych degree to analyze that there was a problem-but he still had a good deal of work ahead of him! Of all the times for her to decide to mope-and it wasn't like she could just state whatever was on her mind! A grin tugged at the corners of his mouth, and she picked up on it:

"What's funny?" Her tone was injured that he could have a humorous thought run through his mind!

"You know I care about you terribly! It's just-it ran through my mind, one of the numbers from *My Fair Lady*!

She twisted a pack of crackers savagely! "Let my guess! *Why Can't a Woman Be More Like a Man*? I mean, I know how easy it is for you, from your lofty perch, to condemn people who are weak!"

He looked shocked, and then smiled in relief! "Ah, there! It came out easier than I anticipated! I certainly never intended to grieve you by my attitude! I know you're still conflicted by what the Lord has given you! I can't say I understand your tormenting yourself! I've honestly tried to help you clarify issues through Scripture, and yet, you think I use the Bible to justify what we have- You know how much we tithe and give to spread the Gospel! I think Rose Reynosa was wrong to breach her position and put at risk, not only her own company and its employees, but also Deborah and the entire lot of us! And then, what can you do but confess and correct your course? Try to cover it up, while you keep on!"

Her features turned miserable. "I wasn't trying to make you mad!"

He met her stony gaze with aplomb! "I'm not angry! But I work very hard by Scriptural principles, and I know I'm villainized by a Socialistic liberal press! I'm sorry for your desperate home situation and feeling victimized! We're on opposite sides of the fence on this one! I don't want us to argue, but I must concentrate on this debacle! Admit it or not, she has created a fiasco for people who don't deserve the cost and difficulty she has created for them! You seem not to be hungry at all! I believe I'll take my food and return to my work! I'll walk you to your car first, though!"

⚕ ⚕

"Where have you been?" Summer's irate question as Brenna dropped her bag and keys on the kitchen counter!

"I had an appointment on campus, and then I stopped by to talk to Gray about it!"

"Did you guys get into a fight?" Summer could be exasperatingly perceptive!

"No, he told me his opinion in no uncertain terms, and then said he didn't want to argue! He walked me to my car and went back up to work!"

"You must have made him really ticked! Usually he does most of his stuff from his office here! Especially this late! Just because you have a rich dad to fall back on~"

Brenna moved past her sister and pulled her shoes off, "Will you relax, Summer? I'm not blowing this 'gig'! Gray and I love each other and we're committed to one another! And we're committed to God~"

"Okay, do you always have to go there?"

Brenna sighed, "No, I'm sorry! I just try to make you feel secure and happy in Gray's devotion to us~I know your entire existence has been insecure! I find a decent dad, in my quest~and you learn that yours died~probably before you were even born~"

"Yeah, and he wasn't a war hero~or anything~"

"No~but~mother knew him from their church youth group! It's likely he was a Christian, and just tried the rebellious teenage thing! Summer, it you'd receive Christ, you might still meet him some day~"

A huffy, "That's a long time off!"

"Well, you can hope!" Brenna didn't intend to respond in anger, and Summer flounced away!

⚕ ⚕

Daniel and Diana met with Gray in his office! It wasn't just the money, although it was a hefty sum! It was more the ticklish situation of dealing with the criminal entity! They weren't sure which way to turn!

308

"We can't run to Erik Bransom with every problem we encounter~"
Diana's serious eyes reflected the lovely blue of her ensemble!

"Righto! Quite right!" Gray's tone sounded heartier than he felt! "But
he is Mallory's step-father~"

Daniel scoffed. "You know, the state lottery commissions have to be
aware that things like this happen routinely! Either that, or they don't want
to know! Mallory doesn't alert Erik to everything, either! I'm not sure it's
an FBI issue, but if it is, Erik has gotten raked over the coals routinely
for involving himself with anything that directly protects or aids our
businesses! Frankly, it scares me to death, trying to pay off gangsters to
make this go away! I mean, do we ask for a receipt? All I have to go on is
a few TV programs! Where, usually, everyone ends up shooting everyone
else! This is a lot of money!"

Diana rummaged in her bag, "I'll call Erik!"

⚰ ⚰

Brenna listened to a rundown of the kids' afternoon! Quite a few
disagreements and scuffles to tattle on one another about, but they were
all still living and basically unhurt! "Okay, you know it's not nice to spit~or
pinch~" Her phone jangled and she went in search of it! Alex! She was
mentally exhausted. Still, she answered, then listened to his news, stunned!

"You're both here, in Tulsa? We can't! Gray's working late down town!"

She caught Summer making a face! Summer wanted to be around Alex
at every opportunity! Feeling trapped, she suddenly acquiesced! "Warn him
about what he's letting himself in for! Can you give us forty-five minutes?"

Disconnecting, she issued orders for everyone to use the restroom,
wash up, find shoes! Going out to dinner didn't seem like a totally bad
plan! The fridge and pantry seemed to run low quickly, no matter how
much Gray tried to keep up!

"Forty-five minutes! I'm starved! Why's he in town?" Summer always
grumbled, no matter what!

"Because there's been some kind of ministerial meeting in Oklahoma
City, and mother's oldest brother has been attending it! I guess he pastors
a church, and he wants to meet us!"

Luke paused, hopping on one foot as he tied a tennis shoe on the other!
"Are we gonna have to go live with him?"

Brenna laughed. "I'm pretty sure you're not invited to do that! Besides that, you live here! It's no big deal! Alex originally told me my aunts and uncles would try to box us out of the little bit of money our grandfather has accumulated!"

Luke's expression registered doubt! "I'm starved, too! Call back and make the time earlier! We're all ready to~"

"Okay, I'm not ready! I'm gonna change and redo my makeup~" Even as she spoke, she wasn't sure why she would do that! She looked okay! And her plan had been to order pizza and start the kids watching a movie so she could get alone with the Lord to grapple with Him about her conflicted feelings! Maybe at her morning devotions~

※ ※

"You were planning to what?" Erik's gruff voice came out crankier than ever! "Whose screwball idea was that?"

Diana answered diffidently, and he thundered "Y'all put your heads together, and that was your best plan? You're right, it's not exactly on my playground! Who was that Miami PD detective that worked gangs? You know, the one that *El Diablo* turned himself in to?"

Daniel entered the conversation, "I guess we're stumped! Who are you talking about? We never heard of this *El Diablo*. Doesn't that roughly translate to, The Devil?"

"Okay, I'll call David; he'll remember! Whatever you do, don't try to pay extortion~to these thugs! If they don't kill you, you can get yourselves in legal hot water! This woman has created a real mess!"

"Yes, because Deborah was threatened if she involved the police," Gray's worry reflected on his features and in his voice.

"Yeah," Erik grumbled, "They say that on the all the TV shows! Guess that's where the general population, including the thugs, gets their tutorials! Deborah and all involved will be safer with the authorities involved, than with trying to wing it!"

※ ※

The saddest words of tongue or pen,
Are those which say what might have been!

Brenna fell in love! Shaking hands dazedly and staring into the depths of tawny brown eyes, she let herself go! Either the rest of the kids took their cues from her, or they also sensed an atypical sense of love and acceptance! A big teddy-bear of a man, Uncle Jerome lavished hugs all round, before distributing candy bars with a mischievous, "You have to promise you can still eat your dinner!"

Brenna laughed. That wouldn't be a problem with this crowd! Her biggest regrets of the moment were the absences of Gray and Jacob! Summer managed to position herself between Alex and the new-found, kindly uncle—which might have rankled with Brenna, except that Jerome had immediately launched into a narrative about Simon! Surreal, to discover a real person behind the long-since-deceased man's name! If the story was opening wounds, it was also releasing infection and pouring in soothing balm! There wasn't a dry eye at the table as a few disjointed tidbits coalesced to bring a better perspective for their fractured lives! Before the beverages were delivered, Jerome had explained to Summer how he knew for certain that Simon had received Christ and the gift of eternal life! And although drug usage had overwhelmed his friend's physical body, he knew for certain they would meet again in Heaven! Without a second thought, or embarrassment at making a decision in front of heartless siblings, Summer accepted the same free gift!

At once jubilant, but at the same time sad at Gray's missing the epic moment, Brenna considered sending a text! But before her finger pressed the first key, Summer bolted from her place with a delighted cry! There stood Gray!

Summer's words poured out! About wanting to make the decision, but not wanting Gray to miss it–Then, he was overcome with emotion, as were also some diners at nearby tables!

Gradually, the heightened emotions eased off, and the normal turmoil of their placing orders took over! As the kids enjoyed candy bars, and the adults attacked chips and salsa, Brenna conveyed her thanks to Alex!

"Thank you for bringing us together! It's too bad the Grand Duchess, Anastasia, didn't have an uncle like ours!"

Alex laughed, still of the persuasion, that with a large enough sum of money at stake, anyone would have met the same fate as the poetic heroine!

"But, that's such a bleak outlook," she reasoned!

His response was filled with admiration! "I'm amazed how your outlook can be anything but bleak! I feel more regret than I can ever convey, at not having been there for you; and yet, I feel like I would have loused up the parenting thing~and your life wouldn't be the shining light that it is!"

Tears sprang to her eyes! He was right! As engaged and caring as he might have been, he was unregenerate! He didn't have answers for being a wise parent! Especially~he would have been what? A single parent? With her being batted back and forth between him and her mother like a ping-pong ball? How many times had he been married; how many stepmothers for her to have adjusted to? Too many variables to consider~about what might have been~With clarity she suddenly saw that the suffering which God had allowed her to endure, had molded her into who He wanted her to be! What had Alex just said; that he saw her as a 'shining light'? She prayed desperately for it to be true, that she might yet light the way for more!

※ ※

Uncharacteristically, Gray wasn't ready to head straight to their room! Having put in an exhausting day, he seemed to crave the turmoil that was his family! On the other hand, Brenna sought moments alone with him, to get her balance restored! Although she didn't know either Deborah, or her lottery-playing-fiend-of-an-aunt, she still felt a certain empathy! Why was it okay for so many people to have more than they could take care of, while others, especially those stymied by ethnicity and prejudice~? Since no one seemed to miss her in the general confusion, she sank down in the middle of her bed with her Bible!

"Lord, You know I want to please You! Just let me know what to do!"

Opening her Bible, her eyes fell on John chapter eight! Where Mary took expensive ointment to anoint Jesus' feet prior to His crucifixion! It was the traitorous and covetous Judas Iscariot, who spoke against the sacrificial act! Implying Mary should never have been in possession of anything costly~and she certainly had no business wasting it! He used the smokescreen of helping the poor, which elicited Jesus' response in verse eight:

> *John 8:8 For the poor always ye have with you; but me ye have not always.*

Brenna regarded the words in wonder! According to the words of Jesus, there would always be the less fortunate! Despite high-sounding rhetoric and government programs, there was no eraser, no magic wand-for lifting the whole of the world's societies from Satan's various bondages! Of which a major one was poverty-leaving a trail of hunger and desperation! And according to Gray, Rose Reynosa, was doing better than she could ever have imagined! That demon of covetousness for more, would now cause her to lose what she had! An *Aesop's Fable* from a childhood reader came to mind: the one about a dog carrying a large steak in his mouth! As he loped across a bridge, he caught sight of his reflection in the water! The reflection of his steak appeared larger than the actual one, so he snapped hungrily at the reflection! To alas, lose the real thing!

As she sat pondering in wonder at being led to chapter and verse, something overwhelming dawned on her! Summer had been issued into the Kingdom! They were all out there talking ninety to nothing about Uncle Jerome and the whole evening! And here she sat like a bump, chasing philosophical ghosts through her mind, missing epic family moments she had barely dared dream of!

⁂

In Miami, Daniel breathed a sigh of relief, that Rose's loan shark and his associates had been booked in by the Miami Police Department! The criminal was out the large sum he had leant! He wouldn't be needing it in the pen! Still, he, or his higher-ups, or lower-downs, or someone, would be looking to recoup the loss! Aware of that, the overworked gang unit promised to keep an extra eye on Deborah's corporate interests!

Since she was actually creating a previously unimagined sense of community, the possibility was great that her neighbors would help keep watch! They had been known to! The chief detective smiled, remembering!

"Maybe you could contact that group of senior citizens again! They were quite the colorful bunch!"

Daniel laughed agreement! "They are! But they get things done! Great idea! We'll contact Steb! We'll also use some of our scraped up cash to beef up security!"

Relieved with that victory, they still faced the hurdle of facing down Rose and convincing her to relinquish the reins of her company! At least until she could get help with her problem!

True to form, with the positive outcome of the thugs ending up behind bars, she was smilingly insisting on her, 'No harm; no foul,' philosophy!

Diana and Mallory, whose fashion lines were poised to sustain the biggest hit, disagreed! Her careless and heedless actions needed to be dealt with, before she did meet with catastrophe!

To everyone's relief, even Nita chose to side with earning profits and prevailing good sense, rather than with her sister!

Manny's eyes were sad as he made his decree to his sister-in-law! "We love you very greatly! And for that reason we cannot allow this behavior to continue! It is destructive to you, first-"

"No! You just wish everything for yourself!" Screeches of rage made the entire group cringe! They hadn't expected the scene to be pretty! "You wish to control everything-"

Manny shook his head, and Nita put a supportive hand on his shoulder before he spoke softly, "That is not true! But if it were true, it would have been you and your foolish actions that opened the door for me to do so! We have all spoken together extensively, and Deborah will preside over both enterprises! Pablo, will remain as COO!"

His face showed deep concern. "You still do not even get it, that you have endangered our lives, first of all; but secondly, you have risked what we are trying to achieve among the Latino culture-both here in Miami, and in Texarkana; but also reaching all the way to Honduras-and possibly beyond! We are gaining political clout and economic power, and showing our ability to be successful, and then to handle success wisely-" he hesitated, wishing his words would break his defiant sister-in-law! As a staunch Catholic, he was loathe to relinquish her and her 'weakness' to the Baptist pastor!

꒦ ꒷

"Well, that was nerve-rattling!" Brenna's breathless whisper in Gray's ear as they found seats at their gate! "I guess all's well that ends well! You really accomplished miracles-" She broke off as her phone rang. Her face brightened, "It's Jacob!"

Gray nodded. Having not heard from his son in a couple of days, he was glad for the call, too! Satisfaction gave way to fear at Brenna's horrified expression!

"What are you saying, Jacob? That's not-well-what did-she say-Summer-wouldn't-"

Gray reached for the phone, but she swung away! "Okay, well let me call-and make-sure-she's okay- Okay; call you back!"

To Gray's total exasperation, she moved away from him to make her next call! He fought panic, unable to discern what the newest issue was! He tried again to approach and she danced away, terror on every feature!

"She doesn't answer!"

"Who?" he demanded!

He listened as Brenna left a panicked voicemail! "Summer? Would you please call me~"

He watched, numbly, as she repeated the call~to be sent to voicemail each time!

"Brenna! What did Jacob say about Summer?"

As emotion overcame her, she sobbed, unable to explain! Terrified, he pressed his oldest daughter's number in his speed dial!

"Sorry," Summer answered immediately, apology ready! "With Aunt Diana and Uncle Daniel in Miami, they said we could come over and swim! So I was across the pool and didn't hear my phone! What's wrong? Why you keep calling and calling? Is Bren okay? And the baby?"

"Yes, she's fine! Jacob just rang up, and said something's wrong with you!"

Summer laughed uneasily! "Well, I'm fine! I called him earlier to tell him I got saved! Well, he asked me why? And I told him lots of reasons! Then I started telling him that someday~when I get to Heaven~hopefully not any time soon~I will meet my father~er~um~I mean my biological dad! You're my father! Well, he got all upset and told me I sounded like our mother did~like I'm suicidal~which I told him~"

With a light chuckle, Gray sank woozily back into the chair! Fatherhood wasn't for the faint of heart! "All right, then, dear; enjoy your swim! Brenna and I will see you soon. Give the other children our love!"

⚑ ⚑

Brenna disconnected from her call, trying not to be aggravated! First, she had felt that the magazine interviewer had acted tacky from their first meeting, deliberately misconstruing every answer she supplied! Then, he asked her to set up an interview for him with Mallory, (probably his hope from first contacting her)! And then bringing up the expunged legal difficulty in Boston!

Now, she stared at an email that informed her that other items of interest had come to the editor's attention, causing him to scrub her article until a later date! She sighed, 'Guess fame and fortune are hard come by'!

Chapter 31: SURRENDER

Brenna sat on the upper deck of an English Channel ferry, staring in wonder as the White Cliffs of Dover emerged from fog! Summer hopped up, camera in hand, determined to capture every moment of the enchanting trip!

"Cripes, Summer, don't go overboard!" Jacob's amended word choices were an improvement, and Brenna laughed nervously! She hated to be the ever-nagging big sister, but she was glad for Jacob's order for Sum to be careful! The other kids couldn't mask their excitement as the ferry approached the dock! Gray appeared, distributing passports to the older kids for entry back into Britain! With a wink and a smile, he stepped back, motioning Brenna to precede him!

With entrance formalities behind them, they emerged into the charming maze of streets in historic Dover!

"Look," Emily's finger and wistful gaze directed attention to the ancient fortress perched atop the cliffs, overlooking the Channel, "Is that another castle?"

Brenna couldn't help smiling at Em's broadened vowel, 'Cawstle'!

"I believe it is, but we need to catch the train! Jacob needs to get to London to catch his flight!"

"I don't want him to leave~" the little face turned petulant!

"Why not? He just teases the daylights out of you!"

"Oh, yeah; I forgot!" With the sentiment forgotten, she skipped blithely ahead to join Terry!

Gray laughed, and circled Brenna's waist with his arm as they surged toward the train station! "Stay together, children," he admonished good-naturedly, once again!

"There's so much to see," Brenna defended their tendency to scatter!

"Indeed, souvenir shops! We have accumulated frightfully a lot! We are on a time constraint; but once we board and get settled, we can enjoy a brunch! Lovely morning, what?"

Brenna settled in contentedly against the window in the first class car! Always, when she settled down following activity, she could feel the baby's movements! A nice feeling and reassuring! The next thing she knew, the train was slowing and travelers around her were gathering their belongings! "I wanted to watch the scenery!"

"Yes, but you seemed exhausted, Love! And that with jet lag~ And, the scenery you missed was extraordinarily ordinary!"

⊰ ⊱

James 5:20 Let him know, that he that he which converteth the sinner from the error of his way shall save a soul from death, and shall hide a multitude of sins.

David and Jeff spoke softly to one another regarding one of the 'Camp' men who seemed to be making enormous strides in the right direction! Through the years of the camp's existence, some men's lives had been miraculously salvaged! Other stories seemed less spectacular! Pastor John Anderson's constant encouragement to his sons, was that their work made an eternal difference! Even men who accepted the Lord, and then didn't seem able to pull it together for the victorious life available to them; were on the road to heaven rather than eternal destruction!

Still, Jeff felt that Warren Weston could succeed beyond the camp's boundaries! David would have agreed more readily, were it not for what was at stake!

Warren had requested an early release for good behavior from the Massachusetts Corrections System! And his behavior since his arrival at the Arkansas camp was better than average! But David's concern was that if Weston headed to Colorado to work with Jacob at his heavy equipment company, he might be after his son's newly acquired wealth! David could tell that Gray had reservations!

Dreading the confrontation, David told Jeff to send the resident to his office!

Weston appeared, hat in hand, shifting nervously from one foot to the other!

David plunged in, "Okay, we've received paperwork from The Commonwealth of Massachusetts! Tell me again, why you've chosen Colorado~"

"Well, I could smart off to you and tell you I've heard it's a pretty place!"

David waited! The fact that Weston had already refrained from his chronic sarcasm must be a good sign!

"Well, you know, like I did when the kids came to visit me! I mouthed off to Brenna~she's a~a good kid~ya know? And my son~I guess he wanted me to say I was proud~I never knew he~cared what I thought~I said stupid stuff about him coming into money~and all that~all the wrong stuff, that even the little kids could tell was real stupid!"

David sat regarding the man silently.

"Hey, if you're telling me, 'No', I get it! My times about up! When it is, I'm not sure what I'll do or where I'll go~I guess~I missed a bunch of good~chances to be a dad~If Mr. Prescott wants me to back away~well, I get it~Jacob and Millard couldn't have gotten that game~into the~marketplace~just a couple of neighborhood kids~from a 'declining neighborhood'~ I'm not too bad of a mechanic, though! I think I could be of help to Jacob and the Alvaredo kid with their equipment!"

David nodded slowly! "Yeah, you're a great mechanic! One of the reasons I'm reluctant to turn you loose!" He laughed easily! "You're also quite a talented artist! Maybe you can develop your skills and get some of your pieces into the art galleries that abound~"

"Art galleries that abound~" Warren's words parroted David's blankly! Then the light dawned! "Art galleries that abound ~out in Colorado? Does that mean~?"

David nodded slowly! "You know that Jacob isn't interested in spiritual things? Alvaredo's a Christian, but he rides the fence about it!" David paused, "Been there; done that! The most miserable time of my life! Colorado is a chance for you, Weston! If you stay close to the Lord, you can reach lofty heights! Or you can fall off the shelf!"

☙ ❧

Brenna's eyes filled with tears, and she met Gray's equally emotional gaze with wonder! Welcome little Levi Alexander Prescott! Seven pounds and one ounce, eighteen inches long on the dot!

Gray clasped the tiny bundled body protectively! "Well, the other children are eager to begin tossing him about~"

Brenna laughed, "I just realized there's a blessing in disguise with all of them coming down with colds at the same time! They have to keep their distance for that reason, if nothing else! Give the poor little guy a chance!"

"Ah, in God's infinite wisdom~although I sympathize with the children feeling so stuffed up and miserable! Not to complain, because colds are something they will get over~"

Brenna rose to give the little blue stocking cap another kiss!

"Take it easy, Love," Gray cautioned anxiously.

"Okay, but I feel fantastic!" A rapturous sigh! "You know, I thought I accomplished something great when I received my Bachelor's Degree~but right now, I can't even describe~I feel like singing *Hannah's Song*! What a miracle~ It's true that God's plans for us are light years beyond our own capacity to plan our lives! When I think about the day we met, I was trying to run from you! I didn't have any money, and I thought your father had sent you to pressure me~"

"Into buying our business services! But no, I was on my own mission, to pressure you into marrying me!

"And at that moment in time, I didn't want either a husband~or a baby!"

❦

It was hard for Gray to tell Summer, 'No,' but he felt he had no choice! "Summer, that will accomplish little we don't know, and it will be expensive! With what Alex and Jerome have told you and your mother's telling you your father's name was Simon~have you searched him online for a photograph to see if there's a resemblance?"

Gray was afraid to begin the process of exhuming bodies! What had seemed like a good idea at first, now just seemed fraught with risk! If DNA didn't match, there might be no end in Summer's tormented search!

"I have searched online! But I don't see family resemblances in people! And the pictures I've found aren't real clear! Just like everyone carrying on about Levi looking just like you~they see something I don't! Sorry!"

His phone indicated a message and he frowned! It seemed as if Alex Hamilton planned to do double duty as a grandfather to make up for his missed years fathering Brenna! His third time 'just happening to be in town' in ten days! And could he pop in and see Brenna and Levi?

But between Gray's courteous upbringing and a new idea for helping Summer, he agreed cordially!

"Okay, Dear, Alex is on his way from the airport~"

Summer frowned, "What; again?"

Gray shrugged, "I thought you liked him, and Levi is his grandson!"

"It's just kinda funny! I never knew anyone to take on so much about a baby before! No one ever welcomed our arrival and came visiting with toys and blankets and clothes! For a cool guy like Alex to go so far~out of his way~so often~"

Gray felt fresh profound sympathy for his daughter! "Well, actually, he's doing what grandparents are supposed to do! And my parents are too, even though, Levi is their sixteenth grandchild! It's hard for me to grasp that there are so many children of the world who have not been planned for and welcomed!"

"That's why I'm not sure abortion's such a bad idea~"

Gray bit back a response! Summer was growing in grace since her salvation, and the Holy Spirit could convict and lead in her life! His taking her to task on every word she uttered would probably be counterproductive!

Brenna laughed as Alex arrived with yet another New England Patriot's outfit and a team football!

"Between you trying to make him into a New England Patriot, and Mallory's Red Sox stuff, what chance does he have?"

"Well, you're from Boston! Don't tell me you're a turncoat! And I'll encourage Mallory to keep up the good work, too! My grandson needs positive influences in his life!"

Brenna laughed again. Mallory was an exemplary influence on anyone whose path she crossed, and for higher stakes than team loyalty!

"So, how are things with Kayla? Or should I ask?"

"Let me feed him, and I'll fill you in!"

"He just ate! Sorry! I didn't know you were flying in!"

"Then I should probably head back to the airport"~body language and facial expression belied his words.

"Well, unless you're on a time constraint, stay for tea! Make yourself at home!"

"Can I hold him and watch him sleep?"

"Sure; he's turning into a spoiled baby at being held so much!"

"I'm his grandfather! That's my job!"

Gathered for tea, Gray took a chance! "I'm sorry to pump you for information~about the past~every time we see you~"

Alex looked up from devoted attention to his grandson, surprised. "Hey, no problem; what haven't I told you?"

"Well, of course, Simon is deceased, but what about his family?" Gray tried to sound discreet, but Summer nodded emphatically!

"Do I have grandparents, and aunts and uncles and cousins? I wanted to do DNA testing to make sure~but~uh~and Gray said for me to see if I have any family resemblance to pictures!"

Alex focused on Levi, who tried to force heavy eyelids open, adorable little features contorting, and lithe body squirming! This was a tough conversation! If anyone had ever verbally accused him of being responsible for someone's death, it was Simon's family! At last, he spoke unsteadily!

"They were good people, and they were heartbroken! They blamed me, and~uh~your mother, and Richard, too! Something to the effect of, 'church youth groups should be purer from evil influences'! Of course, I wasn't part of the church~just met Irene~and then some of the kids~uh~er~outside of church activities~"

Neither Summer nor Brenna could respond!

"I think they moved out west within a year~to escape the ghosts~Ohio, Idaho, Iowa; I'm not sure where!"

Although Summer was pretty much geographically challenged, she frowned! "Those states are all back east!"

"Everything's 'out west' from Boston," Brenna reminded

She watched enviously as Alex cradled Levi and fed him a bottle! What would it have been like~if he had known~would he have been a doting father~as he was proving to be a grandfather? No way to know! Love for her mother hadn't prevailed over her grandfather's irate threats and demands that he get away and stay away!

She listened, only half-way interested in his reconciliation with his wife! But to her surprise, she liked Kayla and was glad for Alex's chance to stabilize a relationship!

⊰ ⊱

Alex Hamilton pulled his high end rent car up to the curb at 2018 Dennison Lane in Bristol, Iowa, and surveyed a neat but modest home! The residence

321

of Martin and Della O'Connell! He hesitated, knowing what he needed to do, but knowing it was going to be unpleasant! Well, as long as he had made the journey this far-

⊣ ⊢

Brenna regarded the unknown phone number in puzzlement! With calls dying down about Mallory's ocean find, she was unsure-

"Hello, this is Brenna Prescott." Her answer cordial and professional. "How may I help you?"

A long pause on the other end nearly caused her to disconnect, but then a timid, thin voice came, barely audible-

"Yes, this is Brenna; with whom am I speaking? How can I help-"

Her knees dropped her suddenly into her office chair, and she stretched to reach a tissue.

"You-you want to meet me? Um-uh-yes, Ma'am; I'd like that very-much-" Forcing out her voice past the lump in her throat, she jotted down a date and time! Alex was full of surprises!

Disconnecting, she placed a call to him, "I just got off the phone with your mother! It seemed a little surreal! You couldn't have given me a heads up?"

He laughed apologetically! "My mother told me basically the same thing! They never knew they were grandparents, and now they're great-grandparents! My relationship with my parents hasn't always been smooth, and when I found out about you, well, I wasn't sure how they'd react! I mean, they used to bug me to no end about when I was going to give them grandkids, but my marriages never seemed that stable, and society seemed so loused up-I didn't have a clue-well, we've been over that already-They're coming to see you next week? I hope that works for you-"

"It does, I guess! I'll be nervous-"

"Would it help if I flew in at the same time?" his voice was eager. "I'll get another chance to see Levi!"

Brenna laughed, "Yes, I think it would help a lot! Don't buy out the stores for him, though! He's growing so fast, he isn't going to be able to wear everything, even once- Hey-um- thanks for how you've been-you know after the response I got from Richard-"

"Yeah, I know! I talked to your Uncle Jerome again, and don't be surprised if Richard doesn't still come around- Uh-in the meantime, maybe you should warn Summer that I went to Iowa to face Simon's parents~"

For the second time, her knees plopped her suddenly into her chair! "Really! Uh~how did that go?"

"Well, tense, at first! Martin and Della are their names! My appearance jolted them to no end! Della pulled out her Christianity trump card about their responsibility to forgive me~So, that being said, they let me in the door and listened to me say my piece! I'm glad I'm not a Christian, so that if I don't want to forgive or like people~"

His words worried Brenna, about being glad not to be saved, but she bypassed the issue! "So, did you tell them about Summer?"

"I did! That was my sole reason for facing them! They were pretty surprised, I think! Simon had a sister, Amber, who was a little older. She has kids in college now, so Summer has a couple of cousins about her age! I think when they get over the shock, they may reach out! I hope so. You know, it's funny what Summer said about not being able to see family resemblances; but her cousin Bethany, well, it's scary how much they look alike!"

⚔ ⚔

Summer turned her face toward towering peaks, glad for a chance to return to southeastern Colorado to visit Jacob! She gazed around the historic, but stark building Jacob and Tim ran the heavy equipment business from! It definitely needed a woman's touch! Dusting and mopping to begin with~the furniture was all makeshift! Junk salvaged from surrounding stores and businesses that were closing their doors! She frowned at Warren! One of her reasons for wanting to come was to make sure he didn't fleece her brother out of any of his newly acquired green!

"Why don't you go to the lumber company and get some stuff to build a decent looking counter to go across here?" Hand motions indicated her concept!

Her step father squinted at her strangely! Last he knew, she wasn't his boss! He worked for Jacob; not for her! Still, with the equipment in tip-top shape, her project intrigued him! Clarifying her thoughts on the project, he went in search of his son for permission to use the pickup and make sure he was onboard with the idea!

Warren smirked! Since the idea was Summer's, Jacob opposed it! What else was new? These kids would rather fight than breathe! It brought back memories of Irene! And family life! A hectic, dysfunctional family life-but something-

"Yeah, she's thinking something that we can move around," he expounded to Jacob, including Tim, who was just putting in his appearance. "It'll look more businesslike immediately, but we can shove it out of the way when we get ready to redo the floor!"

Jacob shot a killer glare and Summer stuck her tongue out at him!

"Nothing's wrong with the floor!" Jacob's frustration boiling over! "I thought you wanted to come visit; not take over!"

Warren's gaze traveled from one to the other! "I gotta say this! It's like music to my ears to hear you guys fighting again! Look, I know she's just a girl, and I don't pretend to know about business and taxes and stuff! But, I think if you have all this money coming in, it's called investing to put some of it in this here other business of yours!"

Summer bristled at the 'She's just a girl comment'! Not sure why! Warren had always been an idiot!

"I'm gonna go get some buckets and brushes and stuff to start cleaning this pig sty! When I get back, you can go get the stuff for building the counter!"

ᛁ ᛒ

Brenna wasn't sure whether to be miffed at Gray, or not! He was claiming work demands as an excuse to send her and Levi alone, to meet with Alex and his parents! Lacking confidence in her mothering ability, she felt extra concern! Not just on trial for herself with grandparents that were alien to her, and vice versa; but on trial as a mother!

She spoke reticently, "Is there anything I can help you clear up? Or that Terry can help with-to free you up-"

"No, I think not! Thank you, though, Love, for the offer! Charm their socks off!" He gave her a hard kiss and planted a gentle one on his son's cheek! "What's for them not to love, after all?"

'Yeah, really; what'? She watched as he loped easily down the stairs, leaving a hint of cologne!

ᛁ ᛒ

Warren paused to watch in wonder, as Summer, on hands and knees, attacked layers of wax and film on undulating, worn linoleum! Quite the worker! Nothing she ever exhibited at home~Brenna did most everything that Irene couldn't~Brenna did most everything~

"Watch your eyes, Jacob muttered at him! Thought you were building a counter!"

Warren flushed! Though his step-daughter had grown right cute, and was crawling around with her backside in the air, his thoughts were more appreciative of her efforts than they were lustful! Without responding, he returned to his project! Guessed it was a good thing for Jacob to finally get protective of his sisters!

⇥ ⇤

Between Alex and Kayla, Brenna had no opportunity to exhibit her mothering skills to her newly met grandparents, good or bad! Latham and Sandra Hamilton were amazing! Open and easy to talk to, Brenna felt like it was Christmas! Her first time ever, to have doting grandparents! They laughed and talked and made over every word she said like she was the last word in both cute and wisdom! They kept snapping pictures as though they could make up for the lost years! Grandparently, in every sense of the word, yet modern and vibrant! Brenna guessed that Sandra's timidity on the phone had made her sound older and frailer than she was! Evidently shy at making the contact!

"She has to post the pictures to Face Book now," Latham explained good-naturedly! "She's a good photographer, though! Even with just a phone! She has a big kit and caboodle of other expensive cameras too! We've~uh~traveled a good bit~say, are you familiar with a travel blog called, *By the Seaside with Nanci Burnside?*"

Brenna laughed that she wasn't, proud of grandparents who had traveled to the far corners of the planet!

"Well, this Nanci (Burnside) Higgins who owns the blog~she's bought quite a few of Sandra's pictures and articles from some of our trips! Sandra buys lots of cute clothes, too, from Mrs. Higgins and her associates!"

"Oh!" Realization overtook Brenna, making her glad Gray wasn't along for the evening!

"What, Dear?" Sandra picked up on her new-found granddaughter's confusion!

"Nothing! I guess I'm just so blown away by your adventures! World travel was something I always felt was way beyond my reach! But then, we had this great trip to Europe! I wish Gray were here so you could meet him!"

Sandra hugged her warmly! "We, will, Darling! Of that you can be certain!"

Chapter 32:   TRIUMPH

Brenna experienced acute guilt as Sandra and Latham lavished her with invitations, gifts, and pride in her, while Simon's parents still hadn't made gesture one toward Summer!

Gray listened to her anguish thoughtfully, "It isn't like you wrote the script, that both a father and doting grandparents would come to you~while Summer still has no one~"

She nodded, "It has to bother her, though! Remember how jealous she was of me, just getting those cute new purple jeans?"

Laughter chased the frown away, "Ah, the purple jeans; yes! How could I have forgotten them?"

She sniffed defensively! "They were cute! I liked them!"

"I did, too; and then you were so overwrought when the first pair disappeared during your abandoning ship! A miracle that you were not lost, as well! But back to Summer~it concerns me greatly, too; I must admit! I have made it quite a matter of prayer~that her Aunt Amber, or her cousins, or someone would reach out to her~"

"The way family can behave brings me back to that first night of meeting Alex, and his story of the Russian royal family's demise! I thought he was terribly cynical!"

"Cynicism usually comes as a result of expecting too much from people, and the corresponding disappointment! The Bible cautions us repeatedly not to put confidence in men, ultimately! That confidence in God is well-placed! Sometimes, I think He purposely causes people in our lives to fail us, so we see His love and dependability by contrast!"

Brenna blinked rapidly, fighting the tears sparkling on her lashes! "It's just that Summer has known nothing but disappointment! And Alex went and humbled himself to the O'Connells again! He told me he's glad he's not a Christian so that he doesn't have the responsibility of loving and forgiving people!"

"Hmmm; it sounds as though we should pause for a prayer meeting!"

⛩ ⛩

Jacob frowned as Summer pulled away for a cleaning job!

"You okay?" Tim looked up from a heavy equipment and supplies catalog to inquire of his partner!

"Yeah, her and all her Christian garbage still keep me worried!"

"She's a trooper! She'll be fine!"

Jacob snorted! "You weren't the one to find my mother-"

Tim set the catalog aside! "No; I can't begin to imagine! I didn't know that you-"

"Yeah, it was me, and it wasn't the first time! But-that time-that was it-And what about that professor of yours?"

"What about him? He didn't hang himself because he was a Christian eager for heaven! He was a died-in-the-wool atheist! People commit suicide all the time, and it's sad-really cruel to those left behind feeling like abject failures-"

"People that commit suicide go to Hell, if there is such a place! Because according to the Commandments, it's a sin to kill! Brenna and Summer, going on and on about our mother's being in a better place-they make my skin crawl! It's just a nice story to help them cope! But then, what happens when they can't cope anymore? And they believe that Jesus is up there with arms wide open to tell them killing themselves is fine-"

"Why don't you come to a singles' activity with us Friday night? We have lots of fun-"

"It's church; right? Count me out!"

"Yeah, but it isn't boring stuff! It's a lot of fun and playing games, a chance to get acquainted with other people dealing with the same questions! Our pastor's cool, and he really makes stuff relevant! Just once! Give it a try?"

Jacob looked at him shrewdly, "I'll think it over!"

⛩ ⛩

Summer studied her bank book with elation! An additional ninety dollars! Well, make that eighty-one-with the tithe taken out! Her brain went into tug-of-war mode! Tithing was a principle the Bible stuck with all the way through! And Brenna had done it, from her first days as a Christian, even though struggling with a crummy job and college expenses! And look where she was now? Just a coincidence? That she gave when she didn't really have it to give? Because she believed God would bless her? And she knew Gray did it! No telling what he earned; and how much ten per cent of that was! Probably in a stratosphere her brain couldn't grasp! Still, ninety dollars looked so much better than eighty-one! Maybe when she got a little more of a balance accumulated she could start!

⊰ ⊱

David listened to a news flash from Daniel!

"The sprinkler system-" his first thought-was to ask if it triggered!

"Yeah, it kicked in! So, there's some water damage-it'll slow production down some-at least it won't bring it to a screeching halt!"

"So, how did Rose respond to it?"

"I didn't hear! But the fire was arson-if it wasn't tied to her gambling debt, it's an awfully funny coincidence! If it doesn't have her attention, it has Deborah's! And local law enforcement, which had relaxed its vigilance, will be on higher alert again!"

"That's good! What's the latest on the Colorado vigilante group?" David and Mallory usually took their cue from the Faulkners' silence about Alexandra and her mining operation in the Colorado Rockies! But since Daniel's call was about violence and the threats to their various enterprises, he asked!

"Well, the Forestry Service and their law enforcement arm, run periodic patrols through all of the National Forests! No sign of our threat! But disappearing in millions of acres of forests would be easy enough for a novice! These guys are pros at disappearing until they're ready to strike!"

"Yeah, I hear ya," David acknowledged! "We have some news about Halsey and Pritchard! They took plea bargains! Guess they'll get a couple of years in the slammer, at best! And that's for the illegal dumping! Their corporate espionage and theft from *DiaMo*, as well as the cold blooded attempt on Brenna's life-didn't get a blink from the Federal Prosecutor!"

"That's sad! They can beat up on people all day long, but threaten Mother Nature, and they get the book thrown at them! Shows again how topsy-turvy our value system has grown! Well, I could keep you all day, but I figured you should know about the fire at the plant!"

"Yeah, thanks! Have a good evening! Tell your family our family says, 'Hi'!"

⊣ ⊢

Jacob frowned as he watched Tim help Summer roast a marshmallow! What was up with that? When did this take hold? Plus, their attention to each other left him feeling like a real social outcast among the group of people he didn't know and felt uncomfortable around! Maybe he should do a disappearing act, go back to the shop and call to rat on Summer to Gray and Brenna! He spun toward his pickup, and there stood Andy McGuire in his path!

The pastor thrust his hand out, "Hi, I'm Andy! You're here with your sister, and she left you high and dry? That's the worst! Hang with me, and I'll introduce you around! Glad you could make it! You own the heavy equipment company in town, right? With Tim? Hey, I heard you're a computer genius, too, and that you developed *Yeti Treasure?*"

Jacob was unsure whether he was aggravated to be thwarted in his escape plan, or pleased at the friendly intervention of Pastor Andy!

"Actually, my pal, Millard, from the old days in Somerville, Mass, is the geek! I would never have had the Yeti run-in, or the where-with-all to get a game concept protected and marketed, except that my big sis~"

"Whoa! You've had a Yeti run-in? You're kidding; right?"

Jacob's turn to laugh! "Yes and no! It was a guy in a costume, sent to scare us off from a diamond deposit! And it worked! I mean, what do I know about forests and forest creatures? My whole frame of reference was Boston and suburbs! So, this dude sent us running and diving over a gate~"

Andy laughed and Jacob realized he was disarmed by the open friendliness and interest!

⊣ ⊢

"Do you tithe?" Summer extinguished a flaming marshmallow and pressed it into a Hershey bar on graham cracker half!

Tim squirmed! "Why? I usually put a few dollars in the plate when it goes by! My folks have never been rich!"

Summer scowled, "Why not?"

"Well, just hard-working, and a Hispanic background~"

"Well, you don't have to be rich to tithe! So, that's an excuse~for not?"

"Well, let's face it, people like the Faulkners can tithe! Cause they're filthy rich!"

Summer sighed! "That's what I'm trying to figure out; the cause and effect! Do people tithe because they're rich? Or are they rich because they tithe?"

"They're rich because they're born rich!"

"Well, not always!" She mentioned some of America's wealthy, vaulting to the heights from humble origins!

"Well, take the pro athletes! They're rich because they have prowess, and they're in the right place at the right time! None of them ever get up and say that when they started tithing, God gave them a pitching arm!"

Shaking her head at him in wonder at the logic, she rose! "You just helped me! I'm going to start!"

"Uh~how did that help you decide?"

"Because you're the kind of Christian I don't want to be like! I don't want to be a cowering Christian! I want to be a towering Christian! Like Gray and Brenna! Or Mr. Faulkner~Thanks! Ciao!"

⚔ ⚔

Brenna cradled a coffee cup in both hands, watching steam rise, as she considered Gray's suggestion!

"That's scary!"

His rich, soft laugh elicited a smile from her, "What's funny?"

"You were never scared growing up in your neighborhood, never scared to take people to task you thought were wrong, not afraid to tackle a college degree with no encouragement or money, not scared to travel across country in the dead of winter in an unreliable automobile~"

She shook her head! "You're wrong! I was terrified at every juncture!"

"Ah then, you've made my point for me! You always fought through your fears! Even prior to your salvation! And then your faith in the Lord was astounding! Why back away now?"

"I'm not sure my company's stable enough to support a family man! That's a whole other level above paying Jacob or Summer an hourly amount! We're talking about insurance and retirement and social security withholdings~"

"All things that are actually my strengths!"

She feigned ire! "Ah, I see how you are! Here it finally is! You're pressuring me to buy your package!"

"What can I say? I've held off as long as I could; mentioning it!"

They laughed and she turned back pensive! "The whole idea is overwhelming to me! I don't know where to look for someone, and if I send out feelers, I might get an applicant I don't' want-but there are so many regulations on who you have to hire!"

"All very good points! And pitfalls to avoid, if possible! I mean, I don't have a problem with you taking it easy and regrouping~"

"What?"

"Well, you have more than you ever imagined~and I'm glad you're contented with it! Godliness with contentment is great gain~"

"And yet~ I'm only twenty-four, and I haven't finished my course! I should be, what, satisfied, but then, not?"

"Yes, do you remember the Bible story of Israel's defeat at Ai; due to Achan's sin?"

She nodded, "Actually, I love it, but I'd lost sight of it! Before Joshua knew the reason for the defeat, he threw himself on his face, and said, 'Would to God we had been content on the other side Jordan'! When you think about it, that was a crazy conclusion for him to jump to! God's plan from the outset had been for them to cross over Jordan! Into the Promised Land! As Christian's we can get contented too soon! With doing less than God wants us to do! I want to go forward boldly~"

"And you shall! Are you quite ready to go? Perhaps we should rescue Alex and Kayla from our son!"

⊣ ⊢

Jacob turned his attention to counting floor tiles! He should probably blame himself for dummying into this situation again; but it was Tim and Summer's fault! Once again, they had promised to stick to him and run interference, but then, the second they all stepped through the church door, some woman had shooed them away to be in a worship team~whatever that was~

Suddenly freezing, he decided going to his truck for his coat would be a good cover for escape! Evidently not moving quickly enough on the idea, he nearly bumped into Pastor Andy, who smiled affably!

"Mornin', Weston!

"McGuire!" he returned evenly! "I was just on my way to the truck for my coat!

"Yeah, I hear ya! Cold in here! Soon as I put this box down, I'll adjust the thermostat! You're here alone? How about giving me a hand?"

Trying not to mumble under his breath at being trapped, Jacob complied, answering the pastor's question.

"My partner and my sister are both around here someplace! I guess they got drafted to be on a wor~"

The assistant pastor's pleasant demeanor turned to a sudden scowl! "Just place a copy on each chair! Be right back!"

᚜   ᚛

Mallory and David finished a fast food meal with their Miami friends, Bryce and Lisette and their two toddlers!

"Seriously, Dude, why do you only ever look us up when you're in trouble with the local gangs?" Bryce's tone sounded good-natured enough~

"Well, we're not exactly in trouble with them~it's Rose Reynosa, sadly by association, Deborah and all her family and workers!"

"And also by association, David and Mallory Anderson; and by association with them, Bryce and Lisette Billingsley!" Lisette's tone more strident, with no attempt at cajoling humor!

"Well, insurance settled on the damage, and Deborah hired David to bring in a team to clean up and renovate the plant following the fire! We didn't want to come to town, and not call you~" Mallory's explanation! "I can't believe how tall Mark has gotten, and we hadn't even met~" she bounced eight month old Hannah on her knee as she made eye contact with her~"you! You're quite the little beauty!"

The baby clapped her hands, smiling, and gyrating exuberantly in response to attention from the beautiful newcomer!

Mallory caught her in an affectionate squeeze, "Whoa! Look at you! You already have the cheerleader thing going on! I never realized it's genetic!"

Lisette couldn't help laughing as she reached for her baby

"Well, if you guys feel like we've put targets on your backs here, you can always move to Dallas!" David's suggestion.

Bryce met the serious gaze, "And why would we do that? Are you guys ever there except to pick up your mail? What did you think of the Canary Islands? Our family went there once when Blythe and I were kids! Makes me miss my parents just thinking about it! It's an interesting place to dive!"

"Yeah, we didn't get to dive! After our scary experience diving the Red Sea, we haven't embarked on any more diving excursions!" David's haunted expression at the memory belied his laugh! "We mostly looked at Geology-Volcano related sites! The kids thought we were there to get canaries, and they all freaked out en masse when they realized we were boarding the plane-without any-"

"Speaking of canaries, do you still have the Hyacinth Mackaws?" Lisette's curiosity!

Mallory laughed, "We do! Did you ever know what Daniel and Diana's response was, when I first got them?"

"Yeah, kind of! The Faulkners aren't really animal people!"

Mallory nodded at her friend's vague response! "Yeah, Diana doesn't like anything that makes added messes, and Daniel just said that family life and kids all yacking at once-having parrots in the mix would be one thing too many! We now understand what he was talking about! They multiply pandemonium when we're home! But the kids all love them-can't say I'm disappointed not to have canaries, too!"

Bryce laughed. "What we won't do for our kids! Seriously, it's been great to see you!"

"You, too!" David was glad for the warm-up! "We're heading home late tomorrow afternoon once I get the job under way! You guys want to meet us down at Reuben's in the morning for the specialty of the house: Cheese Blintzes?"

"Yeah, let's do it, Bryce! Want to?" Lisette's eager expression was tough to resist!

"Sounds good!"

⊰ ⊱

Brenna caressed her sleeping son's face as she turned her Bible page! "I guess I read you right to sleep!" She continued her reading softly, trying to concentrate on the content when her mind tended to wander to Gray!

Yes, she wanted to keep advancing in faith in obedience to God's will for her life! But how could Gray be so certain that she should hire a full-time Geologist? Maybe God was trying to tell him *Prescott* should, and he misunderstood!

She reached for her coffee cup and sipped, "Okay, Lord, make it clear!"

⊰ ⊱

Jacob dipped his burger into a puddle of ketchup as he listened to Summer and Tim complain about Pastor Andy!

"Well, he studied hard for our lesson," Jacob's defense of a guy he barely knew, "and he bought a book for everyone that came! I agree with him; that y'all can practice the music some other time, but not when you're supposed to be in Bible class! And besides that, you guys said you wouldn't desert me, if I'd come with you again!"

Tim popped up to refill his soft drink, and Summer jabbed her cup at him!

Jacob frowned, "What, is he your slave? You have two hands and feet!"

She stuck her tongue out at him! "You sound just like Warren did, all the time we were growing up! He's getting up anyway~"

Tim got the drinks and sank back into his spot sheepishly! "You're right, man! We did promise to hang with you! I guess it's amazing that you stayed, but I'm glad you did!"

"Yeah, I keep trying to leave, but then, he's always in my way, with that hand stuck out there~I don't get it! Why does he do what he does? He doesn't get paid much, and then he spends a chunk of his own money to get books for us? Most of the kids just forgot about them~left them on or under the chairs~"

Tim flushed, guiltier than ever! "Did you hang onto yours?"

"Yeah, man! I've never had many people ever give me gifts! I told him thanks, too! He asked me to tell him what I think about it when I finish!"

"You're going to read it?" Summer's expression and tone registered pure incredulity!

"Yes! I'm still not the best reader! It may take me five years! But like I said, not many people have cared enough about me to buy me something! And fewer yet ever cared what I think!"

⊰ ⊱

335

Brenna read another first class letter through the mist of tears! Gray was absolutely amazing! Well, he was-but he was a gift from the Lord! She softly quoted a verse:

James 1:17 Every good gift and every perfect gift is from above, and cometh down from the Father of lights, with whom is no variableness, neither shadow of turning.

Everything from the gracious hand of God! Membership into every prestigious Geological association out there, an all-expense paid trip to the most expansive Earth Science convention in the US, and a new wardrobe from *DiaMal, Corporation*!

"Gray, how do you think of all this?"

He kissed her hand chivalrously, then with a sly wink, he admitted! "Mallory helped me out! She described your employment ap that first week you arrived here! A degree with mediocre grades and little else to recommend you! No family, no phone, no real address! I wonder how many applications I've discarded, of people only needing a chance to get started! All of these credentials will help you personally, as well as corporately! You need to strengthen your corporate image, not only to attract more contracts, but also to draw good professional employees!"

Her breath caught raggedly at the scope of his implication! "What are you saying, Gray?"

"I'm saying, what drew you all the way from Boston to Tulsa?"

"*GeoHy!*" Her immediate response! "Like him, or not, your brother-in-law is legendary among Creationist Geologists!"

Gray grinned. "Actually, I like him quite a lot better now! I used to think he was only a legend in his own mind!"

She smiled at the observation before turning her attention back to the assortment spread on the bed before her!

"I'm afraid to ask this, but why have you reserved a booth for me at the convention?"

He drew her near and placed a kiss next to her ear! "You're a very smart woman! You'll figure it out!"

Chapter 33: FULFILLMENT

Brenna drummed impatiently on the edge of her desk! But Brad Maxwell's number rolled over to voice mail! Strange, at least he had emptied his full message box! Having left several messages in the past, she disconnected! Her plan wasn't hiring Brad; but asking for the names of some of the other Geology grads who had begun the fated course! She hated to contact the University! Either, they would be protective of the information she sought, or, if they realized she was hiring, they might try to force someone on her for 'equal employment'! And, she was in favor of not vetting applicants by race or ethnicity! With her, the issue was hiring someone with similar philosophy! And in the field of Geology, highly indoctrinated with Evolution and the Old Earth Model, scientists of her stripe were few and far between! She considered contacting Tom Haynes, the educator who had put together the courses for Mallory and Alexandra!

"Lord, I've prayed about this before! Maybe hiring will put my new little company in a bind I can't handle! And that's why You have shut the door on me finding~But I don't want to be content on the wrong side of Jordan! I want to hire and grow~maybe I can get Gray to ask Daniel~except if I'm going to do this, I need boldness to contact these intimidating people~Just call me, as in John Bunyon's, Pilgrim's Progress, little Much Afraid! Gray's right; I've fallen backwards in faith and boldness! Or have I gleaned more wisdom?"

Confused, she went to check on Levi!

✥ ✥

Malik Owens winked at his gorgeous bride, Sheena! "We're on an adventure! Relax! You haven't smiled for the past hundred miles!"

"That's because I've needed to stop for the last hundred miles!"

"Well, we're almost there, Baby!"

"That's what you've said for the last hundred miles!"

⚐ ⚑

Gray watched an Animated DVR with pride! It was reminiscent to him of Diana and Caramel Du Boise' *Fear Not* Sparrows! But now, rather than a family of sparrows teaching kids to trust in God's provision without panic and fear, this featured a community of Dinosaurs teaching on Creation and the origins of all things! Cuter than cute! Brenna's brainchild and her rationale behind majoring in Geology and minoring in Elementary Education! To reach the open minds of young children before they became totally propagandized by the system!

Brenda Brontosaurus: "I thought scientists had to be good with math and numbers!"

Professor Reginald Rex: "That's a common myth about Scientists! Sometimes it's hard to sort out fact from fiction!"

Tillie Taractadyl: "You can prove they're terrible with numbers because they use the terms millions and billions interchangeably!"

Brenda: "I wish they were bankers! My account balance is a big Gigantasaurus egg!"

Pamela Panoplosaurus "Well, Brenda, be glad they aren't bankers, because they'd probably try to prove you're one hundred fifty billion dollars in the hole!"

Professor Rex "Well, they try to prove lots of stuff with no basis in fact! The sad thing is that they purposely miss out on the beauty of our Creator and His Creation!"

Sammy Sinosauropteryx: "Yes, and cause everyone else to miss out, too! It's very sad, that under the pretense of searching for truth, they ignore facts and forge lies!"

Professor Rex: "Yes, Sammy, but that's how the enemy works! He causes men to fall in love with the reasoning powers the Creator granted them, rather than glorifying Him for it! That was the beginning of their errors!"

Cynthia Centrosaurus: "Well, it just chaps my armor that they use our noble history to cobble their hypotheses~Is that the word I mean?"

"Great job, Sam! You said Millard helped, too, and some of his cronies? Do I owe you or any of them? It's just so perfect! Brenna stressed that it be colorful and the different dinosaur species adorable! I hope she'll be pleased~"

Sam nodded, "Why wouldn't she? You know, when she breaks this at the convention~I mean, it's not a lot of time to get it done! I should have thought of it before now~"

"What, Man? Spit it out, if time is indeed of the essence!" Gray slid the master into a sleeve!

"Well, you know how movie releases can typically spark toy sales? And Diana and Caramel produced toys and lamps and furnishings with the *Fear Not* concept~"

Gray clapped his brother-in-law on the back with enthusiastic force!

"Brilliant, my dear fellow! I shall have to enlist the aid of my entire family to accomplish the feat, at the same time maintaining the surprise element for Brenna!"

Sam laughed. "Well, we are part of an amazing family, but to get design, production, and delivery within the next three weeks?"

"Righto! Quite right! We shall be forced to enlist the aid of Heaven!"

Daniel closed his Bible and answered the buzz on his intercom!

"Yes, Amy, what is it?"

He frowned at her answer! A job seeker? Showing up in person? He sighed. Guessing he was still mourning Al's silence and the fiascos caused by Brad Maxwell, interviewing someone was the last thing he felt like doing! He sat, fingers steepled contemplatively! Pushing the button again, "Amy show him in! Bring coffee and offer him coffee or a choice from the refrigerator!"

"He has his wife with him! Do you want both of them? She's real gorgeous!"

He hesitated. After so many years, Amy remained basically clueless! 'What did gorgeous have to do with anything? And what numbskull showed up with his wife, looking for a job?'

He rose courteously as the office door opened and the receptionist stood back with the tray of beverages!

⚑ ⚐

Gray shuddered at a scary-looking rendering of Cynthia Centrosaurus! Evidently the toy designer had not taken even one second of time, to view the film! This one would never do! At least, he was eliminating contenders. Usually exhibiting great equilibrium, he gasped with frustration when his phone buzzed!

Noting that Jacob was the caller, his aggravation turned to concern!

"Good afternoon, Jacob! It's a pleasure to hear your voice! Is all well?"

He relaxed as his son assured him they were fine!

"I was wondering if it would be okay for me to fly home," Jacob's uncertain voice when he got to the purpose of his call!

Gray tensed again, not sure why Jacob should need to return 'home', unless Warren was pushing for it! Well, possibly for a visit with Millard~

"Well, I don't see why not! You've certainly been working very hard, and you have plenty of money for the fare!" Even as he spoke, he sank into his chair! Parenting was fraught with challenges!

"Okay, well I've already booked the flight! I get in tomorrow afternoon! Should I take a cab, or can someone meet me? I have a few things I want to talk to you and Brenna about! And I need to check out my newest little brother!"

Gray did some mental gymnastics to grasp his son's meaning. "I thought you were asking me if you could fly home to Boston!" He choked up and couldn't go on!

"No, Sir! I have no home in Boston! I have a home here in Colorado, and there with you and Bren~"

Gray laughed aloud with relief! "Certainly we can meet you! Send your flight information!"

⚑ ⚐

Alex Hamilton shared an updated picture of his daughter and grandson with the world of his friends, who probably cared little to none! Most of them were years ahead of him in the parenting/grandparenting game, and it was mundane to them! Even their own!

Feeling stung by the O'Connell's rejection, for Summer's sake more than his own, he nevertheless, reached out to Richard once more!

Dear Richard,

I'm sure you were trying to protect me from the possibility of a fraudulent paternity suit, and I find that amazingly kind in view of our long ago falling out about Irene! For many of my youthful escapades I feel profound sorrow and regret! I'll not enumerate them here!

If you continue your choice to avoid Brenna and Irene's other children, I understand! Sometimes life seems to throw one curveball after another! Brenna's search for us, amazingly, wasn't a quest to latch onto money! I'm amazed by that, too, in a day and age of scams and tricks!

I have many regrets about missing her childhood and 'being there' for her! The amazing thing is that, I'm afraid my failing to be there for her worked more in her favor, than if I had been there! She is an incredible lady now, is happily married, and has a sweet little son named, Levi!

I know Brenna would be delighted to have a relationship with you! My parents adore her (and Levi, or course)! And yet, I'm not asking you to reconsider your response for Brenna's sake, so much as for Jacob and Summer, and the other children!

Jerome met them all when he attended a convention in Tulsa a few months back! I'm not certain how much you two stay in contact, but the children loved him immediately! I know that it's been a rather short time since all of this bombarded my world, and if you need some time to adjust and consider-well, you're certainly your own man, and the choice is yours~

Thank you for your attention and consideration,

Alex Hamilton

⊰ ⊱

"Could we please just order pizza in, and all eat at home?" Jacob's plea when Gray suggested the city's prime steak house!

"Certainly; I mean I had promised the other children–" Gray thought Jacob looked remarkably well, filled out and tanned!

"Pizza! Pizza!" Emily bounced up and down eagerly!

Terry gave his brother an affectionate high-five! Although his mouth had been watering at the thought of a juicy filet mignon, he deferred readily to Jacob's suggestion. "Okay, we can go with pizza! Let's just get plenty! And with lots of meat!"

Settled around the sizeable rustic oak kitchen table, Jacob got his turn with Levi! It wasn't easy to get a turn, and the kids made Jacob nervous!

"They treat him like a sack of potatoes! Aren't you scared they'll hurt him?"

"Terrified, at first!" Gray acknowledged with a laugh! "But then he grew a little tougher, and they dote on him so! We're more concerned about his being horrifically spoiled, than sustaining physical injury!"

Jacob nodded; living in Colorado didn't isolate him from facts! "I hear Alex comes around quite a bit, and his dad and mom, too!"

Brenna flushed guiltily, "How's Summer doing?"

He grinned broadly! "Summer? Oh, Summer's doing just great! Especially whenever Alvaredo's around! Which, is most of the time!"

Gray frowned! "Brenna, my Love–"

"I considered him, Gray, but he chose Colorado and Jacob's Heavy Equipment Company over me! I suppose Summer could pick worse–"

"She's terribly young, and she's up there, far from home–Supervision is the word of the day–"

"Yeah, I got em in my sights at all times!" Jacob's features dead serious! "I put a word of warning on him, and unbeknown to me, Warren had already informed him, 'that he has a gun, a shovel, and an alibi'!"

Brenna laughed, pleased that her step dad was turning into a person! Growing serious, she pinned Jacob with a long searching look!

"What about you? All the single women up there throwing themselves at you?"

He flushed! "Well, Tim kids me a lot that so many of the local girls are into heavy equipment! A few stop in often to say, 'Hello'! Not exactly throwing themselves at me! I kinda have my eye on somebody, but-Well, she came to help Alexandra when she broke her ankle, but then she went back home-"

"Janni Anderson?" Brenna bit back a retort and finished lamely,"Well, yeah, she's cute; that's for sure-"

⚔ ⚔

Daniel couldn't help liking Malik and Sheena as he visited with them over lunch! He figured they took the meal as a positive sign that he was considering hiring! He wasn't! Even as he stayed engaged in the conversation, he racked his brain about who might be on staff at Boston University, sending beleaguered graduates his way in Tulsa! First Brenna; and now Malik! And his wife!

Alexandra didn't need him; probably Mallory didn't either! That left the possibility of Brenna! Crazy for the couple to make such a long trip-his thoughts broke off as Diana entered the café!

He rose courteously at her approach, and Malik followed his example!

She extended her hand as Daniel made the introductions! "Amy said I could find you down here! So-another Geologist?" She laughed light-heartedly as she settled into the offered chair, "What about you Sheena? Do you have a passion for rocks?"

Sheena patted Malik's arm possessively, "Only for this one!"

⚔ ⚔

"Dad, could we talk privately, please?" Jacob's soft request barely carried above family hubbub!

"Certainly!" Gray laid aside the newspaper, rising to lead his son to his office! 'Hmmm; he had thought something was on his eldest son's mind! Amazing how your children could create such alarming feelings!'

"I don't know where to start-" Jacob's troubled expression doubled his father's anxiety!

"Well, just start anywhere-but start! Would you like for Brenna to join us? What's it to do with?"

Totally unable to utter a word, Jacob began to cry! Sobs shook him, and he dug the heels of his hands into his eyes, trying to stem the unaccustomed flow of tears!

"There, there, now!" Gray's inexperienced attempt at providing comfort!

"It's-it's Pastor Andy-"

Gray frowned, familiar with the assistant pastor of the Silverton church Summer attended!

"Yes, Andy McGuire! What about him? What's troubling to you about him? He seemed to me a pleasant enough fellow-although-" He broke off awkwardly!

"He-he bought us all-books-with his own money-And he doesn't even make very much! Nobody ever just did anything that nice for me-" he cut himself off, laughing through his tears! "Well, except for Brenna-and then-you! I-I've thought that I-I don't need this Christianity-thing-"

Gray pulled his glasses off to blot at copious tears, saying nothing, allowing his son to continue-

"I-thought it was-for suckers-And I've been mad at both God and Brenna-"

"Yes, for your mother's death," Gray supplied quietly!

Jacob nodded, "Well, I'm slow-" He held his hand up to halt Gray's defense- "I may not be a super-fast learner-but I've finally figured out-that people that have what you and Brenna have-are a world better off-for a multiplicity of reasons-"

Gray laughed, "A rather big word for a slow learner-multiplicity-"

"I want what you and Brenna have, but I can't figure out what I have to do-"

"Why actually, Jacob, you have already done it! When you made the decision in your heart, that you need Jesus; it's not the words said in the prayer, as much as your humble realization! But I shall lead you in a prayer if you wish it! You can repeat the words after me!"

At a slight nod, Gray commenced a phrase at a time, with Jacob repeating:

Dear Heavenly Father, I know that I'm a sinner, but that You sent Your Son to die on the cross for my sins! I invite Him into my life to be my Savior! Thank You for loving me and making a way so I can be in heaven with you some day! In Jesus' Name; Amen!

᪥ ᪤

Gray grinned inwardly! Brenna's excitement was palpable! Directly to the airport when church dismissed, for her flight to Ontario, California, where Malik and Sheena Owens would meet her flight! Owens was a literal Godsend! Oops! He forced his attention back to the sermon! Well, he was sitting here in church and praising God for His wondrous works! But attention to the Word through the sermon was important!

His heart overflowed with excitement! With Brenna's booth set up presenting information about her corporation, *Brenna Prescott Geological Exploration, Inc.*, pre-registered guests were already showing remarkable interest! And her DVD, *A Day with Dinosaur Friends*, already showed strong sales! Worried that irate attendees might return to demand their money back when they saw the exact nature of the products, he reminded himself to be more positive! Of course, the movie, professionally produced, with the accompanying merchandise, were intended to surprise her!

⚍ ⚎

Too hyped to sleep, Brenna got up and brewed coffee! Before her on the coffee table lay a glossy booklet to promote her company! Beginning with her receiving her diploma; moving from Boston to Tulsa; embarking upon an advanced degree; waving her passport; boarding the *Rock Scientist*, as expedition Geologist; dealing with the media regarding the *Rock Scientist's* finds; pointing out a significant rock formation to Mallory on a large wall monitor; trudging around the higher elevations in Colorado! It all made her seem more experienced than she felt!

The glossy left out her crowning accomplishment! Levi! She missed him; he changed and did new things with each day that passed! And she supposed she felt guilty in spite of Gray's injunctions that she shouldn't! She laughed softly before speaking aloud in the hushed suite, "Okay, I won't! It's a week for me to enjoy and network! And I worry about 'sticking' Gray with the kids, when they are what he has yearned for! I guess every day, I'm amazed anew that he really loves me! That he really loves the odd assortment of all of us! That I haven't done something to 'blow the gig', as the kids refer to it!"

Opening the closet door, she surveyed elegant ensembles with coordinating shoes and handbags! A small fortune in fine jewelry snuggled in a jewelry roll in her handbag! Manicured nails and fresh hairstyle bespoke Gray's attention to detail to make her a professional from head to toe!

And Warren was saved? Go figure! Wonders never cease! And Summer, and now, Jacob-of course, her list was long of people still needing the Lord-beginning with Alex-Lots of prayer requests! Regardless of how many answers the Lord provided, her life was a continuum of need-rather than individual moments in time, needs, plural!

Philippians 4:19 But my God shall supply all your need according to his riches in glory by Christ Jesus.

Chapter 34:   FRUITION

Brenna settled back into the leather comfort of the first class seat! An amazing week, and now she was headed home to Gray! How could it get any better?

The week was an amazing time of making new acquaintances and networking, assisted by her personable new staff Geologist and his lovely wife! There had been a couple of rough moments when a prominent scholar in the field of Geology and the keynote speaker at the convention, Phelps Hensley, had thrown a fit about Brenna's DVD and accompanying line of merchandise!

The event planners, trying to appease him, had asserted that everyone, including small children, knew 'the truth' that origins lay in Evolution! Brenna's merchandise, though misguided, seemed basically harmless! Sadly, she almost agreed with their assessment! So many voices from cradle to grave screamed the message they wanted the populace to hear! Still, there was not one complaint or return! Maybe when the attendees returned home and their kids watched the DVD's, problems would arise!

She smiled at the attendant and asked for a cup of coffee before opening her Bible! She reprimanded herself sharply for having become so spoiled! So much to be thankful for! And how could she assess the cash outlay on Gray's part, in arranging the professional completion of her educational children's video and its associated products, as well as airfare, hotel suite, rental car, and the booth space? Surely that should all count as some kind of birthday present!

Except that he seemed to have completely forgotten–not even a verbal birthday wish throughout the day's phone chats! The previous year–flowers, balloons, jewelry, an elegant meal out–

Pressing fingertips to temples, she counted softly to ten! And all of the years prior to that one-nothing special at all, ever! Her disjointed and dysfunctional family had never made a point of celebrating one another! Her mom, usually strung out, no dad, no grandparents! She frowned! Strange that Alex and Kayla hadn't phoned or emailed! Neither had Sandra and Latham!

She smiled to herself! What was the point of finding your dad and grandparents, if it wasn't good for Birthday presents? Come to think of it, Jacob and Summer were conspicuously silent, too! Okay, Gray was up to a big shindig-

≒ ≓

Brenna pressed her temples in total bewilderment! Such a lavish party with such a perfect blend of friends; and yes, family, too! To the dazed young Geologist, the family surrounding her was the greater gift, even than the exquisite and lavish things heaped upon her! One part of her brain told her it was the Lord, heaping on blessings! Part of her mind played the verse from James that attested that every good and perfect gift was from the Lord! The other half of her mind thought surely He couldn't approve of such extravagance!

Hugs, and tears, and thanks; and hugs, and tears, and thanks, again! Seemed totally inadequate! Her brain, brimming with experiences, challenges, and triumphs from the convention, seemed to be approaching overload!

Gray sat beaming at her proudly, eyes burning with ardor! She caught her breath at the honest sincerity that was her mate! Part of her wanted the quiet moments alone with him, while her schitzo-side wanted the party never to end!

Gray had literally assembled guests from the ends of the earth! His brother, Parker, and his family won a prize for traveling the greatest distance-from Abuja, Nigeria! Second runner up would be a Chemist, Donovan Cline, who spent a great deal of time between Egypt and Jordan, searching for artifacts related to the ancient Israelite's wilderness wanderings! Then, the O'Shaughnessy's had traveled from Boston, and Shay appeared well and robust!

And the gifts! World famous jewelry designer, Herb Carlton, and his wife, Linda (Mallory's aunt), presented her with a jewelry suite themed to cute shoe charms! Daniel and Diana bestowed a five piece coordinate outfit for the coming spring in a monochromatic violet color scheme; as well as a Geological sample featuring large Amazonite crystals combined with Smoky Topaz crystals on matrix! Delia's gift of linen table coverings for the new dining room table in their work in progress home, brought squeals of delight!

"You're the woman I've been searching for all my life," Brenna's grandmother's, laughing admission to the Irish Linen CEO!

Brenna was further bedazzled by that! 'Who had leisure and money to worry about finding table linens for humongous tables in gigantuous dining rooms? Evidently, lots of people, because Sandra was still gushing to Delia about how many linen orders her friends would place, once they became aware of the luxuriant products!

So, people were using her birthday celebration as an occasion to network? Somehow, they didn't seem the least bit tacky!

And at last, she met Deborah Rodriguez and her talented family members, including the infamous Aunt Rose! And Deborah's gift was a cute, flippy summer outfit that featured a lot of ruffles in a rich hyacinth color! The coup de grâce, a coated canvas handbag that pictured a couple of Hyacinth Mackaws, and trimmed out with leather in the same rich color and jingling with a flirty assortment of signature charms!

"Oh! To die for!" Diana's outburst showed her genuine admiration of the young designer, with a pang of envy combined!

Mallory grasped the canvas espadrilles that were trimmed in hyacinth leather piping and tied at the vamp with a delicate piping bow! "So cute! It's absolutely amazing what the human mind can conceive! Although, my spoiled rotten birds should get some credit, too!"

Brenna smiled shyly at the man seated to her left who had said little since his arrival! Evidently a joint maneuver between Gray and Alex to coax him to attend! She assumed he heartily disapproved of her! In much the same manner he had so viciously opposed her mother! Trying not to let him affect her, she turned her radiant smile on her other grandparents!

Sandra's ebullient voice seized the moment! "Well, we're a little miffed at our son-that we have missed out on such a major portion of your life! We regret having missed birthdays and other milestones in your life!"

Brenna shot a surreptitious glance at Summer, always sympathetic to her sister's less successful quest, before fastening her gaze on paternal grandparents!

"Our gift, I guess, tends toward the selfish side on our part!" Latham besieged by sudden guilt! "In light of some of these other gifts, we should feel ashamed!" He laughed! "We should! But we don't!" He handed her a thick envelope, continuing his explanation as she tried to delicately unseal the missive!

"We're combining a couple of things! The blog that purchases Sandra's photographs, has requested a photo array from Greenland! A place which we have yet to visit, that has been on our personal bucket list! We assumed also, it must be of tremendous interest to you as a Geologist!"

Brenna nodded, dazed, before returning her attention to the envelope! As a Geologist who had barely been out of Massachusetts, the world was her playground! They couldn't pick a wrong destination! The trip, conveniently arranged for summertime when the frozen islands were the most accessible, with details worked out for Summer to oversee her younger siblings!

When Gray shot Summer a questioning glance, she met his gaze levelly! "I can do it! We've all talked, and we want you guys to go without worrying about all of us! We'll do what we're supposed to, and Aunt Niqui has agreed to be on standby~"

Brenna's eyes brimmed with tears as she studied the itinerary! The trip included Latham and Sandra, Alex and Kayla, Gray and herself, and of course, Levi!

Alex' eyes twinkled as she met his gaze, "I can look after the baby while you do your Geological exploration!"

She nodded, before acknowledging her appreciation:

"Thank you~" she hesitated awkwardly~ At some point in time, shouldn't she call him Dad, or Father, or Daddy~"

"You can keep calling us Alex and Kayla! I forfeited some important things~by~turning loose~never checking! I'm grateful every day when you answer your phone, or when you let me see the baby~"

"We have a gift, too!" Kayla squeezed her husband's hand affectionately as emotion choked his voice! She continued, "We want to fund your advanced studies~but due to your busy schedule and the frivolity of campus life~we've made arrangements with Dr. Thomas Haynes and his company! Your study will be fully accredited, and Dr. Haynes has numbers of very successful graduates to his credit!"

"You guys are awesome! Thank you! That's what I had decided would be the best course of action, but Gray and I hadn't gotten a chance to talk it over~"

Gray nodded enthusiastically, "Exactly! Bravo! My thinking also, which I hesitated to mention! I practically lost you down that rat hole of a campus! Between handsome fraternity men, and crazy professors~"

She laughed, "It'll take a lot more than that for you to rid yourself of me! But it really is the best course! Professor Stone's idea~to appoint group assignments~ I was ready to call on our brother-in-law for a favor to get me out of that!"

Daniel laughed, whereas Summer huffed indignantly!

Going back and forth between Tulsa and Colorado, Summer was aware of some things the others were not privy to. Things she couldn't divulge; not even the Summer who delighted in whispering tidbits of gossip!

'Brenna's two study partners~Brad was dead, following a macabre series of events! But, Tim Alvaredo? Tim was strictly all right!'

Richard Williamson took note of his newly acquainted granddaughter as her skin flushed delicately and a dreamy smile coaxed dimples from young cheeks! She was Irene made over, all right!

'Please God, help me do a better job second time around!'

Chapter 35: IRENE

Brenna, stunned at the gamut of emotions she was experiencing, sat clinging to Levi, afraid that if she met Gray's solid gaze, she would fly to pieces completely!

Back from an astounding adventure in Greenland, she now sat on a deck chair in Richard and Betty Williamson's back yard!

Though sad to have never met her real grandmother, she immediately liked her grandfather's second wife! With a broad, pleasant face and easy laugh, Betty was fun to be around! Brenna's aunts and uncles had shared that marrying her had helped Richard lighten up!

Brenna considered thoughtfully, realizing it was important to be serious about the Lord's work, without being joyless! That meant a daily dealing with bitterness! Even as she joined family camaraderie like she had never dreamed of, she confessed having bitter feelings toward people and experiences! At the moment, her toughest struggle was with the O'Connell's; not just for Summer's sake, but for Alex's, who had looked them up on Summer's behalf and asked their forgiveness!

'Lord, I've put this in Your hands before; but I guess I haven't left it there! Help me trust You! It was when You instructed the disciples to forgive seventy times seven, that their response was, *Lord, increase our faith*! Help me have faith, that what I consider wrongs, are events planned by You for my ultimate good! So consequently, I shouldn't chafe and fret against them!'

She smiled a welcome as one of her cousins, Jerome's youngest son, approached, balancing a plate loaded with barbecue and Betty's remarkable side dishes!

"Do you mind?"

"Not at all"! She swung her feet around, making room for him to sit "Kenny, right?"

"Close! Kevin!"

She laughed, "Close only counts in horseshoes and hand grenades! I apologize, Kevin! I'll get it! So, how do you like living in Connecticut? I hope to see more of the US!"

"It's the armpit of the earth!"

She laughed when he turned suddenly sullen and spewed his opinion! "Well, okay then: I'll cross it off my bucket list! But, I always thought Somerville, Mass was the armpit! Of course, we all have two armpits, so maybe the earth does, too!"

A smile played despite his best efforts!

She continued, "I have this amazing friend who grew up in a small town in Arkansas! And she was actually pretty happy! Her dad was really involved with her life, and she had a lot of good friends! She got saved when she was seven, and really got involved in church because she wanted to! Still, as a junior in high school, when she was introduced to Edna St. Vincent Millay and <u>Renascence</u> in lit class, she started to develop a wanderlust! Now, she's seen lots of the world, but can't wait for the oases of getting back to Murfreesboro!"

His body language reflected a certain resistance to her story; still, he continued teasingly, "So at least this *Murfreesboro* doesn't pretend to be an armpit! Because I'm fairly certain you had a good point that there can only be two!"

"Yeah; no, she never said it was an armpit! Just that she was starting to feel trapped and closed in! You know:

All I could see from where I stood
Was three long islands, and a wood!

"Hmmm; I hate English, but I think I remember that! I don't know what I'll ever need all this stuff for! I want to join the Marines!"

She nodded slowly, "Yeah, that's one way to get out of town! And I'm grateful for all of the Marines and every military person who defends this country! Not a bad calling! There are other escapes from the armpits, though! Kevin, knowledge is the key! If you want to see and do more; to be more, education is really important! Even in the Marine Corps, education separates the officers from the rest!"

He scowled, "Thought you seemed cool! Look at these saps!" He waved a sweeping arm at the relatives scattered in conversation groups! "Your mother is the only one who broke free! I've always admired that!"

Tears started! "Sorry I'm not cool, Kevin! I loved my mother, but what she did with her life! There was little that was admirable! She had a sense of family, and I understand now, why she never took the abortion route! But, you can't imagine all she put us through! Her immorality and drug use! Your parents really love you! Please don't resent who they are and what they ask of you, like my mom did! You'll be free soon enough! And realize that freedom isn't all it's cracked up to be, either!"

She cried harder, "But more than that, God loves you so much! Kevin, I know you know this, but He loves you so much, that if you were the only person on earth, He still would have sent His only begotten Son to die on the cross for you! His salvation is the center of life! My mother knew that, and never once breathed a word to any of us about it! I never even heard until my third year of college-and then not from her-Has there ever been a time, Kevin, when you asked Jesus to come into your heart and save you?"

"No; not yet! I'm gonna do it later! But I plan to have some fun first! Ciao! Been nice-"

Brenna watched sadly as he headed across the yard toward the gate!

冯 岊

Brenna and Jacob sat late, watching the summer sky deepen into inky purples as they visited with their grandfather and Uncle Jerome! It seemed strangely serene, although having some of the blanks filled in raised other questions in Brenna's mind! Questions that would require thought and formulating into words!

"So, Latham and Sandra gave you a trip to Greenland?" Richard's voice a mixture of question and statement of fact!

Jacob answered for Brenna, before asking his own probing question. "They did! Did-umm-you know-them-back-then?"!

Richard shook his head, barely perceptibly! "Our little church was so broke! We were so broke! But I came out of Bible college with the impression that no one should have money, and if they did, it was-rich men can't get into heaven-I'm not sure if that was taught or implied-"

"Well, I saw that in the Bible the other day!" An eager Jacob trying to share his limited Bible knowledge with the two pastors!

Jerome's deep laugh filled the silent night! "But in that same passage, the Scriptures are careful to say that what is impossible with man, is possible with God! Meaning, that it's harder to make wealthy people see their need for God and His redeeming grace! We use a possibly overworked phrase that states, 'God is able to save people from the uttermost to the guttermost'! Even though we say it repeatedly, we tend to try harder to reach those in the gutter than in the upper echelons of society! So, to answer the question about the Hamiltons; we knew of them! Knew all about the big house they were building~"

"I would never have had the boldness to go up and knock on a mahogany door like that~" Richard's painful admission

"I think it was teak, but anyway," Jerome trailed off following a withering stare from his father~

Brenna laughed, "We get the point; we don't want to start any additional family rows!" She sobered, and Richard took note of her beautiful features as she continued, "So~uh~our mother~resented being poor for the sake of the Gospel?"

"Well, I don't think that had anything to do with it~"

"That had everything to do with it!" Jerome spoke forcefully! Willing to back down about which exotic hardwood the door had been, he was prepared to cross his father on this one!

"She just rebelled about doing right~" Richard's defeated response! "I've had years to mull it over and over~"

Brenna nodded, convinced that they were both right! At last she spoke, "It's just so ironic, though, that her rebelling and trying to grab for better things, outside of God's will~never worked~Whatever she had, growing up in your home~had to have been more~than she~ended up with~More than we ever had! At least~a real family~"

Jerome shifted uncomfortably, and Jacob spoke up! "We're not saying he wasn't an autocrat! Or that your family was like <u>Little House on the Prairie</u>! We don't need any raw truth!" He shuddered exaggeratedly! "But~we were just there! Nobody loved us! No autocrat in our house! We all did pretty much what we pleased~" He grew emotional, "Except Brenna~even before she met the Lord~I mean, she used to brag and tell us crazy things she was doing~she lied a lot~"

He moaned with fake pain as Brenna kicked him, but continued his narrative as he moved beyond range of her retaliation!

"Like I was saying, she made us go to school! Which Mother wanted us to do, but she never would have made us! She wanted to be a fun person and be friends with us! When she wasn't strung out~"

Jerome nodded agreement, "She always needed to be liked, and be the life of the party! Popularity~and she thought not having designer things and 'the image' held her back~"

Jacob nodded, "And Warren~did you know Warren Weston? My biological dad? He always ignored us, even when he was around; I mean, he'd yell at us, but mostly to be quiet and not bother him! Brenna was the bossy big sister! On steroids! Even before she did, what we called, 'Getting religion', she obsessed about going through our backpacks and everything to make sure we weren't starting to 'use'!"

"You should be glad!" Annoyed, she popped up to refill her iced tea!

He laughed, still loving to tease! "I am glad! That's really what I'm trying to get to! I'm glad you're such an amazing and caring person! And yes, I know, in a sense, you're like Mom was! But still, when everything in the neighborhood was so dog-eat-dog, you were different!" He paused grinning, "I mean you were the neighborhood liar and bragger, but~"

He defended himself, nearly helpless with laughter, until her attack subsided; then he continued, "You were the neighborhood shrink, trying to straighten out a weird and warped assortment of folk; the one to go to, whenever they had problems! We all laughed when you decided to go to college! Most of us were dropping out of high school! We were behind; nobody cared about grades~"

"How did you go to college? Richard's softly asked question!

"I wanted out of there!" Brenna's words spoken more forcefully than intended! "I didn't know the first thing about the Lord, or salvation~Gray feels like the Lord really had His hand on me, though, even~" She paused, breathless~ "Were~were you praying~did you know about all of us~"

"No!" Jerome's assured voice! "We didn't know that Irene was right over in Somerville! Or that she had you kids~"

"We did pray, though, that wherever she was~" Richard's voice choked off! "I hate that she didn't really meet the Lord~until almost too late~ I'm not sure how I failed to show Him to her~"

"Well, if she didn't want to see it~" Jacob's attempt to alleviate the pain in his grandfather's voice! "Anyway, the important thing is that she did get saved, and we'll all get to see her again! But, we all blamed Brenna when mother OD'd! Brenna's taken a lot of abuse from all of us~she really deserved a good guy like Gray! None of the rest of us deserved him-it's amazing! Can-uh-I ask you guys something? How do you know if you're called to preach?"

≒ ⊨

"I'm whining when I promised myself I wouldn't"! Agent Caroline Hillman as she completed making a report to Bransom! Thinking she was tough, springing tears humiliated her!

The senior agent regarded her steadily, long past his issues about female agents! Hillman was good, and discouragement at fighting the rising flood of crime and scams wasn't a female/hormone issue! Every good agent struggled with it! Bransom recalled a watershed day in his career, when Pastor John Anderson had introduced him to the Lord! Since that time, the feeling of losing the war with its overwhelming feelings of giving up had ceased to plague him! So, the bad guys continued to pop up! Like targets in the field training courses! He'd keep taking them down! What did he have better to do? And besides that, he got paid for doing it! Credit the bad guys for providing job security!

He nodded understanding before reminding her, "Interpol is hot on the trail of *the Ghost*, even as we speak! Thanks to your persistence! Just stick with it, here a little, and there a little! Still, I feel a new concern for Nick and Jennifer Mo'a'aloa! With Sharon Saxon more involved than we knew-and Jennifer shot both Robert, Sr. and Bobby!"

She nodded, "Which also brings us back to Mallory and her safety! She's the one who took Bobby out after he survived the shooting! And it's probable that Sharon had more love for her son than she did for her philandering mate- I know you hate to hear that, because you like to hope there are no threats to Mallory-"

Erik glanced up sharply, offended at the suggestion that he suffered from denial-but, she was right-

≒ ⊨

Gray wiped Levi's chin gently with a paper napkin! With teething, the baby drooled constantly! And, he was fussy!

When Gray made eye contact with Brenna across the table, she laughed. "I know! This is the same booth! I'm hungrier now than I was that day!"

Satisfaction glowed in his eyes! "And more beautiful than ever!"

He spoke softly to the server, ordering for both of them, before reaching for her hand! "I know this is just a bistro where people who work downtown grab quick lunches! Not saying it's shabby, but not a totally romantic spot-except to me~"

"And therefore, to me, also! My life's definitely been an adventure! I can't imagine my life without you! When I think about my goals, that brought me to Tulsa, "she broke off, laughing, "and it was really Mallory, that I admired the most! I'm not even sure as I look back, why I came here instead of heading to Dallas!"

He chuckled softly, "A bit of an odd thing! I'm not certain you ever told me that, before! How positively fortuitous for me, that you ended up in my brother-in-law's office, and he sent me the assignment of performing a background check on you! I'd had a bit of a conversation with the Father, after which the background request arrived in my in box! Oh, how I willed the international flight to fly faster!"

He quoted softly:

"Psalm 37:4 Delight thyself also in the LORD, and he shall give thee the desires of thine heart."

Look for the next exciting Christian Novel from Paula Rae Wallace:

Alexandra